Daleks .... machines housing brains as malevolently twisted as any in the cosmos...Daleks!

"OUR IN-FOR-MA-TION IS AC-CU-RATE," one shrilled. "IT IS VER-I-FIED THAT THIS IS THE DOC-TOR."

"Well, I never denied it."

"THIS IS THE DOC-TOR." This one's mechanically produced voice was lower, more gravelly, but just as shrill. "THE DOC-TOR IS AN EN-E-MY OF THE DA-LEKS. THE DOC-TOR IS TO BE EX-TER-MIN-A-TED."

"NEG-A-TIVE. THE DOC-TOR IS A TIME LORD. HE WILL BE OF GREAT VA-LUE TO US IN OUR PRO-JECT."

"THE DOC-TOR WILL NOT BE EX-TER-MIN-A-TED." Did I hear an unspoken "yet" tacked onto that line? "HE WILL HELP US IN OUR SEARCH."

"HE WILL NOT WIL-LING-LY CO-OP-ER-ATE WITH THE DA-LEKS."

"THE DOC-TOR WILL CO-OP-ER-ATE WHEN HE LEARNS WHAT IS AT STAKE. RE-LEASE HIM."

Friendly Daleks? I rubbed my wrists as they opened my shackles. Somehow, I felt less than total relief. I wasn't sure I wanted any part of a project the Daleks were working on, even to save my life. Anyway, working for the Daleks wasn't likely to bring me job security for very long.

DOCTOR WHO AND THE VORTEX CRYSTAL

by
William H. Keith, Jr.

This book is published by FASA Corporation
P.O.Box 6930
Chicago, IL 60680

Cover Art by: Harry Quinn
Maps by: Dana Knutson

INTRODUCTION

Doctor Who And The Vortex Crystal is a solo gameplay novel based on the adventures of the popular BBC television series, *DOCTOR WHO*. In this game, you take the part of The Doctor as he attempts to unravel a mystery that threatens the existence of the entire universe. During the course of this perilous adventure, you will be making important decisions. Each decision will lead to consequences, leading to another decision point, and so on as you go.

This solo adventure is played using a simplified version of FASA's *DOCTOR WHO* Role Playing Game. The rules of the game, as well as some background information on The Doctor and his universe, are explained below.

Background Information

The Doctor

The intrepid time traveller known as The Doctor (and never addressed by any other name) is a native of the planet Gallifrey. Not only is he Gallifreyan, but he is a member of an advanced race of beings known as Time Lords. Though Time Lords resemble humans on a superficial level, they have two hearts, immensely longer life spans, and are able to regenerate when near death. (For a fuller discussion of regeneration, see **Playing The Game** below.)

In this game, The Doctor is in his Fourth Incarnation. Tall and thin, with curly hair and a wide, open smile, the Fourth Doctor has been affectionately described as "all teeth and curls". He wears a floppy, broad-brimmed hat, a long coat with deep pockets, and a multi-colored scarf that trails on the ground as he walks. The Fourth Doctor is also known for his insatiable curiosity.

Though a Time Lord, The Doctor is actually a renegade whose actions are neither guided nor approved by his former brothers on Gallifrey. As a group, Time Lords have withdrawn behind the walls of their capital, holding to a policy of strict non-intervention in the affairs of lesser races. The Doctor and a handful of other Time Lords disagree with this policy, working when and where they can to stop injustice and to help beings in trouble.

The Doctor has only recently been able to travel again among other worlds, as he spent much of his third incarnation in a long exile on Earth. During that period, The Doctor made a number of friends, several of whom now accompany him in his time travels. Currently, he has two such Companions, Sarah Jane Smith, an independent-minded freelance journalist, and Harry Sullivan, a former Royal Navy doctor serving with a world-wide security organization known as UNIT. Though Sarah and Harry's relationship is sometimes rocky, they are intensely loyal to The Doctor. He, in turn, is quite fond of them, and would do anything necessary to rescue his Companions if they were in danger.

Not all renegade Time Lords are benevolent, however. One of The Doctor's bitterest foes is a renegade known as The Master, who is mentioned in passing in this adventure.

The TARDIS

Long ago, the Time Lords of Gallifrey learned to control and travel through time and space, a feat they accomplish with a time machine popularly known as a TARDIS (an acronym for Time And Relative Dimensions In Space). The TARDIS travels by dematerializing from our normal, four-dimensional space-time universe, and dropping into the Temporal Vortex, the center of all Time/Space. Once within the Vortex, the TARDIS operator can go anywhere, anywhen in the universe.

It is difficult to adequately describe the TARDIS in three-dimensional terms because most of its physical existence is outside the three-dimensional plane altogether. For example, the TARDIS is *dimensionally transcendent*, which means that it is much larger inside than out. Also, because the TARDIS is not a normal physical object, it cannot be harmed by normal physical objects, an effect known as *temporal invulnerablity*. Finally, the timeship is equipped with a *chameleon circuit* that allows it to imitate objects as a form of camouflage.

Like any machine, TARDISes can break down, especially when they have been in service for centuries. The Doctor's TARDIS, for example, which is an old Type 40 model, has a number of quirks and minor operating flaws. Great skill is necessary for precise time and space maneuvers with The Doctor's TARDIS, especially on short jumps, because the timeship is slightly out of tune. In addition, the chameleon circuit for The Doctor's TARDIS is out of order, leaving it in the shape of a blue police call box from Earth's England in the mid-1960s.

Playing the Game

To play **Doctor Who And The Vortex Crystal**, you will need this gamebook, and paper and pencil to record clues and other information. Two six-sided dice are recommended but not necessary for play, as noted in the Designers Notes on page 12.

This book is divided into three sections. First is **The Adventure**, which is presented as many numbered parts. These parts are called PARAGRAPHS, even though some are quite long and may contain many actual paragraphs. Play begins at the beginning of **The Adventure**, at Paragraph **100**. In contrast to most books, you will not read these paragraphs in sequence, but will move forward and back according to the italicized instructions given at the end of each. These instructions describe your options and direct you to the next appropriate paragraph(s) elsewhere in the book.

Attribute and Skill Statistics

As in more conventional roleplaying games, The Doctor has attributes that describe his innate abilities of Strength, Dexterity, Charisma, Mentality, Endurance, and Intuition, as well as several skills that will be needed to determine the outcome of various encounters during the adventure.

For this solo game, you will be using slightly modified attributes and skill statistics from FASA's *DOCTOR WHO* **Role Playing Game**. Consult the Attributes and Skills Table below. The third column lists the arabic numbers that you will be using for the Doctor's attributes and skills in **The Vortex Crystal.**

ATTRIBUTES AND SKILLS TABLE		
Attributes	**DR WHO:RPG**	**Vortex Crystal Stat**
Strength (STR)	Level IV	8
Endurance (END)	Level IV	8
Dexterity (DEX)	Level IV	8
Charisma (CHA)	Level V	9
Mentality (MNT)	Level VI	10
Intuition (ITN)	Level VI	10
Skills		
Brawling	Level IV	8
TARDIS Operation Skill	Level IV	8
Computer Systems	Level IV	8
Stealth	Level IV	8
Haggling	Level V	9
Negotiation/Diplomacy	Level VI	10

Saving Rolls

In playing this adventure, you will confront various situations testing your skills and abilities. To determine the outcome of these situations, you will usually roll 2D6. Sometimes the outcome of a situation depends merely on a lucky roll of the dice. For example, you might be instructed: *Roll 2D6. If the result is 8 or more, go to* **215**. *If the result is 7 or less, go to* **210**.

In other situations, you will have to make what is known as a Saving Roll. For example, the instructions might read:

Make a Saving Roll against your DEX. *If the roll is successful, go to* **534**. *If it fails, go to* **538**.

To make this Saving Roll, find the number of your DEX, which is listed as 8 on the Attributes and Skills Table. Then, roll 2D6 and add together the results. On a roll of 8 or less, your effort using DEX ability would succeed. If the result were 9 or more, your attempt to use DEX would fail.

Sometimes the instructions will add further complications, directing you to add or subtract a number from the die roll result. This number is called a *die modifier*, and represents unexpected difficulties or advantages in the situation. In this game, a successful roll is always *equal to or less than a certain number*. Therefore, a minus modifier is a bonus, making it easier for you to make a successful Saving Roll. A plus modifier will make a successful roll more difficult.

Combat

Occasionally, you will have to fight, either verbally or physically. Verbal Interaction represents an attempt to persuade another person to do something, while Combat Interaction represents hand-to-hand combat.

The instructions tell you which skills and attributes are called into play by the game situation, and, in some cases, you will be able to choose your strategy. Generally, you will begin by making a Saving Roll against one of your attributes. Then, you will roll 2D6 or 1D6 for your opponent's skill (the opponent's roll), subtracting this result from one of your own attribute or skill statistics. Next, you will make a modified die roll to represent your own skill. If the modified roll is *equal to or less than* your opponent's roll, you win. If it is greater, you lose.

Verbal Interaction

As an example of Verbal Interaction, let's say that you are trying to bluff, bluster, or convince six suspicious soldiers into believing that you are, in fact, an officer in their army and that they must follow your orders. You will be relying on your CHA more than anything else in this confrontation. Your instructions might be:

Make a Saving Roll against your CHA score. If it succeeds, you win a bonus modifier of –3. If it fails, the modifier is +3.

Then roll 1D6 to represent the guards' reaction, subtracting 1 because they are conditioned to obey without question. Subtract the result from your own CHA score. This is the guards' roll.

Next, roll 2D6 to represent your own tactics, and apply the modifier. If the modified roll is less than or equal to the guards' roll, you are successful. If the modified roll is higher, you have failed.

Let's say that you have a CHA of 8 in the above situation. You make a Saving Roll of 4. As this is less than 8, you win a bonus modifier of –3.

Rolling 1D6 for the guards' reaction gives you 5 – 1 = 4. Subtract this from your CHA of 8, which gives a result of 4 for the guards' roll.

Now, you must roll 4 or less on 2D6 to succeed in Verbal Interaction with the guards. You roll a 9, then apply the –3 modifier, which makes it a 6. As this is higher than the guards' roll of 4, you have failed in the attempt.

After making your Saving Rolls, the instructions then usually direct you to other numbered paragraphs, depending on whether you won or lost the Verbal Interaction.

Combat Interaction

Hand-to-hand combat works the same way. Let's say you are fighting two guards armed with submachine guns in a lift. In this struggle, you will need your STR and your *Brawling* skill. The instructions might read as follows:

Make a Saving Roll against your STR. If it succeeds, you win a bonus modifier of –3. If it fails, the modifier is +2.

Then roll 2D6 for the two soldiers, and add 4 for their training. Subtract this from your DEX score + your Brawling *skill. The result is the soldiers' roll. To determine your own actions, roll 2D6 against the soldier's roll, applying the plus or minus modifier. If your modified roll is less than or equal to the soldiers' roll, you have won. If it is greater, you have lost.*

Let's say that you have an 8 for your STR, DEX, and *Brawling* Skill, and you roll 7 on 2D6 in the above situation. As this is less than 8, you win a modifier of –3.

Then you roll 2D6 for the two soldiers, getting a 7. Add 4 for their training, which gives an 11 for the soldiers' roll. Subtract this from your DEX + *Brawling* Skill (8 + 8 = 16 – 11 = 5). This means your modifier must be a 5 or less to win the encounter.

You make a roll of 6, and apply the –3 modifier, giving you a 3. This is less than 6, and so you have won the encounter.

The instructions would then direct you to other numbered paragraphs, depending on the outcome of the Combat Interaction.

For example:
If you win, go to **200.** *If you lose, go to* **203.**

Damage

Hand-to-hand combat may result in injury, and this will reduce some of your attributes, especially END and DEX. When this occurs, subtract the amount specified by the instructions, and apply it immediately. The losses are cumulative.

Several defeats in combat may result in The Doctor being unable to defend himself in future combats. It is possible to restore your attribute scores by resting at certain paragraphs or to eliminate the losses through regeneration, however.

Regeneration

Time Lords have the ability to regenerate when they are close to death, transforming their bodies and even their characters, thus cheating death. In this adventure, The Doctor is in his Fourth Incarnation, but may be forced to regenerate during play.

Regeneration is not automatic, however. First, you will make a roll using 2D6, subtracting 1 from the roll if your character has an MNT of 9, 2 if he has an MNT of 10, and 4 if his MNT has been raised somehow to 11. If the modified roll is less than a certain number (usually 7, but possibly lower with very serious injuries), The Doctor has successfully regenerated.

Regeneration Effects

First and foremost, regeneration allows your character to continue with the adventure by ignoring what otherwise would have resulted in his death. Although The Doctor's previous regenerations each resulted in drastic changes of his appearance and personality, it is sometimes possible for Time Lords to control their regeneration and to determine the outcome to some extent. There is, however, a period of mental and physical instability for a period of time after a regeneration.

Each time The Doctor regenerates, roll 1D6 on the following table to determine losses to his attribute scores:

REGENERATION EFFECTS TABLE						
Die Roll	STR	END	DEX	CHA	MNT	ITN
1	–0	–1	–1	–1	–1	–1
2	–1	–1	–1	–1	–1	–1
3	–2	–1	–1	–1	–1	–1
4	–2	–2	–1	–1	–1	–2
5	–2	–2	–2	–2	–2	–2
6	–2	–2	–2	–2	–3	–3

For example, if the die roll after a regeneration is 3, The Doctor's attributes become:

STR	4	CHA	6
END	6	MNT	10
DEX	6	ITN	9

In time, your character will recover from the effects of regeneration. Roll 2D6 each time you move to another paragraph after a regeneration, whether or not that paragraph calls for the use of attributes. If the result is 8 or more, the attributes remain reduced for that paragraph. If the result is 5 or less, The Doctor's attributes are restored to their original level, and further recovery rolls are no longer necessary. Recovery from the effects of regeneration is complete, even if the attributes have been reduced several times by the effects of multiple regenerations.

When combat has caused reductions in attributes, these losses are restored through regeneration.

Loss Of Attributes

Attributes can NEVER be reduced below 2. However, a character forced to make Saving Rolls against a STR or DEX of 2 will not last long.

Clues

From time to time, you will be told that you have won a Clue, identified by a letter, e.g., Clue A. Each time you encounter a clue, write down the letter on a piece of paper and save it. If you come across the same clue more than once, write it down EACH time it comes up.

Some clues are necessary to move you in certain directions during the game. Others count for points toward the solution of an important mystery. The more clues you have, the better your chances of solving the riddle.

Exploring The Tower

The second section of this book is entitled **Exploring The Tower**. It maps out and describes the interior levels and rooms of a tower in Tharesti, a city on the planet Gathwyr, where this adventure takes place. The text will direct you to turn to this section anytime you must enter, leave, or move around within the Tower. Its various rooms may provide clues or important encounters, and from here you will be directed back to **The Adventure** section again.

Paragraphs are keyed to a map of the tower floors by the codes **T-1**, **T-2**, and so on. Simply find the appropriately coded paragraph and read it. You may have the opportunity to study the room more closely, or you may be told to make a die roll that results in the arrival of unfriendly forces. Or, searching the room carefully may yield clues to solving mysteries or lead you in other promising directions.

The paragraph descriptions of the various rooms will either lead you to OTHER room descriptions, or back to a numbered paragraph in **The Adventure**. Simply read the room description, make your decisions or roll your dice, then follow the instructions.

The map of the tower is included in the **Exploring The Tower** section to help you orient yourself. Remember, however, that your character does NOT have a map and so doesn't know that there may be a room around the corner until he gets there. The maps should be used sparingly in play.

Exploring The Ship

Exploring The Ship is laid out in the same way as **Exploring The Tower**. It describes the interior of a spaceship that may be encountered during the adventure. You may discover clues by searching various areas coded as **S-1**, **S-2**, and so on. A map of the two decks of the ship is given. As with the Tower, use this map only sparingly.

Designer's Note

While there is only a single general plot line to **Doctor Who And The Vortex Crystal,** there are many ways of arriving at the end. The design of this solo gameplay novel allows you to play it through a number of times, with major or minor variations each time. There is no 'correct' solution, though some solutions will be more elegant than others.

After you have run through the story a few times, you might try varying things a bit to increase the challenge. You might try playing The Doctor with all his skills and attributes reduced by 1 or more, or worse, handicap him by reducing his stats permanently after he regenerates.

You might decide to create a completely new character to play the adventure, using the character generation system in FASA's DR. WHO: RPG. Use the following table to translate skill levels from that system to arabic numerals:

Skill Level	Vortex Crystal Stat
I	2
II	4
III	6
IV	8
V	9
VI	10
VII	11

Another twist might be to continue using The Doctor, but to give him an entirely new set of stats (rolling 1D6 for each) every time he regenerates. Use the first column in the above table to represent the roll of the die, then read across to the second column for the resulting new stat. With this method, The Doctor's stats could never rise higher than 10, but they could drop significantly lower.

Doctor Who And The Vortex Crystal can be played without dice. In the upper corner of each page is printed a number ranging from 2 to 12. To simulate the throw of two dice, simply flip through the pages and then stop randomly. The number on the page would be the number 'rolled'. The chance of rolling a specific number and stopping at a particular page are the same. To simulate the roll of one die (1D6), use the following table:

2D6 Roll	1D6 Equivalent	2D6 Roll	1D6 Equivalent
2	1	8	5
3	2	9	4
4	3	10	4
5	3	11	2
6	1	12	5
7	6		

Using this method, **The Vortex Crystal** can be played anywhere.

THE ADVENTURE

100

    The planet did not look inviting. Our TARDIS had materialized on a rocky plain, a tortured landscape pocked by craters and shrouded in billowing mist. I eyed the area with distaste.

    Somewhere on this planet, which the TARDIS computers identified as Gathwyr, was the source of a temporal disturbance registered by our instruments. The traces were vague and fleeting, however, and could have been broadcast from a locus anywhere within 10,000 kilometers of where we were now. Finding the source of that anomalous wisp of disturbance in the Temporal Vortex was going to be a considerable problem. Like looking for a needle in a haystack, as Earthfolk would say.

    I'd first been alerted to the fact that something strange was happening here when we hit a storm within the Vortex. Piloting us through those entropic currents had taxed to the limit even my skill with the TARDIS controls, but we'd come through.

    Afterward, the currents had vanished, leaving behind only some kind of temporal static. That bothered me, plucked at my curiosity. As I'd explained it to my Companions, the 'static' represented an interface between the normal universe and the Space-Time Vortex. But it was an interface that shouldn't have been there.

    What was it?

    "There's nothing out there but fog, Doctor," Sarah Jane said, disappointment in both her face and her voice. "Are you sure this thing is working right?"

    I winced. My two Companions had not been overly

impressed with my TARDIS piloting skill since the last time I'd tried to return them to their own time and place. Sarah Jane had this habit of crossing her arms, then smiling sweetly as she asked, "Do you have the right time, Doctor?" and as for Harry Sullivan, well...

None of it was my fault, you see. The spatial coordinates had been right, but that glitch in the temporal governor had brought us down 140 million years off the mark. For my part, I've always been fascinated by Earth's Upper Jurassic fauna, but neither Sarah Jane nor Harry could seem to muster the proper scientific spirit. That Allosaurus, for instance... Fascinating!

"These readings say the air out there is breathable," I told my two friends, "but if something's wrong with the plumbing, we can't quite trust them, can we? Shall we check it out for ourselves?"

Without waiting for an answer, I opened the TARDIS door and went out. Is "this thing working right?", indeed!

Harry and Sarah Jane followed with only the slightest, pro forma show of hesitation. The air outside was cool, the ground under our feet warm. I squatted and scooped a handful of rich, black sand, letting it trickle through my fingers.

"Volcanic," I said. "That explains the mist. Subsurface magma pockets heat the ground, causing condensation of water vapor in low-lying masses of cold, moist air."

Sarah arched an eyebrow, unimpressed. "Meaning?"

"Fog. Lots of it. And volcanoes too, unless I miss my guess. Smell them?"

They wrinkled their noses. "Sort of. More like rotten eggs," Harry said.

"Brimstone. Burning sulphur...but faint, far off. I'd say there are probably quite a few active volcanoes here. Gathwy is quite young, geologically."

"Oh, great," Sarah said mournfully. "More thundering dinosaurs with kitchen-knife teeth and big appetites?"

"Oh, hardly," I said casually. "There *is* one dangerous lifeform here, though."

"I knew it," she said. "What?"

"It's man," I told her, grinning. "Come along. Let's have a look around, shall we?"

We set off more or less randomly. The ground rose slightly ahead, and I wondered if we'd be able to get above the fog for a look around. I checked my pockets first. I had a TARDIS homing beacon (Type A, a Temporal Field Indicator), my sonic screwdriver (of course!), and the usual odds and ends such as string, a yo-yo, and jelly babies. I also had with me a temporal interference sensor.

I was quite proud of that last, a palm-sized gadget I'd worked up in the TARDIS workshop on our way here. It responded to the faint traces of disturbance at an interface of the Space-Time Vortex with normal space, the 'temporal statis' that had brought us to Gathwyr in the first place. The sensor showed no reading now, but if that disturbance recurred, I would be able to get a directional reading on it.

Harry came up behind me, looking around at the encircling fog. "But what would people be doing here?"

"Remember, this is the far future for you, Harry. Gathwyr was colonized during Earth's Imperial period. The civilization slipped back a bit when the Empire fell, of course, but they managed to build an admirable culture, as human ones go. They've been on their own for quite a few centuries now, pretty much minding their own business and..."

Sarah's unmistakable scream interrupted my dissertation. I bounded down the sandy slope toward where she stood, one fist against her mouth, eyes staring.

"Sarah! What is it?"

She pointed. Sprawled among volcanic shards on the black sand was a body, a human dressed in mottled black and grey tunic and trousers, a ragged uniform of some kind. The tunic appeared scorched and burned, and the rifle alongside the body was partially melted, as though by a blast of terrific heat. The man's face was locked in a grimace of rage or terror, and the cloth around the wound in his chest still smoldered.

Harry was at my side, looking solemn. A Royal Navy doctor attached to UNIT, his inspection of the wound was swift and professional. "A burn," Harry said. "Possibly electrical. This didn't happen long ago, either."

"Yes. A few minutes...an hour at most."

"Then...then, whatever did that—"

"Is still around. Yes." I was examining the rifle, and noting something very curious.

"I told you the Gathwyrans slipped back a bit when the Empire fell. See this weapon? It's typical of primitives. Uses explosive chemical propellant in metal cartridges to shoot a bit of metal..."

"Yes, Doctor, we know," Harry said impatiently. "It's called a gun."

I gave him a sour look. "If you know so much, can you tell me why this man was killed by—at first approximation—a 10 million-electron volt particle beam?"

"Wrong technology?"

"Decidedly. Of course, he could have been fighting someone much more advanced..."

"There are more bodies over there," Harry said, motioning with his chin. As the fog thinned, I could see them now, the bodies crumpled and sprawled along the hillside. There were also dozens of small craters lined with black glass, some still trailing wisps of smoke. I guessed that several hundred people had died here, and recently.

"It looks like they were trying to get up this hill," I said, eyeing the slopes. "And someone, or something, blasted them down. Hmm."

You may choose either to climb the hill or head back for your TARDIS. If you elect to go up the slope in hope of discovering what killed the men, go to 125. If you decide that discretion is the better part of valor, and that observing from the safety of the TARDIS might be preferable to exposing yourself to whatever killed the soldiers, go to 118.

101

I dropped it.

I'd hoped to grab the yo-yo and bluff them with it. Maybe make them think it was a bomb or something, but the slippery thing flipped out of my fingers and bounced down the hill with an embarrassing clatter.

A rifle butt came down on me out of nowhere, and all I saw was a dazzle of blinding light that faded swiftly into enveloping dark.

Go to 138.

102

This called for fast thinking. I had noted the positions of the sensor helmet-wearing troopers before I made my break, and now I was slipping through the fog in what I thought should be the direction to carry me clear of them. It would take them time to get organized, time to arrange a search. That is, if they decided to follow me at all. It would take time for them to track me down on foot, and those black-clad troopers had seemed unusually nervous, continually glancing over their shoulders into the fog. No, they probably wouldn't follow me into the fog. If I could just get out of rifle range, I would be safe.

Then I heard the electronic hum of a vehicle overhead.

Impossible! That keening was characteristic of anti-gravity vehicles, and this culture couldn't possibly support that kind of technology. Not with rifles and submachine guns for weapons!

Just then, a rock glowed white in front of me, sizzling hissing, and turning to vapor with a vicious crack as lightning seared through the fog.

I stumbled, suddenly blind. The dazzle had wiped away my vision—temporarily, I hoped—but leaving me quite helpless Which way? That way, I thought...

Then there was another ear-splitting crack and a wave of heat engulfed me. As I pitched forward, the darkness seemed to rise like a black flood to engulf and drag me down.

In those last seconds of consciousness, I realized just how badly I'd been hit.

I was dying.

As a Time Lord, you have a chance to regenerate before you die, repairing the damage done by the enemy beam and thus escaping death. If you do not regenerate now, you will die. Roll 2D6. Subtract 1 if you have an MNT level of 9, 2 if you have an MNT level of 10, or 4 if you have an MNT level of 11.

If the result is 7 or less, you have regenerated. Go to **150.** *If the result is greater than 7, go to* **113.**

103

I couldn't let them take me! I threw myself behind a boulder, heard rocks hiss and crack, then felt a wave of heat pass over my back. I scrambled downslope, away from that vehicle and its gunner, painfully aware that they could see me through the fog while I was effectively blind.

The beam caught me squarely in the back, blinding me in a glare of light that dazzled my eyes and numbed my brain and…slowly…faded…to…black.

Go to **138.**

104

Maybe I could get back to the TARDIS. There, at least, I might be able to track my friends, might be able to attempt a rescue. I no longer had my homing beacon, but my unerring sense of direction would lead me straight to my goal. That way…No, that way…

There was only one problem. The TARDIS was surrounded by black-uniformed men with nasty weapons and nastier voices, a milling crowd that I could hear long before I got close enough to the TARDIS to see it. I hung back among the boulders and the grey fog, waiting for my chance.

"Hands up, rebel," an amplified voice boomed from above. "Surrender or die!"

The machine descended on me like a mechanical hawk, a great, black, metal craft defying gravity with an electronic hum, tracking my movements through impenetrable fog.

The technology of these people shouldn't even have been up to sophisicated, all-weather sensor helmets. Now they were coming at me with an anti-gravity vehicle. Something was definitely askew here.

The machine's hum fell through the octaves as it settled to the ground a few meters in front of me. Helmeted troopers swiveled a large and unpleasant-looking device to point at me, and one of the men announced again, "Surrender or die!"

Some choice.

Go to **107** *if you want to do as he says. Go to* **103** *if you want to dive into the fog and try to escape.*

105

With the towers as a guide, we marched along the crest of the hill. My temporal interference sensor was giving only indefinite readings, much too weak to be certain yet of direction. If we were to find any answers at all, it would be where there were people. The city offered our one hope of finding someone to talk to.

Still, the nagging feeling that we were being watched continued. Once I heard the scrape and clatter of boots in volcanic gravel, and twice I thought I heard voices in the mist, somewhere off to the side.

You can change your mind and return to your TARDIS, at **121.** *Or you can continue ahead to* **124.**

106

I did a perfect, four-times-over somersault, landed on my feet, and started running. The yammer of gunfire came after me, but I dodged among massive boulders sunken in the volcanic slag. Hitting a loose patch of gravel, I slid, putting as much distance as possible between me and those gun-happy soldiers. Troopers wearing sensor helmets would be able to track me in the fog, but if I got far enough, fast enough, maybe...

It was odd, though. I could still hear gunfire behind me, but none of the bullets were coming my way. Then I sensed movement in the fog, and saw dim shapes slipping through the mist up the hill.

Suddenly, two of them stepped out of the mist in front of me, their rifles levelled.

Go to **155.**

107

My captors crowded me into the small, open-topped aircar and kept their guns pointed at me as we lifted above the fog toward our destination. The city was called Tharesti, and the sight of its white towers against the blue sky filled me with a nameless dread.

"The Tower of the Masters," one of them said, pointing out the tallest of the towers. "That's where we're taking you. And you won't be coming out alive."

I decided to enjoy the scenery while I could. Unfortunately, the fog and the rapidly approaching white towers were all there was. Gathwyr thus far had been singularly lacking in scenic charm. Nor did it seem likely to get much better.

Go to **142**.

108

There were dozens of them, grim men in black uniforms. Most of them surrounded us, though a few others clustered about the door to the TARDIS. Several wore peculiar helmets, great, bulbous things that masked their faces and gave them an ominous, insectlike look. Odd...I could have sworn those were heat and motion sensors on those masks, devices far in advance of this culture's late-Iron Age technology. I'd seen similar devices before, but where?

"What have we here?" said one of our captors, who paraded around, looking us up and down. Judging by the gold of his throat and jacket sleeves, he was an officer. "They don't look much like rebels, now, do they?"

"Hello! I'm The Doctor," I said, trying my friendliest grin. "You might find this rather hard to believe, but we're travellers. Tourists, you might say. We landed here and..."

"SILENCE! Search them!"

Rough-handed men began going through our pockets. The leader seemed puzzled by some of the things he found in mine—the sonic screw driver, the homing beacon, the interference sensor, and especially the yo-yo. "What are these...?"

"Not weapons."

He grunted and handed the collection to an aide, while I experienced a sinking feeling at the pit of my stomach. We'd have to get some or all of those devices back or we could forget about finding that temporal disturbance.

One of the men turned from the TARDIS door, saying, "It seems to be locked, Armsleader."

The officer turned to me. "Is that...that device yours also?"

"Yes. Actually, it's my space ship. If you'll just..."

Two of them helped me back to my feet. I hadn't even seen where the blow had come from.

"After this, simply answer the questions put to you!" The leader's brow furrowed, then cleared, as if he had finally reached a decision. "We'll take them back to the city," he told his men. "The Masters'll know what to do with 'em."

I pondered this repeated reference to some 'Masters'. The thought of one Master seemed bad enough. But more than one?

You can try to break away into the fog and go to **123**. *Or you can go along with your captors to* **119**.

109

They called the city Tharesti, its stark towers piercing an impossibly blue sky above the sea of fog. There were clusters of ominous, black-clad sentries at the massive, clamshell gates that opened with a ponderous grinding at our approach. Inside those gates, few people were *not* in uniform, and those were a grey and cheerless lot.

My captors steered me through twisting streets, ever upward toward the tallest of the city's towers.

"The Tower of the Masters," the officer observed. "You won't be leaving it alive."

Go to **151.**

110

You are trying to convince Harry to leave the submachine gun where he found it. To persuade him will require charm and either tact or persuasive argument.

First, make a Saving Roll against your CHA score. A successful roll will be equal to or less than your score. If the roll succeeds, you win a bonus modifier of −2. If the roll fails, the modifier is +3.

Next, roll 2D6 to represent his stubbornness, and subtract this from either your *Haggling* or *Negotiation/ Diplomacy* skill. This is Harry's roll.

Finally, roll 2D6 for your argument or use of tact, and apply the modifier. If this result is equal to or less than your *Haggling* skill rating minus Harry's stubborness, the roll is successful. If it is greater than your skill rating minus Harry's stubbornness, it has failed.

If the roll fails, go to **140***; if you succeed, go to* **115**.

111

I followed the crest of the ridge in the direction of the party with Harry and Sarah. They were heading toward the blank-faced towers visible in the distance along the ridge.

Black specks appeared in the air close by those towers, specks that grew with alarming speed into some kind of aircraft streaking toward me. I slithered back down the ridge into the cloak of fog.

Just as I was thinking the fog would keep me safe, I heard the high-pitched whirr of a hovering machine somewhere in the mist above me. Now, that was curious! These people shouldn't have anti-gravity technology. Yet that aircraft defied gravity with an electronic hum that was nothing like the roar of a hovercraft or other conventional vehicle. It was floating directly overhead, pacing me through the fog.

"Surrender or die!" the amplified voice boomed at me. Then a nearby pile of rocks glowed white before changing instantly into molten, hissing liquid. It appeared that whoever was in the vehicle could see me, even though I couldn't see them—another small mystery of technology. Where was this stuff coming from?

"We see you down there," the voice continued. "Surrender or die!"

Some choice.

You may do as the voice says, and go to **107**, *or you can attempt to run and hide at* **103**.

112

Obviously, if I went along with this bunch, my opportunities to help Sarah and Harry were going to be limited. Besides, I had a sudden curiosity about the rebels. The real rebels, that is. The ones who had left beam-charred bodies strewn all along the slope of the ridge. Who were they? What were they trying to accomplish? I had a growing feeling that I was going to need plenty of help if I was going to survive—much less accomplish anything—on Gathwyr.

Maybe I could still make it back to the TARDIS. I was certain I could find it in the fog, even without the homing device. Once inside, I'd have a good chance of finding—and rescuing—my Companions.

The officer's aide was examining my yo-yo curiously.

"Here," I said, reaching out. "Careful of that."

As he looked up to meet my eyes, my hand struck down and snatched the yo-yo from his fingers.

Make a Saving Roll against your DEX *score. If you succeed, go to* **134**. *If you fail, go to* **101**.

113

Unfortunately, your regeneration attempt has failed. You are dead, and in all probability, your friends will soon be dead as well, if they aren't already.

Go to **541**.

114

Before I could say a word, there was a chattering crash close by my ear as Harry opened fire with his machine gun. The recoil jolted him back a step and sprayed bullets harmlessly into the air, but then the air was full of the smash and rattle of gunfire.

"Harry! You idiot!" I yelled, and knocked him to the ground, only partly because I wanted him down out of the line of fire. The gun went skittering away somewhere. I think the recoil had surprised him.

I heard Sarah say, "Oh, Doctor," and then I was looking up at a scowling black-uniformed man who held a wicked-looking gun pointed at my face.

I gave him my best smile. "Hello there! Please forgive my friend, here. I think you startled him."

Go to **116**.

115

"Oh, very well," Harry said, and he dropped the gun. He sounded hurt, but if Harry Sullivan's going to be on the same planet as me, I would rather have him sulking than armed.

Go to **118**.

116

We stood there in the fog with our hands in the air, while black-uniformed troopers crowded close about us, going through our pockets and shoving us this way and that. Their leader gave us a close inspection. By the gold at his collar and sleeves, he appeared to be an officer.

"Rebels." The man pronounced the word as though it were inexpressibly sour. Going through the collection of objects in my pockets, he seemed puzzled, too, but handed the lot over to an aide without comment.

"Oh, no sir," I said. "I'm The Doctor, and these are my friends, Sarah Jane and Harry. You really must forgive Harry. He gets a bit excited sometimes."

"Steady on, Doctor."

"Quiet, Harry. I'm trying to save your life."

"You can save your explanations," the officer said. "Save them for the Masters."

That word chilled me. "Masters? More than one?"

"You'll find out. If you live." He summoned a soldier, a man wearing a bulbous-eyed mask that had to be a sensor helmet of some find. It seemed curiously out of place alongside this planet's unsophisticated technology. "Proctor, take those other two on ahead."

"Now, wait a minute…"

When they helped me to my feet and I was again able to breathe, the officer favored me with a smile. "Next time, just

26

answer questions, rebel. I'm sending them on ahead so your friends can't free all of you with one attack. Now, move."

They led me up the ridge to the crest. There, the fog thinned away to tatters and the sky was impossibly blue. In the distance loomed the white, blank-faced towers of a city, and we began moving in that direction.

Go along with them to **109**, *or watch for a chance to get away at* **123**.

117

I stood up carefully, breathing hard, the soldier unconscious at my feet. Our scuffle seemed to have gone unnoticed. I'd escaped, at least for the moment.

But what about Sarah Jane and Harry?

Listening for sounds of pursuit, I maneuvered through rocks and slithered across gravel, trying to get closer to the searchers without being seen. I could hear voices calling to one another through the fog. "Over here! They went that way! There!"

There was a long pause, and finally I heard someone shout, "O.K.! We got two of them!" So, my Companions had been captured.

Well, perhaps I could backtrack to the TARDIS. Once there, I might manage a daring rescue.

Putting my hand into my pocket, I experienced another icy shock. My coat pocket was empty. The homing beacon, the temporal disturbance tracer, even my sonic screw driver and yo-yo were missing. I looked back into the fog, chewing at my lower lip. The objects must have spilled out during my fight with that soldier. The sound of jackboots crunching through gravel in that direction discouraged me from going back to look. I'd have to make do without those gadgets.

I checked my other pocket. Yes, there was still half a

27

package of jelly babies. Things might not be so bad after all.

I could hear the scuffling of a large body of soldiers moving through gravel up ahead. Following my ears, I trailed them back up the slope of the ridge.

At the crest of the ridge, the fog thinned out to reveal the strikingly blue sky overhead and the blank-faced, needle-tipped spires of a city off to my right. There was a paved road along the top of the ridge running straight toward the city. In the distance, I could make out a party of soldiers on the move in that direction.

And they had Sarah and Harry.

You can follow them to **146**. *Or you can go back down the ridge, looking for your TARDIS at* **152**.

118

"Oh, Doctor, I'm scared," Sarah said. "Can we get out of here?"

"I don't much like this either," I said. I was feeling vulnerable. "In fact, I've got a very bad feeling about this place. C'mon."

The TARDIS was only a few meters behind us in the fog. Once inside, we should be safe enough from whatever terror it was that had swooped down upon those poor souls.

"This was a military expedition of some kind," Harry said. "Look at the weapons."

As the fog thinned, we could see bodies scattered all along the slope, with dozens of primitive rifles, pistols, and light automatic weapons still clutched in literal death-grips. Whoever they were, I doubted that these dead men had been part of an organized military force. Their clothing was ragged and made up of odds and ends rather than proper uniforms. "Yes, well, their guns didn't help THEM much. Let's get back to the TARDIS."

The sound of metal scraping on rock stopped us, and we saw shadows coming out of the mist, shadows that materialized as men in black uniforms, and carrying guns. Many of them wore heavy, black helmets that masked their faces, giving them an eldricht, bulbous-eyed, insect look. Sensor helmets? That seemed a bit out of place with this planet's technology.

"Hold it right there, rebels," a voice said, amplified through the mask's speakers. "Put your hands up!"

It appears that you are surrounded. You can obey your captors by raising your hands and going to **108**. *Or you can make a dive for the protection of the encircling fog at* **126**.

119

The Armsleader jabbed a finger at me. "This one seems to be the leader. Take those other two rebels on ahead."

"No!" I said. "Wait!"

A rifle butt connected with my solar plexus. When I could breathe again, the officer said, "You speak when I ask you a question, got me?" He seemed to relax a bit as Sarah and Harry vanished into the fog up the ridge. "Your rebel friends may still be around. I'll not have them trying to rescue all of you. Now move!"

They prodded me along up the ridge to where the fog was thinned by sunlight, and there was blue sky overhead. Off to the right, stark white towers arrowed up above the fog sea, and it was toward this that our captors led me. Strain as I might, I could see no sign at all of Harry or Sarah.

I hoped those two would keep their heads about them. This lot didn't seem to be forgiving types, and that mention of "Masters" worried me. What was going on here on Gathwyr?

You can continue going along to 109, or you can watch for a chance to dive down the slope of the ridge into the fog at 123.

120

None of us liked the look of those towers much, and the fog shrouding both slopes of the ridge had a clammy and claustrophobic feel. There was the prickling sense of being watched, of being shadowed by unseen followers.

"Let's try this way," I said and pointed to the left, away from those silent towers. Harry and Sarah followed, both of them nervously looking over their shoulders.

Then we heard the sound of metal scraping on rock. We WERE being followed, of that I was certain now.

You can try to return to the TARDIS at 130. You can get off the ridge, and try to hide in the fog at 135. Or you can continue ahead to 124.

121

"I don't like this," Sarah said. "Shouldn't we be getting back to the TARDIS?"

"Well, if you insist." I was trying to sound casual but was wondering the same thing myself. We were altogether too vulnerable out here on the ridge, despite Harry's gun.

We about-faced and started back toward the TARDIS. Though it was completely masked by fog, my homing beacon let us retrace our steps without hesitation.

"Almost home free now," I said, reaching for my TARDIS key. "Once inside, we'll..."

There was a slap-clatter of guns being brought to the point, the sinister click of drawn bolts.

"Halt!" Throw down your guns!" a man's voice called out, as black shapes materialized from the mist.

If you want to do as they say, go to **116**. *If you want to try to dive for the fog and hide, go to* **114**. *If you're worried about what Harry might do with his submachine gun, go to* **131**.

122

They called the city whose towers gleamed white above the fog Tharesti, and they led me along the ridge toward it at a quick march. My captors seemed nervous, as though expecting an attack from out of the mist at any moment.

You can keep going with them to **133**, or you can try to escape to **128**.

123

There was a moment's confusion as our captors milled forward in the swirling fog. When one trooper stumbled, several heads swung in his direction. That was our chance! "Run!" I whispered. "Quick!"

The three of us darted into the fog. Shouts and commands echoed behind us, followed by the staccato clatter of automatic weapons and a whirring overhead like a hover of angry wasps.

I heard a familiar scream ahead, and called, "Sarah!"

There was no reply. I turned to Harry, then realized that Harry was no longer at my side. "Sarah! Harry!"

Still there was no answer, save the scrabbling sound of men behind me, but getting closer. I chose a direction and began moving, treading on the loose rock as lightly and as silently as I could.

What had become of my Companions?

There seemed to be considerable confusion in the mist around me. I found an inconspicuous spot tucked between a pair of massive boulders and waited for the ruckus to die down, then crept cautiously out and up the side of the ridge There were voices up there, and the rumbling of squads of jack-booted men marching in step.

For just an instant, the fog thinned enough for me to catch a glimpse of Sarah and Harry being marched down the road, surrounded by black-uniformed troops.

Then the fog closed after them, and they were lost from view.

All this running around out here is hard work. Reduce your END and STR each by 2. You can try to go back to the TARDIS at 104, or you can follow your friends to 111.

124

The ambush was sudden and complete. Sarah screamed once, and then there were black-uniformed men on every side of us, holding weapons to our heads and ordering us to raise our hands. A pair of troopers grabbed Harry from behind and efficiently disarmed him. They wore massive helmets that masked their faces and gave them an eldritch, bulbous-eyed insect look. They had seemed to come out of nowhere. It was a mystery how they had managed to trail us invisibly in the fog.

"Good morning," I started to say, but a harsh-featured soldier jammed a rifle butt against my chest.

"Silence, rebel." Another trooper peered into my face then looked me up and down. From the gold on his collar and jacket sleeves, I judged him to be an officer. "Strangers...in a restricted zone...carrying guns," he said. Blast Harry and his submachine gun! "You don't look much like a rebel," he said "Could be Latham and his gang are getting desperate." There was a polite chuckle from several of the soldiers. He gestured and then rough-handed men were searching me, going through my pockets.

The leader seemed puzzled by some of the things they found. There was the sonic screw driver, the interference sensor, the TARDIS homing beacon, and my yo-yo. The man carefully examined each one before handing it to an aide. He sniffed at a jelly baby suspiciously. "This is...?"

"Not a weapon."

He grunted and handed the package to his aide.

"Look," I told him. "This is all a mistake. You see..."

The soldier with the rifle slammed it into my solar plexus. When I could breathe again, the officer smiled. "Maybe that will teach you to speak only in reply to a question." He gestured again. "Yavikk! Garrol! Take those two on ahead. The rebels are still around. I don't want to risk a rebel attack to free them all."

"No!" I said, stepping forward. But before I could speak another word, I was on the ground, rubbing a bruised jaw and glaring up at the soldier who glared right back down at me.

"No nonsense, rebel. On your feet!" When I looked around, my Companions were gone, swallowed up with their captors by the fog.

Want to try to escape? Go to **112**. *If you want to go along peacefully, go to* **122**.

125

There were more bodies as we neared the crest of the hill, hundreds of them in grotesque sprawls, clustered so thickly it was difficult to walk without treading on them. All were armed with relatively primitive weapons such as repeating rifles, light auto-fire weapons, revolvers, and automatic pistols. All bore the smoldering marks of violent death by high-energy beam.

Harry picked up a submachine gun and snicked back the bolt. The design was similar to what he would have known in his own time on Earth. "Maybe we should arm ourselves, Doctor."

I've never cared for guns. They have a nasty tendency of inducing false bravado in their bearers, of making all-too-vulnerable flesh and blood feel invincible just when a healthy dose of caution is needed most. "Well," I replied. "Those things didn't help THEM much, did they?"

Harry looked around nervously, but he kept the weapon.

Someone like Harry carrying a loaded submachine gun makes you nervous. You can ignore him, and go on to **140**, *or you can try to talk him out of carrying it and go to* **110**.

126

There was chaos among the swirling fog and moving shadows. It had always been my experience that the more people you put in an army, the easier it is to confuse them.

"There they are!" I yelled and pointed. "They're getting away!"

Then I gave my Companions a shove back into the fog. "Run! As fast as you can!"

We pounded through the mist, yells and orders rising behind us. There was a staccato rattle and a whirring overhead like angry wasps.

"Halt, rebels!" The amplified voice boomed after us. "Halt or we shoot!"

Idiots! What did they think they were doing now?

A shadow loomed up in front of me. I collided with it in a tangle of arms and legs and scarf, and the two of us went down, rolling across black gravel. "Keep running!" I yelled to my Companions, then grunted as the soldier I was fighting caught me in the stomach with a knee. His head loomed over me, nightmarish. He was masked in a metal helmet with bulbous lenses, which gave him an eldritch, insect look.

You can surrender at **129**, *hoping that Harry and Sarah will get away. Or you can fight by going to* **127**.

127

You will need your STR and *Brawling* skill to defeat this soldier. Make a Saving Roll against your STR score. If the result is equal to or less than that score, the roll is successful and earns you a bonus modifier of −2. If the roll fails, the modifier is +3.

Then, roll 1D6 and subtract it from your *Brawling* skill to determine the soldier's fighting skill. The result is the soldier's roll. Roll 2D6 for your own attack, and apply the modifier from your Saving Roll above. If the result is equal to or less than the soldier's 1D6 roll, you have won the fight. If the result is greater, you have lost.

If you win the combat, go to **117**. *If you lose, go to* **132**.

128

It looked like my best chance to rescue Harry and Sarah would be if I were someplace other than in the presence of the grim-looking troopers and their unpleasant-looking weapons. But how?

"There!" I shouted, pointing out across the fog sea. Of course, it was an old trick, but these boys were so nervous, it had a chance of working. "There! What's that?"

They looked, and I did a swan dive into the mist in the other direction.

Make a Saving Roll against your DEX *as you land head-first and then roll down the loose rock and gravel of the ridge slope. If you succeed, go to* **106**. *If you fail, go to* **141**.

129

"All right! All right!" I said, my hands in the air. "You've got me!"

The trooper gestured with his gun and led me back to the soldiers gathered around the TARDIS. With one raised palm, he saluted an officer wearing gold on his collar and sleeves. "Armsleader! I captured this one, but the others got away."

"No matter. They won't get far." The officer looked me up and down with an expression of sour distaste. "Who are you, rebel?"

"I'm The Doctor," I said, mustering my brightest, friendliest expression. "I believe there's been a terrible mistake. My friends and I were simply…"

"SILENCE! Search him."

The Armsleader seemed puzzled by some of the objects in my coat pockets. The yo-yo, especially, intrigued him. "Some kind of garrote? A weapon?"

"Certainly not! We are travellers—strangers here—and don't know anything about these rebels of yours."

The man's mouth twitched in something distantly related to humor as he handed the contents of my pockets to an aide. "No? Well, the Masters'll know what to do with you, I expect. Take him."

Masters? As in more than one? This did not sound good.

They led me up the ridge to the crest, where the fog thinned and shredded, revealing the white, needle-tipped towers of a city rising in the distance. There was a road along the ridge, and the armed troop pressed me on at a stiff pace, heading toward the towers.

I only hoped Harry and Sarah had gotten away.

Go to **109**.

130

The homing device led us unerringly back toward the TARDIS. We were half running now, our feet sliding in the loose volcanic rock underfoot. The fog had taken on a menacing, sinister quality, as though someone were out there, watching. We only felt it at first, but when we heard the scrape of metal against rock from out of the mist, we knew that someone or something was pursuing us down that slope toward the TARDIS.

"Almost there," I said, reaching for the TARDIS key. "Once inside, we'll…"

A sudden sound brought me to such a sudden halt that Sarah and Harry collided against me from behind.

"For heaven's sake, Harry," I said quietly, "put that idiotic thing down."

Harry only clutched the gun tighter, peering into the fog ahead. "But Doctor…"

"Please, Harry. For all of us." My hands went up above my head, and then Harry saw the shadows around us taking form.

He nodded, and very slowly put the submachine gun on the ground, then raised his own hands. "I see what you mean, Doctor."

Go to **108**.

131

Harry was bringing his gun up.

"Whoa there, Harry!" I said and stepped in front of his gun. Inspiration seized me and I raised my hands. "I give up!" I called loudly. "You've got me!"

Soldiers surrounded us within moments, grim figures in black uniforms. Many of them wore armored masks over their faces, which gave them blank, bulging-eyed, insect expressions. This was strange indeed, as advanced sensor equipment was beyond the technology suggested by these people's machine guns and rifles. There was something here that was not quite right.

"Fade back, Harry," I muttered out the side of my mouth. "Take Sarah and slip away, if you can." It wasn't much of a chance, but it was all we had.

Harry balked. "I say, Doctor, we can't!"

"For once, Harry, do as I say!" The soldiers were closer now, advancing slowly. One of them strode up to confront me. Judging by the gold at his collar and cuffs, he was an officer. "Who are you, rebel?"

"Oh, I'm The Doctor," I replied, with my brightest, toothiest smile. "So pleased to meet you. I'm a traveller here, and…"

"Silence!" He made a curt motion to one of his aides, who began going through my pockets. I carefully kept my eyes on the officer's face, hoping Sarah and Harry had been able to slip away. I'd learned centuries ago that humans tend to see what they expect to see. The fact that Harry and Sarah looked nothing like these black-clad commandos would not register for several precious moments, and in that time, they might be able to vanish into the fog.

"Hey!" Stop those two!" I closed my eyes and surrendered to the inevitable. Behind me, I heard a flurry of shots, then the sounds of struggle and scrabbling across loose rocks.

"Got them, Armsleader," a voice called.

"Very good. Take them on ahead. We'll follow with this one."

When they pulled me up off the ground and I'd managed to catch my breath again, the officer smiled at me with a horrible show of teeth that sent chills down my spine. "Let that be a lesson to you. You will speak only to answer my questions."

"But what about my friends? You're making a terrible mistake! We're not rebels."

"We'll let the Masters decide that." Again that chilling smile. "If they decide you're not rebels, they might possibly even let you live. Move!"

Masters? More than one? I didn't like the sound of that.

Someone gave me a shove, and I was led up the slope.

Go to **136**.

132

The butt of the soldier's gun swung out from nowhere and connected with the back of my skull. Then there was nothing but tiny, dancing lights as I faded into darkness.

Subtract 2 from your END *and 2 from your* STR. *Go to* **138**.

133

There was an unpleasant number of black-clad sentries standing about the massive, clamshell gates to the city, gates that ground open with a ponderous groaning at our approach. Inside, there were few people visible who were not wearing uniforms. Those I could see seemed a grey and cheerless lot.

My captors led me through twisting streets, up and up toward the tallest of the needle-capped towers.

"The Tower of the Masters," the officer announced with something distantly related to a grin. "Take a last look at the sky, rebel. Once in THAT place, you won't be seeing it again."

Go to **151**.

134

"Hold it! All of you, hold it!" I slipped the string over my finger, and snapped my wrist down and out, letting the yo-yo flip to the end of its tether and spin. Not a soldier moved, and every eye fastened on that spinning toy. "Onc wrong move and I set this off!" I warned. "You don't want to be around when I do!"

Step by step, I backed away from the troops. No one moved, I don't think anyone even breathed until I snapped the yo-yo back up its string into my hand and hurled it at their feet. Soldiers scattered in every direction, diving for the ground. While they scratched gravel, I turned and vanished into the fog.

Those troopers wearing sensor helmets would be able to follow me, of course, but they would be reluctant to follow too closely if they thought I was carrying a bomb. Sure, what I'd thrown at them hadn't exploded after all, but they would be cautious now, uncertain what other tricks I might have up my sleeve. If THAT had not been a bomb, perhaps the next device would be. This group did not seem to be particularly heroic. My guess was that they were ordinary people stuck with a job they'd really rather someone else would do.

Make a Saving Roll against your MNT. *If it succeeds, go to* **139**. *If it fails, go to* **102**.

135

We stepped off the crest of the ridge and started down the side, loose rock rasping and skittering away beneath our feet. Fog swirled about us again, thick and clammy.

"Doctor!"

"What is it, Sarah?"

"I heard something. There..."

I heard it too, and recognized the scrape and clatter of boots on volcanic gravel.

"I don't like this, Doctor," Harry said.

For once, I agreed with him. "Maybe we should try going back."

Go to **124**.

136

From the top of the ridge, I could see the towers of the city. Tharesti, they called it, shining white and stark against a deep blue sky. There was a road along the ridge, and they started me along the pavement toward the city at a forced-march pace.

Who were these rebels the soldiers were so concerned about? I could tell they were nervous, the way they kept peering around at the sea of fog that lapped at our feet and filled the valleys on either side of the ridge. Obviously, the bodies we'd found had once been part of the rebel forces. Perhaps, they had been burned down while trying to reach this ridge-top road and access to the city. Their recent victory did not seem to have filled my captors with any particular sense of enthusiasm or confidence. In fact, they looked scared.

The officer, the one the troopers called "Armsleader", paced at my side. "Expecting an attack?" I asked in my most innocent voice.

"We're always expecting an attack. You people don't know when you're beaten."

"I think you must have me confused with someone else. I'm not a rebel, remember?"

"Shut up and march."

And then the firing began.

You can stay low and wait for the firing to stop at **137**, *or you can watch for a chance to escape in the confusion by going to* **145**.

137

With the officer at my side, I hugged the pavement. Meanwhile, soldiers all around me popped away with their automatic rifles at unseen shadows within the fog on either side. SOMETHING was moving down there. Twice I caught glimpses of crouched, slinking figures in the mist, and once I heard a yell of pain as bullets found their mark.

Then the firing stopped, and we were moving on at a half-run. I gathered from snatches of conversation that the soldiers had beaten off the attack, but expected more rebels at any moment.

As we neared Tharesti, I received another surprise. Flying vehicles emerged from ports high up among the towers and began to circle above our heads and skim along the top of the fog. They were anti-gravity vehicles of some kind, which was surprising. The technology of this civilization, as revealed by their rifles and submachine guns, was scarcely up to primitive ground effect hovercraft, much less anti-gravity vehicles. It was all getting curiouser and curiouser.

There was an ominous number of black-clad sentries clustered about the massive, clamshell gates that swung aside with a ponderous grinding at our approach. There were few people inside those gates not in uniform, and those I saw were a grey and cheerless lot. There was dread in many of the eyes that followed our procession, apathy in most of the rest. Gathwyr had fallen a long way from the glory days of Terra's Imperium.

My captors steered me along twisting streets that led up and up toward the tallest of the city's towers.

"The Tower of the Masters," the Armsleader observed. "Take a last good look at blue sky, rebel. You won't be leaving that place alive."

Go to **151**.

138

Consciousness returned like an unwelcome relative, loud, rude, and unpleasant. I forced my eyes open and winced at the glare of blinding light.

A small eternity or two later, my surroundings came into focus, and I sat up very slowly, holding my throbbing head. The intolerably brilliant glare faded to a single, naked electric light bulb dangling on a cord from a high stone ceiling. Blocks of rough, grey stone walled me in, forming a bare cell not quite as wide as my outstretched arms and twice as long. The heavy door was made of wood bound in strips of iron, and secured by a rust-gilded lock that looked centuries old. It was set into one of the shorter walls, with a narrow slot of a window set high up and closed from the outside. My only furniture was a pile of dirty hay, a filthy bucket, and a brown pottery jug half full of tepid water. There was a crude drain set into the brick floor at the far end of the chamber.

Without a window, without ventilation, the air was terribly foul and stuffy.

What to do? My pockets were empty. All my tools, including the sonic screw driver, were gone.

No, not quite empty. There was still half a bag of jelly babies in one pocket, and the key to the TARDIS was hanging around my neck. I still had my somewhat battered hat, my coat, and my scarf. Now why hadn't they taken that? Maybe they didn't particularly care if I hung myself in my cell.

Somehow, I couldn't see any way to turn what I had into

a weapon...at least, not yet. Perhaps the first step was to establish contact with my captors.

"Hey! Hallo out there! Is anyone there?"

The speed with which the slat was drawn back from the peephole in the door suggested that a guard was standing close by on the outside. Red-rimmed eyes glared in at me.

"Oh, hello! I'm The Doctor, and I think there's been a mistake."

"No mistake, rebel." The voice was gruel-thick and cold. "Shut off the racket or we'll start the interrogation early."

"Look, there's no need to be unfriendly. Can you tell me where I am?"

"The Tower of the Masters." There was a dry, rasping sound that might have been a chuckle. "'Course, you'll find out about THEM a little later. I imagine they'll have a few questions to put to *you*."

The peephole snapped shut, cutting off that chuckle.

Masters? As in more than one? This did not look good.

I sat down to think things over.

Though the circumstances are unpleasant, at least you can sit and rest here. You may restore ENT *or* STR *reduced by wounds or fatigue (but not by regeneration) to their original levels. Make a Saving Roll against your* MNT. *If it succeeds, you think of a risky but possible way to get out. Go to* **149**. *If it fails, or if you decide you'd be better off waiting to see what happens, go to* **156**.

139

The military mind tends to be one-track and inflexible at times. They assumed I was moving away from them as quickly as I could. Instead, I slipped around through the fog until I could approach them quite closely from the other side, following in their footsteps. When I was certain they were making their way back up the ridge and not following me, I slipped under the cover of a tangle of boulders set into the slope and waited.

How to find the rebels? Good question.

And how to find my TARDIS? Another good question. My homing device was gone, and my circling maneuvers in the fog had left me with the vague impression that it was THAT way. Or was it? No, THAT way.

And I had no ideas at all about how to rescue my friends. They'd been marched off into the fog, and here I was with no homing device, no temporal disturbance detector, no sonic screw driver, not even my yo-yo. I had my hat, coat, scarf, and half a package of jelly babies, none of which offered much potential for being cobbled together as a super-weapon.

Well, TARDIS or rebels. Which?

If you decide to hunt for the rebels, go to **144**. *If you decide to hunt for your TARDIS, go to* **154**.

140

I could see the sky from the crest of the hill, and in the distance to our right, there were the white towers of some very large buildings, or possibly a small city, glittering in the morning sun. At my feet was a paved road, alongside which ran confused markings in the gravel, as though heavy machines or vehicles had moved there. I stooped, touching the marks. Those tracks were highly compressed, the product of something quite massive. What could have made them?

I stood, looking each way. To left and right, the ridge stretched off into the mist. Ahead and behind, the hill dropped into impenetrable fog. There was no sign of life, except for those enigmatic towers.

I could not shake the feeling that we were being watched.

*If you decide to go along the ridge to your right, in the direction of the towers, go to **105**. If you wish to go straight ahead, down the hill, go to **135**. If you want to go to your left, go to **120**. You may also go to **130** if you decide that the security of the TARDIS would afford a much better vantage point for exploring this world.*

141

Unfortunately, there was a boulder in my path, hidden in the fog. My swan dive ended when the trajectory of the top of my head intersected the surface of the rock with sufficient force to turn the universe black and very, very painful.

*Ouch! Reduce your END by 2. Go to **138**.*

142

The aircar approached the tallest of the gleaming white towers.

"The Tower of the Masters," one of my captors said with an unpleasant grin. "Take a good last look around. You won't be seeing daylight again, ever."

"These 'Masters'," I said. "Who are they?"

"You'll be meeting them soon enough, rebel."

"Yeah," another said, then snickered. "I wouldn't be too eager about that, if I were you."

The tower swallowed the aircar. We stopped in a broad, cold-lit vehicle area, where my escort quick-marched me under close guard to a wide, central pillar. There, a door hissed open at the touch of an ID card placed by one of the guards against a wall-mounted scanner, revealing a lift. Checking which floor we were on, I noted that it was Level 20.

*Go to **143**.*

143

The door opened again at Level 2. The decor here was more primitive. Slick, bare stone walls, narrow corridors lined with massive, iron-bound doors, and blackness fitfully lit by electric bulbs at uneven intervals. The guards half dragged me along a passageway to where a soldier held one of those doors open, gave me a shove, and sent me sprawling face down inside.

I was in a stone cell not quite as wide as my outstretched arms and twice as long. Light came from a naked electric bulb dangling beyond my reach from a high, vaulted ceiling. The only furniture was a filthy bucket, a pile of dirty straw, and a brown pottery jug half full of tepid water. There were no windows or ventilation, and the air was thick and foul. The door had only a small, vertical peep slot, now closed from the outside.

I was locked in, of course. My tools, including my sonic screw driver, had all been taken from me. I had my hat, coat, and scarf. Why hadn't they taken that, I wondered? Perhaps they didn't care if I hung myself in my cell. I still had my TARDIS key on its chain around my neck. A half-full package of jelly babies was still in one pocket. All in all, I could think of no way to convert my meager assets into a doomsday weapon powerful enough to blast me free and rescue my friends.

Things did not look good. I sat down to think it all through.

It may not be pleasant, but the cell offers a place to rest. You may restore END *and* STR *levels reduced by wounds or fatigue (but not regeneration). Make a Saving Roll against your* MNT. *If it succeeds, you have an idea for a way to get out. It's risky but could work, with a bit of luck. If you want to try it, go to* **149**. *If the roll fails, or if you would prefer to stay where you are and see what happens, go to* **156**.

144

How to find the rebels? What did I know about them? Only that a large number had recently climbed up that volcanic ridge in a valiant but hopeless charge that had resulted in dozens of them being burned down by unknown energy weapons. Their bodies and weapons lay strewn across a quarter-kilometer strip at the foot of the ridge. How could I find their base?

Make a Saving Roll against your MNT. *If the roll succeeds, you have an idea and believe you know how to find the rebels. Go to* **147**. *If the roll fails, you have no ideas about how to find the rebels. Maybe you can find your TARDIS instead. Go to* **104**.

145

I hugged the pavement, the Armsleader at my side, as soldiers around me blazed away at shadows and fog. SOMEONE was down there, hidden in the fog. Twice I caught a fleeting glimpse of crouching figures darting through the mist. The troopers wearing sensor helmets were trying to direct the fire of the unhelmeted soldiers, pointing out targets and giving the commands to fire.

If I was going to get away from this grim and cheerless lot before they dragged me into that city, now was probably my only chance. Besides, I was possessed by an intense curiosity to meet the other side in this war. The only rebels I had seen so far were those scattered bodies on the slope of the ridge. Had they been killed trying to take the road and gain entrance to the city? Brave men, if so. They'd been cut down by weapons more advanced than rifles and machine guns (another mystery of Gathwyr that I wanted to solve) and had kept on coming. Perhaps the rebels were attacking now because they knew these soldiers were not armed with advanced weapons.

Or was there more to it? I shook my head. There was only one way to find out.

"Over there!" I yelled and pointed. It was an old trick, but men under fire were rarely discriminating. When someone shouts and points, they look and fire—not necessarily in that order. As heads turned and bullets stitched into the mist where I'd pointed, I rolled off the road and down the slope, into the clammy embrace of the fog.

The soldiers with sensor helmets would not be stopped by fog. I was on my feet and running as fast as I could, zigzagging as I went, expecting any moment the sledgehammer blows of bullets in my back. Behind me, I heard the chatter of automatic fire, heard bullets chirring through the air above my head. Then rocks skittered out from under my feet, and I was plunging headlong down the slope.

Make a Saving Roll against your DEX *to keep from landing on your head. If the roll succeeds, go to* **148**. *If it fails, go to* **153**.

146

"Hey! There he is! Stop him!"

I spun around, heart pounding. While I'd been watching the group marching Harry and Sarah toward the city, another group had emerged from the fog fifty meters behind me. The sound of automatic rifles rattled in the air, and lead hummed and whirred close above my head.

Make a Saving Roll against your DEX *as you try to leap clear of the gunfire and dive for cover in the fog. If the roll succeeds, go to* **169**. *If it fails, go to* **158**.

147

I had an idea for finding the rebels. By going to the bottom of the slope and backtracking along the broken, boulder-strewn ground, I found the place where the rebel bodies lay.

It was obvious, really. From what I'd seen of the soldiers and their equipment, this rebellion was fighting tough, well-armed, well-equipped troops. That told me that the rebels would be short of supplies, especially guns and ammo. I remembered that first, chilling view of the ill-fated remains of the rebel attack—bodies and weapons scattered as far as the enshrouding fog let us see.

No rebel commander would abandon that many weapons! True, many were half-melted and twisted by the force that had burned the attackers down, but many were in perfectly serviceable shape. I remembered Harry's submachine gun. The survivors might have been scattered so completely that it would be hours before they returned, possibly at night, to get those guns. Even if the attacking rebels had been wiped out to a man, which was unlikely, SOMEONE from the rebel base would come sooner or later to retrieve those weapons.

That the soldiers had not retrieved those guns bespoke either a shortage of manpower in the government forces or a supreme and overmastering confidence.

I found the battlefield, with its scattered bodies and weapons, just as I'd seen it before.

The TARDIS was nearby, but it seemed likely that the government soldiers would have mounted a guard on the blue-painted police call box squatting in the gravel a few score meters from the place of battle. It must surely seem an inexplicable phenomenon to them. Sure enough, when I crept close enough to see, I could make out the black-clad forms of a half-dozen soldiers crouched around the TARDIS door.

If I could get past those people, I'd be in a position to rescue Harry and Sarah and to get on with tracing those enigmatic disturbances in the space-time continuum, which is what had brought us to Gathwyr in the first place. But one against six?

As I watched from behind a dew-wet boulder, the guards shifted nervously, heads and guns turning at each twisting of fog or scrape of rock. There was no chance there. I eased back into the fog and returned to the debris-cluttered battlefield. Safely out of earshot of the guards, I gathered up an armload of what looked like working weapons, found a comfortable boulder, and sat down to wait.

It wasn't long before I heard stirrings in the fog, sensed more than saw the stealthy movement of grey figures, and caught once the scrape of boots on rock.

Then from out of the fog in front of me the butt of a rifle came up to point dead in my face.

Go to **155.**

148

By a minor miracle of acrobatics and flailing arms, I landed feet first in a cascading shower of gravel, then caught my balance in a wild breakneck scramble down the slope. The air above my head was filled with whirring objects and the crack and chatter of guns. I ran, cutting back and forth partly to make myself a tougher target, and partly to keep my descent down the slope from becoming a headlong, bone-crunching anticlimax.

A jumble of boulders loomed grey and massive out of the fog ahead. I skidded the last few meters, and scrambled around behind them, gasping each breath now. The gunfire had stopped. For a moment, I could rest.

But something was moving in the fog. As I looked up in

alarm, two bearded men clad in rags materialized from the mist, their rifles aimed steadily at my face. It seemed that I had found the rebels. Or rather, the rebels had found me.

There were shouts and the sound of boots scraping on loose gravel from behind. The two rebels started, looking upslope wildly. Government soldiers must have followed my wild descent, and now they were closing in for the kill.

The rebels are distracted. You can break away from them and run for it to **163.** *Or you can go with them to* **159,** *even though it may mean fighting hand-to-hand with the soldiers when they appear.*

149

If I was going to get out of here, I would have to take the guards by surprise, perhaps catching just one of them off guard. And I had an idea how to do it.

That electric lightbulb was dangling on its cord a meter beyond my reach. I took the wooden bucket and turned it upside down directly underneath the bulb, then stood on the bucket. The light was still centimeters beyond my reach, but I was able to make a noose of the end of my scarf, catch the cord just above the socket, and gradually pull the bulb toward me.

The cord showed obvious signs of age. It also showed signs of being the sort hurriedly installed by connecting it directly to a central wiring core. That meant a slow, steady pressure would pull the cord out of the ceiling fixture, without cutting the power.

I had the bulb in my hand. I kept pulling, slowly, slowly, with bits of dust and dirt floating down from the hole in the ceiling through which the cord was passing. Then I felt resistance, and knew that the cord had been pulled through as far as it would go. But I had enough cord to work with.

I unscrewed the bulb, plunging the cell into darkness, then went to work on the empty socket. My scarf was the best insulating material I had at hand, and so I worked the end of it through the socket. In darkness thick enough to touch, I had to work carefully, and by touch alone.

And if I slipped, it would mean disaster.

Make a Saving Roll against your DEX. *If the roll succeeds, go to* **171.** *If the roll fails, go to* **176.**

150

Consciousness returned, sharp and insistent. Alive! I was alive!

Regeneration is always a bit of a tricky thing for Time Lords. If they can choose their own time and place for it, there's not much to it, of course. I've known Time Lords— and Ladies—who changed bodies as casually as they changed their clothes. But in the case of a body gone suddenly wrong—hit by a death ray, for instance—the process can be rushed and the results unpredictable.

This time, at least, I'd managed to maintain control for a critical few seconds. My hand explored my face—same chin …same brow…the nose…yes, yes, same nose, unfortunately. I'd regenerated successfully, but I was still me—the old me, I mean, and not a new one. That was a relief. I rather liked myself the way I was, at least for now.

I opened my eyes.

"We thought you were dead."

The speaker was a man well along in years, with a worry-worn face and a grey grizzle of a beard. He wore ragged clothes, heavy boots, and a submachine gun hung by a sling from his shoulder.

Behind him were other men, clad as he was, bearing a motley assortment of arms and expressions. We seemed to be in a camp of some sort. Lean-to shelters were camouflaged with artfully planted masses of brush and leaves, and there was a small army of armed men and women all around, watching silently.

"I'm Latham," the man said. "We found you on the slope below the Tharesti Road. You're not one of us, and you're not a Blackie. I don't think you're from the Crystal City, either. Maybe you'll tell us just who you are?"

I sat up, a bit gingerly, but I felt surprisingly clear-headed, considering what I'd just been through. "I'm The Doctor. Pleased to meet you, Latham!"

It appeared that I'd found the rebels, or rather, that they had found me.

Go to **157.**

151

We entered The Tower of the Masters after a climb of endless, broad steps through a graven stone door three stories tall. The floors were seas of white and black marble, the foyer inside the doorway a great, hollowly echoing chamber with the dry, sterile feel of government buildings on a hundred thousand worlds across time and space.

The soldiers hustled me through to a curved wall at the center of the room. One of my captors touched an ID card to a sensor on the wall, a door opened, and we entered what could only be a lift. I took careful note that we were on Level 5.

Go to **143.**

152

I plunged back into the grey fog. Getting back to my TARDIS was the only hope I had now. I touched the key still hanging by its chain around my neck. If I could get back within the comforting extra dimensions of the TARDIS, I'd have a decent chance of tracking Harry and Sarah and getting them away from those people before...before...I didn't want to think about before what. These people were distinctly unfriendly, and seemed to be playing for keeps.

Finding the TARDIS should be simple enough. We had materialized about fifty meters from the scattered bodies we'd found, and those bodies were strewn across a good quarter-kilometer along the ridge. By getting to the bottom of the slope and backtracking, I'd find the bodies, and then the TARDIS, even without my homing beacon.

But who had these men been? They were not part of those soldiers we'd run into, that was certain. The soldiers were dressed in black uniforms, heavy jackboots, and helmets, and a number of them also wore those curious, bulbous-eyed fright masks that had to be sensors of some kind. The bodies we'd found had been dressed in ragtag clothing, and the faces I'd seen—young, old, bearded, clean-shaven—had been in marked contrast to the stark, military uniformity of the soldiers. Perhaps the dead men had been part of some sort of militia unit fighting the soldiers, possibly rebels.

I pondered those sensor helmets, too. They represented a technology quite advanced from the rifles and submachine guns I'd seen so far. The helmets didn't fit, and that bothered me. Just what, exactly, was going on on Gathwyr?

I found the cold, grey forms of bodies in the half-light of the fog. A moment later, I saw the TARDIS again. But on guard around the TARDIS door crouched six soldiers.

From my hiding place among a cluster of boulders about eighteen meters from the TARDIS, I could tell that they'd not yet seen me. They were watchful and very nervous, their heads and guns twitching about at drifting tatters of fog, at imagined noises or shadows. They had the look of troops ordered to mount guard in a lonely and exposed place, waiting for the enemy to close in. Were they expecting another rebel attack?

Things still were not adding up. If those scattered bodies represented an unsuccessful rebel attack, what had killed them? Not the primitive rifles and automatic weapons carried by these soldiers, weapons no more advanced than those carried by the rebels themselves. There was some vital factor missing from the equation. At the moment, I could see no way to find it.

Meanwhile, these people were standing between me and my TARDIS. I could try to talk my way past them, or I could sit where I was until the situation changed. Neither choice was appealing.

All this running around in the fog is tiring, isn't it? Reduce your END *and* STR *each by 2. You can walk up to the guards in an attempt to confuse and distract them long enough to get into your TARDIS at* **161.** *Or you can go to* **165** *to wait among the rocks to see what happens.*

153

I lost my balance completely and tumbled head over heels, rolling over and over down the slope in a minor avalanche of gravel and small rocks. Then the ground dropped out from under me and I was flying through space.

I can't really say I felt anything when I hit. All I knew was an explosion of darkness. After that, nothing at all.

Reduce your END *by 2, then go to* **164**.

154

Finding my TARDIS would be easy enough. We'd materialized about forty-five meters from the scattered rebel bodies, bodies that were strewn across a half-kilometer stretch of the base of the ridge. By getting to the bottom of the slope and backtracking, I'd find the battleground, and the TARDIS nearby.

The bodies were easy enough to find, but the TARDIS was a bit tougher. The fog was thick enough that I had to do a bit of searching, but sound carried well in the mist. The scrape of metal on gravel brought me eventually to a pile of boulders from which I could see the TARDIS sitting where we'd left it.

Unfortunately, there were six nervous-looking guards sitting there, too, clustered around the door with heads and guns jerking at every twist of fog or imagined sound or movement. They looked like they were expecting the enemy to close in at any moment.

The enemy? Probably that was the rebels, but things still were not adding up. The soldiers I'd seen so far were armed with weapons not different from the rebel rifles and submachine guns. But the dead men had been burned down by a high-energy discharge of some sort—a particle beam, or something very like it. Somehow, I was still missing part of the whole picture.

Meanwhile, these unpleasant people were keeping me from my TARDIS. I could try to talk my way past them, or I could sit right where I was until the situation changed.

Neither seemed an appealing choice.

You can walk up to the guards in an attempt to confuse and distract them long enough to get inside your TARDIS at **161***. Or you can wait among the rocks to see what happens at* **165**.

155

One of the men motioned with his hand across his mouth, and gestured with his gun. The message was unmistakable: keep quiet or die. The other gave a jerk with his gun, and they led me at a quick and silent trot into the mist.

They said nothing. Presumably, these were rebels, members of the force that had left those bodies strewn across the slope of the ridge. With care, they might become my allies. That was just as well, considering I was going to need their help if I was going to rescue Harry and Sarah and have any chance of finding out what was going on here on this planet.

Unfortunately for me, trusting strangers was not going to be a survival trait among outnumbered, outgunned rebel forces. Those who tried it tended to end up dead.

The journey through the fog covered several kilometers, all through an unending sameness of grey fog and black gravel. I was beginning to suspect the entire planet was like this, and wondered why humans chose to live in such desolation. Then the gravel gave way to dirt, to purplish grass and twisted plants, and the low, spreading canopies of red-leaved trees.

There was a camp here, lean-tos made of canvas hung from lines strung between trees, with generous masses of foliage and leaves artfully spread across each structure, providing camouflage against airborne observers. There were people here, rag-clad men and women carrying a variety of weapons and expressions, all watching me in silence. One man, dressed in rags, fur, and knee-high jackboots (taken from some soldier, no doubt) with a submachine gun slung from his shoulder, had the bearing of a leader.

There was a hushed, hurried conversation between my escort and this man. He regarded me with cold eyes, then said, "I am Latham, the leader here. My men say they found you on the slope below the Tharesti Road. You're not a Blackie, and you're certainly not one of us. I presume you're not from the Crystal City. Do you mind telling me *who* you are?" The way he said it suggested that an answer ill-received or not believed would probably be my last.

"Of course I don't mind! I'm The Doctor, and I'm very glad to meet you, Latham."

It appeared that I had found the rebels, or rather, that the rebels had found me.

Go to **157**.

156

I sat waiting for what seemed an eternity, though my inner clock told me only fifty-two minutes and forty seconds had passed. Then I heard the hollow shuffle of boots echoing along the stone corridor outside, the clash of keys in the metal lock. Two soldiers entered, took me firmly by each arm, then led me out and down the passageway.

The building's lifts ran through a shaft at the structure's center. I could see how cross-passages circled the central shaft. A guard used an ID card of some kind to open the lift door. I deciphered the lights on the wall inside, and decided they were taking me up from Level 2 to Level 4.

I thought fast. Wherever they were taking me, the two-to-one odds I faced now in the lift car were certain to be a lot better than any odds I would face when I got there. If the pattern common to imprisonment in totalitarian societies was being followed here, the next scheduled stop on my itinerary would be an interrogation team, which might be anything from a platoon of policemen with bright lights and gruff voices to a bare-chested, hooded-executioner type with blood on his hands.

On the other hand, perhaps my best bet was to wait. After all, I'd not have a better chance to meet the people who were running this show. They were bound to be personally interested in any prisoner dressed as oddly as I was, comparatively speaking, of course.

So, go along with them, or try to make my break? I had to decide immediately.

If you decide to go along with your captors without resisting, go to **180.** *If you want to try to overpower your guards and escape, go to* **195.**

157

Latham watched my expression as I swept my eyes around the camp. "The remnant of Free Gathwyr," he said. "All that's left of it, anyway, after the coming of the Masters." He spat.

"Who are these 'Masters'?"

His eyes widened. "You...don't know?"

"I'm not from Gathwyr," I said. "I'm a visitor...a traveller. I came here with friends."

"Friends?"

"Two of them, Latham," one of the rebels said. "They were taken to Tharesti by the wardens. We saw them."

"That's not good," Latham said. "They won't last long once the Master's interrogators start on them."

"Who are the Masters?" I repeated, more insistent. Repeated mention of these Masters—more than one!—had me worried. If this were some plot of my old enemy...

"The Masters came here from...somewhere else. They are not of Gathwyr." He looked at me with a dawning suspicion. "You say you don't know them?"

"Tell me about them."

"They are...horrible...not human at all."

"What do they look like?"

"I'm not sure. No one who has gotten close enough to see them has lived to describe them. I've seen them from a distance, a very great distance, and can't tell you much about them. All I know is that they kill mercilessly."

I felt a chill at that. Did I know these monsters?

"Anyway, they arrived on Gathwyr several years ago, landing in a great, flat, round ship or vessel of some kind that could hover silently in the sky and kill people with blue fire. The great cities along the coast—Grathen, Telemar, Vandetrin—all of them were destroyed. They spared Tharesti, but only on condition that the people become their slaves. We think there must be only a handful of Masters, because they work through human traitors, creatures like Kolav, who rules now in their name from the Tower of the Masters. They created a slave army, the wardens, who keep the people in line and working, and patrol the countryside.

"A number of us escaped the burning of the cities. Me, I was from Telemar. Elanin here, he was from Tharesti, but escaped soon after the Masters came. His family did not."

"What do they want here?"

He slumped. "I don't know. They want something more than mere conquest, that is certain. Patrols of wardens are sent out constantly into the mountains west of Tharesti, searching for we don't know what. It must be something of incredible value to warrant so much effort on their part."

"Indeed." What COULD they want? I might be able to guess if I knew who these Masters were. Another race of world-conquering megalomaniacs, obviously, but there were so many of those.

Make a Saving Roll against your MNT, *adding a +2 modifier because of the difficulty of the problem. If the roll fails, go to* **175**. *If the roll succeeds, or if you have already figured out who the Masters are on your own, go to* **225**.

You have also won Clue Y by discovering the location of the rebel camp. Record this before proceeding with the adventure.

158

Too slow! Something grazed my head with a sledgehammer blow, slamming me back and down, over and over in the gravel. I tried to open my eyes, and found my vision obscured by a red haze that was gradually swallowed by darkness.

Reduce your END *by 1, and go to* **138**.

159

The soldiers burst out from behind the boulders. There were four of them, all wearing the insect-eyed sensor masks and carrying wicked-looking submachine guns.

One of them caught me with a flying tackle. We went down together, me on the bottom, with my scarf tangled around my left arm. I heard shots, shouts, and scuffles nearby, but I was too busy fighting for my life to see what else was happening.

Go to **160**.

160

You are engaged in hand-to-hand combat with the soldier, and will need your STR and *Brawling* skill to defeat him.

Make a Saving Roll against your STR. If the roll is successful, you win a bonus modifier of −2. If it fails, the modifier is +3.

Roll 1D6 and subtract the result from your *Brawling* skill to represent the soldier's fighting skill. The result is the soldier's roll. Roll 2D6 for your own attack, and apply the modifier from your Saving Roll above. If the result is equal to or less than the soldier's roll, you have won the fight. If the result is greater, you have lost.

If you win the combat, go to **162**. *If you lose, go to* **168**.

161

When I stepped out of the fog in front of those six soldiers, they looked as thunderstruck as if a bomb had detonated in their midst. One or two guns were pointed in my direction, but none of the soldiers did anything but stare. I knew I had to take the initiative, or I would instantly lose any slight advantage of surprise I might still have.

There are a number of possible approaches you can use to get past the guards, who don't look too bright. You can simply stride past them without saying a word, unlock your TARDIS, and walk on in before they recover from their surprise. Go to 177 for this option.

You can engage them in conversation, trying to convince them through fast talk and psychological mastery of the situation to let you through, at 182.

You can show yourself, then run away, hoping all or most of the guards will follow you, so that you can slip around behind them and sneak into the TARDIS. This choice is at 183.

You can engage them in conversation. While their attention is focused on you, you can put them all to sleep with your hypnotic ability. This option is at 184.

You can run at them wildly, shouting orders as if you were an officer, confusing them with bluster, at 188.

162

I stood slowly, looking at the unconscious soldier sprawled at my feet. When I looked up, I saw the two rebels standing there, with the other three soldiers laying in heaps by the boulders. The guns were aimed at me again.

Trusting people, I thought.

Go to 155.

163

The rebels were looking up the hill, distracted by the racket of the approaching soldiers. I saw my chance and broke into a run, making for the safety of the mist.

Another rebel loomed out of the fog almost before I knew it. His rifle butt swung up and jabbed down. There was an explosion of darkness, and I knew no more.

Go to **170.**

164

Consciousness returned with a throbbing of my head and the vaguely uneasy feeling that I had overslept. I opened my eyes.

"We thought you were dead."

The speaker was a man well along in years, with a battered face and grizzled grey beard. Ragged clothes hung on his spare frame, and a use-worn submachine gun was slung across his shoulder.

Behind him were other men and women, clad as he was and with a motley assortment of arms and expressions, all watching silently. I was in a camp of some sort. Lean-to shelters made from scraps of canvas slung across lines tied to trees were camouflaged with artfully placed masses of leaves and foliage.

"I'm Latham," the man said. "We found you on the slope below the Tharesti Road. We saw you running from the wardens. It's obvious you're not one of us. You're not a warden, either. And I don't think you're from the Crystal City. Perhaps you'd tell us just *who* you are?"

I sat up slowly, gingerly touching the lump on the back of my head. "I'm The Doctor. Glad to meet you, Latham!"

It appeared that I'd found the rebels, or rather, that the rebels had found me.

Go to **157.**

165

I waited there in the wet and fog for what seemed like hours, but the guards never moved. An officer must have posted them there, with orders to make certain that no one carted off what must be to them an extraordinarily puzzling artifact—a blue, London police callbox unaccountably materialized on a volcanic, Gathwyran plain.

Or might it be a trap? If they expected the strangers they'd been chasing to come back and retrieve it, surely those six guards would have hidden themselves? Then again, perhaps those six were not all the guards there were. The trap could have more than a single arm.

The thought prickled at the hairs on the back of my neck. What to do? As I lay there considering, I became aware of a sound, an electronic hum in the air somewhere overhead. The machine descended on me like a great, mechanical hawk. Hovering overhead in an effortless defiance of gravity, it was a black metal craft that seemed to have detected me through the fog cover with ease.

"Hands up, rebel," an amplified voice boomed from above. "Surrender of die!"

I pitched to one side, rolling in the gravel as the hovering monster drifted just past my head with a sinister whoosh. Strange! I'd not thought that this culture, with its rifles and submachine guns, would be up to sophisticated scanner tracking techniques, and it most certainly shouldn't be capable of anti-gravity devices! But the vehicle swung through the air without jets or fans or propellers, with nothing holding it aloft but that electronic keening and the will of its occupants.

I was trapped, my back up against the boulders. The machine's hum fell through several octaves as landing legs silently extended and the black device settled to the ground a meter or so in front of me. It was open on top, where several helmeted troopers perched in a well deck around a nasty, swivel-mounted gun of some unearthly kind.

"Surrender or die," a voice repeated.

Some choice.

Go to 107 if you choose to obey the voice. Go to 103 if you'd rather chance another dive into the fog.

166

Working by touch in the pitch darkness, I felt the guard's neck at the angle of his jaw, probing for his carotid. Good. He was unconscious, not dead. I hadn't thought there was enough juice in that line to kill him, and I was glad.

So, what now? Somehow I had to find Sarah and Harry, but finding them in this stone mountain would be no easy matter. If my experience with other totalitarian governments was any guide, there were probably hundreds of cells on this level alone. And how many other levels? Besides that, it was quite possible that my friends weren't even in one of these cells. One or both might be somewhere else, being questioned.

THAT was an unpleasant thought. I had to hurry.

Somewhere there must be a central cellblock control center, a place where prisoners' effects are kept and cell assignments made. If I could get there, I might be able to find out there where Harry and Sarah were being held. All I had to do was find the place.

I cast about for the gun, but couldn't find it. Just as well. I dislike guns, as a rule. I turned and made my way to the open door. Which way—left or right?

If you want to go to the left, go to 172. If you decide to go to the right, go to 178.

167

You are attacking the lone guard in the lift, hoping to disable him before he can sound the alarm or before more guards arrive.

You must use your STR and *Brawling* skill to stop the soldier from sounding the alarm.

Make a Saving Roll against your STR. If it succeeds, you win a bonus modifier of –4. If it fails, the modifier is +2.

Roll 1D6 for the soldier's skill, and subtract 1 for his surprise. Then, subtract this from your *Brawling* Skill Rating. The result is the soldier's roll. Next, roll 2D6 for your own attack, and apply the modifier to it. If the result is equal to or less than the soldier's roll, you have won. If the result is higher, you have lost.

If you win, go to **208**. *If you lose, go to* **223**.

168

With the return of consciousness came the awareness of a throbbing, consuming pain extending from my battered skull to the bottoms of my feet. My eyes snapped open. I'd been fighting with that soldier, and I'd lost.

I sat up, then very slowly let myself slide to the ground again, my head spinning. When I could finally pry my eyes open, I began to wonder who I was.

"We thought you were dead, stranger."

The speaker was a grizzle-bearded man in rags, gleaming military boots, and with a submachine gun slung over over one arm. He reached out and adjusted the bandage on my head. "It was fortunate for you that Gowan saw that you were still breathing after he killed the warden who had knocked you down. The warden was about to shoot you."

I sat up, very slowly. "My thanks to Gowan," I said.

The man nodded. "I am Latham, the leader here." He

regarded me with searching eyes. "You are not one of the wardens. You obviously are not one of us. I rather doubt you are a Thol. Just *who* are you?"

"Yes, well, I'm The Doctor, and I'm very pleased to meet you, Latham. Very pleased." I looked around. We were in a camp in the shelter of an open woodland. It was composed of lean-tos, mostly scraps of canvas stretched from lines tied to trees, clustered under protective canopies of purple-red leaved trees. The lean-tos were artfully camouflaged with clumps of foliage, obviously as a precaution against observation from the sky. There were dozens of men and women in the camp, of every age from children to elders, all ragged and lean, with a motley assortment of weapons and expressions.

It seemed that this was the rebel army that those soldiers had been so concerned about.

Go to 157.

169

My dive took me off the crest of the ridge and into the protection of the swirling fog. Shots whined and thuttered all around me, smashing rocks and ricocheting in every direction. I was on my feet in an instant, zigzagging down the face of the ridge in a madly twisting attempt to make myself an impossible target and to keep from crashing headlong down the slope at the same time.

I paused at the bottom, listening. I heard nothing. Perhaps I'd managed to elude them! Nevertheless, my options at this point seemed rather limited. I could try to rescue Sarah and Harry single-handedly, of course, but that didn't seem promising. I could try to find my TARDIS again (assuming of course, that the soldiers hadn't seen fit to guard it), then somehow try to track down Harry and Sarah in that immense city I'd seen them being marched toward. That was unlikely n such a large city. Even with the TARDIS, my resources were limited.

What I needed even more than my sonic screwdriver at his point was allies. There were simply too many unfriendly people running around on this planet for even me to deal with alone. And my only hope for allies seemed to be among the rebels that had these soldiers so worked up.

So, which was it to be? Find the TARDIS, or try to find he rebels?

Go to **144** *to try to find the rebels. If you'd rather look or your TARDIS, go to* **104**.

170

I opened my eyes slowly. My head throbbed with pain, and the universe seemed to be dipping and circling wildly. Gradually, the sky learned to stay in place above me, the ground stayed put beneath me, and I was able to sit up slowly.

I was alone on a gravel plain, the landscape still obscured by the clammy, eddying sea of fog. I remembered the rebel I'd nearly run into, remembered him raising his gun. He must have clubbed me in the head with it and left me there for dead. There was no sign now of either rebels or soldiers. Just gravel and fog and the deepening realization that I was going to have to win allies on this world if I were to have any chance at all of rescuing Harry and Sarah.

I must have made a great impression on them by running from those pursuing soldiers. That must have been why the rebel clubbed me down..

As I slowly got to my feet, I heard a high-pitched, keening hum from above. I looked up, but whatever was causing the sound was hidden by the fog. That hum sounded remarkably like some sort of pocket anti-gravity drive, which made no sense at all. Anti-gravity was far beyond the rifles-and-machineguns-technology I'd seen so far on Gathwyr. What was going on?

Rocks turned white hot close by my feet, then vaporized in a flash of light, heat, and a gunshot crack. I dove in the other direction, rolled, came to my feet and ran, zigzagging across the plain. The electronic hum of the invisible hovering vehicle sounded close behind and above me, pacing me unseen through the fog.

"We see you, rebel," an amplified voice boomed out. "Surrender or die!"

Some choice.

If you want to do as the voice says, go to **107**. *If you want to keep running, go to* **103**.

171

It was mighty hairy working in pitch dark, by touch alone, on live electrical wires. If I slipped just once, they could give me a hefty shock, at best. At worst, they would blow every fuse in the building and kill me, too.

I broke the light bulb and used the metal rim as screwdriver to detach the wires from the socket. Then I used a bit of broken glass to painstakingly cut back the insulation, exposing several centimeters of bare metal on the ends of two wires that I was careful to keep widely separated. Still using my scarf as a substitute for rubber gloves, I tugged the wire strands far enough across the cell that they would reach the door. Finally, I emptied the half-full jug of water on the stone floor just inside the door. Then I stood behind the door, the free end of the cord in my hand.

Well, no time like the present, I thought, and began to shout, "Help! Help! Guard! Help! Let me out!"

Keys clashed in the lock. Then the door swung open.

spilling light into the cell. A guard strode in, pistol drawn in his left hand, his right hand still holding the keys in the lock. When his foot came down in the puddle of water, I rammed the electrically charged wire into the door's metal framework.

There was a sizzle and a snap, an acrid smell, and the guard vaulted across the cell, crashing into the wall with a clatter of helmet and equipment. The lights in the corridor faded, brightened again for a moment, then went dark. Somewhere in the distance there was a chorus of muttering voices.

I had only moments in which to work.

If you were brought to the cell while unconscious, go to **166.** *If you were brought to the cell conscious (and so remember the way out of here), go to* **173.**

172

I moved down the lightless corridor to the left, feeling along the wall at my side. I was operating completely on guesswork now. That Harry and Sarah must be prisoners someplace in this building, I knew, but it was pitch black, and there must be hundreds of cells on this level alone. There might also be other prison cell levels. It was just as possible that my friends weren't even in the cell area now, but were someplace else, undergoing interrogation.

That thought was not at all pleasant. I had to find some sort of central prison block control area, a command center where I could find out where my Companions were being held. Then I could think about rescuing them. For now, I would have to concentrate on not being captured myself.

I'd gone about thirty steps when the lights flickered on, dimmed slightly, then came on full. Somewhere, someone had been on the ball and thrown a circuit-breaker switch. My chances had just diminished by a percentage I didn't want to think about.

Walking briskly, I kept going. It was unlikely that any guard would take me for an insider, but it was worth the try.

After passing many more locked doors like the one through which I'd escaped, I paused to peek into several of them. All were cells identical to the one I'd just left. About half were occupied by dirty and bedraggled, rag-clad men who reminded me of those bodies we'd seen on the slope of the ridge. Taking care of rebel prisoners must be a full-time career here on Gathwyr.

The corridor ended at a branching. One passageway went to the left, the other to the right, and the way straight ahead ended in a blank stone wall. The curve of the passageway suggested that the direction I'd just come from led toward the center of this large, circular building. Perhaps at the center I would find the cell-block control area or possibly a stairway or lift to take me to another level.

But back THAT way I heard crashing noises, as if large numbers of jackbooted men were pounding on the double along a stone-floored passageway. I could hear the echoes of yells and shouted orders.

Left or right?

Go to the left at **191**, *or go to the right at* **196**.

173

The guard in the cell was unconscious, not dead. I hadn' thought the charge would be enough to kill him, but it had given him a nasty jolt and knocked him cold for the moment. In a pouch on his belt, I found the ID I had seen guards use to open the lift doors. That might well be my key out of here and who knew what other important uses.

I searched but couldn't find the gun. It was dark, and my time was rapidly running out. It was just as well. I never have liked guns.

I entered the darkened passageway and turned right, back toward the lifts. I was playing entirely by ear now, as they say on Earth. That Harry and Sarah must be somewhere in this building structure, I knew. But it was pitch black, and there must hundreds of cells on this level alone. There might well be other prison levels, too, and it was just as possible that my Companions weren't even in the cell area now, but someplace else, undergoing interrogation.

That thought was not pleasant. I had to find some sort of a central prison block control area, where I could find out just where they were being held. Then I could think of rescuing them. For now, it would help if I could keep from being captured myself.

The lights in the passageway flickered on, dimmed, then came up to full brightness again. Someone had been on the ball and thrown a switch on a circuit-breaker box. My chances had just lessened considerably.

Go to **174**.

174

I reached the lift. So far, all was quiet, but I couldn't count on my luck holding for much longer. To find Sarah and Harry, I had to find the central cell control area. From what I could see, this entire level was laid out like a giant wheel. Lifts were at the hub, and corridors were the spokes leading past the cells. I could search this level more thoroughly, or I could call a lift and start exploring other levels. Which should it be?

Go to **200**.

175

"These conquerors," I said. "Do they look something like humans, only made of metal? Bright silver?"

Latham shook his head. "These...these creatures are nothing like humans. And they're impervious to our bullets. The best we can hope for is to pick off the patrols of traitor humans the Masters send against us. If there were more of them..." He spread his hands. "That would be the end of us."

So, they weren't Cybermen. Or Movellans or Sontarans or any of the other more-or-less humanoid, megalomaniacal conquerers I'd encountered across Space and Time.

I sat and thought hard for several moments. Obviously, we were going to have to learn more about these Masters Latham was talking about. Obviously, too, we would have to get Sarah and Harry out of their hands, and quickly. When I questioned Latham, he answered me that the life expectancy of rebel prisoners in the hands of Gathwyr's Masters was lamentably brief. Unless those captives had information or talents the Masters desired very much, their days, or perhaps their hours, were numbered. If the captives were allowed to live, their existence would not be very pleasant and would continue only as long as it served the purposes of the Masters.

"But what is it they search for?" I asked at last. Gathwyr had been a peaceful, backwater world without exceptional value, without strategic location. "What could they possibly want?"

Latham gave an eloquent shrug. Speculation in that direction seemed a dead end.

I tried to probe further. "You said something earlier, something about a 'Crystal City'."

"The Lost City," someone said with a chuckle.

"Myths," said another.

Latham shrugged. "Off to the west, there's supposed to be a lost city, from where our ancestors came centuries ago. The People of the City are supposed to come out and trade for food once'n a while, but I think it's just an old legend. Like the story of the man who went looking for 'em, and came back a month later an old man!"

There was laughter, then silence. I thought a moment, then shrugged, too. Lost cities would have to wait. "I've got to rescue my friends," I said at last.

He shook his head slowly. "An impossible task."

"Nothing is impossible." Only improbable, terribly difficult, or very, very silly, I added to myself.

"That is," Latham went on. "We attacked this morning with our entire army. Our plan was to show ourselves, draw a large part of their army out on the Ridge Road, attack and overwhelm them, then storm the gates of Tharesti." His hand made a brutal, chopping gesture across his throat. "The result was a slaughter—for us. There were Masters on the ridge, Masters waiting for us with their fog-piercing sensors and their blue fire." His voice raised in pitch, his eyes widened. "They killed hundreds of our people, burned them down in agony, and we couldn't even get near them!"

Gowan laid his hand on Latham's shoulder. "Gently, Latham. There was nothing more you could have done."

"I could have died," Latham said quietly. There were tears on his face. "I could have died there, on that hill, with my son. But the blue fire passed above me, and around me, and I lived."

"I'm sorry, Latham," I said. "But if we're going to strike back at the Masters, we'll have to learn more about them. We've got to find a way inside that city."

Another of the rebels, one who had been sitting close by, said, "There is a secret way in, Doctor. Some of us escaped that way when Tharesti was taken."

Gowan's face clouded. "That way is certain to be guarded, Elanin. It's much too dangerous."

"Tell me more," I said.

Elanin took a stick, sketching lines in the sand at our feet. "The city is built at the end of the ridge, as you know. On the far side of the city are cliffs, like so."

"Go on."

"The cliffs are riddled with caves, some of them quite large. There is one cave, quite a wide one, that enters the face of the cliff thirty meters above the sea. There are passages running through the rock up and into the lower levels of the city."

"And every person in the city knew of those caves," Latham said. "Gowan is right. They are certain to be heavily guarded. Why, we've not even considered an attack by that way. Every tunnel could be guarded, and held against any number of attackers by just a few men with automatic weapons." He shook his head. "It's foolhardy, going that way."

"If the cave system is as complex as you say, maybe they can't guard it all," I suggested. "One person might be able to slip in."

"Aye, but how would he know which ways were guarded?" Gowan said. "Besides, if the Masters know about those caves, they would seal them off, or watch them with sensors or cameras or traps. It's hopeless."

I had to admit that Gowan made a good case. Of course, there was another way. If we could get into my TARDIS, a simple spatial transition could drop a whole army of rebels inside the city. What they could do once they were inside was anyone's guess, but it was something to think about. And if they were unwilling to come along, well, I always have preferred slipping into tight places alone. You're not as conspicuous if you don't have an army clattering along on your heels.

But I had to decide which way to go.

You have learned something. Record that you have acquired Clue B. You are also feeling rested, and may restore END *and* STR *levels if they have been reduced by fatigue or wounds (but not regeneration).*

You can try to convince the rebels to help you get your TARDIS back, then accompany you inside the city, at **210**. *You can enlist their help to get your TARDIS, then enter the city alone, at* **215**. *Or you can try to convince them to help you find the caves Elanin mentioned, so that you and a small party (possibly just you and a guide) can slip into Tharesti, at* **218**.

176

There was a snap, a flash, and a jolt through my entire body that smashed me back across the room and left me stunned and shaking. When I could move again, I crawled back across the floor, retrieved my scarf and the broken light bulb, then made my way back to where the light cord was dangling.

I had no choice. I would have to try again.

Carefully, meticulously, working through the scarf, which turned my precisely trained hands clumsy, I set to work once more.

Make another Saving Roll against your DEX. *If it succeeds, go to* **171**. *If it fails, go to* **193**.

177

I looked neither right nor left, but strode with masterful purpose toward the TARDIS. I was acting on that age-old rule for deceit and deception: If you behave as if you belong there, people will hesitate before challenging you. I was counting on those soldiers' hesitation.

"Halt!" one of them said, as I stepped past him. He was clearly uncertain. "I said, hold it!"

I had the TARDIS key on its chain still around my neck, cupped in the palm of my hand. If this didn't work, I didn't want them getting inside the ship. I could see hesitation fading from their manner, replaced by a growing resolve. Now they were closing in on all sides, a sudden deadly purpose in their eyes. This wasn't going to work.

Try to bluff your way out of this with some fast talking by going to **182**, *or keep trying to get into the TARDIS at* **187**.

178

Halfway down the corridor, the lights flickered on again. Someone, somewhere, had been on the ball and thrown a circuit-breaker switch. Not good. Now I could be seen.

At the end of the corridor was a broad, curved wall with a closed sliding door set into it. There was no door handle or control that I could see, but there was an electronic card reader next to it. That meant this building used an internal security system; doors were opened and access gained to lifts and restricted areas by computer-coded cards carried by the personnel who worked there. If I was going to get around, I would have to find a card.

When the door hissed open, I was face to face with a guard armed with a shoulder-slung submachine gun and holding a green plastic card in his hand. He looked just as surprised as I was.

You can fight at **167**, *or flee at* **181**.

179

You are trying to so bewilder six guards through bluff, fast-talk, and psychological manipulation that you will be able to slip past them into your TARDIS.

Make a Saving Roll against your CHA score. If it succeeds, you win a bonus modifier of −3. If it fails, the modifier is +3.

Roll 1D6 to represent the guards' reaction, subtracting 1 because they are conditioned to obey without question. Subtract the final result (from 0 to 5) from your own CHA score. This is the guards' roll.

Then, roll 2D6 to represent your own tactics, and apply the die modifier. If the result is less than or equal to the guards' roll, you are successful. If it is higher, you have failed.

If you win the combat, go to **190**. *If you lose, go to* **187**.

180

I tried to relax between my two guards as the lift climbed slowly to Level 5.

"I hate going up to see...them," one said.

"Shaddup," the other told him.

"Yeah, but..."

"Shaddup."

He shaddup, and then the door slid open. Within was a chamber with walls made of stone blocks, and bank upon bank of gleaming instrumentation and electrical equipment. There were more guards with guns, and a sickly, burnt-meat smell heavy in the air. A man with the bald skull and sunken-eyed face of a cadaver, and wearing a long, white apron splotched with brown, came forward to meet us.

My knees felt suddenly weak. It didn't look like I was going to be leaving this room soon. Not alive, that is.

Go to **213**.

181

I turned and ran, my footsteps echoing through the corridor. The words "Halt! Halt!" sounded behind me, and then the passageway was filled with the rolling crash of gunfire. I twisted down a passageway as bullets ricocheted past my ears.

Then I collided headlong with a pair of guards who were running toward the sound of gunfire, and the three of us went down in a twisted heap of struggling legs and arms.

Go to **197**.

182

"Hello there!" I said with my brightest, toothiest smile. "I'm The Doctor, and I believe you have something I've been looking for! Have a jelly baby?"

Six blank stares told me I had them right where I wanted them.

Go to **179**.

183

I waited as conflicting emotions flickered across all six faces. Then their guns snapped up, and I turned and ran for my life, zigzagging as I went. There was a baffled pause, then the silence was shattered by the clattering crash of automatic weapons and the chopping, sizzle-hiss of unpleasant objects flying through the air around me.

I could tell from the sounds behind me that at least some of the guards were following. Though they'd not appeared to be very bright as soldiers go, I still had to outfox them. They were too close, their fire too accurate.

I ran as fast as I could, all the while circling to get the TARDIS in front of me once again. I heard the scuff of running boots in the gravel very close behind me, and realized that this was not working out well at all.

I burst from the fog right on target. There was the TARDIS! Panting, my scarf flapping, I dashed around the corner. Reaching the door, I nearly bowled over the two guards who were standing there, rifles leveled at my head. In that instant, I saw that their fingers were tightening on the triggers...

Make a Saving Roll against your DEX *as you try to avoid their fire. If you succeed, go to* **189**. *If you fail, go to* **198**.

184

"Hello there!" I chirped. "I'm The Doctor!" Six blank expressions told me I had them right where I wanted them.

"Listen, you have something of mine that I need, and I wonder if you could tell me if you aren't getting rather sleepy standing out here."

Two of them dropped off immediately, and another was staring at me with that slack-jawed look that said he was going to go any second. I kept on talking, letting my voice drone on and applying the full force of my Gallifreyan hypnotic training.

Make a Saving Roll against your MNT *as you try to hypnotize the six soldiers. Add 1D6 to your roll to represent the difficulty of controlling so many subjects. If the roll succeeds, go to* **190**. *If it fails, go to* **185**.

185

Two of them seemed to shake themselves, looking around blinking. Their eyes widened, and the rifles came up again. It wasn't going to work! As though the event were in slow-motion, I watched their fingers tightening on the triggers.

Make a Saving Roll against your DEX *as you try to avoid their shots. If the roll succeeds, go to* **189**. *If it fails, go to* **198**.

186

You are fighting with two guards armed with submachine guns in a lift. In seconds, the lift door is going to open onto the level to which they were taking you.

You'll need your STR and *Brawling* skill for this struggle. Make a Saving Roll against your STR. If it succeeds, you win a bonus modifier of −3. If it fails, the modifier is +2.

Roll 2D6 for the two soldiers, and add 4 for their training. Subtract this from your DEX score plus your *Brawling* Skill. The result is the soldiers' roll. Then, roll 2D6 against that number for your own actions, applying the modifier from your initial Saving Roll. If the result is less than or equal to the soldiers' roll, you have won. If it is greater, you have lost.

If you win, go to **200**. *If you lose, go to* **203**.

187

I was right—it didn't work. A rifle butt descended out of nowhere and impacted with a crunch at the base of my skull. I had a red-blurred impression of sliding down the face of the still-locked TARDIS door, my fingers scraping along the chameleon circuit-projecting woodwork, and then blackness rose up and swallowed the universe.

Reduce your END *and* STR *each by 2, then go to* **138**.

188

"You six! On your feet! They're attacking!"

All six shambled to their feet, guns pointing uncertainly in six different directions, their blank expressions telling me I had them right where I wanted them.

"You, you, and you," I pointed with sharp, stabbing motions. "Go out there and get ready to ambush them! You two..."

"Who are you, fella?"

One of the group looked decidedly hostile, and his weapon was aimed, from his hip, squarely at my forehead. Suspicion was dawning in the eyes of the others.

You can turn and run by going to **183**. *Or you can go to* **192** *to try to brazen it out by convincing them that you really are one of their officers.*

189

I threw myself against the TARDIS door just as the shots rang out. After some thunderous noise and the sound of shredding air, I was still alive! They had missed!

But, I was out of running room, and I had the distinct feeling that my plan simply was not working this time.

Go to **187**.

190

I had made it! For the first time since I'd left the TARDIS earlier that day, I felt safe. Too bad I was going to have to make an immediate detour back into danger.

The soldiers were still hammering with their gun butts on the outside door when the comforting whirr of the TARDIS dematerialization circuits transported me completely beyond their reach. Not that they could have broken through using mere brute force, but I had friends to rescue and information to win. Adrift in the nothingness outside of Space and Time, I guided the TARDIS toward the structure my scanners had locked onto immediately—the city of Tharesti.

Now, how to find two captured Earth folk held somewhere within an entire city of humans? Not an easy task, but I had an idea that the biggest tower, which was showing the heaviest use of power leaking off the grid matrix and into the hypercontinuum, was the place prisoners would be taken and questioned. After all, it's a standard rule found in the handbooks of universal conquerors everywhere that the most powerful beings get the biggest, showiest palaces, just to show that they're on top.

As I scanned my instruments, I noticed something odd. That anomalous distortion of time, the signal that had brought us here in the first place, was back stronger than ever. It was strong enough for me to get a reading on its direction, which was almost due west. There was no telling how far, as I didn't know how strong the signal was at the transmission point, or its degree of attenuation, but the general direction seemed to be toward the horizon. Thirty kilometers would not be a bad guess.

For a moment, I was tempted to investigate. After all, the reason I was on Gathwyr in the first place was to discover what that signal was. After a moment's reflection, I decided that would have to wait until after Harry and Sarah were rescued.

Assuming they could be.

Make a Saving Roll against your TARDIS Operation Skill. If the roll succeeds, go to 209. If it fails, go to 224.

191

I turned to the left and kept going. The wall was curving gradually inward, confirming my guess that this level was laid out like a wheel, with me now moving counter-clockwise along the rim.

The sounds of running feet and shouted orders were getting close now, coming up one of the passageways of the wheel's spokes somewhere behind me.

*You can run by going to **199**, or you can try to hide by going to **202**.*

192

You are trying to use bluff, confusion, and sheer gall to convince six suspicious soldiers that you are, in fact, an officer in their army, giving them orders in the face of an imminent enemy attack.

You will be relying on your CHA more than anything else in this confrontation. Make a Saving Roll against your CHA score. If it succeeds, you win a bonus modifier of −3. If it fails, the modifier is +3.

Then, roll 1D6 to represent the guards' reaction, subtracting 1 because they are conditioned to obey without question. Subtract the result of the guards' 1D6 reaction roll (from 0 to 5) from your own CHA score. The result is the guards' roll.

Roll 2D6 to represent your own tactics, and apply the modifier. If the result is less than or equal to the guards' roll, you are successful. If the result is higher, you have failed.

*If you succeed, go to **190**. If you fail, go to **187**.*

193

There was another surge of current through my body. When I was able to make my trembling arms pull me up off the floor, I found I was on the far side of the cell. There was a distant murmur of voices from outside.

Several moments later, I heard the peephole open, and a beam of light probed the inside of the cell. It was dark outside. I must have shorted out the power for the entire level!

Whoever was behind the light took in my handiwork— the dangling electric cord, the shattered light bulb—and withdrew. I sat in the darkness rearranging my scarf around my neck. I didn't think I would have long to wait.

I didn't. When the door opened, there was light in the passageway again, though still none in my cell. Two burly, black-clad guards entered and pulled me to me feet, one on either side. Then they frog-marched me out of the cell, to the right, and down the corridor. They said nothing and took no notice of the mess in my cell, but I could tell they were not pleased.

"Could I interest either of you gentlemen in a jelly baby?" I asked. "No? I thought not."

Decidedly unfriendly.

At the end of the passageway, they stopped before a smooth, curved stone wall with a door set into it. There were no handles or controls, but there was a small computer scanner set into the wall next to the door, and it was into this that one of the guards slid a rectangular plastic card. Seconds later, the door slid open, and my captors half dragged me into what was obviously a lift. Through half-closed eyes, I deciphered the control board. We were at Level 2, and one of the guards had entered a command for Level 4.

The sinking feeling in the pit of my stomach was at least partly caused by the lift beginning its ascent. Wherever they were taking me, the two-to-one odds I faced now were bound to be far better than anything I would face when I got there. If the pattern common to imprisonment in totalitarian societies was being followed, my next stop would be an interrogation room. The interrogators might be anything from a squad of police-types with gruff, "'Ello 'ello, wot's all this, then?" voices to a bare-chested gentleman with a hood and blood-stained hands.

Of course, my best bet might be to wait and ride things out. Wherever they were taking me, I was bound to meet with the local bigwigs who were running this show. They would no doubt take a personal interest in any prisoner as oddly dressed as I was (comparatively speaking, of course).

So, which was it to be? A mad dash for freedom in a lift, or stiff upper lip and over the top toward whatever den of horrors they were taking me? I felt the lift slowing. Now was the time to decide.

To go along without resistance, go to **180**. *If you prefer to attack your guards and try to escape, go to* **195**.

194

I sprawled on the floor, watching helplessly as one of the guards got hold of his submachine gun and brought it up into line with my face. His finger tensed at the trigger, and I knew I was about to die.

Make a Saving Roll against your DEX. *If the roll succeeds, go to* **211**. *If it fails, go to* **204**.

195

If these people succeeded in taking me wherever they were headed, my chances for escape would be nil. I'd have to move fast, too. The lift was slowing to Level 4.

"I say," I muttered, looking down, "you're standing on my scarf."

Both men also looked down. My hands snapped up, hard and sharp.

Go to **186**.

196

I hurried to the right, the sounds of pursuit close behind me. The wall curved inward at my left hand, confirming my guess that this level was laid out like a giant wheel, and that I was moving clockwise along its rim. Coming up one of the spokes behind me were my pursuers.

You can run by going to **205**, *or you can try to hide by going to* **202**.

197

You are struggling to get away from two guards armed with submachine guns. You will need to call on your STR, DEX, and *Brawling* skill for this struggle. Make a Saving Roll against your STR. If it succeeds, you win a bonus modifier of −2. If it fails, the modifier is +2. Then, roll 2D6 for the two soldiers, and add 3 for their training. Subtract this from your DEX plus your *Brawling* skill. The result is the guards' roll.

Now roll 2D6 for your own tactics, applying the modifier. If the result is less than or equal to the soldiers' roll, you have won. If it is greater, you have lost.

If you win, go to **220**. *If you lose, go to* **194**.

198

I threw myself to the side as the guns barked and spat white flame. Something hammered into the side of my skull, which seemed to explode in pain and then blackness. I knew nothing more.

Make a Saving Roll aginst your END. *If it succeeds, go to* **138.** *If it fails, go to* **214**.

199

At the next intersection I ran headlong into a pair of guards coming around the corner with submachine guns ready, and the three of us went down in a struggling, kicking tangle of legs and arms.

By the time you reached that intersection, you were out of breath. Reduce your END *and* STR *both by 1. Then go to* **201**.

200

You are in a lift between levels in the core of the Tower of the Masters. You have in your possession a small, green plastic card. By passing it through a slot in computer scanners mounted on walls next to doors, the card will give you access to various rooms throughout the building.

You are attempting to get more information about the Masters, to find and rescue Harry and Sarah, and, incidentally, to find a way out of this place. You may not have much time, however. The alarm may already have been given, and you have no way of knowing whether or not your movements are being electronically monitored.

Besides the green card, you have a half-package of jelly babies, your scarf, your intelligence, your wits, and your intense personal charm. Unfortunately, the usual collection of tools and oddiments carried in your coat pockets have been taken from you.

To explore the Tower of the Masters, turn to **Exploring The Tower** at the back of this book. There, you will find floor plans of the various parts of the tower. Some of these are grouped by size and purpose. For example, both Levels 2 and 3 are prison levels. They arc identical, and so only one floor plan is provided for both.

Each time you enter a room or area, you will find a number. Look up that number and read the accompanying paragraphs to learn what you've found. This gives a basic description of the room, listing what you see at first glance. The paragraph may permit you to go on by having you choose another number from an adjacent area or room on the map, or it may direct you to a paragraph back in the main body of the adventure.

You may also be directed to make a Saving Roll against your MNT or some other attribute if you wish to examine the room more carefully. This may lead to useful discoveries, but increases your risk of being discovered and caught. You may also be confronted with a choice. For example, should I fight, run, or hide? The choice you make will lead you to a paragraph in the main body of the story.

201

You are engaged in hand-to-hand combat with two soldiers armed with submachine guns. Fortunately, these two are as surprised as you are. In this encounter, you will need your STR and *Brawling* skill.

Make a Saving Roll against your STR. If it succeeds, you win a bonus modifier of –4. If it fails, the modifier is +2.

Roll 2D6 for the two soldiers' fighting skill, and add 2 to represent their surprise. Subtract this from your *Brawling* skill. The result is the soldiers' roll. Next, roll 2D6 for your own actions, and apply the modifier. If the result is less than or equal to the soldiers' roll, you win. If it is higher, you lose.

If you win, go to **207**. *If you lose, go to* **194**.

202

I had to find a place to hide. Running blindly through these corridors with unfriendly guards dashing about was certain to get me into trouble. But where could I hide?

The only possibility was an unoccupied cell. Perhaps half of the cells I'd passed had been standing open and empty. I searched along the passageway wall until I found another empty room, one identical to the one I'd just left. I slipped inside, leaving the door slightly ajar. I didn't want to risk locking myself in after I'd just gone through all the trouble of getting out of one of these claustrophobic vacation spas.

After I'd waited what seemed a long time, suddenly the corridor outside was full of running men in black uniforms and helmets, men carrying gleaming rifles and submachine guns at the ready. When the rush was past, I slipped into the passageway and made my way in the opposite direction.

I had to get to the lifts, which I was convinced must be at the hub of the wheel. That would be…ah…yes! That way!

Do you want to approach the lift cautiously, at **206**? *Or is time of the essence, and you must hurry to make each second count, at* **221**?

203

The door hissed open on Level 4, with me standing there above the crumpled bodies of the two soldiers. I stabbed at the buttons to move the lift again. Before the door slid shut, I half-glimpsed a bright-lit room, polished stone walls, and bank upon bank of what looked like electrical equipment. I saw guards and a cadaverous-looking man in a gruesomely stained white lab coat. They saw me, too, and started toward the lift door.

Then the door whooshed shut, and I was moving again. But where to, now? I picked up the computer scanner card from one of the soldiers, then studied the lift's controls.

Go to **200**.

204

I hurled myself to one side just as machine-gun fire thundered in the narrow space. Bullets whined through air turned acrid by smoke, and filled with stinging chips of stone struck from the walls. I collided with the second guard, who had just reached his gun and was bringing it around in a wide arc, butt first. His gun butt connected explosively with the back of my head, and I went spinning away into an endless darkness for at least the second time in too few hours. One could say that, thus far, this had not been my day.

Reduce your END *and* STR *each by 2, and go to* **212**.

205

"HALT!" The shout came from behind me, and quite close. "You...with the scarf...HALT, or we fire!"

You can obey at **219**, *or try to run at* **222**.

206

I approached an intersection in the corridors cautiously, without making a sound. Peering around the corner, I saw a soldier with his submachine gun slung under his shoulder, standing in front of what had to be a lift door. There were no handles or obvious controls, but there was what looked like a computer scanner built into the wall next to the door. The guard was passing a rectangular plastic card through a slot in the reader. A light turned green, and the door slid open.

So, the security doors were accessed by computer-scanned ID cards. If only I could get my hands on a green plastic card, it might be my key out of this place. And one was just about to walk onto that empty lift car. As the soldier entered the lift, I slipped from my hiding place and raced after him. I caught him just as he turned, the card still in his hand.

The man's eyes widened with surprise as I tackled him, driving him back into the lift.

Go to **167**.

207

I stood up shakily, the unconscious soldiers sprawled at my feet. I decided to move more cautiously after this. My encounter with those two had been a close one.

Go to **206**.

208

When I stood up above the body's limp form, I had the green ID scanner card in my hand. The only question now was what to do with it? I left the body in the passageway and stepped into the elevator. I had my key to this building, but now I had to decide what parts of it to unlock.

Go to **200**.

209

Now, to work. How do you penetrate a Dalek fortress?

Very, very carefully.

I let my TARDIS computers select a quiet, out-of-the way spot where I could materialize without attracting attention. I gave some thought to the caves Elanin had mentioned, but decided that would be a bit risky. What I wanted was something like a storehouse or unused basement.

My scanners discovered what looked like just the place, a large, darkened room that my instruments read as being underground, at the very base of the Tower of the Masters. That would be a convenient spot to park the TARDIS while I did a little exploring.

The TARDIS materialized with its characteristic, grinding whirr among dusty crates and the shadows of vast, rusting pieces of heavy machinery. I stepped out cautiously and looked around.

The walls of the chamber were native rock, though it was obvious they had been artificially cut, smoothed, and pierced by ventilator grills, and so were not the natural caves Elanin had mentioned. The room was a little-used basement, crowded with boxes, crates, and machinery, which formed an effective camouflage for the boxlike form of the TARDIS in the shadows against the wall. Across the room, there was an opening in one wall into a low-ceilinged and darkened tunnel that seemed to slant down into the darkness. That must be the way down to the caves. There were no guards at this end, at least, which was a good thing. Sensors, guards, or both, must be stationed farther down among the caverns.

The room itself was circular, with the curved surface of a central pillar perhaps three meters across at its center. There were doors in this wall, doors with no handles or other controls. Mounted on the wall next to each door were small devices, apparently computer scanners. It looked like the Masters relied on an internal security system that allowed access to certain areas only to personnel with the proper kind of ID.

That could pose a problem.

There was a sudden rumble of machinery in the room, and I drew back into the shadows behind a stack of crates, watching. The lift door nearest me slid open, and four men stepped into the room. Close behind them was a pair of sinister, black shapes. The horrible and unmistakable shapes of Daleks!

Two of the men were officers, clad in black with gold devices adorning their starched collars and the cuffs of their jackets. A third was an ordinary soldier with gleaming boots and belt, and a submachine gun held at high port. The fourth was a squat, greasy-looking individual, almost bald, with a chilling half-smile and eyes as blackly unreadable as the Daleks themselves. His clothes were as splendid as the officers' uniforms were severe: white and gold pants, a gold jacket intricately traced with patterns like those on ornamental tapestry, and a red-lined gold and silver half-cloak. The man seemed to be a figure of importance, at least to the other humans.

Sitting on the stone floor near the central column was what looked like an ordinary crate three meters tall and four meters along each side. Leaving the soldier by the lift, the officers and the Daleks gathered by the crate. Producing a small red card, one of the officers slid it through a crack on the side of the crate. There was a grumbling of machinery, and then the side of the box opened up, spilling brilliant light into the darkened room. Three men and two Daleks entered the box, the panel slid shut, and there were again machine noises, this time slowly dying away until the room was silent once more. The soldier left on guard remained motionless in front of the lift door.

Most interesting, indeed. That crate was the disguised head of a secret lift, one descending farther into the depths of rock below Gathwyr. The undisguised lift evidently led up. To get into either one, I needed a computer scanner ID card, something presumably carried by each person with a reason to go anywhere within the tower.

Which direction should I explore? And where was I to get a card to let me do it? I eyed the lone sentry speculatively.

You can sit where you are and wait to see what happens at **230**. *Or you can try to sneak up on the sentry in hopes of overpowering him, taking his ID card, and using it to gain entry to either the lift going up or the secret lift going down at* **270**.

210

As we had no reliable estimate of the government forces' strength within the city, there was no way to accurately gauge how many rebels to take along on this expedition. Led by Latham himself, fifty of his soldiers followed me back to the fog-cloaked plain below the ridge where my TARDIS lay.

"Is it always this foggy?" I asked Gowan, as rebel soldiers moved silently into position. We could barely make out the outlines of the TARDIS and of the six men guarding its door.

"It is here." He reached down and scooped up a handful of black sand. "Have you noticed how warm the ground is? This region is honeycombed with pockets of magma, liquid rock, trapped under the rock. It keeps the surface warm, even in winter."

"Ah! And cold, wet air from the sea settles on top, condensing out as pea-soup fog. Interesting."

"We call this plain the Fog Sea. It stretches for twenty-four kilometers inland, clear across the Dravin wastes up to the foothills of the Thol-Thuril Mountains."

"And it's always this thick?"

"Always, unless it's raining."

"Sounds like some spots I know on Earth. London, for instance."

"Where?"

"Never mind."

"Anyway, the fog is always lying across these plains. Only the sensor helmets the Masters brought for their traitorous servants can...hah! The signal!"

Someone had given the twittering warble of some small, flying creature. Instantly, the rebel host surged forward. By the time we reached the TARDIS, the six guards were dead or unconscious.

"You didn't have to kill them," I said unhappily.

"Argue philosophical views later, Doctor," Gowan said. "Right now, show me how you plan to squeeze fifty men into that thing!"

We would have to move quickly. As I reached for my TARDIS key...

"HALT!" A harsh and metallic voice boomed from the sky. "WE HAVE YOU COVERED! THROW DOWN YOUR WEAPONS IMMEDIATELY AND SURRENDER!"

"Blackies!" someone yelled. "It's a trap!"

Gunfire blazed through the fog as rebels turned their guns to the sky, spraying at the area from which they imagined the voice had come. Fire answered from the sky—blue fire that froze men in agonized poses for endless seconds as they screamed and died.

I yelled to Latham. "You've got to get your people out of here!"

More gunfire answered from every direction out of the fog. More ground troops! The trap was vicious and complete. The wardens had used those six soldiers as bait to sucker us in. Meanwhile, watching us with their fog-piercing sensors, they had taken advantage of the mist to bring in ground and air forces of their own to box us in.

The situation looked hopeless.

*Go to **231** if you want to surrender, encouraging the rebels to surrender with you to save their lives. Or you can try to get into the TARDIS to escape at **254**.*

211

I hurled myself to the side, rolled, and came to my feet just as the second guard tripped over me and fell into the other guard's arms. Machine gun fire barked and thundered in the narrow passageway, sending bits of steel whining down the corridor, but I was away and running once again. Behind me, there was a fresh clamor of shouts and pounding boots.

I swung around a corner and skidded to a stop. A squad of soldiers stood there, their weapons trained on my head. Two seconds later, another squad pounded up behind me, panting and out of breath.

One of the soldiers produced a plastic card, and slid it through the slot of a computer scanner. Moments later, a door opened in the curved wall behind him. A lift! Without a word, I was gestured in between a pair of burly guards who held me firmly from either side.

"You have been far more trouble than you're worth," said the man with the security ID scanner card.

"Why, thank you!"

He sneered. "Old Gustrin'll fix that once and for all. Take him up to Four, boys. We'll see how smart he is after Gustrin and Lord Kolav have played with him for a bit!"

"If'n he's lucky, he'll meet the Masters," the other said.

The guards smiled unpleasantly, as though sharing some particularly foul private joke, and tightened their grip on my arms. The door slid shut on the rest of the soldiers, leaving me alone in the elevator with these two.

Wherever they were taking me, the one-to-two odds I faced now were guaranteed to be a lot better than they would be when we got there. If this was a typical totalitarian setup, the next stop on the itinerary was an interrogation room of some sort, no doubt complete with burly whip handlers and hatchet-faced questioners. If I was to escape, it had to be now, before the car reached Level 4.

On the other hand, perhaps my best bet would be to wait. After all, if I wanted to meet the bigwigs running this show, I'd certainly meet them at the end of this lift ride. Lord Kolav, the guard had said, and someone named Gustrin. They would no doubt take a personal interest in someone dressed as oddly—to their eyes—as I was. Also, I had to admit that I'd caused a fair bit of trouble in the last few minutes. They would wonder about that as well. And these Masters, who were they? Pehaps I would meet them, too.

So, go along with these two, or make my break, a dash for freedom in a crowded lift? The sinking feeling in the pit of my stomach was at least partly due to the slowing of the lift as it neared its stop on Level 4. Whatever I decided, it had to be NOW.

If you decide to go along without resistance, go to **180**.
If you prefer to try to escape, go to **195**.

212

I became aware of my surroundings through a red haze of pain. I knew at once that something was wrong. I couldn't move. That bothered me at first, until I decided that I was still unconscious and not responsible for my body's kinesthetic hallucinations.

Only when my eyes popped open did I realize I was not dreaming. I only wished I had been.

Go to **213**.

They had me chained spread-eagled to a metal rack against the wall, a rack with alarming-looking cables snaking across the floor to various pieces of equipment nearby. The skull-faced character I marked immediately as the proprietor of the establishment. The other people in the room (three that I could see) were typical soldier types with submachine guns and unfriendly expressions.

"Hello," I said. After all, it never hurts to start off a new relationship with a smile and friendliness. "I have a feeling we're going to get along splendidly!"

"Oh, I know we are," the little horror said with a dry, leathery cackle. "Lord Kolav has given very explicit instructions regarding your...ah...treatment."

"Has he now? How very thoughtful of him."

"I have," a new voice answered. Another figure had just stepped into the room, short and swarthy, almost hairless, with an authoritarian manner that had the white-coated character almost cringing. The man wore an elaborate, fancy dress uniform, all brocade, needlework, and gold that would not have been out of place on a Louis XIV tapestry. His pudgy face nearly hid restless black eyes that gave away nothing, and he wore an unpleasant, crocodilian smile.

"Ah! Lord Kolav, I presume."

"I am."

"Lord of Gathwyr?"

"In a manner of speaking. Let us say I represent the Masters to my people, and my people to the Masters." He bowed, ever so slightly, and managed in bowing to convey no trace whatsoever of humility. "I am but a humble servant of both. I, and the Masters too, of course, are very interested in you. We would very much like to know who you are and where you came from."

"Oh well, I'll be glad to tell you anything you want to know."

"Really now," he said, looking disappointed. "There are forms to follow in such things. For example, let Gustrin show you this machine."

The fellow in the white coat bowed and laid his hand on one of the banks of electrical apparatus. "This is a marvelous piece of engineering, really. In their wisdom, the Masters introduced it when they arrived, you see. It represents a ten-thousand fold percentage increase in efficiency over earlier police methods."

"Indeed? I've always said that an efficient police force is a happy police force."

He ignored me. I suspected he was having too much fun to let himself to be interrupted. "You see, if I don't like the answers you give to my questions, I can feed an electric current through your body by way of the metal rack to which you are attached. That current is very finely adjusted to your synaptic neurotransmitter fields, and causes the most exquisite pain at any desired dolorometric level, simply by turning this knob here."

"Show him, Gustrin," Kolav said.

Gustrin demonstrated, and it left me gasping for breath, shaken and weak to the core of my being.

Kolav showed his reptilian grin. "And that was a relatively low setting. Now then, shall we get down to business?"

"There's no need for theatrics," I managed to say through trembling lips. "Ask your questions!"

"It is important that we understand one another."

"I understand! I have nothing to hide!"

"Hmm. We'll see about that. I should add that by monitoring your neurotransmitter fields, the machine will also tell me when you are lying. So you see, it will pay you to answer me accurately, truthfully, and completely, or else…"

Gustrin's second demonstration was set at a higher level, and left me limp and drenched with sweat. I may have screamed, but couldn't really remember. The mind does remarkable things to protect itself in a situation like that.

"Now, then," Kolav said. He seemed quite relaxed. "At the base of the ridge west of the city, there is a remarkable blue box that none of my soldiers have been able to open. Its appearance at the same time we captured you seems to be a singular coincidence. By chance, can you tell me what that box is?"

"It's called a TARDIS. I came to Gathwyr in it."

"You travelled here…in that?"

"I did. You don't think I walked, do you?"

Kolav was studying dials on the machine's console. He obviously didn't believe me, though my synaptic neurotransmitters seemed to be telling the truth.

"And where are you from?"

"Gallifrey."

He was frowning harder now. I very much doubted that "Gallifrey" meant a thing to such planet-bound and isolated people as these, but again the machine showed that I was telling the truth. I began concocting a plan to so confuse these people with the truth—selectively edited as necessary—that I would be able to create an opportunity to escape. The situation was actually beginning to look hopeful. Oh, sure, I might be chained immovably to a torture rack right out of Earth's bloody twentieth century, but this Kolav was not very bright and was far too trusting. I might well lead him a merry verbal chase of truths and half-truths that would land him right where I wanted him, given only a bit of luck, brazen gall, and lightning wits.

"THIS PRI-SO-NER IS TO BE DE-TAINED FOR SPE-CIAL QUES-TION-ING!"

My eyes shot wide open at that grating, electronic drone, which I had heard so many times before.

Daleks! Parts of a hideous puzzle began to fall into place. The heavy-machine tracks on the ridge, the rebel soldiers killed by what looked suspiciously like the effects of a particle beam. I should have guessed it at once!

Kolav and Gustrin both had turned to face the newcomer. There were three of them, stocky, black metal machines, which had drifted through the door from an adjoining room. "B-but Lords..."

"WE HAVE BEEN MON-I-TOR-ING THIS IN-TER-RO-GA-TION FROM THE NEXT ROOM. THIS PRI-SO-NER IS KNOWN TO THE DA-LEKS! WE WILL QUES-TION HIM OUR-SELVES!"

This looked like it was simply not going to be my day at all.

The interrogation has weakened you. Reduce your END *and* STR *each by 4. Then go to* **233**.

214

Somewhere in a far-off and giddily spinning darkness, I realized the wound was very serious. In fact, I was dying.

As a Time Lord, you have a chance to regenerate before you die, repairing the damage that the soldier's bullets have done to your body, and thus escaping death. You must regenerate or die. Roll 2D6. Subtract 1 if you have an MNT *of 9, 2 if you have an* MNT *of 10, and 4 if you have an* MNT *of 11. If the result is 7 or less, you have regenerated. Go to* **150**. *If the result is greater than 7, go to* **113**.

215

Though we discussed the possibility of my smuggling fifty of Latham's soldiers into the city, we finally decided against it. There was simply no way of guessing how strong the government army inside Tharesti was, or what we would encounter once we'd made the shift into the fortress. Besides, I could tell by watching the eyes of Gowan, Enlil, and Latham that the physics of a TARDIS were totally beyond them. Squeeze fifty men into a police call box? Ridiculous!

Better, I thought, to slip unobserved and alone into Tharesti for a quick look around. But to do that I needed help to get into my TARDIS. Latham and a few dozen of his ragged soldiers accompanied me to the fog-shrouded spot where she lay.

"Is it always this foggy?" I asked Latham as rebel soldiers moved silently into position. We could barely make out the outlines of the TARDIS or of the six men guarding its door.

"It is here."

I reached down and scooped up a handful of black sand. "The ground is warm."

"That's right. This area is honeycombed with underground pockets of magma, liquid rock pushed up from deep beneath this planet's crust. Those pockets keep the ground around here warm even in winter!"

"Aha! And cold, wet air from the sea comes across the warm ground and turns to pea soup fog. Interesting."

That's right. I don't know about the 'pea soup' you mention, but we call this plain the Fog Sea. It stretches for twenty-four kilometers inland, across the Dravin Wastes to the foothills of the Thol-Thuril Mountains."

"And it's always this thick?"

"Always, unless its raining."

"Lovely weather. I know spots like this back on Earth."

"On where?"

"Never mind."

"Anyway, it's always this thick. Only the sensor helmets the Masters brought for their traitorous servants in Tharesti can...hah! The signal!"

Someone had given the warble of a small, flying animal. Instantly, the rebel host flowed forward, shadows against the mist. By the time we reached the TARDIS, the guards had been mowed down, lying either dead or unconscious.

"You didn't have to kill them," I said indignantly.

Gowan rose out of the mist, a stained knife dripping in his hand. "We can argue philosophical views later, Doctor. Right now, I'd like to know how you expect this...this box to go anywhere."

I would have to move quickly. I reached for my TARDIS key.

"HALT!" A harsh, metallic voice boomed from the sky. "WE HAVE YOU COVERED! THROW DOWN YOUR WEAPONS IMMEDIATELY!"

"Wardens!" someone yelled, and then gunfire blazed through the fog as rebels turned their guns on the sky, spraying at where they imagined the voice might be originating. "It's a trap!"

In response came a searing blue fire that transfixed rebel soldiers into stiffly agonized poses as they screamed and died.

I called to Latham. "You've got to get your people out of here!"

More gunfire came from out of the fog in every direction. The trap was vicious and complete. The wardens had used those six soldiers and the TARDIS as bait to sucker us in, while moving up forces by ground and air to box us in. The situation looked hopeless.

*You can surrender at **231**, encouraging the rebels to surrender with you to prevent loss of life, or you can try to escape by reaching your TARDIS at **254**.*

216

At the next forking of the way, I let Elanin get a short distance ahead of me, then slipped off in the other direction. Something about Elanin struck me wrong. It wasn't anything I could put my finger on, exactly. It was just that he seemed entirely too sure of himself in a time when he should have been questioning everything. Also, his hatred of the Masters seemed a little too pat.

"Doctor?" Elanin's voice echoed hollowly down the tunnels from behind. I took another turning, one leading up. "Doctor!"

Soon the voice faded away entirely.

*Go to **246**.*

217

The band of soldiers guarding my TARDIS was no match for the swift, silent, and deadly rebels of Latham's command. Latham himself bade me farewell at the TARDIS door.

"I hope you succeed, Doctor," he said. "You're sure you won't take a few troops along?" He looked at the TARDIS dubiously, obviously wondering how more than one person could fit inside without treading on someone else's toes.

"No, Latham. This trip is intelligence-gathering only, and that's best done alone." And a rescue try, I added to myself, don't forget a rescue try. No sense worrying Latham with my own, additional personal plans. Anyway I was certain he knew. "I'll be back as soon as I can. Watch for me!"

*Go to **209**.*

"We can lead you to the mouth of the caves, Doctor," Gowan said, "but it is a long and difficult climb, as well as being extremely dangerous. The Masters are certain to have that route guarded."

"Don't worry about it, Gowan. Even Masters let their guard down once in a while."

Elanin spoke up. "Perhaps I can be The Doctor's guide. He'll need someone who knows the passageways. I can take him."

"You, Elanin?" He was young. "Why?"

"You don't know what the Masters have done to my people...to my family." Hatred worked at his face, subtly twisting it. "I would do anything...anything...to strike back at them." He shrugged. "It is a small thing, but perhaps I can help."

"The way is difficult," Latham said, nodding. "You could become hopelessly lost if you tried it on your own."

"All right, then," I said cheerfully. "When do we start?"

We set out almost at once. Latham gathered a small party of rebel soldiers, and we headed across the plain the Gathwyrans call the Fog Sea.

The city of Tharesti was built on a high and rugged promontory rising from the sea, with the ridge reaching inland like the backbone of some vast, beached animal. The fog thinned markedly where the ocean waves broke across beach and rocks. The prevailing wind was a gentle sea breeze that kept the fog drifting inland, thickest above those warm spots marking subsurface pockets of molten rock.

The opening to the tunnels was a crevice beneath a jumble of fifty-ton boulders just above the beach. "There are dozens of openings," Latham said, looking up at the cliffs above. "Maybe Elanin's right. They can't guard them all, and they certainily can't guard all the openings down here. But they're guarded. They MUST be. Where they'll have guards is higher up, where the tunnel maze enters the city."

"Maze?"

"Oh, yes! These tunnels cross, recross, and intersect in a labyrinth that riddles this rock." Latham grinned. "Don't worry, though. If anyone can find the way through, Elanin can. His father was a smuggler before the Masters came, and I have no doubt he learned secret ways through the rock that the authorities never dreamed of!"

We said our farewells there on the beach. Latham gave us electric torches, fist-sized lamps that cast steady, silvery beams across the black rock as we started in.

The caves Elanin led me to were ancient volcanic lava tubes, smooth-walled and so low that I had to walk in a knee-wracking crouch. The mouth of the cave opened on the beach below the cliffs, then wound back and forth upward into the headland, branching and re-branching with other tunnels that seemed to honeycomb the rock. The promontory was basaltic rock, a remnant of some volcanic upheaval from millennia past. More recent upwellings of lava must have forced these passageways through the stone, lining them with smooth, fresh rock, leaving them hollow when the molten rock at their cores flowed on into the sea. Fascinating.

But Latham and Gowan were right. No militant occupier of the city above us could possibly ignore these caverns as a possible route straight through their back door. These caves were guarded. They had to be. So, why was Elanin so confident, striding purposefully ahead without hesitation?

You are concerned. If suspicious of Elanin, you can either try to slip away from him in order to find your own way through the rock at **216**, *or you can engage him in conversation to try to learn more about him at* **227**.

On the other hand, it may be that Elanin is completely trustworthy. He escaped through these caverns and is supposed to know them well. Perhaps he is expert enough to spot any traps or sensors hidden along the smooth tunnel walls. If you choose to trust Elanin and go along with him, go to 228.

219

I skidded to a stop and threw up my hands. O.K., boys! You've got me!"

They approached slowly, guns at the ready.

Go to 229.

220

I stood up over the limp forms of the soldiers somewhat shakily, breathing hard. That had been entirely too close, but at least the sounds of pursuit were more distant now. I started out again, moving toward what my direction bump told me was the center of this level. Perhaps there I would find stairs or a lift that would get me off this level, and quickly.

I moved stealthily. Running headlong into armed guards could be decidedly hazardous to one's health.

Go to 206.

221

I had to hurry! More soldiers would be along at any moment, and I didn't have a second to spare! I raced down a passageway, swung around a corner, and collided headlong with a pair of soldiers. With a clattering of helmets and submachine guns, in a flailing of tangled arms and legs, the three of us went down together in a struggling heap.

Go to 201.

222

This passageway intersected with another several meters away. I dove for the corner as shots rang out and chips of rock blasted from the walls stung the air.

Make a Saving Roll against your DEX. *If it succeeds, go to* **261**. *If it fails, go to* **258**.

223

The last thing I remembered seeing was the soldier's gun going up, up, up above his head. Then the gun butt came whistling down, and everything went quite dark.

Go to **212**.

224

The TARDIS computers sought out a quiet place deep beneath the tallest tower in the city. When I brought my hand down on the controls to fold back into normal space and time, suddenly I was thrown across the console by a shuddering blow that sent the TARDIS control room careening. Alarms sounded, and mechanisms throughout the ship's extra-dimensional structure groaned and trembled with the strain. The forces battering at her hull were tremendous! Quick! More power! More power!

Make another Saving Roll against your TARDIS Operation Skill. If it succeeds, go to **226**. *If it fails, go to* **232**.

225

Daleks! By the Big Bang, Daleks, of course! The Masters could not be any other creatures in the entire universe but the Daleks!

"These Masters," I said carefully. "They stand about man-high? Black, but made of metal, with a dome head with a single projection, like a stalked eye? With two arms, one of which kills with blue fire?"

"Yes! Yes! That's them! How do you know?"

"Your 'Masters' are a particularly virulent life form known as the Daleks. The machine part is actually a kind of vehicle for the creature inside, a horrid little mutation so twisted it can't walk, can't even *exist* apart from its life support machinery. And so twisted in mind that it seeks to dominate the entire universe at the expense of every other living being in the cosmos."

"But where did these...these Daleks come from?"

"Oh, they got their start a few thousand years ago on the planet Skaro. It was at the end of an interminable stalemate war between the Kaleds and the Thals, when a brilliant Kaled scientist named Davros was trying to..." I broke off suddenly. "Look, are we going to sit here and discuss ancient history, or are we going to get my friends out of there?"

Latham had an expression of absolute defeat on his face. "Doctor, I fear we cannot help you. If these Daleks were men, like you or me, we could fight them...kill them. But I saw this morning what comes of charging the Dalek blue fire. You tell us now that these Daleks come from another world. What hope do we have against enemies like that?"

I drew myself up straighter. "I am from another world, Latham. The machine that brought me here is resting on the plain at the foot of the ridge."

"You look singularly more vulnerable to bullets than do these Daleks. And I haven't seen you spitting blue fire."

"That blue fire is a sub-molecular particle beam, Latham, not magic." He hefted his submachine gun. "Compared to this, it's magic." Suddenly, tears were streaming down his face. "They killed so many of us! I led my people in, struggling up that hill, and we never even came close! We never touched them! They burned us down, hundreds of us, and killed and killed and killed…"

Gowan placed a hand on Latham's shoulder. "Gently, Latham. There was nothing more you could have done."

'I COULD HAVE DIED!" He sagged, wiping his face with agony-clawed fingers. He repeated, more softly. "I could have died. I should have died with my son. The blue fire burned above, beside, and all around me, but it left me untouched. It burned Kalis down where he stood. I heard his screams…"

His voice dwindled away. "I'm so sorry, Latham," I said. "But the fact is, the Daleks are NOT invincible. I've faced them and I've beaten them more times than I care to think about. What we need is a plan!"

I was thinking furiously. If we knew just what it was the Daleks wanted on Gathwyr, we'd know better how to fight them. And I had to get Sarah and Harry out of their clutches.

"To begin with, Latham, we need intelligence, and that's best done by one going in alone."

One of the rebels sitting in our little group spoke up. "There IS a way into Tharesti, a secret way."

"Not THAT way, Elanin," Gowan said.

"What way?" I asked.

"Tharesti is built at the peak of the ridge overlooking a cliff, a sheer drop of a couple hundred meters to the Blackstorm Sea. The cliffs are riddled with caves, a series of interconnecting passageways, really, some of which lead into the lower levels of the city. Gowan and a number of others used them when they escaped from the city."

"Aye," said Latham, "but you don't think the Masters have left those passages unguarded, do you? Everybody in Tharesti knows about those caves. They were used as warehouses for shipments of cargo from the other cities."

"The Masters can't watch every passage."

"But YOU don't know which ones they ARE watching. Besides, they might have sealed them up, or guarded them with sensors or visual probes. Going in that way is pure foolhardiness."

"I don't think we need to worry about the caves," I said, interrupting what was rapidly becoming an acrimonious exchange. "I've got another way into Tharesti, if I can just have the use of a few of your troops."

Go to **217**.

226

Somehow I brought her back under control, and the shudderings and groanings ceased. What had gone wrong?

A quick study of the TARDIS instruments showed the problem. The anomaly—that strange twisting of time that had brought us here in the first place—was much stronger now. It was a rippling fold of time and dimensions that had created something like a powerboat's wake across the normally placid surface of the space-time interface. We'd hit that wake when we first came to Gathwyr. Now that wake was a mountain, a wall, a savagely twisting storm struggling with the dimensional fields of the TARDIS.

As I watched, the disturbance gradually faded and became a shimmering flicker of unreality. It was still there, but lurking, quiescent.

Shaken, I put my hands to the TARDIS controls once again. This time, she responded smoothly.

Go to **209**.

227

"Hold it, Elanin," I said. "I'd like to talk to you."

He watched me with guarded eyes, his face eerily lit by his torch.

"I'd like to know why you're so eager to hand me over to your Masters."

"They're not my Masters!" He spat the words with a hatred I'd rarely heard before. He might be hiding something, but his speech betrayed one certain fact. He hated the rulers of Tharesti.

If you want to pursue the conversation and try to learn more about Elanin, go to **269**. *If you wish to drop the subject, go with him to* **228**. *If you want to slip away from him and find your own way through the maze, go to* **216**.

228

I decided I would have to trust both Elanin and his hatred of the Masters. His confidence could simply be a certainty that the wardens would not have bothered guarding so many tunnels deep in the rock, but would have concentrated their defenses higher up, nearer to what might be only a handful of passages opening into the city itself.

The path led ever upward, doubling and redoubling back on itself in a zigzag through the heart of the rock on which Tharesti was built. Time after time, we came to a place where the path branched into two or three tunnel openings, and each time, after only a moment's hesitation, Elanin would choose one of the ways and we would press on. At last, the passage leveled off, and Elanin pointed to a low opening in the wall ahead. "That opens into the main cave, which runs directly into the lowest level of the Tower of the Masters."

"Is it guarded?"

"If there is a place that would be watched, that is it. There is certainly a guard on the main cave entrance farther down, but it may be that they've not thought to put a guard on this small side opening behind the main opening."

That made sense. The twisting, turning route we'd followed coming here had been incredibly complex. Without Elanin as my guide, I certainly would have become hopelessly lost among the dozens of choices we'd encountered along the path, places where the road had forked or opened into unexpected side galleries and turnings. The Masters of Tharesti might well discount anyone being able to find his way through the maze and into the very bowels of their chief fortress.

Elanin was hanging back, his face pale and eerily lit by the pale gleam of our lamps. "Coming?" I asked.

He looked uncertain. "Doctor, I volunteered to bring you here…"

"That's O.K., Elanin. I travel better alone. Can you find your way back all right?"

He nodded.

"Off with you, then. I've got to go and see what measures our friends up here have taken to keep mice out of the basement."

The opening was a small one. I turned my electric torch off so that a stray gleam would not betray me, and then pressed close to the opening, peering through.

I could see that the cave on the other side was lit by lights dangling from cables strung along the rock ceiling. This must be a heavily travelled thoroughfare, but there was no sign of movement now.

I put the torch in my pocket, got down on my hands and knees, and wiggled through the opening. It was a tight fit, but I squeezed through to the other side, dusty and dishevelled, but…

Go to **268**.

229

They marched me through stone corridors toward the center of the level, where more soldiers stood guard at what must be a lift. One of them opened the lift door by sliding a green plastic card through a slot in a computer scanner mounted on the wall. Two soldiers, one holding my right arm and the other holding the left, then frog-marched me into the car. I deciphered the lights on the wall inside. We were on Level 2, and they were taking me to Level 4.

I did some fast thinking. Wherever we were going, the two-to-one odds I faced now were better by several orders of magnitude than what I was certain to face when this ride was through. If the typical pattern of totalitarian states was being followed here, my next stop would be a visit with interrogators. They might be anything from traditional policemen types, complete with a courteous "'Ello, 'ello, 'ello...wot's all this then?" to a bare-chested fellow with black hood and blood-stained hands. Besides, these guards had the green computer pass cards that would be my own key to the freedom of this building.

On the other hand, perhaps my best bet was to ride things out. After all, I DID want to meet this city's bigwigs. If anything would bring the Masters out of the woodwork where I could see them, the chance to question me personally might be it.

So, which would it be? A mad dash for freedom on a lift, or stiff upper lip and over the top into whatever den of horrors these people had planned for me.

The lift slowed. Whatever my decision was to be, I had to make it now.

To continue along without resistance, go to **180**. *To attack the guards and try to escape, go to* **195**.

230

I crouched there in the shadows, watching the guard.

Daleks! What in all the thundering novas of space were Daleks doing here? And why had they bothered conquering the Gathwyrans? Genocide was more to the Daleks' taste. That is, unless there was something here they were looking for— something they needed human slaves to help them find. But what?

I caught the whisper of movement behind me.

"IN-TRU-DER! IN-TRU-DER!" One of the black monsters drifted out of the darkness toward me, its particle gun already dropping into line with my chest. "IN-TRU-DERS MUST BE EX-TER-MIN-A-TED! EX-TER-MIN-ATE! EX-TER-MIN-ATE!"

Make a Saving Roll against your DEX. *If it succeeds, go to* **276**. *If it fails, go to* **280**.

231

There was no way out of this one. I threw my hands in the air. "We give up!" I yelled. "Don't shoot!"

"What are you doin'!" Latham hissed in my ear.

"Don't be a fool, man. If we surrender, we can talk to them…find out what this is all about…"

"Talk? To THEM? You're crazy!"

Soldiers closed in from all sides, many of them wearing grotesque masks, advanced sensor gear that pierced the fog, probably by infrared, or possibly radar. More shots rang out, and I saw a number of rebels dashing off into the fog, crouched low and zigzagging to avoid the fire. Was Latham with them? I couldn't tell.

An aircar descended out of the fog, the man in the open turret on the fantail swivelling a nasty-looking, double-barreled device to cover me. Rough hands shoved me toward it.

Aircars didn't belong in this culture that seemed to boast only submachine guns and slug-throwing rifles! Someone had been doing some serious interfering, bringing anti-gravity and advanced sensor devices to Gathwyr.

The aircar itself offered no clues. I was bundled inside with some unfriendly looking guards, and we rose above the clouds with a keening burn, then swung into line with the towers of the city.

"Tharesti," one of the guards said. "I don't think you're going to like it there."

Go to **142.**

232

I tried again, and bounced. The noise from the TARDIS instrument column filled the control room with hideous groanings and the sounds of disintegrating machinery. The TARDIS, poor old girl, was breaking up!

I grabbed the controls, steadying myself against the dizzying gyrations of the control room and the protests from the bucking hull. What was going on?

Make another Saving Roll against your TARDIS Operation Skill. If it succeeds, go to **226**. *If it fails, go to* **234**.

233

"WHAT ARE YOU DO-ING HERE, DOC-TOR?" The Daleks ringed me in, their human slaves having been rudely hustled out the door while making strident, but markedly undetermined protests. There was no doubt who ruled here.

"I don't really know," I said. "I just dropped in and…"

"DO NOT TRY TO DE-CEIVE US, DOC-TOR!"

"Who, me? Never! I…"

'YOU ARE HERE SEARCH-ING FOR THE VOR-TEX

CRY-STAL. YOU WILL TELL US WHAT YOU KNOW A-BOUT THE VOR-TEX CRY-STAL."

Daleks are not known for their witty or scintillating conversation. Generally, their talk runs to monologues that tend to get a bit dry and repetitious—especially the "Ex-ter-min-ate" parts. Well, even Daleks have their place in the cosmos, I suppose, but sometimes I wish Davros had instilled his creations with the means for intelligent conversation. Or, was that capability lost when he did away with their sense of right and wrong?

"I'm sorry, but I really don't know what you're talking about."

That caused the Daleks to form a huddle on the far side of the room. As Daleks can whisper no more than they can carry on witty repartee, I was able to listen in.

"IT IS THE DOC-TOR. WE MUST EX-TER-MIN-ATE."

"WE MUST EX-TER-MIN-ATE. HOW-EV-ER THE DOC-TOR MAY BE OF USE TO US."

"THE DOC-TOR HAS ES-CAPED US BE-FORE. HE SHOULD BE EX-TER-MIN-A-TED NOW."

"NEG-A-TIVE. HE MAY BE OF USE TO US. WE WILL NOT EX-TER-MIN-ATE YET."

"WE WILL NOT EX-TER-MIN-ATE YET."

"TAKE HIM TO A CELL WHILE WE CON-SI-DER A PLAN OF AC-TION."

And so, my execution was stayed, at least temporarily.

You have collected Clue A. Record this, then go to **275**.

234

With a keening wail and a final, convulsive shudder, the TARDIS materialized.

But where? The power systems were drained after that titanic struggle in the twilit spaces between dimensions, and it would be hours yet before the TARDIS energy reserves would be up to working levels. I couldn't even energize the control room viewer to see outside.

Well, nothing for it. I used the manual level to crank open the door. Then, with some minor trepidation, I stepped outside.

Black-garbed soldiers ringed me in, their weapons levelled with deadly intent. Gravel crunched underfoot, and beyond the soldiers was impenetrable fog. The TARDIS had apparently lost her battle to breast the dimensional shock waves of that peculiar temporal distortion. Unable to break through and materialize at her destination, she had rebounded back to the plain at the foot of the ridge, probably only a few score meters from our point of departure. She must have materialized in the very midst of a large, government force.

"Hands up, rebel," a gold-braided officer said. "We've got you."

I had no choice but to comply.

Go to **291**.

235

Had I come this way before? These tunnels were so alike, all confusingly twisted, confusingly alike. I didn't remember this joining. Which tunnel had I come out of, the left or the right?

Go left to **249**, *or right to* **242**. *Or go to* **244** *to turn around and go back the way you came* .

236

I was beginning to realize that all these lava tube passageways were monotonously the same. I could wander back and forth in them until I starved to death, and never come close to exploring them all. This way...I MUST have come this way before...yet nothing looked familiar. That tunnel to the left, for instance, had I passed through it once already?

Go left to 245, or straight ahead to 238. Or double back to 248.

237

A dead end! A rockfall had blocked the way ahead completely. There was nothing I could do but turn around and go back the way I'd come.

Go to 248.

238

This was hopeless. Never had I been in such a tangled web. Here was another branch. Should I take it left or right?

Go left to 243, or right to 240. Or turn around and go back to 248.

239

I had the distinct feeling that I ought to be heading more to the right, as well as up. Ah, a side gallery, leading to the right, but did it go up? It seemed to be descending slightly. Or should I keep going straight ahead?

Take the gallery to the right at 243, or go straight forward at 242. Or backtrack at 235.

240

And then I was out! The tunnel deposited me in a vertical shaft of raw, jagged rock lining a chimney running up and down as far as I could see.

The strange part about it was the silvery tube, a metal pipeline three meters thick, that ran straight as an arrow out of the depths below and vanished into the darkness overhead. What was it?

You can climb up the shaft at **263**, *or you can descend the shaft at* **256**.

241

The tunnel continued to descend. How had I gotten this far off track? Here were two more choices. Left or right?

Go left at **237**, *or right at* **243**. *Or you can turn around and go back the way you came at* **248**.

242

Here was a three-way branching, where unimaginable pressures had smashed in the walls of three tunnels and joined them in a scramble of rock and debris. One seemed to lead up, another straight ahead, the third slightly down. Which way?

Go up at **237**, *straight ahead at* **247**, *or down at* **249**. *Or turn around and go back the way you came at* **236**.

243

Here was another branching. Great galloping galaxies, was I NEVER going to find the end of this? Left or right?

Go left at **247**, *or right at* **245**. *Or turn around and go back at* **239**.

244

The path seemed to be rising a bit, and twisting toward the right. Just when I thought I was getting somewhere at last, it dropped away sharply. There was another side gallery off to the left. Should I take it? Or go straight?

*Go left at **241**, or straight ahead at **249**. Or turn around and go back at **235**.*

245

No, this couldn't be right. My sense of direction said THAT way, but this tunnel was going THIS way. Or, had I gotten completely turned around?

*Go straight ahead at **243**, or back the way you came at **248**.*

246

The passageway branched again to the left and right, but both seemed to be leading down. Which way?

*Go to the left at **239**, or to the right at **244**. Or you can turn around and go back the way you came at **248**.*

247

The path rose, and kept rising, gradually moving upward. I MUST have moved up through this rock about thirty meters by now!

Ah! Left or right?

*Go to the left at **237**, or to the right at **238**.*

248

Funny, I didn't remember that branching. I must not have noticed it, coming the other way. Left or right?

*Go left at **241**, or right at **245**. Or you can turn around and go back the way you came at **246**.*

249

Ah! This was better! The passageway was rising steeply now, rising and twisting off to the right. This might be the way after all!

Go right at **237**. *Or turn around and go back the way you came at* **236**.

250

When the lift door opened, a guard stepped out, a rifle slung, his eyes widening in surprise.

I stepped back. This lift seemed a bit crowded. The guard fumbled at his rifle, bringing it around.

You can turn and run at **273**, *or you can attack the soldier at* **285**.

251

The lift door hissed open. I stepped forward, then halted in mid-stride. Two black-uniformed soldiers were just turning to face me.

"There he is!" one shouted, and they lunged for me.

If you want to fight, go to **279**. *If you want to try to close the door on them and escape to another level, go to* **287**.

252

I was very curious, and prowled among the crates and machinery. Layers of dust suggested that they had not been moved for a long time. With one exception, that is. One large crate, perhaps two meters high and three meters long and wide, was resting close by the lifts. I ran my finger along the wood, but found no dust.

Curiosity is a major vice of mine, as it is for every true scientist. Why would all the other crates be covered with dust, and this one be clean? I picked up a pinch of dust and let it powder in the air close by the crate, whistling softly. Come to that, why would there be a strong draft blowing from the room INTO a sealed crate. I could see the dust wafting toward nearly invisible seams, could feet the tickle of moving air on my cheek. How very odd.

I explored further, and found traces of an almost invisible seam on one side. I pressed lightly where the smudge of myriad fingerprints stained the wood, and a panel popped open, revealing a small computer scanner. So, slide a computer scanner ID card through the slot, and something happened. What?

You have your captured green ID card. You can run it through the scanner and see what happens at 295, or you can find a hiding place and wait at 298. Or you can return to the lift and continue exploring the building.

253

The lift doors opened and I stepped out, practically into the arms of a pair of guards waiting outside. The best defense is a good offense, or at least a smooth line. "Hello there!" I piped. "I'm The Doctor..."

"You!" one shouted. They'd obviously been on the lookout for me.

You can fight at 279, or you can jump back into the lift and try to escape at 287.

254

All chaos had broken loose, with running men, shouts, gunfire, and confusion in the fog. I grabbed at the TARDIS key on its chain around my neck and whirled to the TARDIS door.

I never saw the source of the blow that struck me down from behind. All I knew was that a sudden swirling darkness rose up to swallow me.

Go to **316**.

255

Racing down the passageway, I peered through the peepholes of those cell doors that were locked shut. I felt an odd and queasy mixture of emotions. There was guilt that I couldn't help the poor, ragged wretches I'd seen in those cells, hope that I would find Harry and Sarah, dread that I would not, and anger that if I did find them, I would not be able to get them out.

"Stop that man! Stop him!"

Guards! A pack of a dozen, at least! Feeling like a peeping Tom spotted by the police, I turned and ran for it.

Too late! Soldiers closed in from that direction, too. I was trapped!

There was nothing to do but hold very still, slowly raising my hands above my head.

Go to **296**.

256

I braced myself against the rocks for long minutes, considering. Leading up was a fairly direct path toward the city above me, but what was there going down? The lack of corrosion on the silvery metal suggested that this tube or pipe or whatever was a fairly new construction. Its structure also suggested that it led somewhere…from the city of Tharesti to some unknown destination far below.

Unknowns bother me. The very foundation of science is the desire to eliminate them. And that's what I wanted to do with this one. Ironic, I thought, that I'd climbed up through those caverns all this way just to climb back down again following this vertical shaft. Ah, well, such is the nature of scientific curiosity. Sometimes you never know where it's going to lead you next. I started my descent.

It was tricky, for I soon found that I could not descend, hold on, and hold the electric torch all at the same time. The torch went in my pocket, and the descent became a nerve-wracking blind struggle for footholds in the darkness. Eventually, though, I became aware of a dim glow coming up from below, reflections along the walls of the rock-lined chimney from some light source below me.

One foot. One hand. Next foot. Next hand. Crabwise, I eased myself down.

Rocks shifted under my foot. I grabbed for a ledge, and felt it crumble under my hand. There was a roar of cascading rock, and the hideously sickening chill of sudden free-fall.

I was falling!

Make a Saving Roll against your DEX. *If the roll succeeds, go to* **320**. *If the roll fails, go to* **324**.

257

This room was someone's idea of a nightmare, and I began to understand why those rebels we'd found lying on the slope in the fog had charged so valiantly against what must have been hopeless odds. The rulers of this world were monsters.

There was no one here now, fortunately. I searched through the room, looking for some sign that Harry or Sarah had been here, half-terrified that I would find the evidence I sought. But there was nothing.

I moved toward a half-open door leading into an office or small room. Perhaps I would find something there.

You can leave this level by calling a lift. Go to the beginning of **Exploring the Tower** *and roll 2D6 as you summon a lift with your ID card. Or, if you prefer, you can explore the small room, which is described under* **T6** *in* **Exploring the Tower**.

258

My dive ended with a perfect somersault, and then a skull-jarring collision with the wall. From my upside-down tangle on the floor, I looked up into the black barrels of a half-dozen guns pointed at my nose.

Go to **229**.

259

The lift door opened, and I saw the back of a soldier's black uniform, the oily gleam of the submachine gun slung upside down from his shoulder. There was a guard outside the lift door! At the sound of the sliding door, he turned.

You can attack him at **278**, *or you can try to reach the lift control panel and escape. To escape, make a Saving Roll against your* DEX. *If the roll succeeds, go to* **293**. *If it fails, go to* **299**.

260

When the lift door opened, all I saw were soldiers! I had a blurred glimpse of them raising their weapons, of a room filled with electrical apparatus and what looked like the nastier means for interrogating prisoners. A fish-faced cadaver of a man in a stained white smock was there too, pointing at me.

I leapt for the lift control box, stabbing blindly at the buttons.

Make a Saving Roll against your DEX. *If it succeeds, go to* **293**. *If it fails, go to* **299**.

261

I executed a perfect somersault across the floor as bullets snapped through the air above me, then I landed on my feet, turned the corner, and dashed down the next corridor.

Gasping for air in deep, shuddering gulps, I stopped next to the door of a prison cell, and leaned against the wall. The sounds of pursuit were close behind me.

What to do now? Keep running? Or try to find a place to hide?

Keep running at **181**, *or look for a place to hide at* **202**.

262

I decided to check the office carefully. The filing cabinets were locked, and the papers scattered about on the desk were meaningless to me. At a quick glance, they appeared to be medical records for individual soldiers. Was this chamber of horrors also a doctor's office? I shuddered at the thought.

I opened a desk drawer, and time stopped for a moment. Inside was a cardboard container the size of a shoebox. The two wristwatches inside were most definitely not of Gathwyran manufacture. The numerals on their faces were Arabic, the calibrations were for twelve hours. Utterly useless on a world that had a day (I remembered from a computer report taken aboard the TARDIS earlier) of twenty-six-and-a-half hours. Besides, I recognized them. Sarah's had the slender gold band, and Harry's the black leather strap. Now I knew they'd been here.

I debated about whether or not to take the watches with me, and finally decided against it. It was better to leave no sign that I'd been here, no clue that I was on the trail of my two friends. Regretfully, I closed the drawer again, untouched, vowing that if Harry and Sarah were alive in this place, I would find them and bring them out.

For now, I decided, I'd do best to make myself scarce before the doctor, or something worse, returned.

Go to **Lift** *in* **Exploring the Tower**, *first rolling 2D6 as you summon it with your computer scanner card.*

263

I hung there, braced against the rocks for long minutes, considering. The presence of this silvery structure here was baffling. The labyrinth of tunnels I'd been following was supposed to lead up into the lower levels of Tharesti. What could this pipeline or tube possibly lead to so far below the city foundations?

Though I might be curious, I was not foolhardy. Descents are always more difficult than ascents—at least controlled descents are—and I would not be able to descend, hold on, and carry my electric torch all at the same time. A descent in darkness to an unknown destination would be suicidal.

I could also try going back the way I'd come, but I had no particular interest in facing that labyrinthine horror of passageways again. At least, not without a ball of string at least as long as the one I gave Theseus at the Palace of Minos. (Oh sure, I know they all say Ariadne gave him that string, but that's another story). In any case, I wasn't going down and I wasn't going back.

That left only one direction—up.

I quickly found I didn't need the torch for climbing. There was light coming from above, a faint glow from hairline cracks far above me, as though bright light in a large room was penetrating the seams of some hidden panel or door. The rock walls of the chimney were rugged enough that I had no trouble finding hand- and footholds all the way to the top.

When I got there, however, it was a disappointment. The metal tube vanished into a square metal ceiling that capped the chimney. The light was coming from the seams between this metal plate and the rock around it. From the fused and glassy condition of the rock, I guessed that a hole had recently been melted through the rock floor of a large cave or room into the chimney, which until then had been closed off. The tube and the metal cap had been inserted later, and the joints imperfectly sealed in a rushed and sloppy job.

But what WAS the job?

Near the top of the chimney, I found another side opening like the one through which I'd come. I didn't particularly look forward to re-entering the labyrinth, but it looked like the only other choice was going back down the way I'd come.

You may decide to descend the shaft by going to **325**. *Or you can explore the side gallery by going to* **322**.

264

The door opened, and my senses were assaulted by daylight and noise. The main floor! Broad glass doors looked out into sunshine, and both civilians and soldiers walked this way and that on unknown errands.

This level seemed to be a large, open rotunda with black marble floors and an arched, cathedral ceiling three stories above me. The lift shaft was a massive pillar rising from the center of the circular floor and vanishing into the ceiling overhead. There were two balcony levels, one above the other, ringing the walls above and joined to platforms encircling the elevator pillar by narrow, railed bridges or catwalks.

I looked toward the main doors again. No one seemed to be paying me any attention, and the way to the outside was open.

You can return to the **Lift** *for further explorations by going to* **Exploring the Tower**. *Or, you can explore this level more carefully by going to Level 5 in* **Exploring the Tower.** *Or you can walk toward the main doors to leave the building entirely by going to* **281**.

265

I crossed the bridge to the catwalk circling the rotunda wall. The balcony areas seemed to have no purpose beyond simple ornamentation, with railings that looked like late Victorian iron mongery mismatched to walls of pseudo-Neoclassical plaster cast. There were no doors or offices on this level. The balconies offered a view of the rotunda floor below, and nothing more.

Movement caught my eye back across the bridge. The lift doors had opened again, and soldiers were coming out onto my level. When they saw me, the soldiers began trotting across the bridge.

I knew what I had to do. Very slowly, making no sudden moves, I raised my hands.

Go to **296**.

266

There were several civilians present, men and women in severe grey uniforms bent over stacks of paperwork at their individual desks. One of them, a young woman, quite attractive behind her harsh, steel-rimmed glasses, looked up at me with questioning eyes.

You can say "Sorry, wrong floor," then turn around and go to **Lift** *in* **Exploring the Tower**.

If you prefer, you can walk over and engage the young

lady in conversation, hoping to learn something about the whereabouts of Harry and Sarah and the layout of the tower, without giving away the fact that you don't belong here. Pursue this course of action at **297**.

267

The door opened, and I was assaulted by daylight and noise. This was the main floor, and the way to the outside! Broad glass doors opened into sunshine, and people, both civilians and soldiers, walked this way and that on unknown errands.

This level seemed to be a large, round rotunda with black marble floors and an arched, cathedral ceiling three stories high. The lift shaft was a massive pillar rising from the center of the floor and vanishing into the ceiling overhead. I could see two balcony levels, one above the other. The balconies ringed the walls and were joined to platforms encircling the lift column by narrow, railed bridges.

The sudden noise of an echoing crash dragged my eyes back down to the main level. Soldiers! The drumming echo was the sound of jackboots marching in unison across the polished marble floor, which reverberated from the ceiling far above. At least ten black-uniformed troopers were marching into position between me and the main door.

They may not yet have seen you. You can nonchalantly turn around and summon a lift by going to **292**. *Or you can nonchalantly wander out to explore the main floor without attracting attention to yourself at* **294**. *Or you can try to nonchalantly walk past them through the door and out of the building at* **281**.

268

"Hands up!"

I climbed up off my knees, and turned to face the squad of black-uniformed guards who stood there, just far enough up the tunnel that I'd not been able to see them from the other side of the wall.

A gold-heavy officer grinned unpleasantly as he gestured for one of his troops to search me for weapons. "Well, well, our informant's information was accurate! Now we have another one of these…strangers…"

Another stranger. Harry and Sarah must be here! Our clothes, our unfamiliarity with Gathwyran history and politics would set all of us off enough to label us as strangers. And the informant? Elanin, obviously. I raised my hands slowly and let the soldiers lead me up the sloping floor of the tunnel.

The tunnel was a virtual highway, nine meters high and five across, running up into the rock. The tang of the cool breeze at my back suggested that this tunnel opened in the cliff above the sea. A short walk brought us to the point where the tunnel opened into a large, underground room about forty-five meters across, with a massive, central pillar. The room was stacked and strewn with crates and various pieces of massive, long-disused machinery, all covered with a layer of dust. I remembered what the rebels had said about the tunnels being used to bring in cargo in days when there was active trade among the Gathwyran coastal cities. This room must be one of the lower levels of a Tharestian building, perhaps even the Tower of the Masters I'd heard Latham's people speak of.

A door opened in the side of the pillar, and soldiers stepped out. A lift shaft! This was a basement level, then.

The soldiers were followed by a squat and greasy-looking man. He was balding, with black slits for eyes that gave away nothing but the queasy feeling that here was a man not to be trusted.

Imagine my surprise to see coming up behind him none other than a pair of Daleks!

"YOU HAVE SUC-CEED-ED IN CAP-TUR-ING THE DOC-TOR," one of the twin black horrors rasped in strident, metallic tones. "YOU ARE TO BE CON-GRAT-U-LAT-ED, KO-LAV."

The slimy individual smiled, giving a chilling show of teeth. "It was nothing, Master. The rebel informer told us exactly where he could be picked up."

"EX-CEL-LENT. WE WILL TAKE HIM FOR IN-TER-RO-GA-TION."

The other Dalek drifted forward, its vision-sensor stalk roving up and down as it scanned me. "THE DOC-TOR IS AN OLD EN-E-MY OF THE DA-LEKS." This one's voice was pitched lower, harsher. "THE DOC-TOR MUST BE EX-TER-MIN-A-TED."

That sounded familiar.

"THE DOC-TOR CAN BE OF GREAT VA-LUE TO US," the first Dalek replied. "THE WORK IN THE HU-MAN LABS DOES NOT GO WELL. THE DOC-TOR WILL HELP US WITH OUR QUEST."

"THE DOC-TOR MUST BE EX-TER-MIN-A-TED."

"NEG-A-TIVE. THE DOC-TOR WILL BE PER-SUA-DED TO HELP US. HE WILL NOT BE EX-TER-MIN-A-TED."

Well, now that would be a switch if the first Dalek had his way. I wasn't sure I wanted to be too closely involved with any Dalek scientific operation, however. In any case, I heard clearly the unspoken "yet" at the end of that Dalek's speech. He might be willing to spare me for now, but there was always later. I'd ruined too many Dalek enterprises in too many pasts and futures for them to forgive me quite that freely.

It was very unlikely that any task I undertook for the Daleks could be counted on for much in the way of job security.

Go to **305**.

269

You are engaging in a dialogue with Elanin, trying to learn what he knows about the Masters, and whether or not he is leading you into a trap. This encounter requires that you bluff, using your CHA and either your *Haggling* or *Negotiation/Diplomacy* skill.

Make a Saving Roll against your CHA. If it succeeds, you win a bonus modifier of –3. If it fails, the modifier is +2. Roll 1D6 for Elanin's reaction and subtract this from either your *Haggling* Skill rating or your *Negotiation/ Diplomacy* Skill Rating. The result is Elanin's roll. Then roll 2D6 for your own tactics and apply the modifier.

If the result is equal to or less than Elanin's roll, you win. If it is greater, you lose, and Elanin will give you no more information.

If you succeed, go to **302**. *If you fail, go to* **284**.

270

As you sneak up on the guard, make a Saving Roll against your DEX. If the roll is successful, you are able to reach the guard without being seen. The surprise of your attack will give you a considerable advantage. If the roll fails, your loss of surprise will give you a considerable disadvantage. If you fail the Saving Roll against DEX, it means the guard catches sight of you when you are still several meters away from him. You may now try to persuade him that you are lost and in need of directions, using this as an excuse to get close enough to him to attack. This bluff requires CHA and some fast talking.

Make a Saving Roll against your CHA score. If it succeeds, you win a bonus modifier of −4. If it fails, the modifier is +2. Roll 1D6 −1 for the guard's response, and subtract it from your CHA score. The result is the guard's roll. Then roll 2D6 for your fast talking, and apply the modifier. If the result is equal to or less than the guards' roll, you win. If it is greater, you lose.

If you lose, the guard does not believe you, and will not let you get close enough to attack him. If you win, you will have achieved the element of surprise by getting close enough to the guard to jump him.

For this attack, you will now need your STR and *Brawling* skill.

Make a Saving Roll against your STR. If it succeeds, you win a bonus modifier of −3. If it fails, the modifier is +2.

Then roll 1D6 +1 for the guard's ability, and subtract the result from your *Brawling* skill. The result is the guard's roll. Now roll 2D6 for your own actions and add the modifier. If your earlier bluffing attempt was successful, you may subtract 2 MORE from this roll. If the final result is less than the guards' roll, you win the combat. If it is greater, you have lost.

If you lose in the attempt to bluff your way out of the situation, go to **317.**

If you win the combat, go to **319.** *If you lose the combat round, go to* **321.**

You may also decide to surrender to the guard, who doesn't appear to be the kind of person likely to believe your story. Go to **317.**

271

I examined the service area carefully, looking for anything that might useful. But everything was so primitive! For people with anti-gravity technology, their tools certainly weren't state-of-the-art. For that matter, these people shouldn't even *have* anti-gravity, not with primitive submachine guns and rifles for weapons. Why, that cross-latch ratcheter on the table had more in common technologically with a submachine gun than with advanced anti-gravity. And what about that manual wrench? Why, they weren't even up to sonic screwdrivers here, yet!

That meant they must be getting their anti-gravity technology from someplace else.

"Hey you!"

That wasn't my name, but I turned anyway. The man behind me was obviously a mechanic. His coveralls were black with grease, and he had the general bodily dimensions of a Terran gorilla. Holding a manual wrench in one hand, he was slapping it repeatedly against his free hand with a decidedly unpleasant emphasis.

It would be foolish to fight. You can run, making a try for the lift at **289**. *Or, you can try to talk your way out of this one at* **307**. *Who knows? Maybe you can get some information out of him.*

272

The door had no sooner opened than I heard a shout. "That's him! Stop him!"

I had a blurred impression of soldiers, lots of them, descending toward me with guns raised. I dove for the lift buttons.

Make a Saving Roll against your DEX. *If it succeeds, go to* **293**. *If it fails, go to* **299**.

273

I turned and ran, bolting for a side corridor and safety. Then a rifle shot rang out, an explosion that caught me squarely between the shoulder blades, smashing me forward and down and into a wildly spinning darkness.

Go to **313.**

274

Here were row upon row of parked grav vehicles, but not a soul around. Because of the extensive experience I'd had with anti-gravity technology of other worlds and times, I didn't expect any trouble figuring out how to control these devices.

Choosing a sporty, open-topped two-seater, I climbed into the right-hand control seat, and began checking out the controls. They seemed simple enough: a floor-mounted stick for steering, parallel switches for power control...but what was this? The bloody thing needed an ignition key to start it.

Well, only one thing for it, then. I leaned down, fishing around under the dashboard for the ignition wires that had to be there.

Make a Saving Roll against your DEX. *If it succeeds, go to* **303.** *If it fails, go to* **306.**

275

The lift that ran through the core of the Tower took me and a nervous-looking clutch of human guards from the interrogation room on Level 4 down to Level 2. By watching the lighted buttons over the guards' shoulders, I could keep track of the levels.

I slipped a hand in my coat pocket as the lift slowed to a stop. I'd forgotten all about the jelly babies, but half a package was still there. Somehow they'd made it through all that had happened since we'd come to Gathwyr.

Level 2 was a cell-block area whose grim grey passageways radiated out from the central lift shaft. There was door after steel-bound wooden door with tiny, slide-paneled peepslots in them and massive iron locks. It looked like one of these cells was going to be my home for a while.

Make a Saving Roll against your MNT. *Add 4 to your roll, because this is a tough problem. If the roll succeeds, you have an idea for escaping. Go to* **323**. *If the roll fails, or if you would prefer to wait in the cell and see what the Daleks have in store for you, go to* **327**.

276

I rolled across the floor as blue fire dazzled my eyes, washing across the crates where I had been crouching. First, there was an explosion, then a pillar of fire ate its way up the rapidly charring wood as acrid smoke wafted through the room.

"EX-TER-MIN-ATE! EX-TER-MIN-ATE!"

The black horror drifted around, following me as I scrambled to my feet and dodged past machinery and packing crates, keeping the crates between me and that lethal Dalek cannon.

Blue fire flickered again, scorching the air above my head and filling my nostrils with the sharp tang of ozone. My back scraped against rock as the Dalek swung around the last line of boxes in its way. There was no more retreat now, no place else to run.

"DO NOT EX-TER-MIN-ATE," another of the strident Dalek voices rasped, this one a bit higher and sharper than the voice of the first.

"THIS IS AN IN-TRU-DER! IN-TRU-DERS MUST BE EX-TER-MIN-A-TED!"

"THE IN-TRU-DER IS THE DOC-TOR. HE MUST

NOT BE EX-TER-MIN-A-TED!"

That was odd. A reprieve from a Dalek? The argument between the two was becoming interesting, even if the speakers were something less than good conversationalists.

'THE DOC-TOR IS AN EN-E-MY OF THE DA-LEKS! ALL EN-E-MIES OF THE DA-LEKS MUST BE EX-TER-MIN-A-TED!"

Now, that was more like the usual, predictable Dalek line.

"NEG-A-TIVE. THE DOC-TOR IS A TIME LORD. THE DOC-TOR MAY BE A-BLE TO HELP US IN OUR QUEST. THE DOC-TOR WILL NOT BE EX-TER-MIN-A-TED."

With that, the human guard shoved me toward the lift. Somehow, I felt less than total relief. I wasn't sure I wanted any part of a project the Daleks were working on, even to save my life. Anyway, working for the Daleks wasn't likely to bring me job security for very long.

Go to **305**.

277

I heard the hiss of a lift door opening, the crash of jackboots, and shouted commands.

I whirled, looking for a place to hide. Too late! I had a blurred impression of soldiers, rank upon rank of them, closing in with weapons levelled.

Someone snapped, "Hands up!", and I complied.

Go to **296**.

278

You are engaged in hand-to-hand combat with a single soldier armed with a submachine gun. To succeed in this tussle, you will need your STR and *Brawling* skill.

Make a Saving Roll against your STR. If it succeeds, you

win a bonus modifier of –3. If it fails, the modifier is +2.

Then roll 1D6 + 1 for the soldier's fighting skill, and subtract this from your *Brawling* skill. The result is the soldier's roll. Roll 2D6 for your actions and apply the modifier. If the result is equal to or less than the soldiers' roll, you win. If it is greater, you lose.

If you win the encounter, you may return to either Levels 6 and 7 in **Lift** *in* **Exploring the Tower**, *and continue your investigation. If you fail, go to* **308**.

279

You are engaged in hand-to-hand combat with two soldiers, both armed with submachine guns. Make a Saving Roll against your STR. If it succeeds, you win a bonus modifier of –3. If it fails, the modifier is +2.

Then roll 2D6 for the two soldiers, and add 4 for their training. Subtract this from your DEX score plus your *Brawling* Skill. The result is the soldiers' roll. Then roll 2D6 for your own actions. If the result is less than or equal to the soldiers' roll, you have won. If it is greater, you have lost.

If you win this encounter, return to the description of the level where you encountered the guards in **Exploring the Tower**. *You may also turn around immediately and go to another level by going to* **Lift** *in* **Exploring the Tower**. *(The lift door closed during your combat, and you will have to summon it again with your green card.) If you lose the encounter, go to* **308**.

280

Blue fire surrounded, then engulfed me. For one stark, burning moment, I was suspended in dazzling agony, and then the darkness closed in.

Go to **326**.

281

Hands in pockets, a whistle on my lips, I strode toward the door with a jaunty and carefree step. A backward glance, a worried look, a trace of fear, and the hounds would be on me in a flash. The rotunda was filled with soldiers. Were they looking for me, or were they there by chance? I dared not look at them, but it felt as though an entire squad's eyes were burning holes in the back of my head.

There was the door. The city lay spread out below me in the sunshine, its narrow, winding streets enclosed by the protecting wall. Beyond, the grey blur of the Fog Sea stretched off endlessly to the west, with a trace of dim and distant mountains purple above the mist on the horizon.

I put my hand to the door.

"Hold it, you!" I head the clatter of guns being brought to aim behind me. "You! At the door! Hands up!" Next came a more horrible sound, the ratcheting snick of machinegun bolts being drawn.

You can run through the door at **301**. *Or you can turn around very, very slowly, and put your hands up at* **296**.

282

When the door opened, I wished it hadn't. Before me was a military barracks, its wood floors polished by years of soap and scrub brush details. There were lockers, double bunks in precise rows, and dozens of soldiers. Most had removed their jackets and were in various poses of conversation, card-playing, reading, or the like, but two were in full uniform, standing close by the lift doors with rifles at high port.

Those rifles snapped down, trained at the end of my nose. I put my hands up, moving very, very slowly.

"Sorry. Wrong floor," I said.

Go to **296**.

283

The door opened, revealing a pair of smartly turned-out sentries just beyond it, holding gleaming rifles trained at the end of my nose. Behind them was a desk piled with paperwork, where an officer heavy with gold braid was rising to his feet. There were other desks in the room, whose walls were festooned with banners and flags, and numerous other officers.

Somehow I'd stumbled into Tharesti's military headquarters.

"Sorry, wrong floor," I said. Putting my hands up slowly, I was careful not to make any sudden moves.

Go to **296.**

284

I couldn't get anything out of Elanin. He certainly sounded sincere in his enthusiastic support of Latham's fight against the Masters. That didn't mean he was telling the truth, though.

You can decide to trust Elanin on the basis of what he has said, or at least go along with him for now at **228.** *If you fear Elanin is leading you into a trap, you can watch for an opportunity to lose him by slipping into one of the side tunnels you have been passing from time to time at* **216.** *It may be that you can find your own way through the mountain and into the city.*

285

You are engaged in hand-to-hand combat with a single soldier armed with a rifle. You will need your STR and *Brawling* skill for this attack. Make a Saving Roll against your STR. If it succeeds, you win a bonus modifier of –3. If it fails, the modifier is +2.

Roll 1D6 + 1 for the guard's ability, and subtract this from your *Brawling* skill. The result is the guard's roll. Now roll 2D6 for your own actions and add the modifier. If you have achieved surprise as described in Paragraph **270**, you may subtract 2 MORE from this roll. If the result is less than the guard's roll, you win the combat. If it is greater, you have lost.

If you succeed, the lift is now clear, and you can take it to any floor desired. Go to **Lift** *in* **Exploring the Tower**. *If you fail, go to* **308**.

286

I pressed the button for the floor I wanted, but the expected surge of acceleration didn't come. Instead, a panel slid open alongside the button array, exposing a slot. A voice spoke, a rather harsh, metallic voice with the even, measured tones of a rather primitive electronic vodor. "DESTINATION LEVEL IS SECURITY ZONE. PLEASE VERIFY."

The slot looked like a computer ID card scanner. A double security system, with certain floors reached only by inserting a card? It looked that way. I fingered my stolen green card speculatively.

You may insert the green card in the slot and punch the number for your destination floor again at **309**. *Or return to* **Lift** *in* **Exploring the Tower** *to choose another floor instead.*

287

You are engaged in a hand-to-hand struggle at the door of a lift. You are trying to break free and punch a floor number, while two soldiers are trying to stop you and drag you out. You will need your STR and *Brawling* skill for this attack.

Make a Saving Roll against your STR. If it succeeds, you

win a bonus modifier of –3. If it fails, the modifier is +2.

Roll 1D6 + 1 for the guard's ability, and subtract this from your *Brawling* skill. The result is the guard's roll. Then roll 2D6 for your own actions, and apply the modifier. If you have achieved surprise as described in Paragraph **270**, you may subtract 2 MORE from this roll. If the final result is less than the guard's roll, you win the combat. If it is greater, you have lost.

If you win, go to **311**. *If you lose, go to* **304**.

288

The door opened.

That this was some kind of scientific laboratory was obvious. There were benches with reagents, flasks, and chemlab apparatus racked tabletop to ceiling. There were men and women in white lab coats bent over the blue glow of Bunsen burners. There was a mass of some very strange and obviously cobbled-together, high-energy physics gear against the far wall. And there were heads turning, eyes widening, and a sudden exclamation of "Who are YOU? What are you doing here?"

"Uh, excuse me. I must be lost," I said. "I say, what's going on in here?"

"This is a restricted area, and you'd better go!"

Actually, that sounded like an excellent suggestion, but the next voice I heard froze marrow and blood and rooted me to the spot.

"NEG-A-TIVE! THE DOC-TOR WILL RE-MAIN." A pair of Daleks glided into view from the other side of the lift shaft wall. "NOW YOU WILL COME WITH US, DOC-TOR. YOU WILL BE OF GREAT SER-VICE TO THE DA-LEKS!"

"Oh?" The cold had settled around my heart, icily

penetrating the very core of my being. "And what if I refuse?"

"YOU WILL CO-OP-ER-ATE OR YOU WILL BE EX-TER-MIN-A-TED."

Somehow, I knew they were going to say something like that. Still, as they led me toward the lift, it struck me that they were acting rather pleasantly—for Daleks, that is...

Go to **305**.

289

You are engaged in hand-to-hand combat against a large, strong mechanic armed with a spanner. This guy is big, and you will need all your STR and *Brawling* skill for this one.

You have a choice in tactics. You may either attack the mechanic, or try to get the spanner from him and attack him with that. For either approach, make a Saving Roll against your STR score. If it succeeds, you win a bonus modifier of –3. If it fails, the modifier is +3.

If you choose to attack the mechanic, roll 1D6 + 2 for his ability, and subtract this from your *Brawling* skill. The result is the mechanic's roll. Then roll 2D6 for your own tactics, and apply the modifier. If the result is equal to or less than the mechanic's roll, you win. If you win, go at once to **312**. If you lose, go to **314**.

If you choose to get the spanner away from the mechanic and attack him with it, follow the same procedure, but subtract 1D6 from your *Brawling* skill rating to represent his defense. If you succeed, you have managed to knock the spanner from his hand. If you fail, you have automatically lost and must go to **314**.

If you have knocked the spanner from his hand, make a Saving Roll against your DEX score. If you fail, the mechanic recovers his spanner and hits you with it, sending you straight to **314**. If you succeed, you have the spanner and may attack the mechanic with it.

To carry out this attack, roll 1D6 for the mechanic's defense and subtract this from your *Brawling* skill. Add 2 to represent your advantage in holding the spanner. The result is the mechanic's roll. Then roll 2D6 + the modifier you won earlier.

If the result is equal to or less than the mechanic's roll, you win and go to **312**. *If you fail, the mechanic takes the spanner away from you, bashes you with it, and sends you to* **314**.

290

The lift door opened, and I stepped into a laboratory, looking about. There were no people present. Luck was with me.

That it was a laboratory was obvious. Bench after bench was arrayed around the lift shaft column. Some of the benches held Bunsen burners, flasks, and racked bottles of reagents. Most of the lab space, however, was taken up with what looked like strange and cobbled-together, high-energy physics gear. There was a hyperwave detector, a Klevin molecular chamber, a gravitometer, and was that a Temporal Vortex probe? Yes! It had to be!

What would the Gathwyrans be doing with physics gear like this? All the equipment had a rough and ready look to it, as though electronics gear had been dismantled from a few dozen more primitive devices and breadboarded into something far in advance of contemporary Gathwyran science.

I moved over to the Temporal Vortex probe. Primitive, of course. Why, the temporal displacement detector alone was twenty times the size of the little hand-held unit I'd cobbled together aboard the the TARDIS. This one didn't look like it carried even one one-hundredth of the power of mine.

There on the lab bench, lay my detector, partially disassembled now. They'd been busy here, and someone had had brains enough to know that my detector had something to do with anomalous signals through the Temporal Vortex. It also suggested that the scientists here were concerned about those strange Vortex signals that had brought us here in the first place.

I wondered why they should be, as Gathwyr had nothing like a transtemporally oriented physics.

You have picked up some clues here. Add Clue C to the list of clues won so far. If you have already learned who the Masters are, go to **315**. *Otherwise, make a Saving Roll against your* MNT. *If it succeeds, go to* **315**. *If it fails and you do not yet know who the Masters are, go to* **318**.

291

They held me there at gunpoint as the officer spoke into a tiny radio handset. Moments later, the keening hum of an anti-gravity drive descended through the fog, and a small, open-topped grav vehicle settled lightly to the gravel nearby.

"Who's been bringing you advanced technology?" I asked the officer, keeping my voice nonchalant. "That sort of gear doesn't go with submachine guns and rifles, you know. Those sensor helmets your men are wearing, too..."

"Silence!"

Why do harmless inquiries from curious strangers so often elicit the word "Silence!" generally barked at several score decibels more than are necessary for normal conversation? Soldiers hustled me into the aircar, the keening warble gathered voice and power, and we rose above the grey-white surface of the fog.

Go to **142**.

292

"Just a minute, you!" The voice behind me was sharp with authority, and I knew it was aimed at me. The lift door had already closed behind me. Pretending not to hear, I calmly slid the card through the scanner and willed the door to open again. "Hold it! Stop, you!"

The door opened, and I stepped inside. At the sound of running feet behind me and the click of drawn machine gun bolts, I lunged for the lift buttons.

Make a Saving Roll against your DEX. *If it succeeds, go to* **293**. *If it fails, go to* **299**.

293

Made it! The door slid shut on faces darkened with anger and surprise, on aimed guns, waving fists, and shouting voices. There was the thud of something heavy hitting the door, then the pounding of fists. Could they override the closed door before the elevator carried me away?

As the lift began moving me to safety, I breathed a sigh of relief. The only problem was that when I stabbed at the control panel, I didn't see which button I pushed.

Now I was afraid to look. Where was I going?

To find out to which level you are going, roll 1D6. A result of 1 through 5 indicates the first digit of the level you will reach, 1 through 5, respectively. A result of 6 is taken as a 0.

Next roll 2D6, add the results of the two dice together, and subtract 2. If the result is 0 through 9, the second digit of the level to which you are going is 0 through 9. If the result is 10, the second digit is a 0. Read the first and second digits as the level to which the lift is going. Results greater than 50 are considered to be 50.

For example, roll 1D6 for the first digit. The result is

"6." This means the first digit will be "0." Roll 2D6 and subtract 2 for the second digit. If the results were 4 and 7, adding these together yields a 11. Subtracting 2 will give you 9. The second digit is "9." The destination floor is "09," or Level 9. Go to the description of this level in **Exploring the Tower.**

If, by chance, you pushed the button for the same level from which you were trying to escape, the door will open in a few seconds. Go directly to **299**.

If your die rolls result in a floor number of "00", you have hit the "Door Close" button by mistake. The door will open in a few seconds at the same level from which you were trying to escape. Again, go directly to **299**.

294

Hands in my pockets, I strolled away from the lifts toward the far side of the rotunda. There were soldiers everywhere, many more than civilians, who had that grey, oppressed look that I'd seen before on other worlds, in other times. This was a conquered people, and it seemed to make little difference that the conquerors—the visible conquerors, at least—were their own people. It was an alien spirit that had been imposed on them, a spirit of slow death and fear.

On the other side of the lifts, there were glassed-in offices, places where civilians were queued up to pay taxes and buy licenses under the eyes and guns of guards. There seemed no purpose in going THAT way. All things being equal, I would rather face soldiers than bureaucrats. Deep down, soldiers are human.

"You! Let's see your papers!"

But then, there were bureaucratic soldiers. This one was the Gathwyran equivalent of a noncom, I thought, his face all jaw and nose below slitted black eyes. Several soldiers with leveled submachine guns backed him up.

He eyed my coat and scarf. "You're an odd-looking one. Let's see those papers."

"Odd, indeed!" When in doubt, the best defense is a powerful offense. "I want to talk to your commanding officer!"

"You'll show me your papers first!" The slight edge in his voice brought those submachine guns straight into line with my heart.

"Papers? Papers? What would I be doing with papers?"

"That's what I thought. Take him, boys."

I thought of running, but I wouldn't have gone more than a few steps before they cut me down. Besides, I did not want these nervous-looking children with guns to open up with automatic weapons in a place where stray rounds could kill civilians. My running might precipitate a massacre.

Slowly, I raised my hands.

Go to **296**.

295

I slipped the green card into the slot on the crate, but nothing happened. I tried again, and had just about decided that the thing wasn't working right when I felt the hard coldness of a gun barrel probe just behind my left ear.

"Wrong pass," a voice said. "You called us instead."

I turned, my hands carefully in sight. A squad of soldiers had stepped out of the lift behind me and were arrayed across the room, their guns levelled.

"You need a red card to go down there, unless, of course, the Masters want to interview you...personally." The soldier smiled unpleasantly and gestured with his gun. "Who knows? You may get to go down there sooner than you think!"

Go to **296**.

296

Taken captive, I was led with very little ceremony to an out-of-the-way corner of Level 4, where they thought they could keep an eye on me. I learned that this was the floor they called their "Place of Interrogation." The psychological theatricality of such places is the same on a thousand human worlds across Space and Time. Here were the same grey walls and filth, the chains and racks, the cadaverous-looking interrogators with their heavy boots and hard eyes, the racks and implements of torture.

My captors shackled and chained me to a wall, and left a pair of grim-eyed soldiers with grim-looking submachine guns to stand guard.

When the officers and other soldiers had gone from this cheerless place, I tried getting information from my two guards. Information? I would have been glad for some old-fashioned conversation…insults…a demand for silence… anything!

"Good morning," I tried, forcing a brightness I surely didn't feel. "I'm The Doctor!"

Nothing. Not a flicker of amusement even. Not even a strident shriek of "Silence!"

"Say, you wouldn't happen to know the whereabouts of a couple of friends of mine, would you? A man…young, dark-haired…named Harry. Something of a klutz, actually, but a good sort. And Sarah Jane…a pretty, dark-haired girl. She's a reporter, but you musn't hold that against her."

No response. The two soldiers just sat there and watched me rattle my chains, with no more emotion than if I had been a particularly boring episode on the telly.

I must have hung around there for an hour or so, and then finally my guards showed some signs of life—at a sound from the direction of the lift. They turned, looked, and both grew death-white at the sight of something just beyond my range of view. One just stared. The other stood, wiped his mouth with the back of a greasy hand, and took a faltering step backward.

And then the Daleks glided into view.

Daleks! Super-technological horrors, gleaming black machines housing brains as malevolently twisted as any in the cosmos...Daleks!

"OUR IN-FOR-MA-TION IS AC-CU-RATE," one shrilled. "IT IS VER-I-FIED THAT THIS IS THE DOC-TOR."

"Well, I never denied it."

"THIS IS THE DOC-TOR." This one's mechanically produced voice was lower, more gravelly, but just as shrill. "THE DOC-TOR IS AN EN-E-MY OF THE DA-LEKS. THE DOC-TOR IS TO BE EX-TER-MIN-A-TED."

"NEG-A-TIVE. THE DOC-TOR IS A TIME LORD. HE WILL BE OF GREAT VA-LUE TO US IN OUR PRO-JECT."

"THE DOC-TOR WILL NOT BE EX-TER-MIN-A-TED." Did I hear an unspoken "yet" tacked onto that line? "HE WILL HELP US IN OUR SEARCH."

"HE WILL NOT WIL-LING-LY CO-OP-ER-ATE WITH THE DA-LEKS."

"THE DOC-TOR WILL CO-OP-ER-ATE WHEN HE LEARNS WHAT IS AT STAKE. RE-LEASE HIM."

Friendly Daleks? I rubbed my wrists as they opened my shackles. Any project the Daleks were involved in meant trouble, big trouble, for every other sentient life form in the universe.

And one of the Daleks, at least, was confident that I would want to cooperate.

I felt ill.

*Hanging about the dungeon was restful, if not pleasant. You may restore your END and STR if they have been reduced by wounds or fatigue (but not regeneration). Go to **305**.*

297

"Hello!" I said brightly. "I'm The Doctor, and I wonder if you could help me?"

"What can I do for you?" She seemed a bit taken back. I had the feeling that people were not encouraged to ask questions in Gathwyran society.

"Actually, I seem to be a bit lost, and I seem to have lost a couple of friends of mine."

"Friends?"

"Yes, a tall, dark-haired chap—about this tall—and a girl. Brown hair, attractive, has a nasty habit of putting her nose in where it isn't wanted."

"Well, have you checked with the Proctors?"

"Proctor?"

"Yes, of course, the Tharestian Military Authority. Their headquarters is on Level 31 of this building."

"Ah, I see. Can you tell me anything about this building? I mean, where things are? I've never been here before."

"I suppose it can be a bit confusing. You came in through the main level?"

I grinned. "Is there any other way in?"

"Well, if the Proctors brought you here, they might have flown you in on Level 20. That's the gravcar dock. But then, if the Proctors brought you in, you'd hardly be wandering around free, would you?"

She smiled, and I laughed. It seemed the appropriate thing to do.

"Anyway," she continued, "the building entrance is on Level 5. That's below us. I suppose you have a green card?

"Of course."

"You must have used it to get here. Just use it to call the lift, and punch the number of the level you want to go. Five is the entrance rotunda, 6 and 7 are just public viewing areas above the rotunda, 8 through 10 is Record Files, 11 is the Library, 12 up through 18 are offices. Uh…was there a particular office or department you were looking for?"

"No, no, keep going. You're doing splendidly."

"Yes, well, 19 and 20"—she pointed up—"are grav docking levels. Beyond that are the Warden barracks, and the military headquarters levels are on 31 and 32."

"What's beyond that?"

"Main Administration, but I doubt you want anything THERE. Besides, you need a red card for restricted levels."

"Ah, right, I forgot. And below Level 5?"

Her face soured. "I don't think you want to go THERE, either."

"Ah. And to find my friends, I should visit the HQ, is that it?"

"That's your best bet." She lowered her voice. "They're not very friendly there, but they should be able to tell you what to do. Uh…your friends aren't in any trouble, are they?"

"Well, I hope not. As I said, Sarah has a habit of sticking her nose where it doesn't belong, but I'm sure they didn't come looking for trouble. I'll hop up to 31 to see what I can find out. Thank you so much for your trouble!"

"No trouble at all."

My green card summoned a lift. Where to next?

To proceed, go to **Lift** *in* **Exploring the Tower**. *Roll 2D6 before you board the lift, then continue your explorations by choosing a level.*

298

No, I didn't like the look of that crate at all. Until I knew more about it, I wasn't going to mess with it.

But if not that, what then? I prowled the room, then found a comfortable niche behind a stack of nice, dusty, non-threatening crates, from which I could watch the lift and the crate both.

I didn't have long to wait. The lift door slid open, and a soldier walked out. He took his place by the door and another man stepped out, a fat, balding, greasy-looking fellow wearing gold finery elegant enough for one of the more extravagant Renaissance Medicis on Earth. His filigree cloak swirled about his broad hips as he stepped up to the dustless crate, the dim light sparkling from the cloak's gold threadwork.

And behind him came two squat, black, menacing creatures. None other than Daleks!

They stood by while the richly dressed human slid a red scanner card through the slot on the crate, then stepped back as the crate blossomed open. From where I watched, I could see it was a lift of some sort. Man and Daleks stepped in, then sank into the floor as the crate closed again over them. The guard was left standing alone beside the more conventional lift in the center of the room.

Where did a secret lift from the bottom level of the Tower of the Masters lead, I wondered? And how was I going to find out?

There seemed only two choices. I could stay where I was, watching that guard and waiting for something else to happen. Or, I could sneak up and attack him so that I could go somewhere else. Somewhere else? Up or down?

None of my choices looked very hopeful at the moment.

You can sit there and watch the guard at **230**, *or you can sneak up on the guard at* **270**.

299

Stabbing desperately, I lunged for the panel of buttons, and fell flat on my face. Someone had hold of my feet, was dragging me back out of the lift. I struggled vainly until the butt of a rifle descended. A second time, it seemed like the universe had exploded—this time in darkness.

Go to **304**.

300

I stepped into the broad tunnel, peering down its length. It was not dark, as I'd first thought, but lit by electric lights strung at intervals from its rocky ceiling. As I walked down the sharply sloping floor, I could smell the sea more strongly.

This was one of the ways cargo had been brought into and out of the city. If the Tower of the Masters had been the government center before the Masters arrived, which I thought likely, perhaps special cargos such as luxury items had been brought in this way.

Some distance along the way, I noticed a jumble of rocks against the wall to my right. A dark crevice attracted my attention. I stooped and peered, but could see nothing. It was pitch black in there, no place to explore without a light. I kept on going, with frequent glances over my shoulder and up the slope. There was nowhere to hide along here, and anyone coming from either direction would be certain to spot me instantly. As the sharply descending path leveled out, I could see a flat rectangle of sky-blue light ahead of me in the distance. The outside!

Just this side of it, the floor of the cave had been melted and fused into a metal-smooth deck. There were vehicles parked there, grav vehicles ranging from flimsy little two-seaters to bulkier, open-topped eight-seaters with twin-mount gun wells on their sloping afterdecks. There were people there too and—. No, it couldn't be! Did my eyes deceive me, or were those really the drifting, menacing black shapes of Daleks?

There was a place off to the side of the grav vehicle deck where crates and boxes had been stacked in a temporary supply depot. I approached at what I hoped was a casual walk, then slipped behind the cover provided by those crates. It was a good position from which to spy on the activity on the dock.

It was an obviously military operation. The humans present were all soldiers in starched black uniforms and gleaming leather, though most wore something like Terran overseas caps instead of helmets or heavy sensor masks. They seemed to be preparing a large grav vehicle for an expedition, loading its boot with containers of supplies and what looked like various long-range sensor devices. As I watched, a similar eight-man vehicle keened in through the opening, hovered briefly, then settled to the deck with a dwindling whine. It was crewed by four humans and a Dalek. Interesting, that piece of information. It was doubtful that there were many Daleks on Gathwyr. Whatever mission they had here would be delegated to their human slaves, unless what they were doing was very, very important. But what could it be?

The sensor gear might give a clue. I couldn't see clearly, but it LOOKED like the sort of electronics that would be necessary in tracking down a temporal disturbance. I thought about my vanished, hand-wired unit. Were the Daleks looking for the same time/space Vortex anomaly that had brought me to Gathwyr? That wouldn't be good, but there didn't seem to be much I could do about it. Nothing that I could use as a weapon was handily within reach, but I spotted a table near the crates that had some small gear on it. There were electronics parts, hand-held electric torches, and the like for the work that was going on in the grav craft innards.

An idea suddenly occurred to me. With one of those lights, I might be able to explore that crevice I'd seen on my way down here. Though there was nothing concrete to go on, it was possible that it might open into the volcanic caves that must honeycomb the rock on which Tharesti was built. If so, they might lead me back to the city by a different way. I was also thinking about that mysterious crate back there on the main level. Some cavern-exploring might be just what I needed right now.

Then again, I could forget it and just get the heck out of there.

You can try to get a light, then go back to explore the crevice at **328**. *Or you may nonchalantly walk back up the slope the way you came at* **329**.

301

I ran, slamming through the door and out into sunlight. They would never open fire with so many civilians present. Then a volley of shots shattered the air, and I was rolling down the steps as the roar of automatic weapons pounded on and on. Darkness closed over the sun and the bright blue sky.

Go to **313**.

302

There are those who prefer the rubber hose, the bright lights, the barked questions, and cunning rationality of an interrogator to learn the answers to questions. Me, I prefer a friendly manner and a bag of jelly babies. Under my gentle persuasion, Elanin admitted the truth.

"Yes, I'm working for the Masters!" The agony in his face suggested it was scarcely a willing cooperation. "My family is not dead. Not yet, at least. The Masters told me that if I would join the rebels, then let them know when and where the rebels are moving, they'd let my family live." His shoulders heaved and trembled as he sobbed, "I couldn't do anything else!"

"Of course not." I was thoughtful. Latham and his men didn't seem ever to have seen the Masters close up. "No, of course not. You've seen the Masters up close?"

He nodded, a convulsive jerk. "They captured me... operated on me..."

"Operated?"

He turned his head and pulled back a hank of hair, exposing a faint, purplish scar behind his right ear. "It's how they communicate with me, tell me what I'm to do. They told me you were coming, said that if I brought you to them, they'd...they'd..."

"I know. Let your people go. What about these Masters? What are they like?"

"As tall as you. Maybe just a bit shorter. All metal... and black, black as night. They have a thing like an eye on a metal stalk, two arms, one of which is a gun of some kind."

I nodded. "Where I come from, those are called Daleks. They're not nice people."

"No."

"Do you talk to them through that? Are they listening to us?"

"I...I don't think so. I just hear their voice...when they want to talk to me, and they can hear me speaking then. I can sort of feel it when it's on."

"Hmm. I see. It's not on now, then?"

He shook his head.

"The question is what to do now. I could turn around and walk out of here." I saw pain twist his features. "Of course, that might not be so good for your family."

I would have to make a decision quickly. But what decision was there to make? I wanted to meet Tharesti's Masters, or at least study them close at hand. Going along with Elanin's original plan would certainly accomplish that, and might save his family as well. My capture didn't guarantee their safety, but I knew how Daleks worked. My escape might very well guarantee their deaths.

"Let's keep going," I said, and Elanin nearly collapsed where he sat.

On and on, up and up, past multiple, branching passageways that crossed and recrossed in an endless tangle. How did Elanin stay on course? Did the device in his ear have anything to do with it?

At last, he stopped, put out his light, and motioned for me to do the same. He pointed at a crevice where light spilled into the tunnel from the other side of a rock wall.

"That's the place," he said. "I was supposed to lead you to that opening."

On my hands and knees, I peered through the crack. I could see a broad chamber or cavern, the light coming from bulbs strung from a wire at intervals along the rock ceiling. I could see no sign of life, neither Dalek nor human.

"You're not supposed to come with me?"

"N-no, Doctor. I'm to return to Latham and the others."

"Then you'd better do just that. But don't give the game away, O.K? No more spying for the Daleks?"

"Th...that depends on what they ask of me."

"There are lots of possibilities, Elanin. Lots of them. I

think we can arrange to get your family out somehow." As I said it, I wondered how I was going to accomplish that, while rescuing Harry and Sarah as well. Oh, yes...and myself. "Well, here goes."

I wiggled through the narrow gap in the wall.

Go to **268**.

303

Working quickly and surely, I manipulated the wires leading to what had to be the power system enabler. Ha! Did it! The scraped-down ends of two wires came together, and the machine responded with a rising hum. Gently, gently, the grav vehicle lifted into the air, hovering a meter above the floor. When it comes right down to it, there are remarkably few machines that I can't coax into hearty cooperation.

The craft swung around to face the opening. Let's see... Directional controls...There...Steering...with the stick... like this...

I kicked in the oomph and shot toward the opening.

Roll 2D6. If the result is 8 or less, go to **336**. *If the result if 9 or more, go to* **331**.

304

I remembered pain, the descent of a gun butt, an explosion of darkness, of...

I tried very hard to avoid the twin cliches that came immediately to mind. Groaning "What happened?" or "Where am I?" would have hurt too much.

Consciousness returned then in bleak, red pain and a purple throbbing. I squeezed my eyes open, blinked, and stared into the unblinking artificial eye of a Dalek.

Daleks!

"THE DOC-TOR IS A-WAKE," the creature grated.

163

"THE DOC-TOR IS A-WAKE," another Dalek, its voice a bit shriller than the first, agreed. "OUR IN-VES-TI-GA-TIONS CON-FIRM THAT THIS IS THE TIME LORD KNOWN AS THE DOC-TOR."

"THE DOC-TOR IS AN EN-E-MY OF THE DA-LEKS. EN-E-MIES OF THE DA-LEKS MUST BE EX-TER-MIN-A-TED!"

My eyes were wide open now. I was in a room, strapped to a table. The overhead lights were entirely too bright. I felt like a specimen on a microscope slide.

A very painful specimen. I closed my eyes again, willing the throbbing to cease.

"THE DOC-TOR MUST NOT BE EX-TER-MIN-A-TED."

My eyes snapped open again. That was a change in the tired, old Dalek script. Ever since I'd first met the beasties, they'd been threatening to exterminate me, and it was only by the skin of my teeth that I'd avoided that particularly nasty end.

"THE DOC-TOR MUST BE EX-TER-MIN-A-TED."

Now that was more like the Daleks I knew and loved.

"NEG-A-TIVE. THE DOC-TOR IS A TIME LORD. THE DOC-TOR CAN BE OF GREAT VA-LUE TO US IN OUR SEARCH."

I didn't like the sound of that much more than I liked their shrilling "EX-TER-MIN-ATE". Any project the Daleks were working on promised bad news in generous helpings for every other life form in the universe.

One of the Daleks released the straps holding me to the table, then actually helped me sit up.

The touch of its slick manipulator left me feeling sicker than the blow to my head.

Go to **305**.

305

Have you ever met a friendly, cooperative Dalek? The concept seems a contradiction in terms, and the way these Daleks treated me made me far more nervous than any three legions of black Daleks shrilling "EX-TER-MIN-ATE!"

And the lift to the spaceship was the real surprise.

Tharesti is built on a rocky promontory honeycombed with lava tunnels and caves. One of those caves apparently opened at the base of the cliff under water, but was angled in such a way that a vast, interior gallery existed just above water level, on the shores of a subterranean lake. The Daleks had arrived in a space ship, one of their characteristic, thirty-meter-wide inverted pie-plates. After they had subjugated the Gathwyrans, they had literally gone underground. With a mixture of art, brute force, and science, the Daleks had maneuvered their craft into the cave, and set up their secret base thirty meters below the foundations of the city.

The spaceship was joined with the city through a lift shaft, a thirty-meter-long tube descending from the lowest level of the Tower of the Masters through a natural rock chimney and into the main cargo-hold of the Dalek ship. My captors explained during the long trip down the shaft that they had found it best to keep out of the public eye of their Gathwyran slaves, operating solely through the puppet government of Lord Kolav and his stooges. For that reason, they had disguised the top of the lift shaft (in the lowest level of the Tower of the Masters) as a cargo crate. Only a few, highly placed human officials held the red computer scanner cards that gave access to the Dalek base.

"But why?" I asked as the lift car slowed to a stop. Daleks never confided their secret plans to outsiders, especially to Time Lords who had been responsible for scuttling more than a few Dalek conquest plans in the past. But these Daleks were acting so cooperatively, so uncharacteristically companionable, that I thought it wouldn't hurt to ask.

"YOU WILL BE TOLD IN GOOD TIME, DOC-TOR," said the one who kept a firm grasp on my elbow with his manipulator. "WHEN YOU LEARN WHAT WE HAVE DIS-COV-ERED ON THIS PLA-NET, YOU WILL BE EA-GER TO JOIN WITH US. THIS WAY, DOC-TOR."

And they led me aboard their space ship.

Go to **330**.

306

There was a spark, a crack, and acrid smoke blew against my face, but the vehicle didn't budge. I had the sudden, uncomfortable feeling that I had just cross-circuited the altimeter with the heater.

Try again. The wires were slippery, the space cramped and dark, and I couldn't see what I was doing.

Then I heard the unmistakable warbling keen of an anti-gravity flyer.

When I looked up, it was to see a four-man craft edging through the wall opening into the vehicle area. The crew were black-garbed and wore sensor helmets, and one of them had already seen me.

"Stop, you!" he yelled.

I vaulted out of my almost-stolen craft and raced for the lifts. Funny thing. Grav vehicles can travel faster than a running Gallifreyan. Something smashed into the back of my head, and I sprawled forward into darkness.

Reduce your STR *and* END *levels each by 2, then go to* **304**.

307

You are attempting to convince a very large mechanic not to smash your skull in with a wrench and, incidentally, to learn what you can about this place, the Masters, and anything else that might be of interest.

Your CHA and *Negotiation/Diplomacy* skill will be needed for this confrontation. First, make a Saving Roll against your CHA. If it succeeds, you win a bonus modifier of –2. If it fails, the modifier is +2. Then roll 1D6 for the mechanic and subtract this from your *Negotiation/ Diplomacy* skill. The result is the mechanic's roll.

Then roll 2D6 for your own tactics, and apply the modifier. If the result is equal to or less than the mechanic's roll, you win. If it is greater, you lose.

If you are successful, go to **332**. *If you fail, the mechanic is not impressed with your arguments and comes at you with the wrench. Go to* **289**.

308

The barrel of the gun swung around in a whistling arc and caught me behind my ear. The blow staggered me, sending me to my knees. The gun descended again, exploding the world in darkness and whirling pain.

Reduce your STR *and* END *each by 2, and go to* **304**.

309

Stuff and nonsense! Since when does a machine tell me what to do? I inserted the card again, and stabbed the button. Reluctantly, or so it seemed to me, the lift began to move. In a moment, it stopped, and the door slid open.

"Well, that's more like it. I ..."

Oh no...

A pair of smartly turned-out sentries stood just beyond the

door, their submachine guns levelled at my stomach. Behind them, black-garbed troops were gathering. I saw walls festooned with flags and military insignia. The lift had brought me to the building's military headquarters, sounding an alarm as it came.

Efficient, I thought. A chap tries to wander where he's not supposed to be, and so the lift deposits him neatly in the arms of the local constables. No muss, no fuss.

Slowly I raised my hands.

Go to **296**.

310

That hole in the ceiling had to lead to an exit to the outside. I picked a grav vehicle, a sporty little two-seater, and studied the instuments.

That was the power relay ignition. Steering was this stick on the floor. This way, that way, up, down...right!

The controls were simple enough, though the technology was certainly not Gathwyran. I reached under the instrument panel and began tracing wires. Now, if this was attached to the altimeter, and THAT was attached to the heater, then...ha!

Make a Saving Roll against your DEX. *If it succeeds, go to* **335**. *If it fails, go to* **337**.

311

One of the soldiers sprawled backwards, out of the lift. The other held my foot, but I managed to place it against his chest and give a tremendous heave. With pinwheeling arms, he flew back and out into a heap with his comrade. Panting, I stabbed my next destination on the lift control panel.

Go to **Lift** *in* **Exploring the Tower**. *Because you are already aboard, do not make the initial 2D6 roll for calling the lift. Simply choose a level and proceed to that destination.*

312

I stood up slowly next to the crumpled form of the unconscious mechanic. That fight had been much too close for comfort. I braced myself against a parked grav vehicle as I fought to steady my swimming head.

Now what? Back to the lift and keep exploring...or...? These aircars seemed almost too good an opportunity to pass up. I could hot-wire one and escape the Tower of the Masters entirely. Of course, that wouldn't help Harry or Sarah.

You may continue your exploration of the tower by going to **Lift** *in* **Exploring the Tower**. *Roll 2D6 before you board the lift to determine whether or not it is occupied. If you want to steal a grav flyer, however, go to* **310**.

313

Somehow, somewhere in the black and whirling depths where I found myself, I realized I was getting perilously weaker.

Dying? No! I was a Time Lord, and Time Lords are victorious over...over...

Weaker and weaker. I was dying.

As a Time Lord, you have the chance to regenerate before you die, repairing the damage done to your body by the bullets, and thus escaping death yet again. You must regenerate or die. Roll 2D6. Subtract 1 from the result if you have an MNT *of 9, 2 if your* MNT *is 10, or 4 if your* MNT *is 11. If the result is 7 or less, you have regenerated. Go to* **334**. *If the modified result is 8 or more, go to* **113**.

314

The wrench descended, a whistling, sweeping blow. I ducked. Well, almost.

A well-landed blow would have killed me. As it was, a

blue giant sun went supernova in the back of my head, smashing me forward and down into a vast whirlpool of night.

Reduce your STR, END, *and* DEX *each by 4, then go to* **304**.

315

Aha! My finger traced one of the circuits wired into the main detector unit. I knew that work. Those ceramic-molded circuits, that glossy black, unpleasantly slick-to-the-touch metal...

By the Big Bang, it was the Daleks! THEY were responsible for this planet's uneven technological advances and for its enslavement.

But a larger question was what to do about it? And large question number two, why were the Daleks interested in disturbances in the Temporal Vortex? Had they been led to Gathwyr by the disturbance that had attracted my own attention in the TARDIS?

Questions, questions. I left the lab bench as I'd found it, and started for the lift. My detector would do me no good now without the tools in my TARDIS, and I didn't want anyone knowing that I'd been here.

To continue your explorations, go to **Lift** *in* **Exploring the Tower**.

316

There were dim and painful memories of being dragged across gravel, of being dropped into a vehicle of some kind. I distinctly remember the unpleasantly high-pitched, sniggering laugh of one of my captors. As consciousness slowly returned, I found myself in a grav vehicle, with armed men crowded around me and the towers of the city looming ahead.

"Take a good look," the unpleasant voice said in my ear.

"That's where the Masters'll deal with you once and for all!"

"Yeah," another voice said. "We knew you'd show up at that blue box again. THEY said so, and THEY'RE never wrong!"

"If THEY'RE never wrong," I said, gingerly touching the knot on the back of my head, "how come they use heavy-handed dolts like..."

Once more, something heavy descended, hurling me into a familiar darkness.

Reduce your STR *and* END *each by 2, and go to* **304**.

317

My hands went above my head as the soldier's gun came down into line with my nose. "Whoa, easy there, friend," I said. "I'm all yours."

The guard's hand went to a small box clipped to his web belt, an alarm or signal device of some kind. Moments later, there was a sound behind me. My friend wouldn't let me turn to look, but I could hear something opening, hear the whirr of machinery. A lift, from the sound of it.

"YOU HAVE CAP-TURED AN IN-TRU-DER!"

Great thundering novas! A Dalek!

It was all I could do to keep from turning and facing the monster. Daleks! While wondering what they might possibly be doing on Gathwyr, I sensed a metallic shape drifting up close beside me.

"Well, well," I said. "And what might the Daleks be doing on Gathwyr? Seems a bit out of the way for you folks."

"SI-LENCE!" The Dalek came around in front of me, its eye stalk swivelling up and down as it scanned me, particle cannon aimed precisely at one of my hearts. "YOU ARE THE TIME LORD KNOWN AS THE DOC-TOR. THE

DOC-TOR IS AN EN-E-MY OF THE DA-LEKS. EN-E-MIES OF THE DA-LEKS MUST BE EX-TER-MIN-A-TED!"

"Yes, yes, I've heard it all before."

"YOU WILL BE EX-TER-MIN-A-TED."

"NEG-A-TIVE!" A deeper, raspier voice shrilled from behind me. "THE DOC-TOR WILL NOT BE EX-TER-MIN-A-TED."

Well, THAT was a welcome change in the script. I turned and saw a second Dalek approaching me.

"THE DOC-TOR IS AN EN-E-MY OF THE DA-LEKS," the first black machine started to say.

The second interrupted. "THE DOC-TOR WILL NOT BE EX-TER-MIN-A-TED. HE MAY BE OF USE TO THE DA-LEKS."

Me? Useful to Daleks? Anything the Daleks were mixed up in was guaranteed sure-fire trouble for every other life form in the universe. This did not sound promising.

"THE DOC-TOR WILL HELP US WITH OUR SEARCH."

"Search? What search?"

"YOU WILL O-BEY THE DA-LEKS, DOC-TOR. YOU WILL O-BEY OR YOU WILL BE EX-TER-MIN-A-TED."

Ah, THAT was more like the Daleks I knew. Obey or be exterminated. THAT I could deal with.

I hoped.

Go to **305**.

318

It was all a total mystery. What was all this stuff for, and who had helped the Gathwyrans build it? There was something familiar about that circuitry, something I ought to know, to remember…

Bah. No time for wool-gathering now. Stand here much longer and everybody would come back from lunch, or wherever it was they had gone.

I decided to leave my indicator where it was. It was no good to me now without repairs I would have to make in the TARDIS. Besides, I had more pressing concerns on my mind at the moment. Such as what to do next.

You can continue your explorations by going to **Lift** *in* **Exploring the Tower.** *Roll 2D6 before boarding the lift, and go to* **250** *if the result is 12. On any other result, you may choose any other level of the building as your destination.*

319

I stood up beside the body of the guard. Well, that wasn't so difficult. Making a quick search of the man, I opened a small, leather pouch clipped to his belt and found a green plastic card. Aha! A computer scanner card!

You now have several choices. You either have a computer scanner card already, or have just taken one from the unconscious guard. You have either already used it, or you have figured out that you can call a lift by sliding the card through a slot on a small mechanism beside the lift door. You may use the card to explore the building by going to the section of this book entitled **Exploring the Tower,** *and begin with the paragraph describing the* **Lift.** *You must roll 2D6 before boarding the lift, and go to* **250** *if the result is 12. With any other result, you may board the lift and proceed with your explorations.*

You may also choose to examine that crate sitting nearby. It has a slot in it designed to receive a card like the one you have. If you want to try to put the card in that slot, go to **295.**

Or you can continue to explore the lower level. There is a tunnel leading out of the room at a downhill angle, and you can smell the sea in the air coming from it. You can explore this tunnel by going to **300**.

320

I was falling!

My hand shot out and grasped at a projection of rock. It didn't stop the fall, but it slowed me and swung me around in a painful collision with the chimney wall.

My other hand slipped my scarf off from around my neck, doubled it up, and flipped it out. The loop snagged on the rock, and with a heart-stopping yank and clatter of dislodged stones, I swung there in mid-air, safe. Or at least a lot safer than I'd been a second or two before.

I looked up, then down. It was completely dark above me, and I discovered that one of those clatters I'd heard had been the electric torch spinning off into the depths. Below me was the faintest glimmer of light, just at the edge of my vision. My torch? Or something else?

I decided to climb down to investigate. Besides, it looked like I was closer to the bottom of the shaft than I was to the top. That settled it.

Go to **339**.

321

I lay there sprawled on the floor as the soldier raised his gun, finger tightening on the trigger. Then blue flame seared the air, and the bitter tang of ozone filled my nose and mouth. The soldier screamed, froze for a moment in fire and agony, then collapsed in a heap, still smoldering. The next thing I knew, who but the Daleks should drift into view. By the Black Rings of Cerberus! I thought. Daleks!

There were two of them, their eye stalks swivelling down to examine me, their particle weapons trained precisely on one of my hearts.

"YOU ARE THE DOC-TOR," said the one who had fired its beam at the soldier, its voice strident and rasping.

"Yes," I said, getting up very slowly, "yes, I'm The Doctor. Uh...pleased to meet you?" Well, what DO you say at a time like this?

The second Dalek spoke, its electronic speech sharper, more highly pitched than the voice of the first. "THE DOC-TOR IS AN EN-E-MY OF THE DA-LEKS. ALL EN-E-MIES OF THE DA-LEKS MUST BE EX-TER-MIN-A-TED! EX-TER-MIN-A-TED!"

"NEG-A-TIVE," the first one replied. "THE DOC-TOR CAN BE OF GREAT VA-LUE TO THE DA-LEKS. HE WILL NOT BE EX-TER-MIN-A-TED!"

I wasn't sure I was hearing right. Had a Dalek just spared my life? Even more to the point, a Dalek had just killed a soldier who had been about to kill me. What was the universe coming to?

"I'm not objecting, understand, but how can I be of value to you?"

"YOU WILL COME WITH US. YOU WILL O-BEY THE DA-LEKS. YOU WILL HELP US WITH OUR PRO-JECT HERE."

A Dalek project on Gathwyr? Any project the Daleks were in on was certain trouble for every other life form in the universe. As they led me toward the lift, I was feeling quite sick.

Go to **305**.

322

I opted for the galley. Why not? Warned this time, maybe I could keep an eye on THIS entrance to keep my options open. Squeezing through. I found myself in a short, dark tunnel, leading up. Encouraged, I pulled out my torch, shone it around, then started up the slope.

Fascinating. This was some sort of old smuggler's hole. There was sand on the floor, and the countless tracks of feet and wooden crates. The air was stale and dusty, and the thickly gathered cobwebs caught the beam of my torch like fog.

There was a handle set into the rock wall, quite low, and I could just barely discern a hairline crack where the rock had been cut through and jointed. A secret door!

Carefully, carefully, I took the handle. Pushing didn't open it, but when I pulled, a square section of rock hinged open on silent hinges, and light spilled in from the other side.

I couldn't see much. The opening was close to the ground, and seemed to be blocked by a stack of wooden crates. Well, there was only one way to find out where I was. I crawled through.

I came into a large, circular room, a basement room fifty meters across. The stone walls were lined with crates, boxes, and long-unused machinery heavy with dust. At the center of the room was a massive white pillar from floor to ceiling, with doors in it. A lift? It wasn't the shaft I had seen below in the chimney, but was presumably the lift to this building's upper levels. This was what I'd been looking for!

Across the room was a tunnel opening, broad and three meters tall, leading out and down. I thought I could detect a hint of salt air from that direction. A tunnel to the sea?

I was in. Now what?

You may explore the room more carefully at **341**. *Or you can explore the tunnel at* **300**.

323

I had an idea. One of the guards used a rusty, mechanical key to open a cell door, which swung outward with a bone-jarring creak. I held out my hand.

"Would you like a jelly baby?"

"Get in there, you!"

A soldier shoved me, and I braced myself with one hand against the cell door to keep from falling.

"Really, you needn't get violent. It's just a jelly baby, a great delicacy in some parts of the Galaxy."

A second shove sent me into the cell. A stone-floored and cheerless place, it contained only a pile of straw, a filthy bucket, and a naked electric bulb dangling far out of reach above my head. The door crashed shut behind me, and I heard a rattle of keys.

"They're really quite good," I said. The only reply was a clattering of boots fading away into the distance.

I waited several moments. The door was solid, iron-bound wood, with only a slit for a peephole, now closed from the outside. I set my hand to the door and eased it open. The jelly babies that I had palmed and set into the locking bar mechanism as I'd held onto the door had fouled the lock completely, preventing it from snapping home. I stepped into the passageway.

Go to **343**.

324

Falling!

I tried to get my scarf off from around my neck, worked to snag it on the rocks as they rushed past. For a moment, it caught and held. There was a tug, a horrible shock, then my body crashed into the wall and I fell again, bringing an avalanche of rock and dirt cascading down with me.

I hit something that rang like metal in a storm of noise and pain. Then it became very, very dark.

Reduce your STR, END, *and* DEX *each by 4, then go to* **304**.

325

That side gallery couldn't lead anywhere but back to an endless maze of interconnected tunnels where a person could wander for days, perhaps even weeks, until he starved to death. There was actually no other real choice but down, back the way I'd come.

I began crab-walking down the shaft again, feet and hands splayed across space to find projections of rock, ledges, and crevices to which I could cling. It was a long, dark way down.

Over there? Was that a light below me? I couldn't tell, but I had been descending for a long time. Perhaps a little farther, and...

A rock gave way under my foot. Rock and dirt cascaded into the shaft, and my hands tore free as I hurtled backward into space. Falling! No! I reached out...

Make a Saving Roll against your DEX. *If it succeeds, go to* **320**. *If it fails, go to* **324**.

326

You have been terribly injured by a Dalek particle beam. As a Time Lord, however, you may possibly be able to regenerate, allowing your body to repair the damage. While regeneration among Time Lords frequently causes a complete transformation of both appearance and character, it is sometimes possible to retain control of the process and regenerate without such a transformation.

In order to regenerate, roll 2D6. Add 1 to the die roll if your MNT *is 10, 2 if your* MNT *is 11, and 4 if your* MNT *is 12. If the result is 9 or more, you have successfully regenerated. Go to* **334**. *If the result is 8 or less, go to* **113**.

327

The best thing to do, it seemed to me, was wait patiently for the Daleks to make up their minds about me. Best thing? It looked to me like the only thing. I had my scarf, coat, hat, and half a bag of jelly babies. Not much there for making a weapon. The cell was bare except for a pile of straw for a bed. A naked electric bulb dangled far above my head on a cord from the ceiling. No hope there.

So I waited, and did some hard thinking.

Restore END *and* STR *losses due to fatigue or wounds (not regeneration).*

Make a Saving Roll against your MNT, *then add 4 to the result. If the roll succeeds, you may have just thought of a way to get out of the cell. Go to* **344**.

If the roll fails, or if you would prefer to sit there waiting to see what the Daleks have in mind for you, go to **348**.

328

I would make for a torch, grab it, and head back for that crevice in the wall. It seemed a good way to avoid meeting people I didn't care to meet just now. I watched for my chance, then slipped forward carefully, carefully.

Make a Saving Roll against your DEX. *If it succeeds, go to* **346**. *If it fails, go to* **350**.

329

Wandering out onto that landing area was just too risky. I knew from experience how sharp-eyed Daleks could be, even if they did have only one eye apiece. I started back up the sloping tunnel, hand in pocket, assuming a nonchalant air. After all, if I looked like I BELONGED there, no one would question me, right?

What happens next depends on how lucky you are. Roll 2D6. If the result is 7 or less, go to **Level 1** *in* **Exploring the Tower** *to continue your explorations. If the result is 8 or more, go to* **347**.

330

The Dalek ship was a two-level disk about 20 meters across. I was careful to remember our path as the Daleks led me up the ramp and into their vessel. The airlock opened into a curving passageway to the left and the right, but we didn't follow it. Immediately opposite the airlock entrance was a lift that could be summoned by pressing a button beside the door. It was a tight fit to get two Daleks and one Gallifreyan inside, but we managed somehow. When the car stopped, it was the wall behind us that opened instead of the door through which we'd entered, and we stepped out into the ship's bridge.

I thought the bridge was where they were taking me, but I was wrong. It seemed inconvenient to route all traffic from the first level to the second through the starship's nerve center, but perhaps there were security reasons for this. It looked like there might be another lift across the bridge, one of four doors evenly spaced around the bridge's circumference, and another lift at a low platform in the center of the room. I filed all this away for use later. You never know when you're going to have to find your way around inside a strange space ship.

I was led to the door to the left, out into a curving passageway where we turned right, then walked perhaps a quarter-circle around the bulkhead separating us from the bridge. Outboard was a door with a pressure plate in the center. A Dalek touched this, the door opened, and I was led into a meeting room, a white-painted and sterile-looking chamber with too-bright lights, a round, central table, and a notable absence of any other furniture at all.

Logical, of course. Daleks can't sit down, which might explain in part why they tend to be so short-tempered.

"So, why are you here?" I asked. There was no telling how long this Dalek spirit of cooperation would last, and I wanted to use it to snatch what information I could. "I mean, Daleks have never really needed a reason for moving in on a human planet, but..."

"IN THIS IN-STANCE, DOC-TOR, THE DA-LEKS ARE NOT IN-TER-ES-TED IN CON-QUEST. THE HU-MANS ON THIS PLA-NET ARE SIM-PLY USE-FUL AS WOR-KERS."

"Mmm, slaves, yes. I've heard that before."

"WE HAVE COME HERE BE-CAUSE WE HAVE DE-TEC-TED UN-US-U-AL A-NO-MA-LIES IN THE TIME-SPACE VOR-TEX."

"Anomalies?"

"DO NOT PRE-TEND YOU DO NOT KNOW, DOC-TOR."

"Well…"

One of the Dalek's manipulators reached out, setting a small, plastic box on the table. Inside was the partially disassembled remnants of my temporal interference detector, the device I'd cobbled together aboard my TARDIS on our journey to Gathwyr.

"YOU RE-COG-NIZE THIS DE-VICE, DOC-TOR?"

"Of course." There was no use denying it was mine. The technology in that little bundle of molecular circuits and hyperchips was far beyond anything Gathwyr's technology had ever dreamed of.

"YOU DE-TEC-TED THE A-NOM-A-LY WHILE TRA-VEL-LING IN THE SPACE-TIME VOR-TEX."

"Yes. How did YOU detect it?" Though the Daleks had managed to sneak across time on a number of occasions, their efforts were anything but coherent. Indeed, they were usually the result of capturing and using other people's time-travel technology.

"DA-LEK SCI-ENCE HAS DE-VEL-OPED IN-STRU-MENTS CA-PA-BLE OF MON-I-TOR-ING THE VOR-TEX, DOC-TOR."

"I see." Interesting, but why would they want to? Well, Daleks peeking into the Vortex might be able to spot the movement of a time vehicle there, a TARDIS, for instance. It might be useful to know that a TARDIS was materializing nearby, especially if one of your old enemies tends to appear that way from time to time.

More interesting still was the fact that the Daleks had just TOLD that enemy about their Vortex snooper. Why would they give up such a tactical advantage, unless they'd bumped into something that terrified them.

Now, what would terrify a Dalek? The thought made me very uneasy indeed.

You have won a clue to what is happening on Gathwyr. Record Clue C on a piece of paper, then go to **360**.

331

As the flyer angled up and out through the opening, a shadow fell across the sunlight streaming in. I swerved the control stick sharply, banking to the left, as something black and massive narrowly missed me on the right.

My flyer wobbled like a falling leaf alongside the building. There was a roar of rushing air in my ears, and then I was bringing her nose up, up, and back into a climb.

Hearing a high-pitched yowl above my head, I craned to see another craft close behind me, an eight-man grav flyer. There was a stuttering sound and a winking light among the men packed into the vehicle's afterdeck. More snapping whispers flickered overhead, and I heard the hollow thud of bullets striking the hull of my craft.

I twisted my machine away from the stream of machine gun fire. The surface of the sea of fog rushed up at me, and I felt the sharp tang of cold air close to the ground. As I dipped lower, the fog surrounded me.

Visibility within the fog was less than eight meters, but I could see the blur of boulders below as I hurtled through the murk. More bullets hammered into my craft. I'd forgotten the sensor helmets worn by some of the troops. They could see me even when I couldn't see them, on my tail and drawing closer.

My flyer made an unpleasant, grating noise, staggered, and lost altitude. Ahead of me, a black boulder materialized out of white shadows, and I hurtled toward it.

Make a Saving Roll against your DEX. *If it succeeds, go to* **351**. *If it fails, go to* **355**.

332

"What do you think you're doing, you fool?"

My voice carried the crisp snap of authority, the expectation that when a command was given, it would be obeyed. The mechanic stood there uncertainly, cradling the wrench. I had him half-convinced that I was a policeman or an officer. Confusion and fear were in conflict across his face.

"Uh...who...er..."

I flashed my ID card (too fast to be read) and bore in, not giving him a chance.

"I'm The Doctor. Special Intelligence Sector. You've heard of the SIS, of course?"

"Uh...is that like Military Intelligence?"

"'Is that like Military Intelligence?' What do they teach you people, anyway?"

"I'm a mechanic, sir."

"And a darn good one, too, I'll warrant. Here, have a jelly baby? Sure, go ahead! Are these your vehicles?"

"I service them myself, sir." He drew himself up proudly, speaking around the candy. "Me and my boys."

"And you understand how they work?"

"Well, not the flyin' part, sir. The Masters handle all that. But I keep their power plants hummin' sweet. Yessir!"

"I'm sure you do. Have you seen anyone else come through here?"

"Uh...huh?"

"Maybe a man and a woman. A man this high, dark hair. Woman, pretty, a bit flighty."

"No, sir. No one like that. There was a flight of troops with one o' the Masters went out of here half an hour ago."

"Oh? Where?"

"Usual patrol. Out to the mountains for another search-pass." His eyes narrowed suspiciously. "Where else would they go?"

"Don't get smart with me, mechanic! I'm on the trail of some dangerous fugitives. Top secret." I laid my finger beside my nose. "Mum's the word, right?"

You have here an opportunity to take a grav vehicle and escape from the building. If you want to try this, go to **349**. *If you prefer to go back to the lift and continue your explorations of the tower, go to* **Lift** *in* **Exploring the Tower**. *Roll 2D6 first, and go to* **250** *if the result is 12. Otherwise, choose a level and go there.*

333

I brought the flyer down to within a few yards of the surface of the fog sea, heading west. If the machine had an auto pilot, I couldn't find it. I was still able to hold the craft's course and speed steady enough that I could lean over to study the jury-rigged device on the left-hand side of the control panel.

Interesting. Very interesting, in fact. The circuitry was unfamiliar, but that device had all the earmarks of a temporal disturbance detector hastily assembled from spare electronics parts. There was the monopole antennae, a thousand times bigger than it had to be, of course. And that had to be a dimensional difield probe.

Now what would the Gathwyrans be doing chasing disturbances in the Temporal Vortex? If they didn't have the technology necessary to build anti-gravity flitters, they CERTAINLY were a long way from building time probes. At least centuries from even knowing that there was such a thing as the Temporal Vortex, or that travel through the Vortex to other spaces and times was possible.

My finger traced the circuitry. It was unfamiliar, but that metal was not. It was a peculiar black metal with a greasy sheen that I'd seen before, many times. The device had to be of Dalek workmanship.

I straightened up and concentrated on flying the vehicle as I let the implication of that thought sink in. The Daleks were here on Gathwyr. It was they who had set up shop as resident 'Masters' among the towers of Tharesti. They had imported their advanced, starfaring technology, but for what purpose? A cobbled-together Vortex scanner on the dash of a grav flyer suggested they were conducting a widespread search.

Following the effects of a disturbance in the Vortex, they had come to Gathwyr, just as I had. Now that they were here, the Daleks were seeking the source of that disturbance, using the local humans as workers to further their efforts.

But what was this disturbance? Aboard the TARDIS, it had felt like waves in the Vortex, waves that had buffeted the craft like a high wake on calm water. I had to admit that I still hadn't the faintest idea what caused it. The Vortex is a place of mystery even for the Time Lords who sail the Vortex's endless dark dimensions.

What now? There were several options. I might try to find the source of those disturbances on my own. I had a detector now, cruder than the one that I'd lost, but serviceable nonetheless. I could try to get back to my TARDIS, which would be a better vehicle for probing the Vortex than this rusty flitter. Or I could circle back to find another way into the city, where my friends were still prisoners of the Daleks. There had to be another way in, besides the main gate and the Level 20 aircar port.

*You have a clue to what's happening here. Record Clue C on a piece of paper. If you want to fly on in the grav vehicle, searching for the temporal disturbance, go to **368**. If you left your TARDIS at the base of the ridge west of the city, and want to try to get to it, go to **338**. If the TARDIS was left inside Level 1 of the Tower of the Masters, you will have to circle the city looking for another way in at **340**. Finally, if you want to return to the city to find Sarah and Harry, go to **340**.*

334

At first, I was not entirely certain who I was anymore, but then the memories began welling up from some hidden recess of my mind. I'd regenerated.

Well, not a total regeneration. I knew without having to look in a mirror that the process I'd willed had healed the damage to my body, but that I'd managed that last, slippery measure of control that let me keep my noble physiognomy —the straight, high brow, the piercing eyes, the impressive halo of curls, the nose...yes, well, the nose...

Time Lords have a very fine sense about these things, you know. And a complete transformation, with its attendant horrors of mental confusion and lack of concentration, I couldn't very well afford that now, could I? But I felt fine, just fine. Mind sharp as a whip, my body superbly disciplined and blessedly whole.

But where was I? Oh, yes, preparing to open my eyes and see just that. I quickly shut them again.

When I dared look once more, the black apparition was still there. A Dalek stood beside the table to which I was strapped, peering at me with its stalked, metal optical sensor, humming to itself. Humming? Well, maybe that was me. It was a little hard to sort things out right after regeneration.

Daleks! Great thundering novas! What were those mechanical nightmares doing here on…on…oh yes, Wyrthag? No, Gathwyr, wasn't it? What were Kaleds doing on Gathwyr?

As the memories continued to well, I tried to sit up.

"THE DOC-TOR HAS RE-GAINED CON-SCIOUS-NESS," the Dalek shrilled. Another drifted into my limited field of vision.

"THE TIME LORD'S RE-GEN-ER-A-TION PRO-CESS IS COM-PLETE," the second one said. "HAS HE RE-COV-ERED FUL-LY?"

"IN-STRU-MENTS SHOW CON-SID-ER-A-BLE MEN-TAL CON-FU-SION. HOW-E-VER, RE-COV-E-RY IS PRO-CEED-ING RA-PID-LY."

A pair of Daleks worried about my health? Somehow, the thought terrified me. It seemed a complete reversal of the entire cosmic natural order, something akin to what would happen if it turned out the universe was collapsing, not expanding. Only this was a lot more immediate.

I tried sitting up again, and succeeded this time.

"ARE YOU FUL-LY FUNC-TION-AL, DOC-TOR?"

"I'm thinking about it. What's going on?"

"WE RE-GRET YOUR UN-FOR-TU-NATE TREAT-MENT, DOC-TOR."

"Really? Why doesn't that reassure me?"

"WE IN-TEND YOU NO HARM, DOC-TOR. IT IS VI-TAL THAT WE CO-OP-ER-ATE TO-GETH-ER."

"What happened to 'exterminate-exterminate'?"

"YOU WILL NOT BE EX-TER-MIN-A-TED IF YOU CO-OP-ER-ATE WITH THE DA-LEKS."

Ah! I'd heard just a tinge of the old "do as we say or you will be exterminated" in that last speech. Now THAT was more like the Daleks I knew, comforting and reassuring in its familiar hominess.

"And just what sort of cooperation did you have in mind?"

"YOU WILL AS-SIST US WITH A PRO-JECT OF GREAT IM-POR-TANCE. COME WITH US TO OUR SHIP AND WE WILL EX-PLAIN."

A project of great importance? For which the Daleks wanted my help? Now there was a chilling thought. Any project the Daleks were mixed up with was bound to spell trouble for every other life form in the universe. Just what had I regenerated myself into?

Go to **305**.

335

I was rewarded with a rising, warbling hum and the ecstatic quiver of power flowing through the little machine. Did it? Well, after all, there are very few machines I can't eventually coax into hearty cooperation.

Gripping the control stick, I brought the flyer off the floor, hovered, then guided it toward the opening in the ceiling. Still working to get the feel of the craft, I guided it up and through. Level 20 was another garage level, filled with more parked vehicles. One wall was open to the sky, however, where a broad, ten-meter-wide rectangular opening had been knocked through to create a portal for grav craft.

Roll 2D6. If the result is 9 or less, go to **336**. *If it is 10 or more, go to* **331**.

336

Blue sky surrounded me. I took a deep breath, and relaxed. Free!

The only problem was, now what? Harry and Sarah were still prisoners somewhere in the tower behind me, and I was no closer to unravelling Gathwyr's mysteries than I'd been when we'd materialized on the planet. Was it only a few hours ago?

This grav car, for instance, was a bit of hardware much too advanced for Gathwyran technology. Obviously, it had been introduced from outside by the "Masters", but for what purpose?

Other oddities were the jury-rigged instruments tack-welded onto the dashboard of the flyer, set up so that someone in the left-side passenger seat could read them. It was a highly sophisticated scanner system of some sort, though obviously cobbled together from spare parts. What was that for, I wondered?

The question nagged at me. Might this be the key to what was happening on Gathwyr? Or should I discipline my restless, scientist's curiosity and try to make it back to the TARDIS, which was probably my only hope for rescuing my Companions?

Whatever it was, the decision had to be made now. I had no idea what sort of alarm might have been sounded when I left. For all I knew, the entire Gathwyran air force was close on my tail at that very moment.

You can study the instrumentation on the grav flyer's dashboard more closely at 333. Your TARDIS is either at the base of the ridge west of Tharesti, hidden under the fog layer, or it is parked in the lower level of the Tower of the Masters. If the TARDIS is outside, you may try to locate it by going to 338. If it is in the Tower basement and you want to try to reach it, you are going to need to reconnoiter, hoping to find another way into the building. Go to 340.

337

There was a snap, and acrid smoke wafted out from beneath the panel. I had the sudden, uncomfortable feeling that I had just cross-circuited the flyer's heater controls with its altimeter.

Well, try again. I redoubled my efforts, probing for the wire that...

"Halt! Stop that man!"

Oh no, not now!

I sat up slowly in the aircar's seat. A squad of soldiers was streaming out of the lift, and an officer-type was gesturing in my direction.

I raised my hands as they swarmed around the vehicle, their weapons levelled. "Just thought I'd take her for a trial spin," I offered. The soldiers didn't seem amused.

Go to 296.

338

I have a good eye for distance and an infallible sense of direction. I couldn't see my TARDIS through the sea of fog stretched out below me, but I knew just about where it must be. I dropped lower, and the white mist closed around me.

It was eerie, flying blind through a damp sea of white. Visibility was down to about five meters. I could see the grey shadows of boulders materializing out of the mist and drifting away underneath, then fading into the fog behind me. I slowed, brought the TARDIS down to where I could make out the shadowy mass of the ridge slope on my right, and scanned the ground ahead. Somewhere...somewhere...Ha! There!

I'd been half-afraid that soldiers would be stationed around the TARDIS, but then, I'd been away for many hours by now. The local military was probably not willing to tie up soldiers in watching an inert blue box in the middle of the fog. It looked all-clear.

I lowered the flyer to the gravel and killed the power. Now, home at last!

Go to **342**.

339

Gradually it grew lighter, and then I dropped the last four meters to a sandy floor, and looked around. The cavern was broad and flat-bottomed, aglow with an eerie blue light. From somewhere came the faint, rhythmic pulsing of heavy machinery. The spaceship filled much of the room.

It was thirty meters across, and shaped like an inverted pie plate of dull-finished silver supported on three spindly legs. The ship was at the hub of a web of power cables and lines that trailed across the sand toward the silvery pipeline, which dropped out of the chimney opening overhead and came to rest near the rim of the ship's hull. That pipeline was obviously a lift as well as the conduit for power lines running up toward the city. The door to the car was open, spilling yellow light across the cave floor.

In the other direction, I saw how they had brought a deep-space ship into the heart of a mountain. The roof of the cavern dropped lower and lower to meet the oily surface of a black water pool. It looked like the mouth of a tunnel leading outside, a tunnel that must plunge beneath the surface of the ocean, emerging some distance under water. Somehow, the masters of the ship had spotted the submarine tunnel entrance and piloted their ship here, to rest thirty meters beneath the city.

I let my hand rest on the silver metal of the hull. There was no mistaking it, of course. I'd seen that design on dozens of worlds, across many times. It was a Dalek scout-cruiser.

But what were Daleks doing on Gathwyr? And what was the purpose of hiding their ship here, in the rock beneath the city, tied to Tharesti by power lines and a lift? And how was I going to go about finding out?

I looked back up the chimney. Not THAT way, certainly. After an hour or more of climbing, I was utterly spent. It was sheer good fortune that I'd not made part of the trip here in an avalanche of hurtling stones. There was no way of knowing about the tunnel into the underwater cave, either. That seemed to leave the Dalek ship itself.

I stood rooted to that spot of sand for long minutes. I knew the Daleks. And their methods. If I boarded the space ship, I was almost certain to be detected and caught, but I couldn't forget one other important factor. Harry and Sarah Jane had presumably been brought to the city as prisoners. If the Daleks were aware of them at all, they would have noticed that those two were not typical rebels. Might not the two special unwilling guests have been taken some-where safer than the local equivalent of a dungeon. Perhaps someplace like a cabin aboard the ship, where they could be closely watched? That made a depressing amount of sense, and suggested strongly that there was really only one direction in which I could go now.

On the other hand, what could I do if the Daleks had *me*? There was ONE other way out of this cavern, and that was straight up, aboard the Dalek lift. Once out of this cavern, perhaps I could form a plan to take on the Daleks and liberate my Companions, wherever they might be now.

Go to 370 to board the Dalek ship. Or go to 353 to take the lift to the city.

340

I circled the city, skimming low across the fog, alert to the arrival of other flyers who might have spotted me. Tharesti was built on a mound of rock above the seas of fog on one side and the ocean on the other. Curiously, the fog ended at the shoreline, suggesting that the ground must harbor extensive volcanic hot spots that warmed the layer of cold, wet air rolling inland from the sea. The city towers jabbed skyward from within the city walls, glittering white but curiously lifeless. A city under a grey pall.

I drew the flyer closer to the rock cliffs. There had to be other entrances to Tharesti, aside from the single main gate. Especially a city on the sea.

Aha! Halfway between the breakers of the sea pounding at the foot of the cliffs and the base of the city wall was an opening, a queerly rectangular opening with an obviously artificial planing of the floor into a flat landing apron. As I neared, I could see other flyers parked in neat and orderly rows, another grav flyer landing field, and a handful of humans clustered about several of those vehicles.

I was tempted. I couldn't land without being seen, of course, but could I land without being noticed? It was likely that someone in the city knew of the theft of a flyer by now, but surely they wouldn't suspect that stolen flyer to fly halfway around the city and park again in the very midst of the people from which it had been stolen! The idea had a certain dramatic flair that appealed to me. The alternative was to bank away and head elsewhere. I could decide later just where that would be. Right now, I had to decide whether or not to begin my landing approach.

If you want to try to land, go to **354**. *If you want to head for parts unknown, go to* **357**.

341

I prowled the chamber, examining the crates thick with dust, the nameless pieces of machinery and equipment, which must have remained here unused for years. Lift doors were set into the central pillar all the way around. Next to each was a computer scanner, a machine for reading special cards or IDs when they were placed in a slot. That must be part of the security arrangement for the building.

Odd. One crate was completely without a coating of dust. It was a big thing, three meters tall and four wide on each side. As I studied it, my fingers found a small catch that opened a side panel. Aha! Another card scanner. And the position of the crate was such that...

I looked back to where I'd come through the wall, estimating distances and angles. Yes! This crate was set directly over the spot where the chimney came up under the floor. I suspected that the silver pipeway was, in fact, a lift leading down from this basement level of the city. But down to what?

And they were keeping it secret, even from the inhabitants of the city. Hmmm.

I heard the bump-whine of machinery operating, and dove for cover. Moments later, one of the central lifts opened, and black-uniformed troops stepped out. One was a common soldier who took a sentry's stance beside the open lift. The second had to be a high-ranking officer, from the looks of the heavy gold braid on his shoulders and sleeves. There was a civilian, too, an important one by the look of him. Greasy, fat, and short, he wore a gold-worked cloak, silvery garments, and ornate arm, finger, and neck jewelry that would have put the Renaissance Medicis to shame.

Right behind this apparition was something infinitely worse—the black pepper-pot shapes of two Daleks. What in all the thundering novas of space were Daleks doing on Gathwyr?

The officer walked to the dustless crate and opened the hidden panel, then produced a small, red card and slid it through the scanner slot. Moments later, the crate unfolded like a blossoming flower, and the officer, the richly dressed civilian, and the two Daleks stepped onto the platform the opening revealed. They were sinking into the ground as the crate folded shut above them again.

So, it WAS a lift, one leading to a Dalek base or installation underground.

What was I to do now? I could wait where I was and see what developed, or I could make my move against that sentry, then go either up or down. Before I could use that lift, I was going to need one of those computer cards, however.

I eyed the sentry speculatively.

If you want to wait where you are, watching to see what happens next, go to 230. If you want to sneak up on the sentry, hoping to overpower him, take his card, and then go either up or down, go to 270.

342

I was safe inside my TARDIS. Swiftly, I checked her instruments, her power flow, her field control, and, to my satisfaction, found everything in readiness. There were only two problems. One was the disturbance in the Temporal Vortex. Whatever "it" was, the disturbance had dealt the TARDIS some rough blows earlier. Another rough ride like that one could leave me and my TARDIS hopelessly lost in some dark, extra-dimensional whirlpool of the Vortex.

The other problem was where to go. I could search for the cause of the disturbance. That particular mystery was tugging at my scientific curiosity. I was curious, too, about why the Daleks were so interested in it.

On the other hand, there were still Harry and Sarah Jane to think about. How long would they remain in Dalek manipulators without being harmed? Then again, could I manage to find them? And if I did find them, what more could I do to free them?

Questions, questions, questions. I engaged the TARDIS dematerialization circuits and plunged into the Vortex.

If you plan to search for the cause of the temporal disturbance within the Vortex, go to **375**. *If you prefer to hunt for Harry and Sarah within the Tower of the Masters, go to* **209**.

343

I slipped silently along the passageway back toward the lifts. My plan was working perfectly, and now I was taking things as they came, one step at a time. So what if I didn't know what was coming next?

I heard the sound of footsteps up ahead. Moving swiftly, I came up to where the corridor joined the circular passage-way surrounding the central column. There was a lone soldier there, standing with his back to me. He had just slipped a green card through the scanner on the wall, and was waiting for the lift to arrive.

Now was my chance.

Go to **352** *if you want to attack the soldier. Go to* **364** *if you prefer to wait.*

344

I had an idea. There was no way to reach that light bulb, but if I could put it out and darken the cell, I'd have quite an advantage over anyone who came in to get me. I considered throwing jelly babies at the bulb, but that was likely to get me little more than a sore arm and an acute lack of jelly babies.

No, there was another way. I took my scarf and tied several knots in one end, creating a large, heavy ball that Harry and some of my other Royal Navy friends might call a monkey's fist. Then I took careful aim, and hurled it at the light.

Make a Saving Roll against your DEX. *If it succeeds, go to* **356**. *If it fails, go to* **359**. *If you change your mind and decide to wait where you are, go to* **348**.

345

I walked that last ten meters expecting at any second a shout, a shot, and a sudden commotion as someone on the floor below spotted me and raised the alarm. But nothing happened.

Ah! Here it was, the crevice that I had spotted earlier in the rocks. I got down on my hands and knees and wiggled through. It seemed to be a split in the rock wall caused by a recent landslide or seismic quake, something the locals had not gotten around to investigating yet. Or was it? This might have made a convenient smugglers' hole in the days when Tharesti carried on trade with other cities on Gathwyr.

I found myself in a tunnel with smooth sides and a low ceiling. It was a typical lava tube, confirming my belief that this entire rock was the upthrust remnant of ancient volcanic activity. The tube led more or less up, with a branching immediately before me. I WANTED to go up, I thought, perhaps find another route into the city. But which way, left or right?

My light revealed that a fall of rock completely blocked the way left. Well, to the right it was, then. Onward!

Go to **246**.

346

From cover to cover, I crept out onto the landing strip until I crouched behind the table I'd spotted from my first hiding place. There was an electric torch there, a simple, hand-held job that should give me light enough to navigate within the tunnels I was fairly sure existed in the rock around me.

I chanced a look around. The landing area was bustling with men and Daleks working over the grounded aircars. As I watched, another gravvehicle drifted into the opening from the blue sky outside, an eight-man craft loaded with soldiers. They grounded and were met by a couple of officer types and one of the Daleks. I had the distinct impression that those troops had been out hunting for something, and that they'd just returned with a negative report.

With infinite care, I reached out from behind the table, laid my hand on the torch, and brought it away. No alarm was raised, no shouts or sudden clatter of running men. With the torch in my pocket, I backed away from the table and made my way silently back to the tunnel mouth.

What happens next depends on your luck. Roll 2D6. If the result is 8 or more, go to **347**. *If the result is 7 or less, go to* **345**.

347

"Hey, you! With the scarf! Stop right there!"

Uh oh.

I kept walking, but the gunshot roared warning through the cavern, echoing like thunder from the rock walls. I stopped, turned slowly, bringing my hands carefully into view.

Men with guns were running up the slope after me, followed close behind by a pair of Daleks. I was surrounded by a bustling crowd in seconds.

"YOU HAVE CAP-TURED AN IN-TRU-DER," one of the Daleks shrilled. "IN-TRU-DERS MUST BE EX-TER-MIN-A-TED."

"Yes, Master," one of the soldiers said. "You wanna exterminate him, or you going to leave it to us?"

"THE DA-LEKS WILL EX-TER-MIN-ATE! EX-TER-MIN-ATE!"

"NEG-A-TIVE!" The second Dalek's voice was harsher, deeper than the speech of the first, but still sharp and strident. "I REC-OG-NIZE THE IN-TRU-DER. THIS IS THE TIME LORD KNOWN AS THE DOC-TOR."

"THE DOC-TOR IS AN EN-E-MY OF THE DA-LEKS. EN-E-MIES OF THE DA-LEKS MUST BE EX-TER-MIN-ATED!"

"NEG-A-TIVE. THE DOC-TOR MUST NOT BE EX-TER-MIN-A-TED."

"WHY?"

"THE DOC-TOR MAY BE OF GREAT VA-LUE TO US IN OUR PRO-JECT HERE. THE DOC-TOR WILL HELP THE DA-LEKS."

I think I would have preferred to face a horde of black Daleks shrilling "Exterminate!" What project? Anything the Daleks were mixed up in was guaranteed to spell big trouble for every other life form in the universe. And they wanted me to help?

This promised to be interesting.

Go to **305**.

348

The best thing I could do was to stay precisely where I was. I didn't have long to wait, either. There was a rattle of keys in the lock, and a pair of guards motioned me to my feet. Waiting in the passageway outside were two Daleks.

"YOU WILL COME WITH US," one shrilled.

"Why? Is it time for an extermination?"

"YOU WILL NOT BE EX-TER-MIN-A-TED," the second Dalek said. Its voice was deeper than that of the first, but still shrill. "YOU WILL BE OF GREAT USE TO THE DA-LEKS. YOU WILL HELP THE DA-LEKS IN THEIR PRO-JECT ON THIS PLA-NET."

I didn't like the sound of that. Any project conceived and executed by the Daleks meant certain trouble for every other life form in the universe. And they expected me to help?

"What's the matter? Your castors need oiling?"

"YOU WILL CO-OP-ER-ATE WITH US, DOC-TOR."

"And if I don't?"

"YOU WILL CO-OP-ER-ATE WITH THE DA-LEKS AND THE DA-LEKS WILL CO-OP-ER-ATE WITH YOU."

Somehow, I didn't much like the sound of that.

Go to **305**.

349

"Uh…'mums'?"

"Keep it quiet! I don't want anyone to know I'm here. Might give the whole game away to the wrong people!"

"Uh…right…right."

"Mind if I borrow one of your vehicles?"

"Uh, sure. Which one do you want?"

"How about that little two-seater over there?"

"Yes, sir. She's all serviced and ready to go."

"Excellent work, mechanic. Excellent work!"

I climbed into the grav machine. Let's see. Stick on the floor for steering. Left, right, up, down, right. That would be the power control. That would be…

"Mechanic?"

"Sir?"

"Key?"

"Oh! Here, sir."

The key turned in an ignition lock, and power thrilled through the little flyer. It rose, hovering a meter off the floor.

"Remember! No one must know. No one! Top secret, right?"

"You can count on me, sir!"

I smiled and nodded, then turned toward the opening to the outside.

Go to **336**.

350

From cover to cover, I crept out onto the landing strip until I crouched behind the table I'd spotted from my first hiding place. There was an electric torch on that table, a simple, hand-held job that should give me light enough to navigate within the tunnels I was fairly sure existed in the rock around me.

4

I chanced a look around. The landing area was bustling with men and Daleks working on the grounded grav vehicles. As I watched, another grav flyer drifted out of the blue sky and settled to rest on the landing apron. The eight-man craft crowded with soldiers was met by a pair of black-garbed officer types and one Dalek. I had the distinct impression that those troops had been out hunting for something and that they'd just returned with a negative report.

Somebody coming! I ducked down behind the table again and waited for the footsteps to fade away into the distance. Then I reached carefully up over the edge of the table. My fingers brushed the torch, grasped for it . . .

There was a rattle and a crash as the torch rolled from the tips of my fingers and bounced noisily across the floor. From behind me a voice shouted, "Hey! Stop that man!"

Men with guns surrounded me in seconds, followed closely by a pair of Daleks.

"IN-TRU-DER! IN-TRU-DER!" one of the Daleks shrilled. "IN-TRU-DERS MUST BE EX-TER-MIN-A-TED! EX-TER-MIN-A-TED!"

One of the soldiers yanked me to my feet. "Yes, Master!" he said. "You wanna exterminate him, or you want we should do it?"

"THE DA-LEKS WILL EX-TER-MIN-ATE!" The crowd of soldiers edged back nervously at that, leaving me alone in a widening circle. I closed my eyes. "EX-TER-MIN-ATE!"

"NEG-A-TIVE!" That was a second Dalek's voice, harsher and deeper than that of the first, though still as shrill and strident. "I REC-OG-NIZE THE IN-TRU-DER. IT IS THE TIME LORD KNOWN AS THE DOC-TOR."

"THE DOC-TOR IS AN EN-E-MY OF THE DA-LEKS. EN-E-MIES OF THE DA-LEKS MUST BE EX-TER-MIN-A-TED! EX-TER-MIN-A-TED!"

203

"NEG-A-TIVE. THE DOC-TOR MUST NOT BE EX-TER-MIN-A-TED."

"WHY?"

"THE DOC-TOR WILL BE OF GREAT HELP IN THE DA-LEK PRO-JECT HERE. THE DOC-TOR WILL CO-OP-ER-ATE WITH THE DA-LEKS."

I opened my eyes and met the optical sensor of one of the Daleks as it studied me. The fact was just sinking in that I had been spared by a Dalek. At that point, I truly would have preferred a horde of Daleks shrilling "Exter-minate!" A Dalek project? Anything the Daleks were mixed up with was guaranteed trouble for every other life form in the universe. And they wanted me to help?

Well, this promised to be very interesting.

Go to **305**.

351

I yanked the stick hard to the right and back. There was a scream of tortured metal as the belly of my flyer scraped rock and showered sparks through the air. The flyer wob-bled, bucking wildly. Then there was a terrific explosion close behind me, and the flyer was spiraling in a long, flat roll. Somehow, I managed to land right-side up. I thought for a moment that a shot from the pursuing craft had caught me, but as I looked back, I saw the glare of a furiously burning fire silhouetting the boulder. I had made it past that rock. The people chasing me had not.

My flyer was finished, though. The crash had crumpled the after-end like tissue, and spilled the guts of the engine across the black gravel. I was back right where I'd begun, hours before.

What was that? I WAS back right where I'd begun, or not far from it.

If you left your TARDIS out here on the slope of the ridge, it is not far off and you may be able to reach it at **358**. If, however, your TARDIS is now parked inside the lower level of the Tower of the Masters, go to **362**.

352

I sprang forward.

Make a Saving Roll against your DEX. *It it succeeds, go to* **361**. *If it fails, go to* **365**.

353

The lift seemed to operate with no more than the push of a large, black button on a simple control panel. I punched the button, watched the door slide shut, then felt acceleration as the car started up. Moments later, the walls of the car dropped away, and a box-like chamber blossomed open, leaving me standing on the floor of a large, circular room. There was a central column with what looked like lift doors in it, stack upon stack of crates and wooden boxes piled about the perimeter of the room, and what appeared to be a tunnel in one wall, leading out.

There was also a soldier there, armed with a particularly nasty-looking gun. Nasty-looking because it was pointed straight at me.

"Hold it, you! You're not cleared for that access!"

"Cleared? Cleared?" A wise, old saying from some world or other came to mind. When caught red-handed, attack! "What do you mean, 'not cleared!' I'll have you know I've been cleared at the very highest level!"

The gun didn't waver. "You'll have to show me your card."

"Of course! Listen, I know you're very busy standing there stopping people who don't have proper access, but I wonder if you could tell me if you've seen two people—a man and a woman—who..."

If you want to attack the guard, go to **367**. *If you prefer to try to bluff and bluster your way through, go to* **369**.

354

The key to this sort of derring-do, of course, is to act as though you are supposed to be doing whatever it is you're doing. If the guards see you slinking along, looking suspiciously out of place, they are going to stop you.

I banked my flyer down toward the cliff-face entrance, cutting my speed to a gentle, downward-slanting drift. I cut the power and sprang from the vehicle, then started walking across the polished stone floor. All around me were men installing complex-looking electronic equipment aboard grav flyers, with Daleks supervising each group. There were about eight or ten of the monsters in that cavern, and ten times that many human slaves.

Having no desire to become a slave myself, I started walking. I would have to rely now on luck and nonchalance to get me out of the landing area and up the slope of the tunnel I saw before me.

What happens next depends on how lucky you are. Roll 2D6. If the result is 6 or more, go to **347**. *If the result is 5 or less, no one sees you. You walk out of the landing area, up the long, upward-slanting tunnel, and arrive at Level 1.*

If you want to examine it, go to **Level 1** *in* **Exploring the Tower**, *and continue your explorations. If you left your TARDIS on Level 1 earlier and wish to go aboard, you may do so. Go to* **382**.

355

I jerked the steering tiller hard to the left. Too late! There was a violent shock and the banshee shriek of tearing metal. Then I was flying head over heels through the mist, as fire and horror erupted around me.

For a moment, I held tight to some faint glimmer of consciousness, enough to know that I was splayed out on a gravel flat, that the smoke of my burning machine filled my nostrils, and that the white mist above me was growing black.

I heard the scrape of boots on gravel. Rolling my head to the side, I made out a pair of black boots coming close beside me. Feebly, I started to rise. When I looked up, descending on me was the face of the soldier, the gun held high above his head.

Then the black filled everything, covered everything, and pulled me under.

Reduce your STR, END, *and* DEX *each by 4, then go to* **304**.

356

Hot glass showered down from the ceiling, and my cell was plunged into darkness. I unknotted and replaced my scarf, then took my place against the wall to one side of the doorway.

I didn't have long to wait. There was a rasp of wood sliding on wood, then a beam of light stabbed at the cell's darkness. When the light was obscured again, I guessed it was due to someone peering through the peephole. Next, I heard the jingle of keys and the clash of the locking bar being unbolted. The door was thrown wide and a guard stepped into the cell, gun drawn.

For just a moment, he stood there, eyes blinking in the darkness. I squeezed behind him and slipped silently out into the corridor.

I'd been afraid he'd have friends outside covering him, but he'd come alone, checking on the prisoners. I raced down the hallway as quickly and as silently as I could manage. In seconds, the guard would realize that the cell was empty, and I had to be out of sight by then. I turned several corners, putting as much distance between me and that cell as I could, then headed for the center of the level.

Go to **343**.

357

No, flying into that nest didn't look like a good idea at all. I banked sharply away, brushing close past the sheer rock cliffs.

A shadow fell across my craft as something blotted out the sun. I craned my neck, looking back, and saw another grav vehicle behind me and overhead. It had either swooped on me from high overhead, or had just come up out of the cavern. Either way, it had settled on my tail and was closing fast.

I stepped up my power controls to the limit, and swung the stick around. If I could make it to the wall of fog just beyond the beach, I might be able to escape into the mist.

Something yowled close above my head, then again, and again. I looked back and saw the other flyer was much closer now. It was an eight-seater, crowded with black-uniformed troops. There was a stuttering sound and a rapidly winking light from the vehicle's crowded after-deck. More snapping whispers tore the air overhead, and I heard the hollow thud of bullets striking my hull.

I twisted away from the machine gun fire, dropping lower. I raced across the waves, then across the beach, which was a streaking grey blur below. The fog sea was a white wall ahead, sharply delineated where the cold, wet air from the ocean rolled across the land's volcanic, subsurface hot spots.

Then I was in the fog. Visibility was down to ten meters or less. I could see the ghostly blurs of boulders streaking past, materializing out of the murk ahead, vanishing astern almost before they registered on my brain.

More bullets hammered into my craft. Those troops must be wearing sensor helmets! This wasn't going to be easy. I dropped my flyer closer to the hurtling rush of nearly invisible rocks on the ground.

More bullets struck. My flyer made a grating noise, staggered, and lost more altitude. I was going down!

In front of me, a boulder solidified out of white shadows, grew, swelled to fill the sky ahead...

Make a Saving Roll against your DEX. *If it succeeds, go to* **351**. *If it fails, go to* **355**.

358

I have an absolutely infallible sense of direction. Even in this constant fog, I knew my TARDIS was resting at the base of the slope just over that way. No, that way.

I started off.

Make a Saving Roll against your MNT *to find the TARDIS. If it succeeds, go to* **371**. *If it fails, go to* **373**.

359

Missed!

You may make another Saving Roll against your DEX. *If it succeeds, go to* **356**. *If it fails, go to* **359**. *You may also give up and wait for the Daleks by going to* **348**.

360

It took several hours of questions and verbal maneuvering to get the information I wanted from the Daleks. Daleks are not, after all, well known for their conversational abilities, and they tend to rely on rather arrogantly presented circular reasoning to prove their points. When those points are expressed, over and over in a shrill machine-voice pitched somewhere between a shout and a bellow, it leaves you feeling that their principal conversational tactic is to bludgeon the other fellow to death with individually hurled monosyllables. Understanding them and following their reasoning takes patience, fortitude, and a willingness to either accept or overlook certain Dalek prejudices, such as their belief that they are the dominant and superior lifeform of the universe, destined to rule all creation or ex-ter-min-ate it trying.

But gradually their story unfolded.

The Daleks had been experimenting with various forms of time travel for a good many centuries, usually by borrowing the technology from captive peoples. They had had the Time Destructor, for example, and that took at the very least a basic understanding of trans-Vortex engineering. There was also the Dalek conquest of Earth in an alternate timeline, where they'd been experimenting with temporal displacement between the universes.

So far, though, the Daleks had never managed to infest the universe cross-time to any great extent. If they ever found the secret to that particular door, all space and time was in for very rough going. And here were the Daleks looking for that door.

They'd managed to create a Vortex Probe, a machine that crossed the dimensional boundary into the otherness of the Vortex. As I'd suspected, they'd created the device in the first place as a kind of advance warning system to listen for approaching TARDISes. I got at least a hint that they'd been preparing a rather elaborate trap, with guess-who as the intended victim.

But they'd caught more than they'd bargained for. The Daleks had used that probe not only to peer into the Vortex, but to pry open some of the extra-dimensional nooks and crannies accessed through the Vortex, looking for anything that might help their quest for an open door to time. Well, pry open too many locked doors and you're bound to get a surprise sooner or later. The Daleks had detected a curious ripple in the Vortex's space-time currents, a kind of inverse wave-form that suggested great latent power. Power being a key word for Daleks, they eagerly widened their probe, took a good, close look—and got the shock of their long lives.

They couldn't tell me what it was they saw, exactly. The Daleks themselves were divided within their own ranks as to whether the probe had revealed a natural force of some kind or a very strange, incredibly vast, supremely powerful life form. They were able to discover only two things about this extra-dimensional whatchamacallit: It seemed bent on sucking the universe into some kind of entropic whirlpool through a single, tiny crack between the Vortex and our universe. And that crack was located here on Gathwyr.

Even the Daleks can appreciate a danger to the entire universe. After all, if the universe were suddenly to age a few trillion years by falling through the greatly accelerated entropy gradient they'd detected, there'd be little point in ruling it. Dead star cinders and a handful of ancient red dwarfs circled by the ice-bound shards of crumbled worlds. What challenge is there in conquering a universe like that?

Having found the planet where the gateway to this Vortex monster was to be found, the Daleks were having trouble finding its precise location. After scouting around fruitlessly from their scout-cruiser, they'd gone ahead and conquered the local human population, enslaved the largest city and destroyed the rest, then turned the surviving population to building grav vehicles and electronics gear to their specifications. Their scouting parties were out constantly, quartering the mountain wilderness west of Tharesti, where their detectors told them the crack into the Vortex was to be found. So far, several search parties had failed to return, but nothing concrete had been discovered.

"THIS IS WHY WE NEED YOU, DOC-TOR," one of the Daleks had concluded. "YOU HAVE KNOWL-EDGE OF THE VOR-TEX WE LACK, AND YOU HAVE YOUR TAR-DIS FOR EN-TER-ING THE VORTEX. WE HAVE A COM-MON CAUSE IN THIS. THE DA-LEKS MUST WORK TO-GETH-ER WITH YOU TO SAVE THE UN-I-VERSE.

"IF WE DO NOT ACT QUICK-LY, THERE WILL BE NOTH-ING LEFT TO SAVE."

You have learned much about what is happening on Gathwyr. Record Clues C and G, then go to **400**.

361

Catching him completely by surprise, you have jumped a soldier armed with a submachine gun slung over his shoulder. You need STR, DEX, and *Brawling* skill for this attack.

First, make a Saving Roll on 2D6 against your STR. If it succeeds, you win a bonus modifier of −3. If it fails, the modifier is +2. Next, make a Saving Roll against your DEX score. If it succeeds, you get ANOTHER bonus modifier of

−2, and if it fails, another penalty modifier of +1. Combine the two modifiers into a single plus or minus number.

Roll 1D6 − 1 for the soldier's fighting skill, and subtract this from your *Brawling* skill. The result is the soldier's roll. Finally, roll 2D6 for your own actions, and apply the combined die modifiers. If the final result is less than or equal to the soldier's roll, you have succeeded. If it is greater, you have failed.

If you succeed, go to **366**. *If you fail, go to* **372**.

362

I was stranded outside the tower basement where I'd left my TARDIS.

Now what, Doctor? Set out to try to find the rebels? March back to the city gates and demand the return of your TARDIS? Or just pull up a boulder, set yourself down, and see who finds you first?

Actually, that decision might already have been made. I heard a scrape and a clatter of rock. I strained my ears, listening into the fog. I thought that I'd heard the warble of another grav flyer landing somewhere in the distance. Then the shadows around me suddenly materialized as black uniforms, nightmarish sensor masks, and guns trained on my head.

"That was quite a chase you led us," the leader said. "Hands up! You won't escape us again!"

"He's done in Janic and his boys," someone said. "Their flyer's smeared across half the ridge over there."

"Yeah, well, he'll answer to the Masters for that, too. Move along, rebel!"

There was a grounded flyer nearby. They hustled me aboard, then sent the craft arrowing back toward the city.

We approached from the ocean side of the towers, drifting down toward an opening eked into the side of the cliff halfway between the waves pounding at the foot of the promontory and the base of the walls of Tharesti. It looked like the opening of an old volcanic lava tube that had been widened and improved. The floor close by the opening had been smoothed and paved, and it was lined now with parked grav vehicles. I could see men bustling about several of the machines and there were Daleks supervising nearby.

Daleks? What were those black machine horrors doing on Gathwyr?

Maybe I was about to find out. We floated into the tunnel entrance and settled to a halt at the center of the field.

Soldiers and Daleks surrounded us.

Go to **363**.

363

"YOU HAVE CAP-TURED ONE OF THE RE-BELS," one of the Daleks bleated in shrill tones. The soldier who hauled me out of the grav vehicle seemed too scared to answer.

"THAT IS NOT A RE-BEL," another Dalek said. "I REC-OG-NIZE THAT AS THE TIME LORD KNOWN AS THE DOC-TOR."

"THE DOC-TOR IS AN EN-E-MY OF THE DA-LEKS. EN-E-MIES OF THE DA-LEKS MUST BE EX-TER-MIN-A-TED."

This, I thought, with an acute sense of drama, is it. I was completely surrounded, and the Dalek closest to me was levelling his particle gun at one of my hearts. The human soldiers nearest me were edging back a bit. They'd seen what those built-in guns could do.

"NEG-A-TIVE," another Dalek bleated. "THE DOC-TOR MUST NOT BE EX-TER-MIN-A-TED."

Huh? This was an abrupt change of script. Was my hearing finally going after all these centuries, or had I just heard a Dalek spare my life?

"EN-E-MIES OF THE DA-LEKS MUST BE EX-TER-MIN-A-TED. THE DOC-TOR MUST BE EX-TER-MIN-A-TED," the first one said.

"THE DOC-TOR MUST NOT BE EX-TER-MIN-A-TED. THE DOC-TOR WILL CO-OP-ER-ATE WITH THE DA-LEKS ON THIS PRO-JECT," the other one said.

"What makes you think I'll help you?" I wasn't actually feeling all that brave, but a strong answer will often throw off the most determined enemy and make him miss a step.

Of course, it could also make them angry at me, but angry seems to be a natural condition with Daleks, so I actually had little to risk.

"YOU WILL CO-OP-ER-ATE WITH THE DA-LEKS," was the only further enlightenment I received. The crowd of humans parted, and the Daleks led me up the sloping floor of a tunnel out of the landing area.

Go to **305**.

364

I loitered there, waiting. I didn't want to attack the soldier, as it was too noisy and too risky. On the other hand, if I waited there too long…

"Stop, you!"

Uh oh.

Go to **317**.

365

He heard me.

I was still about eight meters away when he spun around, the gun already sliding off his shoulder.

"Wait!" I shouted, but too late.

The stuttering rattle of the submachine gun ripped the air. There was an explosion of pain, hammer blows lifting my body back and up, and then a very deep darkness.

Go to **313**.

366

I stood over the soldier's unconscious body. At that moment, the lift door opened, arriving to the soldier's summons. I carefully picked up the green scanner card from the floor, then stepped across the body and into the car.

You may choose any level within the tower by going to **Exploring the Tower** *and looking up the description of the level you desire. You are already aboard the lift, and so you do not need to go to* **Lift** *first.*

367

I talked casually until I was close enough to reach out to grab the guard's gun. Then I sprang at him.

You are grappling with the soldier, who already has his rifle out and is pointing it at you. You will need your STR and *Brawling* skill for this combat. First, make a Saving Roll against your STR. If it succeeds, you get a bonus modifier of −3. If it fails, the modifier is +2.

Then roll 1D6 + 1 for the soldier, and subtract this from your *Brawling* skill. The result is the soldier's roll. Finally, roll 2D6 for your own actions, and apply the modifier. If this final result is equal to or less than the soldier's roll, you win. If it is greater, you lose.

If you win, go to **374**. *If you lose, make a Saving Roll against your* DEX. *If it succeeds, go to* **378**. *If it fails, go to* **313**.

368

I flew west, keeping close to the surface of the fog and travelling fast. I'd figured out how to turn the detector on. A blip of green light on a black screen indicated what must be the source of the temporal disturbance. It HAD to be that, as a temporal disturbance was what the jury-rigged circuitry was meant to detect, wasn't it? I caught myself wishing I was aboard my TARDIS.

Minutes passed, dragging toward an hour. It was difficult to gauge my speed, because all I could see below was the white blur of the fog layer. I could see mountains ahead, a purple softness between white horizon and deep blue sky. As the minutes passed, the mountains seemed to grow no larger, no clearer. I began hoping that the power plant carried by my flyer wasn't sharply limited. If it was a pocket fusion plant (something the Gathwyrans were nowhere near able to produce, but not out of line with anti-gravity technology or the ability to snoop into the Vortex), I had nothing to worry about. If it was something more primitive, such as fuel cells or batteries, I was in trouble. Or soon would be when they started to fail.

I had another worry to amuse me. Grav flyers fitted out with sophisticated scanner apparatus suggested that the Masters were in the business of searching for something. The fact that the disturbance was showing on my scope meant that it was probably easy to find, in principle, but difficult to find, in practice. For example, the source of the disturbance might be a fairly sharply defined area, but its position within that area could be hard to pinpoint. Rather like finding it easy to locate the haystack in the field, and more difficult to lay hold of the needle hidden inside.

If that was the case, I could expect a lot of other flyers in the neighborhood when I got close to whatever was causing that blip, flyers manned by unfriendly folks in black uniforms.

That gave me something to think about, too.

The flight is restful, if nothing else. You may restore STR *and* END *levels reduced by fatigue or wounds (but not those reduced by regeneration). You may keep on flying west, following the blip on your screen, at* **390**.

You may change your mind and turn around, hoping to find your TARDIS. If you left your TARDIS on the slope of the ridge just west of the city, you bank your craft around 180 degrees, retrace your path, and begin to search for the area where your TARDIS lies hidden, at **338**. *If you left your TARDIS in the basement level of the Tower of the Masters, things are a bit more difficult. You may turn around, fly back toward the city, then circle Tharesti looking for another way in besides the front gate at* **340**.

369

I began talking fast.

You are trying to use bluff and bluster to convince the guard that you are a high-ranking member of the local security forces, travelling incognito. When he demands your ID card, you try to convince him that you left it in your other coat. He is already half-convinced, as he saw you emerge from the "lift to the Masters' secret base", but he is suspicious of anyone travelling in a security zone without a card.

Your CHA and ability to talk fast will get you out of this. First, make a Saving Roll against your CHA score. If it succeeds, you win a bonus modifier of −3. If it fails, the modifier is +2.

Roll 1D6 + 2 for the suspicious guard, and subtract the result from your CHA score. This is the guard's roll. Roll 2D6 and apply the above modifier. If the result is equal to or less than the guard's roll, you win. If it is greater, you fail.

If you succeed, go to **380**. *If you fail, the guard brings his rifle up to point at you. Go to* **367**. *You may, if you prefer, take a step back and raise your hands, surrendering at* **317**.

370

I had to board that ship.

There was an open door, a frighteningly obvious one with a smooth ramp lowered toward the lift. Harsh white light spilled from the door out onto the sand. From where I was, I could see no sign of cameras, sensors, or electronic warning equipment, but not being able to see them did not mean they weren't there. It was also possible that the Daleks felt secure enough in their underground hideaway that they'd not bothered to set up any.

As carefully and as silently as I could manage, I started up the ramp.

Go to **Exploring the Ship** *to continue this adventure.*

371

Ha! Just as I thought! There was the TARDIS, just where I'd left it. I strode up to the door, took my key from its chain around my neck, opened the door, and slipped inside.

At last!

Go to **342**.

372

I sprawled on the floor, looking at the soldier standing above me. He raised the butt of his gun above his head, then brought it down on me in an explosion of pain that sent me hurtling back into the darkness.

Reduce your STR *and* END *each by 2, then go to* **304**.

373

Strange. I could have sworn that the TARDIS was just over that way. Hmmm, maybe more...uh...THAT way.

Make another Saving Roll against your MNT. *Add 6 to the roll because you are a bit confused. If it succeeds, go to* **371**. *If it fails, go to* **373**.

374

The guard was unconscious. I stood up slowly, rubbing my sore fist. Now, how to get out of here?

The door behind him was evidently the door to a lift, but there seemed to be no button or other control for summoning it. There was a device mounted next to the door. It appeared to be a computer scanner of some sort, equipped with a slot designed to accept a small ID or magnetically charged card.

Searching the guard, I found a rectangular, green plastic card in a leather pouch at his belt. That must be the key to the building's built-in security system, my pass to other levels of the place. But there was also that tunnel in the wall across the room. I thought I detected a whiff of fresh, salt air in the draft from that opening, but I couldn't be certain.

Up, or out? I flicked the card against my chin, considering.

To follow the tunnel, go to **300**.

To call the lift, go to **Lift** *in* **Exploring the Tower**.
Roll 2D6 as soon as you summon the lift, and go to **550** *if
the result is 12. For any other result, go to the description of
the level you wish to visit.*

375

Within the Vortex, the TARDIS was beyond the forces of
the normal universe, beyond the realm of space and time
entirely. I set the TARDIS adrift within the Vortex currents,
going nowhere, nowhen.

The TARDIS sensors probed for the disturbance that had
brought us to Gathwyr in the first place. Yes, there it was,
but faint, only a pinpoint of energy leaking across a
microscopic bridge between the universes. The wakes that had
buffeted the TARDIS before were gone, or were so reduced in
intensity that they were impossible to detect.

A leak between universes? It happened, of course. In a
cosmos as vast as this one, with as many extra-dimensionally
separated, multiple universes, even the most improbable of
events happened at least occasionally, somewhere,
somewhen. Eternity was a long, long time.

Trans-dimensional flows could be dangerous. What
happens to a place, to a world, to an entire star system when
the normal flow of entropy is reversed like spilled milk
splashing magically back into the glass? Or the local sun's
heat refuses to disperse into space, but instead accumulates on
the surface of a world...building...building ...building...

On such worlds, magic may be commonplace, or a
quasar's energies may run rampant through a galaxy before
even the most brilliant of civilizations can come to
comprehend what is happening to them.

Or consider the opposite—the flow of entropy increasing, the random activity of molecules accelerating, or worse, time itself flowing faster. Objects such as chairs, cities, people, and planets might age millennia in seconds, might crumble into dust in the wink of an eye. Or the stars themselves might begin winking out into an icy death, as heat and mass drain away and the thermonuclear reactions in their hearts flicker and fail.

Yes, trans-dimensional flows could be dangerous.

Gathwyr was still here, and so this trickle of energy was probably nothing serious...yet. There is the story from Earth about the little boy in Holland who plugged his finger into the hole in the dike. On one side of the dike was the low-lying countryside, his home, friends, and family. On the other side was the ocean, and death by drowning for all he knew. I crooked my own finger just before my face, wondering what sort of hole I was setting out to plug.

Your reasoning has given you some insight into what is happening here on Gathwyr. Record Clue F on a piece of paper, then go to **395**.

376

I landed squarely on my feet, facing the soldier as he approached with his gun at the ready.

"Aren't you carrying this zealous, pursuit-of-duty bit just a little too far?" I asked.

I could tell by the look in his eye, his bared teeth, the knuckles white against the barrel of his gun that he didn't think so.

You can grapple with him again at **367**. *Or you can surrender at* **317**.

377

His card was still in his hand, lightly held between thumb and forefinger as he reached across to punch in a level for me. I reached out and pulled the card away, then gave him a shove that sent him somersaulting out of the lift and across the floor. He landed with a clatter, then scrabbled for his rifle, which he was pointing at me just as the lift door slid shut.

I had an ID card and was safe aboard the lift, studying the array of buttons on the lift's control panel.

You may go to any level you desire. The lift lights indicate that you are already on Level 1. Go to **Exploring the Tower** *to find the description of the level you wish to explore to continue your explorations. (As you are already aboard the elevator, the initial 2D6 roll will not be necessary.)*

378

The gun exploded in noise and smoke just as I hurled myself to one side. The bullet smashed into the floor close by my head, stinging my face with flying chips of stone. I flipped over in a backward somersault, and sprang to my feet. The soldier's smoking gun followed, tracking...

Make a Saving Roll against your DEX. *If it succeeds, go to* **376.** *If it fails, go to* **379.**

379

I overbalanced as I came to my feet, and crashed backward into a stack of empty crates. There was an ear-shattering smash as I toppled over up-ended wooden crates in a miniature avalanche of splinters and stoved-in boxes. The soldier followed close behind, his rifle at the ready.

I picked myself up with exaggerated care. "You want to be careful where you point that thing," I said. "Your Masters wouldn't care to receive damaged merchandise, would they?"

*You can surrender by going to **317**. Or you can keep talking quickly, hoping the guard comes close enough for you to spring at him again at **367**.*

380

The guard nodded, uncertain, then said, "You'll have to go pick up an ID at HQ, sir. You can't wander around the tower without one."

"Quite right, quite right. I don't know where my head is this morning."

"Shall I call a lift for you?"

"Would you, please?"

He reached for a pouch at his belt, and pulled out a rectangular green plastic card. Beside the door was a computer scanner with a slit evidently designed to receive such a card. He deftly slid the plastic through the slot, and the door opened. Obviously, I was going to need that card of his to continue my explorations. Stepping into the lift, the guard reached up to punch a button for me. I wasn't about to go to the guard HQ, but I'd have to think fast if I was going to avoid just that.

*You may change your mind about having him set your destination, of course, and let him push Level 31. Then go to **283** to see what happens. Or you can make a Saving Roll against your DEX. If it succeeds, go to **377**. If it fails, go to **381**.*

381

He was still holding the card, and I grabbed for it. But he moved just at that instant, and the card skimmed out the door and across the floor. He spun on me, catching me in the face with his elbow, a blow that left me sprawled on the floor. When I managed to look up, it was just in time to see his gun butt whistling down.

Then there was a sickening crunch, a nightmare of black. *Reduce your* STR *and* END *each by 4, then go to* **304**.

382

My TARDIS was still there on the basement level, right where I'd left it. I hadn't had much luck so far in my search for Sarah and Harry. Perhaps it was time to change strategies.

Why were the Daleks here on Gathwyr, anyway? Not for conquest, certainly. Gathwyr was a primitive world, as human-colonized planets go, so primitive the Daleks were busy importing technologies like scanners and antigravity.

Again, why were they bothering with all that? Not for the comfort and enlightenment of the natives, surely. Daleks don't work that way. Their idea of munificence is to rape a planet, then allow the slaves to starve to death instead of putting them through the ordeal of waiting to be shot.

It was clear that the Daleks were after something, searching for something here on Gathwyr. What could possibly be of such interest, of such importance about this world?

Use your head, Doctor! What brought YOU here?

Why, I answered myself, that queer disturbance in the Time Vortex, of course, the one that gave you a nasty bump and dropped you all on Gathwyr in the first place!

Find that disturbance, and I might learn why the Daleks were here. Know why they were here, and I might find the way to rescue Harry and Sarah Jane. Right?

Don't question it too closely, Doctor. Away!

Go to **375**.

383

I touched the button beside the door, and heard the whirr-thump of machinery. Then the door slid open, confirming my guess. It was a lift.

There were no control panels or buttons inside, only a saucer-shaped pressure plate on the floor. With only two levels to travel, it was probably enough just to step aboard the lift to have it take you to the next and only other level.

After the door slid shut, I felt a gentle acceleration, then another whirr-bump as the lift came to a stop.

When the door opened, I was greeted by the sight of Daleks!

Go to **S13** *in* **Exploring the Ship.**

384

Though the light was dim, there was enough to see by. It looked as if the box lids had been sealed shut with some kind of glue or sealant, but a gentle tug was enough to pry one open. Inside, I found electronics parts, a treasure chest of circuit modules, diphasic chips, amplifers, and myriad other components. Evidently, the Daleks were in the business of mass-producing sophisticated electronic devices of some sort. But what?

The diaphasic chips suggested transdimensional physics were involved. A dimensional scanner, perhaps? A sudden chill hit me. A scanner? A Temporal Vortex scanner?

Should the Daleks become able to peer into the Vortex, they could spot movement there, might even be able to predict where and when a TARDIS was going to land. Useful information for a race of pathological killers whose worst enemy generally arrived by TARDIS.

This was grim news indeed. Deep in thought, I closed the box, arranging things so that a casual inspection would reveal no tampering.

You have won a clue about the mystery that surrounds Gathwyr. Record Clue C on a piece of paper before continuing with the adventure.

Roll 2D6. If the result is 10 or more, go to **396**. *If the result is 9 or less, you may return to the passageway at* **S4** *in* **Exploring the Ship**, *or you may go through the bulkhead door to the adjoining compartment at* **S7**.

385

The crates were sealed or somehow glued shut, but it was easy enough to pry one open for a peek inside. Lifting the lid, I found a pile of arms, Dalek manipulator arms.

So, this was a cargo hold for storing Dalek spare parts such as bodies, optical sensors, and arms. An open box nearby contained Dalek particle beam guns, the kind normally mounted as personal artillery on a Dalek travel machine. Too bad it required a power source to fire. I could search these boxes for hours before finding one, assuming any were even kept here.

I pondered why the Daleks would have brought so many spare parts to the planet Gathwyr. There were only two answers that made any sense.

One possibility was that the Daleks were planning to set up a breeding program on Gathwyr. After all, the creatures are only part machine. The familiar and sinister black metal body is actually a shell, a complex and heavily armed and armored travel machine for the vicious little organic horror that rides inside. Though known today as Daleks, they are actually mutants of the Kaleds, a once-human race of the distant past. The Daleks' organic parts are bred with the same efficiency used to manufacture their bodies, and they need fairly elaborate industrial facilities to do it. They just might be intending to turn Gathwyr into a Dalek nursery.

The flaw in that line of thought was that there are plenty of other planets suitable for Dalek breeding programs. Why go to all the trouble of enslaving a human planet first? A second, marginally more realistic possibility was that the Daleks were engaged in some project or search on Gathwyr that was using up Dalek bodies at a fearful rate. They needed the spare parts to keep themselves going.

Which brought me back to an earlier question. Why were the Daleks here on Gathwyr? And what could possibly be making the nearly indestructible Daleks wear out so quickly?

This compartment seemed to hold no answers to my questions. Unless I wanted to disguise myself as a Dalek—impractical on several counts—there was nothing I could make use of here. I carefully restored the boxes so that a casual inspection would reveal no tampering.

Roll 2D6. On a result of 10 or more, go to **396**. *On a result of 9 or less, you may either return to the passageway at* **S4** *or go through one of the other two doors to either* **S9** *or* **S11**.

386

I ran my hand along one of those sleek, sinister cylinders. They were bombs, probably fusion devices with dalekanium imploders. And those crates?

I pried open the lid of a nearby crate. Inside were incendiary explosives, saucer-sized and -shaped packets with magnetic grips and built-in miniature timer-detonators. One of these could melt a man-sized hole through the thickest armor plate in literally a flash.

This find was a treasure trove of sorts, but what?

You may, if you wish, carry one or two of these explosive packets with you, one in each of your large coat pockets. Make a note that you have done so, then continue with the adventure.

Roll 2D6. If the result is 9 or more, go to 396. If the result is 8 or less, you may either return to the passageway at S4, or go through one of the other bulkhead doors to either S12 or S10.

387

Daleks!

"IN-TRU-DER! IN-TRU-DER!" The mingled shrilling of the Daleks echoed through the bridge. "IN-TRU-DERS MUST BE EX-TER-MIN-A-TED!"

The lift was not going anywhere, and the Daleks were closing in. My options seemed a bit limited. There were three other doors equally spaced around the bridge. The one directly across seemed to be another lift door, but the other two might lead out onto this level of the ship. There was also what looked like a weight-activated pressure plate on the raised dais at the center of the room. Another lift?

The Daleks milled closer, and I stepped out of the lift to gain room to maneuver. About the only thing I had going for me was the fact that the Daleks were unlikely to open fire on their own starship's bridge.

You can surrender at 401. You can try for the lift that brought you up, which has just closed behind you. This choice is at 403. Or you can barge through the middle of the Daleks into the center of the bridge, hoping to get to one of the other ways out by going to 402.

388

The Dalek was turning to face me. Behind him was a room crammed with electronics consoles, communications equipment, for the most part. Also behind the Dalek was a table where electronics gear was spread out in a kind of assembly line.

"IN-TRU-DER!" the Dalek shrilled. "IN-TRU-DERS MUST BE EX-TER-MIN-A-TED!"

The door had closed behind me. I could try for that way out, or push past the Dalek toward a door in the adjoining bulkhead.

You can surrender at **401**. *Or you can try for the door behind you at* **404**, *or the door beyond the Dalek at* **405**.

389

I stepped into the passageway. Shadows danced along the corridor's bulkheads as an army of black machines drifted into view. Shrill bleatings of "EX-TER-MIN-ATE" rose from the throng, and weapons swung around at me.

You can surrender at **401**. *The door behind you has just slid shut, but you can try to go back through it at* **404**. *Or you can turn and run for it at* **406**.

390

I left the sea of fog as abruptly as if I'd flown across the shoreline of an ocean. The land, far more rugged now than in the coastal region of Tharesti, rose in jagged, skyward scrabblings, while the distant purple mountains had also solidified into razor-edged peaks among the clouds. The country was wild and desolate, the vegetation hardy, semi-arid scrub brush and isolated, scraggly trees among the up-ended boulders. The rock formations looked volcanic, and recently so, like so much of the rest of Gathwyr's geology.

The blip I had been following had expanded with the mountains, until it was now a soft, pulsing light that filled the crude detector screen on the console of my flyer. The detector indicated that the cause of the temporal disturbance was somewhere in the vicinity, but not precisely where. I could search hundreds of square miles in this desolation and not find whatever it was that I was looking for.

Now, if I had my TARDIS, that would be another story. Once planted in the general area, the TARDIS instruments could locate the source of the disturbance. But the TARDIS and Tharesti were a good many miles behind me now.

What was that? A flash—sunlight glinting from a piece of metal—had caught my eye. I circled back, around, down, settling the flyer to ground.

Go to **445**.

391

I hit the pressure plate at the center of the door, but nothing happened. Though I pounded it repeatedly, the door wouldn't budge.

For a moment, I thought I heard a noise from within, like a far-off, muffled pounding, but when I put my ear close, there was silence again.

Roll 2D6. If the result is 9 or more, go to **407**. *If the result is 8 or less, you may move along the passageway to another of the three doors here at* **S20**, **S21**, *or* **S22**, *or you can continue along the passageway to* **S15**.

If you brought along one or two bombs stolen from the Dalek armory, you may try to blow open the door. If you want to open either **S20** *or* **S21**, *go to* **415**.

392

There were two Daleks in the room on the far side of the table. They must have been as surprised as I was, for neither bleated "EX-TER-MIN-ATE", but only stood there.

Go back out into the passageway at 407. Or surrender to them at 401. If you have not talked to the Daleks yet (either in this room, S22, or elsewhere in the course of your explorations), you may try to talk to them now by going to 408.

393

A Dalek army boiled out of the room after me, bleats of "IN-TRU-DER!" mingling harshly with counter-bleats of "EX-TER-MIN-ATE!"

Surrender at 401, or run for it at 406.

394

The menacing shape of the Dalek closed in. The lift remained obstinately motionless. Apparently, to go up again I would have to get off and call the contraption again.

My only hope was that the Dalek would hesitate before opening fire in the middle of his own ship's engine room. I dashed from the lift, dodging behind a tangle of cables and wiring.

The Dalek horror followed.

You can surrender at 401. You can keep trying to dodge away from the Dalek, in hopes of getting back to the elevator at 409. If you have one or two bombs stolen from the Dalek armory in your pockets, you may either attack the Dalek at 410, or try to destroy the engine room of the ship at 411.

395

With a grind and a groan, the TARDIS materialized on a desolate plain. The computer locators plotted my position at over eighty kilometers west of Tharesti. Mountains that had been only a purple blur from the coastal city were here jagged blocks of volcanic stone stabbing skyward. The TARDIS rested on a desolate plain, a slightly depressed, bowl-shaped field strewn with small shards of broken rock.

I double-checked the TARDIS sensors. Though it was not possible to pinpoint the precise center of the temporal leak in normal space, the TARDIS scanners could come close. Whatever was causing that peculiar, pulsing entropic trickle between the universes was somewhere close by. Very close by.

I stepped from the TARDIS. The air was chill and harsh, and a sharp wind was keening down from the higher mountains further west, bearing with it a taste of snow and glacier ice. The plain seemed empty, but sunlight glinted on metal farther down the valley.

If you have been here earlier in a flyer, go to **442**. *If you have not been to the mountains yet, go to* **445**.

396

There was a hissing sound behind me, and a sudden chill draft. I whirled and saw an open door crowded with Daleks.

"IN-TRU-DER!" one of them bleated, and then they were all joining in a shrill, electronic chorus. "IN-TRU-DER! IN-TRU-DERS MUST BE EX-TER-MIN-A-TED!"

You can surrender at **401**. *You can pretend to surrender, then try to make a break for it at* **412**. *Or you can make your break now, trying to reach the nearest other door leading out of this compartment at* **404**.

397

More electronics parts! This ship was like a wholesale parts shop, but what I wanted to know was why.

Roll 2D6. If the result is 9 or more, go to **396**. *If the result is 8 or less, you may continue your explorations, either in the passageway at* **S4**, *or by going to an adjoining compartment, either* **S6**, **S7**, *or* **S8**.

398

I slipped through the door, breathing hard. The shadows of those sleek, tapered cylinders seemed almost comforting this time.

You may, if you wish, examine the room more carefully at **386**. *If you already know what this place is and have come here because of that, go to* **414**.

399

I pressed the button next to the door, waited for the door to open, then stepped into the lift. My weight activated the machinery and carried me up.

As my head came level with the floor of the bridge, I found a group of Daleks waiting.

"All right, Doctor," I muttered to myself. "Let's see you get yourself out of THIS one!"

Go to **416**.

400

The first thing the Daleks wanted from me was my TARDIS.

"No," I said. You'd have thought it was the first time they'd ever heard the word.

"YOU MUST CO-OP-ER-ATE WITH THE DA-LEKS."

"I will, but the TARDIS is out. What kind of idiot do you think I am?" If the Daleks ever got hold of a TARDIS, the rest of the universe had better watch out. Even if the universe ended at this particular point in time, there were quite a few billion years of previous history the Daleks would just love to play with, perhaps to the point where it would no longer matter that everything came to an end here and now.

"IF YOU DO NOT CO-OP-ER-ATE, THE DA-LEKS HAVE OTH-ER WAYS OF PER-SUA-DING YOU."

"Oh yeah? What?" I had a sinking feeling that I knew what was coming next.

One of the Daleks gestured with its manipulator, and the air above the table turned hazy. A holographic image formed, solidified.

"Sarah! Harry!"

The two couldn't hear me, of course. They were sitting on a bench in a room somewhere, a white-painted room with harsh, actinic lighting. They seemed unharmed, but...

"WE BE-LIEVE THESE HU-MANS ARE KNOWN TO YOU, DOC-TOR."

"You'd better not have hurt them..."

"THEY ARE UN-HARMED. HOW-EV-ER..."

I thought fast. "Look, I can't take you aboard the TARDIS. It won't work with Daleks aboard. Built-in security, you know?" That bit was a lie, of course, but I didn't think the Daleks would have any way of checking up on it. Besides, they needed me to pilot the ship, and I certainly wasn't going to take them anywhere or anywhen. Ergo, the TARDIS WOULDN'T work with Daleks aboard.

"WHAT DO YOU SUG-GEST?"

"That I take the TARDIS myself. I'll help you, but I've got to pilot the TARDIS alone."

"YOU WOULD DIS-AP-PEAR AND NOT RE-TURN."

"Oh, c'mon, now! Where's that keen, cold, calculating Dalek reason I've heard so much about? You've got my friends! Do you think I'm going to fly off and leave them with you?"

There was a pause, the chirp of high-speed data transmissions between the two Daleks, then one said, "WE FIND YOUR REA-SON-ING LOG-I-CAL. YOU WILL LO-CATE THE DIS-TUR-BANCE IN TIME FOR THE DA-LEKS AND HELP THE DA-LEKS DEAL WITH IT. THE HU-MANS WILL RE-MAIN WITH US TO AS-SURE YOUR CO-OP-ER-A-TION."

"Hey, I want to save the universe as much as you guys do!" For different reasons, I added silently. "And if we help you, those two can go free? With me?"

"AF-FIR-MA-TIVE."

I suppose that was as close as I would ever get to having a Dalek's word on a promise. With typical Dalek logic, their promise was likely to last only as long as it was of benefit to them. The moment they no longer considered me useful, the terms of our 'agreement' were liable to change suddenly and drastically.

The two Daleks were to be my escorts back to the TARDIS. I wondered how much they believed of my story about on-board security systems. Would they wait for me to unlock the TARDIS, then rush aboard anyway? The creatures led me back into the corridor, through an inboard door onto the bridge, and across to a lift door. As we waited for the door to open, I pondered my options. I could go along with the Daleks, and hope they didn't try to steal the TARDIS when we got there. Or I could assume right from the start that they were out to double-cross me.

If the latter were true, my best course was to escape now, and try to find the means to cause so much damage to the

Dalek ship that their mission here on Gathwyr would be aborted, THEN try to rescue Harry and Sarah, and THEN try to save the universe...

The lift opened and we stepped aboard.

Hold on a second. That holographic image of Harry and Sarah had shown them in a room aboard this ship. The Daleks would certainly never trust two such prisoners to the dungeons of their puppet human government on Tharesti! If I broke free now, perhaps I could rescue them. The three of us might be able to damage this ship on the way out, and then have a decent chance of saving the universe later.

When the lift deposited us in a curved passageway opposite the ship's airlock, I realized that if I was going to break away, now was the time.

You may try to break away from your Dalek escort at **434**. *Or you may choose to cooperate with them as discussed in the meeting room, and go with them to your TARDIS at* **436**.

401

I raised my hands above my head very slowly. Daleks were not known for taking prisoners, but I had nowhere left to run.

Your fate depends now on chance and the kindness of your Dalek friends. Roll 2D6. If the result is 9 or more, go to **413**. *If the result if 8 or less, go to* **425**.

402

There must have been five or six Daleks on the bridge, enough black metal horrors that I was able to dive between them toward the center of the bridge. For one split second, they couldn't shoot me without shooting one another or the instrument consoles of their own bridge.

*You can surrender at **401**. Or you may dash for the nearest lift off the bridge to the level below by going to **403**. Or you may go through one of the other two doors leading off the bridge to other parts of this level of the ship at **417**. Finally, you can go to the raised dais at the center of the bridge, where a pressure plate on the deck marks a lift going down at **421**.*

403

This was no place for me. I leaped for the lift door, stabbing at the button on the bulkhead beside it.

"EX-TER-MIN-ATE! EX-TER-MIN-ATE!" The cry rose behind me.

*If you have a bomb from the ship's armory, you may use it to escape by going to **424**. Otherwise, roll 2D6. If the result is 7 or more, go to **404**. If the result is 6 or less, go to **422**.*

404

My hand hit the door button. Open! Open!

The cry behind me was shriller now, raising in pitch. "EX-TER-MIN-ATE! EX-TER-MIN-ATE!"

There was an explosion of blue fire, then a spiralling agony. Darkness closed in, and I knew no more.

*Go to **430**.*

405

My hand hit the door button. Open! Open!

The cry behind me was shriller now, rising in pitch. "EX-TER-MIN-ATE! EX-TER-MIN-ATE!"

Then the door was open and I passed through. As the door hissed shut behind me, it cut off the cries of the Daleks.

*Go to **S19**.*

406

I ran, my feet echoing along the passageway. Shrill bleats rose behind me, cries of "EX-TER-MIN-ATE! EX-TER-MIN-ATE!"

Keep running around the passageway to 423. You can go to the next outboard door and try to open it at 404. Or you can run around the passageway to the nearest inboard doorway at 426.

407

An ominous sound echoed down the passageway, the hissing glide of Daleks. I turned, saw the dance of shadows along the bulkheads and then the black metal horrors drifting into view, filling the corridor.

"IN-TRU-DER! IN-TRU-DER! EX-TER-MIN-ATE!" they screeched.

Surrender at 401. Or turn and run for it at 406.

408

Well, the best defense is a good offense. At least, that's what they always say. "You can't hope to get away with this," I said, trying to sound sure of myself. "You've been found out."

"WHAT ARE YOU TALK-ING A-BOUT?"

Well, at least I had them talking, which meant that they weren't shooting or screeching "Ex-ter-min-ate!" I stepped into the room with them. It was small, white-painted, and harshly lit. There were no furnishings besides a single round table that stood in the center of the room. No wonder Daleks tend to be so testy. They can never sit down.

"Why, your plan here on Gathwyr, of course." The two metal creatures exchanged glances by swivelling their optical sensors, then looked at me again.

"YOU ARE NOT A HU-MAN," one bleated. "YOU ARE A TIME LORD."

"Quite right."

"YOU ARE THE TIME LORD KNOWN AS THE DOC-TOR."

"Quite right again."

"WE HAVE BEEN SEARCH-ING FOR YOU, DOC-TOR. WE NEED YOUR HELP."

"Eh?" That was an abrupt switch from the usual Dalek script!

"YOU MUST HELP US, DOC-TOR." The Dalek sounded agitated, even frightened, which startled me more than the change in the Daleks' manner. I needed time to recover my balance. "You want my help conquering Gathwyr? You seem to have done quite nicely on your own."

"WE ARE NOT IN-TER-ES-TED IN CON-QUEST. THE HU-MANS ON THIS PLA-NET ARE USE-FUL AL-LIES AND WOR-KERS."

"Hmmm…slaves, yes. I've heard that one before."

"WE CAME HERE BE-CAUSE WE DE-TEC-TED UN-US-U-AL A-NO-MA-LIES IN THE SPACE-TIME VOR-TEX."

"A…anomalies?"

"DO NOT PRE-TEND NOT TO KNOW! DO NOT PRE-TEND! THE SAME A-NO-MA-LIES MUST HAVE BROUGHT YOU HERE AS WELL."

One of the Daleks turned toward a wall, then set a small, plastic box on the table between us. Inside were the partially disassembled remnants of my temporal interference detector, the device I'd cobbled together aboard the TARDIS on our journey to Gathwyr.

"YOU RE-COG-NIZE THIS, DOC-TOR." It was a statement, not a question.

"Of course." It would have been futile to deny it. The technology in that small bundle of molecular circuits and hyperchips was far beyond anything native to Gathwyr.

"YOU DE-TEC-TED AN A-NOM-A-LY WHILE TRA-VEL-LING WITH-IN THE VOR-TEX."

"Yes. How did YOU detect it?" Although the Daleks had managed to sneak across time before, their attempts had so far been anything but coherent, and usually depended on captured technology and know-how.

"DA-LEK SCI-ENCE HAS DE-VEL-OPED THE CA-PA-BIL-I-TY OF MON-I-TOR-ING THE VOR-TEX."

"I see," I murmured. That capability would let them see a TARDIS coming, as well as where and when it would materialize. The Daleks could do a lot of mischief with intelligence like that.

But why had the Daleks just admitted all this to me? Not only was I their old enemy, but I would certainly be a target—perhaps THE target—of this new technology. Why give up such a tactical advantage, unless they had bumped into something in the Vortex that terrified them.

The Daleks? Terrified? What was there in this or any other universe that could terrify a Dalek? The thought that there might be such a thing on the loose was very disturbing indeed.

You have won important information about what is actually happening on Gathwyr. Record on a piece of paper that you have acquired Clue C, then go to **360**.

409

I dodged among the machines, the Dalek moving clumsily after me. This particular specimen must be their equivalent of an engineer, tending the power plant and the throbbing generators that surrounded us.

The deck space was cramped and narrow, and wouldn't allow me to run for long. If that Dalek closed its manipulator arm on me, it wouldn't need its gun at all to end my explorations.

If you are carrying one or two explosive packets from the ship's armory, you may use one to try to blow up the ship's engine room at 411, or you can attack the Dalek with an explosive packet (which may or may not damage the engine room as well) at 410.

If you don't happen to have any explosives with you, you can keep trying to avoid the Dalek at 427, or you can circle back to the lift at 431 to try to go back up to the bridge. You may also attempt to perform some sabotage on the power plant with your bare hands, hoping to delay the Dalek long enough to let you escape at 429.

410

I reached into my pocket as I backed along the aisle, the Dalek only a few feet away.

"IN-TRU-DER!" it shrilled. "EX-TER-MIN-ATE! EX-TER-MIN-ATE!"

My hand brought out an explosive packet taken from the ship's armory. Though the timer on the saucer-sized package seemed simple enough, I would have to guess at the time delay because the dial had no markings.

I squeezed my eyes shut, gave the timer dial as large a turn as I dared, then leaned forward to snap the packet's magnetic grip onto the Dalek's chest armor.

Go to 428.

411

I reached into my pocket as I backed along the aisle, the Dalek only a meter away.

"IN-TRU-DER!" it shrilled. "EX-TER-MIN-ATE! EX-TER-MIN-ATE!"

My hand brought out an explosive packet, one of the saucer-shaped devices I'd found in the ship's armory only moments before.

The detonator seemed simple enough, a knob that turned around a dial and then ticked off the seconds like a kitchen timer. Unfortunately, the dial was not marked, and so I would have to guess what setting would give me the necessary time delay.

Still, this seemed a good way to mess up the Dalek's engineering room and to cripple their space ship, possibly for good. I squeezed my eyes shut and gave the timer knob a twist, then shoved the device in among the spaghetti-tangled wires of the Dalek power plant.

You don't know how much time you have before the explosion. Roll 2D6. If the result is 9 or more, go to **433**. *If the result is 8 or less, go to* **435**.

412

"O.K., iron-pants, you've got me!" I raised my hands above my head and strode toward them. They scattered back as I stepped through the doorway. For just that instant, my Dalek captors could not shoot me without shooting one another. As the machine bodies crowded around me, I shoved hard at the nearest one, launching myself in the other direction.

"HALT! HALT OR WE WILL EX-TER-MIN-ATE! O-BEY! O-BEY!"

I could sense the black metal hulks turning to pursue,

sense those guns swinging into line with my back.

I had an instant or so to live.

Roll 2D6. If the result is 9 or higher, go to **413**. *if the result is 8 or less, go to* **406**.

413

The Daleks glided closer, filling the passageway. "EX-TER-MIN-ATE!"

Blue fire washed around me as I threw my hands up in front of my face. As a sea of agony, fire, and spiralling darkness engulfed me, from far off I heard someone screaming. Then the darkness swallowed all sound, all sensation.

Go to **430**.

414

This was the Dalek ship's armory, a place I'd visited before. I went to one of the cases and pried open the lid. Inside were explosive packets, each a saucer-sized and –shaped thermal bomb equipped with its own timer and detonator, each able to melt a hole in almost anything. A mere steel alloy door would offer no barrier to one of these. Placed in a vital spot like the bridge or main power plant, one or two of these bombs would ruin the ship. Not to mention the Dalek plans.

I reached into the box.

You may, if you desire, take either one or two packets of explosives with you, carrying one in each of your large coat pockets. Make a note that you have done so, and proceed with the adventure.

Roll 2D6. If the result is 9 or more, go to **396**. *If the result is 8 or less, you may return to the passageway at* **S4**, *or go through one of the bulkhead doors to either* **S12** *or* **S10**, *in* **Exploring the Ship**.

415

I chose the door I wanted open, reached into my pocket, and drew out the flat, dull-grey packet of thermal explosive. The timer device was obvious enough, though the dial was not marked to indicate how much of a time delay was created by turning it. The magnetic gripper on the opposite side welded the packet to the center of the door.

I closed my eyes tight, moved the knob as much as I dared, and stepped back down the passageway. I hoped anyone standing on the other side of that door was well clear of it. The explosive was of the chemical-compound type that burned with fierce heat rather than exploding all at once. Even if someone happened to be leaning against the inside of the door, he should have a moment or two to realize that the door was getting uncomfortably hot.

The packet went off with a white-hot glare that seemed to burn into my brain even with my eyes screwed shut. Holding my outspread fingers up against the dazzling radiance, I could see the door dissolving, melting into a pool of liquid metal where the doormat should have been.

I stepped forward, waving acrid white smoke away with my hand.

If you have just melted a hole in the door to S20, go to 437. *If you have just opened the door to S21, go to* **440**.

416

The Daleks crowded closer. "YOU ARE A PRI-SON-ER OF THE DA-LEKS," one bleated. I was nudged by relentless manipulators off the engine room lift. "THE PRIS-ON-ER IS DAN-GER-OUS. RE-MOVE HIM FROM THE SHIP."

"WE O-BEY!"

"Sort of like closing the barn door after the horse, isn't it? Your ship is pretty badly damaged."

"IR-REL-E-VANT! IR-REL-E-VANT!" The Daleks were more agitated than ever, and seemed to be working themselves into a murderous frenzy. "THE DA-LEKS WILL TRI-UMPH! THE DA-LEKS WILL BE SU-PREME! TAKE HIM! TAKE HIM!"

I was led from the ship a prisoner.

Go to **418**.

417

As I leaped for the door, cries of "EX-TER-MIN-ATE! EX-TER-MIN-ATE!" rose behind me.

Make a Saving Roll against your DEX. *If it succeeds, go to* **438**. *If it fails, go to* **404**.

418

Minutes later I was in an antigravity flyer, slipping low over the fog sea, heading west. The towers of Tharesti dwindled away astern. There were two humans in the vehicle with me, a driver and a guard. For good measure, there was also a pair of Daleks. They'd hustled me up the lift to the lowest level of the city, then through a tunnel to their landing port in a cavern mouth above the sea. It was good to taste fresh, sunlit air again.

I wondered how much longer I would enjoy that luxury.

My questions, my entreaties, my protests all went unacknowledged by human or Dalek. In fact, not a word was spoken until the flyer grounded in a desolate little valley beyond the limit of the fog. In this wild landscape, saw-tooth mountains stabbed at the sky, and the towers of Tharesti were lost completely in the haze to the east.

"YOU HAVE COST US MUCH, DOC-TOR," one of my captors said at last. The wind was blowing very cold. Had the Daleks brought me to this dreary spot just to execute me?

That seemed a bit sentimental for this lot.

"Yes, well, that's the way it is when you're out to conquer the universe. Some days nothing goes right."

"WE DO NOT WISH TO CON-QUER THE U-NI-VERSE, DOC-TOR."

"Eh?"

"WE WISH TO SAVE IT." The Dalek studied me through its optic tube as though I was some sort of scientific specimen. "AND YOU MUST HELP US."

Go to **441**.

419

The bridge! The door to it opened as I palmed the button in its center, and then stepped through.

There were Daleks there, their optical tubes swinging about. "IN-TRU-DER!" one shrilled, which set all the rest of them off. "IN-TRU-DER! EX-TER-MIN-ATE! EX-TER-MIN-ATE!"

You may surrender at **401**. *Or you may jump toward the center of the bridge, hoping the Daleks will get in one another's way, giving you an opportunity to reach a lift (for example, the lift built into the dais at the center of the bridge) at* **402**.

Or you may turn and try to go back out the door you just came through at **404**. *If you are carrying a bomb taken from the ship's armory and you wish to use it on the bridge, go to* **424**.

420

When the lift door opened, I stepped into the lower deck passageway. I breathed a sigh of relief, as there were no Daleks about.

But there would be very soon. They were probably

moving down the lifts from the bridge at this very instant. I looked about. The airlock door out was…yes! There!

"EX-TER-MIN-ATE! EX-TER-MIN-ATE!" Daleks were filling the passageway behind me, gliding forward on silent, invisible wheels. "IN-TRU-DER! EX-TER-MIN-ATE!"

They were closing in!

Surrender at **401**, *or keep running at* **423**.

421

I sprinted up the ramp to the dais in the center of the room, Daleks milling after me. When I stepped on the plate in the middle of the dais, the platform dropped away, carrying me with it. For one horrible moment, I thought the Daleks were going to fire, bridge or no bridge. Then I was safely below the bridge deck, dropping into comforting darkness.

Comforting? In the dim and cable-tangled space where I landed, I could make out the familiar, sinister shape of a Dalek.

Go to **S24**, *in* **Exploring the Ship**.

422

I dashed across the bridge to the nearest lift door as blue fire crackled in the air above me. I dove, somersaulted across the deck, and came up at the door. When my hand hit the button, the door opened, and I fell through. For one nightmarish split second, I lay on the floor of the lift, watching the Daleks advance toward me. Then the door hissed shut, and I felt the car dropping to the lower level.

Though I was safe for a moment, the alarm would certainly be out now.

If you are seeking to escape the ship entirely, go to **420**.
If you have another destination on the lower deck, go to
Exploring the Ship, *to the passageway description of*
S5.

423

I kept running.

"EX-TER-MIN-ATE!"

Blue fire caught and engulfed me. I slammed into a curving bulkhead, clawing weakly at the metal wall as I slid slowly down onto the deck. Darkness whirled, then exploded inside my head, and I hurtled over into nothingness.

Go to **430**.

424

I still had one of the bombs from the armory. Reaching into my pocket for it, I knew I'd have to guess at the timer setting. The Daleks had hesitated, but that wouldn't last for long. One shot from a particle gun and I would die with the bomb in my hand.

I twisted the knob for as tiny a fraction of the setting as I could. As my target, I chose a particularly complex tangle of wiring, screens, and instrument consoles close by the railed balcony where the Dalek commander stood. Blue fire burned the air around me, but I was already rolling across the deck toward a door.

The explosion was a great, nearly silent flare of sun-brilliant heat and light erupting from instrument consoles that sagged and puddled in the glare. The bridge lights died, then flickered on again as auxiliary systems cut in. Good. My sabotage had not killed the power for lights, doors, or lifts. Silhouetted against the light, Daleks toppled, melted, and burned in a Dantean nightmare of white heat. Billowing clouds of acrid smoke filled the bridge.

I saw one Dalek afire, two more lying on the deck, and a great ruin in the corner where I'd thrown the bomb. The rest of the bridge seemed intact, except for a wild noise and confusion. This was my chance to make an exit.

As several Daleks moved toward me with grim purpose, I zigzagged past a ruin of instrument consoles and ran toward a door.

Make a Saving Roll against your DEX. *If it succeeds, you may go either to a bridge lift at* **443** *or a door to the passageway on Level 2 at* **444**. *If it fails, go to* **404**.

425

The Daleks closed in. One of them seemed to be a spokesman, perhaps their commander.

"YOU HAVE CAUSED THE DA-LEKS A GREAT DEAL OF TROU-BLE, DOC-TOR. YOU WILL NOT BE A THREAT TO THE DA-LEKS A-GAIN."

Then they hustled me off to a room on the second level, where a pair of Daleks seemed to have been waiting for me.

It looked like it was interrogation time.

If you have already had a conversation with a pair of Daleks in the room labled S22, go now to **446**. *Otherwise, go to* **408**.

426

I skidded to a stop alongside an inboard door. This was the way back into the bridge!

The Daleks rounded the curving passageway. "EX-TER-MIN-ATE! EX-TER-MIN-ATE!" I saw one's gun swinging about to center on my chest.

You may surrender at **401**. *Otherwise, roll 2D6. If the result is 9 or more, go to* **404**. *If the result is 8 or less, go to* **406**.

427

A Dalek manipulator swung out at me with whistling viciousness, narrowly missing my head. I stepped back again, and ducked as the manipulator swung back, smashing into some conduit piping with a boiler room clash and a shower of sparks.

Make a Saving Roll against your DEX. *If it succeeds, try to work your way back around to the elevator at* **431**, *or try to delay the Dalek by finding something you can sabotage quickly at* **429**. *If it fails, go to* **447**.

428

You must move in close to attach the explosive packet to the Dalek. You need DEX more than anything else in this encounter.

First, make a Saving Roll against your DEX score. If it succeeds, you win a bonus modifier of −2. If you fail, the modifier is +3.

Then, roll 1D6 + 1 for the Dalek's actions, and subtract this from your DEX score.This is the Dalek's roll. Then roll 2D6, and apply the modifier. If this result is equal to or less than the Dalek's roll, you have succeeded in placing the explosive without being hit by the Dalek. If it is greater, you have failed.

If you are successful, go to **432**. *If you fail, go to* **439**.

429

I scrambled backward, just barely maintaining my balance on the slick steel deck. As I righted myself, my hand fell on a bundle of wires protruding from a circuit junction of some sort, giving me a flash of inspiration. Closing my fingers on the wires, I yanked as hard as I could.

Sparks showered across the narrow passage between the generators, followed by a cascade of fire and acrid smoke that sent eerily dancing shadows across the overhead. The Dalek stopped dead in the midst of the commotion, jolted by current from a snapping loose wire.

I found more wires, and yanked again, then turned and ran for the lift.

Go to **399**.

430

As a Time Lord, you have a chance to regenerate before you die, repairing the damage done to your body by the Dalek beam, and once again escaping death.

You must regenerate or die. Roll 2D6. Subtract 1 from the result if you have an MNT of 9, 2 if you have an MNT of 10, and 4 if you have an MNT of 11.

If the roll is 6 or less, you have regenerated. If you have had a conversation aboard the ship about the Dalek purpose on Gathwyr, go to **450**. *If you have NOT had such a conversation, go to* **448**. *If the roll is 7 or more, go to* **113**.

431

There was the lift again, the way back up to the bridge. If I could just reach it before the Dalek came at me again. Just then, the black horror reappeared, its gun trained on me. There, in front of the lift, I would be a sitting duck.

Quick! Before the Dalek could get a clear line of fire, I dove for the lift door.

Make a Saving Roll against your DEX. *If the roll fails, go to* **404**. *If it succeeds, go to* **399**.

432

I ducked under another whistling swing of that robot arm, and slapped the explosive into place on the Dalek's chest, close by the arm, where it couldn't reach. I jumped back as the Dalek scrabbled helplessly at itself. The explosion was a soul-jarring cascade of heat and light that sent me reeling back, my hands up over my eyes to shield them from the glare.

The fire fountain subsided, leaving not much but a memory of the Dalek behind. The deck was seared and blackened, and there was damage to the wiring and generators under the spot where the creature had stood.

I hurried past the smoking ruin to the lift.

Go to **399**.

433

It was not so much an explosion as an intense eruption of heat, as though someone had transferred a bit of star mass into the midst of the engine room. Machinery melted and flowed sluggishly into molten puddles on the deck. The Dalek was in flames. Acrid, billowing clouds of smoke filled the place, blocking my vision.

I made my way toward the lift, guided by the light from small emergency indicators still shining among the shadows of the dead power plant machinery. That meant emergency power systems must still be operating, including those for the lift and its power doors.

There was nowhere to go but the bridge, but what would happen to me when I got there?

With the fumes growing heavier around me, burning my throat and lungs, I really didn't have much choice.

Go to **399**.

434

I couldn't go with them. Me? Work with Daleks? Never! I stepped back from my escorts, then ran as they nearly collided with one another in their abrupt halt and turn. Running for my life, I rounded the curved passageway.

Go to S5 *in* **Exploring the Ship**.

435

I continued to backpaddle around the engineering deck, the Dalek close behind. Why didn't the bloody thing go off?

Roll 2D6. If the result is 9 or more, go to **439**. *If the result is 8 or less, go to* **433**.

436

They escorted me all the way to my TARDIS, and, strangely enough, actually seemed ready to keep their word. As I opened the TARDIS door, none of the Daleks tried to enter, nor was there a last-moment blast of deadly fire from their gun-sticks. It was an eerily strange sensation to dematerialize, with a party of Daleks there outside to see me off.

And then I was safe in the murky realm of the Temporal Vortex.

You may recover STR *and* END *lost from wounds and fatigue (but not regeneration), then go to* **375**.

437

Men and women staggered from the room, covering their faces with their hands against the smoke, coughing and with eyes streaming. There were an older man and woman, a girl who couldn't have been more than fifteen, and a very young man. But Harry and Sarah were not among them.

I stopped the sandy-haired young man, whose clothes weren't much more than rags. "Who are you?"

"I'm Savron," he said. "And this is my family...my father, Marikan, and my mother and sister."

"But what are you doing here?"

Marikan, a grim-looking man with a square-cut, greying beard answered. "We were taken by the Masters to force my other son to work for them."

"Your son..."

"He's with the rebels outside Tharesti. His name is Elanin."

"Elanin?"

"Yes. He's with a man called Latham. They've been fighting against the Masters. If we don't get to them, the Masters may make Elanin betray the rebels!"

I nodded. "I understand. We'll get you out. But first, have you seen two strangers, a man and a woman?"

Marikan shook his head. "We haven't seen anybody else since the Masters locked us in here. Perhaps they're in another room."

The man might be right, but how was I going to find my friends with four extra people now in my charge? I couldn't turn them loose aboard a Dalek space ship, and they probably wouldn't last long on their own.

If you still have another explosive charge from the armory, you may choose to open the sealed room next to this one at S21 by going to **449**. *Or you may lead the party out of the ship at* **451**.

438

The door hissed open, and I tumbled through. Though I was safe, it was only for the moment. Even now, I could hear the Daleks on the other side of the door, which would be sliding open momentarily.

I turned and ran. Behind me, Daleks filled the passageway, and I heard their shrill battle cry, "EX-TER-MIN-ATE! EX-TER-MIN-ATE!"

Go to **406**.

439

The manipulator arm swung around with a whistle and a thwack that sent me flopping back into the instrumentation. I lay there, struggling feebly against a crushing pain in my back and chest, and realized that the bomb was set to go off, with me lying on top of it!

Before I could do anything about this singularly distressing state of affairs, there was a blinding explosion that seemed to burn and disintegrate all space.

Even a Time Lord cannot regenerate after being blown to atoms. Regrettably, The Doctor has been virtually disintegrated by the force of the explosion, and this adventure is at an end. Go to **541**.

440

A woman's form groped through the smoke, followed by a man.

"Sarah! Harry!"

"Doctor!" Sarah tumbled into my arms, sobbing with relief. Harry's face was split with a bigger idiotic grin than usual. For a change, I was delighted to see it.

"Come on, you two. Time for reunions later. Let's get out of here, shall we?

If you have another packet of explosives with you (and if you have not already done so), you may choose to open the door next to this one at S20 in the same way. Go to **453**. *If you wish to escape from the ship immediately, go to* **455**.

441

As we walked that dust-dry valley, I saw at once what the Daleks feared here. The valley floor was littered with scraps of decayed and crumbling metal, fragments of machines that had occupied the spot tens of centuries before. In many cases, the metal had dissolved completely, leaving only a fossile-crisp impression in the hard-baked mud. I looked closely at a dome-shaped fragment that had a long, narrow tube still attached. It had once been a remote manipulator of some sort, just like that of a Dalek. An army of Daleks had apparently marched here, but so long ago that their remains had crumbled away into fragments.

Daleks, here...thousands of years ago?

Nearby was the wreckage of a Tharestian flyer. I could make out the impressions of its grav lifters, with splintered shards of metal scattered around them. Now, that made no sense at all. It was impossible that a Dalek expedition from millennia ago would have had the same grav vehicles their counterparts had introduced to Gathwyr only recently. Moreover, the Daleks themselves admitted that they'd learned how to peer into the Vortex, but not to transport themselves through time. And though these metal remains were very, very old, where were the signs of erosion? These crisp impressions of disintegrated parts would normally have softened and blurred away in a matter of weeks, or even one good rainstorm. No, the answer to this mystery was more complex, more dangerous, than simple time travel.

"I'm going to need my TARDIS," I told the Dalek next to me.

"Why?"

"Because we're not going to get anywhere poking about this junkyard. How long ago did this...massacre happen?"

"THIS SEARCH TEAM DE-PAR-TED TWEN-TY LO-CAL DAYS A-GO. IT WAS O-VER-DUE FOUR HOURS LA-TER."

The hair rose at the nape of my neck. It takes more than three days for metal to disintegrate into nothing. Yet the story made sense. There was no trace at all of weathering, and that supported the Dalek's claim.

"YOU SEE, WE RE-QUIRE YOUR HELP, DOC-TOR," one of my captors bleated. "WE MUST CO-OP-ER-ATE."

Imagine, Daleks asking me for help! That was the closest I'd ever heard a Dalek come to saying "please", and it had me worried. I spoke slowly, quietly. "You ran into something out here you couldn't handle."

"YOU ARE A TIME LORD. YOU MUST DIS-COV-ER WHAT IS HAP-PEN-ING HERE. SOME-THING IS SER-I-OUS-LY WRONG WITH TIME."

It took awhile, but I began to gradually piece together the story of what had happened. The Daleks had been dabbling with their new invention, a device that let them peer into the Temporal Vortex, looking for me. If they could just once predict where my TARDIS was about to materialize and be there waiting for me …

But what they had seen in the Vortex had scared them badly, enough that they weren't going to kill me out of hand, because they needed my help to figure out what was going on in this valley.

Their Vortex scanners had told them that this valley was the center of the temporal disturbance they'd detected. After subduing the local humans, the Daleks had arrived in force. But then their search parties began vanishing. The parties that did return reported that the lost units had been found… as scraps of metal centuries old. Something was very seriously wrong with the flow of time, but its effects were sporadic, seemingly random. And they frightened the Daleks so much that they were now asking for my help in discovering what was going on in the valley.

"If you want my help," I told them firmly, "I have to have my TARDIS."

My captors conferred, then turned to me. "A-GREED."

My eyebrows rose. "You'll trust me?"

"OF COURSE." Daleks have absolutely no sense of humor, but I could have sworn that this one sounded amused. "WE HAVE YOUR FRIENDS. IF YOU BE-TRAY THE DA-LEKS, THEY WILL BE EX-TER-MIN-A-TED."

"I thought you were going to say that," I replied. "Let's go."

The flight back to Tharesti was uneventful, and before long, we had landed and the Daleks were escorting me to the door of my TARDIS.

Somehow, I'd been expecting a last-minute betrayal, an attempt to hijack the TARDIS even though I'd told them that the ship's defensive mechanisms wouldn't work with Daleks aboard. (It would have been easy enough for them to disprove that little white lie.) Besides, the Daleks couldn't be feeling particularly friendly toward me after what I'd done to their space ship.

But they didn't even ask to come aboard. Instead, they gathered around and watched me enter the TARDIS door. It was a very strange feeling to dematerialize with a band of Daleks outside, seeing me off.

You have won several more clues toward solving Gathwyr's mystery. Record Clues C, D, and G on a piece of paper, then continue with the adventure at **375.**

442

The plain was as I'd seen it before, desolate, windswept, and utterly foreboding.

It was curious how regular was the shape of this circular, slightly depressed mountain valley. Why hadn't I noticed that before? In nature, regularity on a scale as large as that of a valley suggests that something other than nature has been at work.

But there was nothing to be seen beyond the shards of crumbling metal that littered the valley floor. If there had been buildings here millennia ago, there were no signs of them now. And if that much time had passed, the regularity of the valley itself would have been affected by erosion, mudslides, and storms.

There is a mystery to be solved here, and you are beginning to see how pieces of the entire puzzle fit together. To solve the puzzle, you must roll 26 or higher. Begin by rolling 2D6; then add 1 for each point of your MNT, *plus 1 if you have collected Clue A, 3 for Clue B, 2 for Clue C, 3 for Clue D, 2 for Clue E, 3 for Clue F, and 2 for Clue G. You may also add 1 for each ADDITIONAL time you collect a clue. If, for example, you rolled 6 and your character had an* MNT *of 11, plus you had collected Clues C (twice), D, and F, you would add 21 to your roll. You would have to roll 6 or higher to solve this mystery.*

You may attempt to solve the mystery now. If you succeed, go to **460**. *If you fail, go to* **456**.

443

Somehow I made it to one of the lifts leading down to the lower deck. My weight activated the control mechanism, which was still running on auxiliary power, and I started down.

I couldn't guess how much damage my bomb had done. Craft as complex as starships tend to have a good many independent back-up systems. Nevertheless, my sabotage had certainly thrown a very large wrench into the Dalek plans. And so, now what?

Go to the passageway at **S4** *in* **Exploring the Ship** *to continue exploring. If you prefer to try to escape from the ship by finding the airlock, go to* **420**.

444

I leaped for the doorway to the upper level corridor. There was still emergency power on the bridge, and so doors, lifts, and some lights were working. I slapped the button and stepped through the door.

Go to **406**.

445

The valley was a junkyard of ancient remnants half-hidden in the dust of centuries. Where heavy metal objects had once stood, there were only clear impressions in the ground, with bits of metal scattered all over the landscape.

As I stooped and studied one peculiar, dome-shaped scrap with a slender tube extending from one side, my blood ran chill and rising hairs pricked at the back of my neck. This was the skeletal remnant of a Dalek. I looked into the long-dead optic sensor, and knew there could be no doubt. Though this had been a Dalek, centuries, even tens of centuries, must have passed since the metal carcass had fallen in this desolate spot.

Or had they? It was curious how sharp and fresh were the impressions left behind by the disintegrated metal pieces. They were almost like fossils, but implanted in dried mud, not stone. If they had been there for centuries, however, the natural erosion of wind, rain, and sand should have long since obliterated all trace of those marks. Indeed, the entire valley should have filled in with dirt. It was as though millennia had passed miraculously without a single rainstorm, flood, or strong wind. The fact that the ground was of dried mud *proved* the existence of floods. But what kind of valley flooded only once in fifty centuries?

Nearby I found what had to be the time-ravaged ruin of a Tharestian flyer. I could make out the imprint of its grav lifters, though most of the hull had crumbled away around them.

Something was very wrong here. While I'd not been given a precise timetable, I knew the Daleks had not been on Gathwyr for more than a few months. These wrecks suggested they'd been here eons before; how was it possible that they'd been here with grav vehicles identical to the type they were bestowing on the locals now?

You may have gained some insight into what is going on here. Record the fact that you have won Clue D on a separate piece of paper.

If you have arrived in the valley by grav flyer, there is little more you can do here. You realize that you can better study this mystery with your TARDIS. Besides, you are worried about Harry and Sarah. If you want to return to the flyer and go back to get your TARDIS, go to 338 if you left your TARDIS on the plain outside the city, and 340 if you left it in the lower level of one of Tharesti's towers.

If you arrived here in your TARDIS, you are becoming a little worried that Dalek search parties might see it sitting in the middle of an empty plain. Return to your TARDIS at 452.

"WE DO NOT UN-DER-STAND YOUR HOS-TIL-I-TY, DOC-TOR." The Daleks made no move to punish, to attack. "WE NEED YOUR HELP. WE WANT TO CO-OP-ER-ATE WITH YOU."

That shook me. After the chase I'd led them, now it was forgive and forget? I'd never known Daleks to think that way before.

"Pardon me if I seem a bit skeptical," I said, "but isn't it the Daleks who claim that they are superior to all life forms in the universe? I mean, I'm just a Gallifreyan who happened to be passing by and..."

"YOU ARE A TIME LORD. YOU UN-DER-STAND THE WOR-KINGS OF THE TEM-POR-AL VOR-TEX."

"Well, I wouldn't exactly call myself an expert, though I do know the Vortex like the back of my hand..."

"YOU WILL CO-OP-ER-ATE WITH THE DA-LEKS OR YOUR COM-PAN-IONS WILL BE EX-TER-MIN-A-TED."

Ah! That was more like the Daleks I knew. "There's no need to get nasty now, is there? What is it you want?"

"WE HAVE EN-COUN-TERED A PLACE WHERE A GATE-WAY HAS O-PENED IN-TO THE VOR-TEX."

"What! From this universe?"

"AF-FIR-MA-TIVE."

This was indeed serious. It sounded like the Daleks had stumbled on an entropic drain, a kind of crack between dimensions. If that were so, the universe itself might be threatened.

"Where is this gateway?"

"IN THE MOUN-TAINS WEST OF THIS CI-TY. WE WILL TAKE YOU THERE."

"Good. We haven't a moment to spare."

Go to **418**.

447

The manipulator collided with my skull in an explosion of light and pain. Then it was as though I were falling... into...darkness...

As a Time Lord, you may attempt to regenerate your body before you die, repairing the damage done to your skull and once again escaping death. You must regenerate or die. Roll 2D6. Subtract 1 from the roll if you have an MNT of 10, 2 if you have an MNT of 11, or 4 if you have an MNT of 12. If the result is 8 or more, your regeneration attempt has failed. Go to **113**. *If it is is 7 or less, you have regenerated. If you have not yet had a conversation with Daleks about what they are doing on Gathwyr, go to* **448**. *If you have already had that conversation and know what they are doing here and what they want you to do, go to* **450**.

448

The universe steadied, cleared, grew light once more.

I had made it! I was still alive!

I dragged a heavy hand up to my face, feeling hair and nose and chin. It even felt as though I'd managed to control the regeneration process this time. Here were the same noble brow, the same firm, commanding chin. I wasn't as pleased to find the same nose, but there wasn't a lot I could do about that.

I also felt the same inside. My mind was sharp and clear, not muddled with the fuzziness so often characteristic of hurried regenerations.

But where was I? When I dared open my eyes, it was to find myself lying on a table in a harsh-lit room. Standing over me were a pair of Daleks.

"Oh...how do you do?" I said cheerfully. "I'm The Doctor."

264

"THE SUB-JECT SEEMS TO BE RE-COV-ER-ING FROM THE EF-FECTS OF RE-GEN-ER-A-TION." The speaker was studying some electronic monitoring instruments up behind my head.

"You're Daleks, aren't you? What are you doing on Wyrgath?"

They ignored me. "IS THERE DAM-AGE?"

"THERE IS CON-SI-DER-A-BLE MEN-TAL CON-FU-SION. NO PER-MA-NENT DAM-AGE."

Daleks! These WERE Daleks! What were they doing here? I couldn't remember. My mind was fuzzy, confused.

I decided to throw them off balance with an original question. "Where am I?"

"YOU ARE A-BOARD OUR SHIP. WE WISH TO TALK WITH YOU."

"Hey! What do you mean, 'mental confusion'?"

"YOU SUF-FERED A RE-GRET-A-BLE AC-CI-DENT. YOU ARE RE-COV-ER-ING FROM THE EF-FECTS OF A SER-I-OUS WOUND."

"Accident nothing. You shot me! I remember…"

"THAT WAS AN ER-ROR. WE WISH TO CO-OP-ER-ATE WITH YOU, DOC-TOR."

"In what?"

Their explanation was most interesting. Dalek science, it seemed, had learned to probe the Temporal Vortex, which was the first step toward conquering time. Actually, the original experiments were aimed not so much at travelling in time as at learning how to detect the approach of a TARDIS through time and space, so that they would know where and when to wait for it.

Instead, their probe had discovered something else, and that something terrified them. The fact that they were willing to tell me all this was proof. After all, I was the one they'd planned to ambush with the probe in the first place.

I couldn't imagine what there could be on the loose in the universe to terrify a Dalek, and I wasn't entirely sure I wanted to find out.

Go to **360**.

449

Working swiftly, I placed the remaining explosive packet on the other door. SOMEONE was in there, and I couldn't leave them to the tender mercies of the Daleks.

The door dissolved in light and heat, and this time, four people came stumbling out. There was an older man with a square-cut, greying beard, and a woman at his side. There was also a girl of not more than fifteen, and a young man barely out of his teens—probably the couple's children.

"That's it," I said, helping the woman past the still-molten puddle of metal on the deck. "Who are you?"

"Marikan," the older man said. "And these are my wife, daughter, and Savron, my son."

"And I'm The Doctor. What were you doing in there?"

"It was the Masters," Savron said. "They locked us up to make my brother work for them."

"Your brother?"

"Elanin, my eldest," Marikan said. "He's with the rebel forces of a man named Latham, outside the city. We must hurry. He may betray Latham if we can't let him know we are safe!"

"I understand," I said. "I think we've worn out our welcome here, anyway. Let's go!"

The only way out is through the bridge at **454**.

450

I became aware of light, then of the harsh, grating sounds of a conversation being carried on at a great distance. Next, I became aware of shapes visible against the light.

Alive! I was alive! I had been able to regenerate, once again cheating death.

I brought my hand up to my face, and let my fingers drag across it. Ah, good. I'd been able to retain control this time, which was not always possible when Time Lords are forced to regenerate in a hurry. Yes, I still had the same noble brow, the same strong chin. Oh well, I thought, the nose is the same, too.

As my vision cleared, I began to pick out the shapes I'd first been aware of. Daleks!

"HAVE YOU RE-COV-ERED, DOC-TOR?"

What were the Daleks doing here?

For that matter, where was here? Wyrgath? No, Wathgyr. Gyrwath? I struggled to assemble wildly scattering thoughts and memories.

"THE DOC-TOR IS SUF-FER-ING FROM SE-VERE MEN-TAL CON-FU-SION," another Dalek voice said. "BRAIN FUNC-TIONS AP-PEAR UN-DAM-AGED."

"Where am I?" An unexpected question would throw them off guard.

"GATH-WYR, DOC-TOR. A-BOARD THE DA-LEK SPACE SHIP."

"Ah, yes." Memory was returning. "Hey! What do you mean, 'severe mental confusion'?"

"WE RE-GRET YOU WERE IN-JURED, DOC-TOR. IT WAS AC-CI-DEN-TAL, WE AS-SURE YOU."

"Accident, nothing! You shot me!"

"'WE DO NOT UN-DER-STAND YOUR HOS-TIL-I-TY, DOC-TOR."

"Well, that's O.K. I don't understand yours, either."

"WE MUST IN-SIST THAT YOU HELP US WITH OUR PROB-LEM, DOC-TOR."

Problem? What problem? Then more memories surfaced. "Oh...yes."

The Daleks had been probing the Temporal Vortex, which would have been bad news at the best of times. They'd discovered something there, and it terrified them.

I closed my eyes, wondering if my regeneration had been a good idea.

"WE WILL TAKE YOU TO THE CEN-TER OF THE EF-FECT WE HAVE NO-TED, DOC-TOR. WE NEED YOUR EX-PER-TISE AS A TIME LORD. OUR SCI-EN-TISTS SUG-GEST THAT THERE IS A GATE-WAY IN-TO THE VOR-TEX AT THIS POINT."

"What? From this universe?"

"AF-FIR-MA-TIVE."

"Then let's go! We haven't one moment to lose!"

I meant that quite literally.

They took me out of the ship and up the lift, then down a tunnel to a grav car port. There, a pair of Daleks, two black-garbed humans, and I squeezed into a flyer, and went winging off to the west, leaving the city of Tharesti dwindling astern.

The trip took minutes even at what must have been a speed of hundreds of miles per hour. Because of the sea of fog covering the ground below, it was hard to gauge distance at first. When the fog eventually dropped away, the land rose into rugged badlands extending toward high, saw-toothed peaks on the horizon. There was a valley up there, a perfectly circular, desolate valley littered with shards of crumbled stone and struggling patches of scrub vegetation.

"THIS IS THE CEN-TER OF THE EF-FECT OUR SCI-EN-TISTS NO-TED," one of the black metal creatures bleated.

"Right. Let's have a look, shall we?"

You may recover from losses to END *or* STR *due to wounds or fatigue (though not regeneration) during your trip. Then go to* **441**.

451

I led the group through the passageway to one of the doors leading to the bridge. Checking carefully, I found the bridge deserted. All the Daleks must be out hunting for me.

At the moment, that suited me fine. I signalled the little group to follow me onto the bridge, and led them to one of the lifts. Moments later, we reached the lower level, and raced for the airlock.

"I know these caverns," the father said. "I used to meet …ah…business partners down here. There's a way from this main cavern that winds down through the mountain and comes out above the beach."

"Good! You lead the way, then!" I waved them on past me into the airlock and down the ramp.

I was torn. Sarah and Harry MUST be somewhere aboard this ship, but I'd still not found them. Should I go back and hunt for them, or follow the freed hostages out? If only I could get back to my TARDIS, I might have a better chance of rescuing my friends. It was painful to think of those two in the manipulators of the Daleks.

Go back to search for Harry and Sarah at **457**, *or leave the ship at* **459**.

452

I returned to my TARDIS and took the old girl safely into the murk of the Vortex. My scanners now showed the distortion as simply a subtle warping of the continuum. The source of it was very close by—around me, in fact.

Curious. When I materialized, I should have materialized in the very center of whatever was causing the disturbance, but there'd been only that desolate valley and its melancholy debris. Yet, whatever was causing the anomaly was definitely reaching into the Vortex. I studied the TARDIS instruments carefully. Yes! There was a severe strain in the space-time fabric, and a small but measurable flow of entropy from that empty valley into the Vortex. In the few minutes I'd been out there, I must have aged a bit faster than normal. I checked the TARDIS master clock. Yes! It had FELT like I'd been outside in that valley for perhaps fifteen minutes, but within the TARDIS, at most, a few seconds had passed.

The remnants of the Daleks out there suggested that periodically—and unpredictably—the entropic flow increased a thousand-fold or a million- or billion-fold. When that happened, objects—be they Daleks or people—aged a thousand years in a few moments of time.

Now, what could warp time that badly? A black hole could, of course. If there were a black hole in that valley, however, the entire planet would have fallen in and vanished from space within microseconds of the hole's appearance. The TARDIS could, for short periods. So could a sufficiently powerful interstitial time-space transmitter such as a Tom-Tit. The Master—not these self-styled Dalek Masters, but THE Master—had once done something like that at Cambridge during one of my earlier regenerations.

Think, Doctor, Think!

You have a chance at understanding what is going on, now that you are beginning to see and reason out parts of the puzzle. To solve it, you must roll 26 or higher. Begin by rolling 2D6, adding to the result 1 for each point of your MNT, *plus 1 if you have collected Clue A, 3 for B, 2 for C, 3 for D, 2 for E, 3 for F, and 2 for G. You may also add 1 for each ADDITIONAL time you have collected any of these clues. If, for example, your character has an MNT of 11, and had collected Clues C (twice), D, and F, you would add (11 + 2 + 1 + 3 + 3) to your die roll. To make 26, you would need a roll of 6 or more.*

*You may attempt to solve the mystery now. If you succeed, go to **460**. If you fail, go to **456**.*

453

I waved Harry and Sarah back out of the way, placed the explosive charge carefully against the door, set the timer, then stepped back myself. Again, the passageway was bathed in light and choked with smoke.

A man and woman and a boy and girl came out of this room, coughing and gasping against the smoke.

"Hello there," I said. "I'm The Doctor. I don't suppose you folks would like to leave here, would you?"

"I'm Marikan, the older man managed to say after a brief coughing fit. "This is my family. My wife, my son Savron, my daughter...."

"I'm delighted to meet all of you, but this really isn't the time or place for extended introductions. The Daleks will be by any moment now."

"Yes," Marikan said, "The Masters. We must get to the rebel forces with Latham in the hills."

"You know how to reach the rebels?"

"Certainly! My other son Elanin is with the rebels. We were brought here to force him to betray them. I only pray it is not too late!"

I thought of those still bodies on the slope in the fog. Elanin was going to have a lot to answer for.

*Go to **454**.*

454

Harry, Sarah, Marikan and his family, and I raced through the passageway to one of the doorways leading to the bridge. I peeked in first. Good! It was deserted! They must all be out looking for me.

"I hope you know a quick way out of these caverns, Marikan," I said as we made for the lift to the lower level.

"Are you kidding? I used to have to meet...er...business associates down here."

"Oh, really? Cav-e-at emptor?"

"What?"

"Never mind." When the lift came to a halt, we stepped into the lower level passageway. The airlock door stood open, inviting. "Hurry up! Go on!"

I took another look around the passageway. I could hear movement down those corridors, and saw the dance of shadows along the far bulkheads. The Daleks were coming! I raced down the ramp after the others.

If your TARDIS is hidden on Level 1 of the city, go to **458**. *If the TARDIS is outside the city, go to* **462**.

455

"Come on," I said. "We've got to get out of here!"

We raced through the passageway, found a door to the bridge, and peeked in. Good! It was deserted. The Daleks were probably out looking for me.

We slipped across the bridge to one of the lifts, got in, and descended to the lower level.

I knew I had to get Harry and Sarah out of these caverns and away from the city. But to where?

The lift door opened, and we stepped out.

"YOU ARE OUR PRI-SON-ERS," a Dalek screeched. "SUR-REN-DER! SUR-REN-DER! O-BEY! O-BEY!"

"Oh no," Sarah groaned.

"I couldn't agree with you more," I muttered. As the Daleks closed in, we raised our hands.

Go to **461**.

456

I just couldn't figure it out. The whole situation simply made no sense at all.

As I rematerialized in the valley, I scanned the landscape through the viewer. Its stones, shards, and sun-dried mudflats remained stubbornly silent.

Before going further, roll 2D6. If the result is 9 or more, go to **463**. *If the roll is 8 or less, you must decide what to do next.*

If you have NOT rescued Harry and Sarah yet, and if you have collected Clue X, you may try to rescue them at **464**. *If you do not have Clue X and want to search for them, go to* **469**.

If you have visited the rebel camp and have Clue Y, you may go there to decide what to do. If Harry and Sarah have been rescued and sent to the rebels, go to **466**. *If Harry and Sarah have not yet been rescued and you want to go to the camp, go to* **467**.

Finally, you may stay where you are and keep trying to puzzle things out. Go to **465**.

457

As I stepped into the passageway, the waiting Daleks closed in on me from both sides. Behind me, I heard the airlock door hiss shut. I was trapped.

Go to **401**.

458

Marikan led us to a crevice among the rocks behind the lift tube in the chimney. "This is it," he said. "In my old business, I sometimes needed alternate routes down here. Of course, THAT wasn't here then." He nodded toward the lift. "The Masters have put in some improvements since then."

"You're going to reach Latham's rebels, then?"

He nodded vigorously. "I have information they can use. Perhaps the plague of the Masters can be broken at last! Besides, I have to find out about Elanin."

I arrived at a sudden decision. "Marikan, I want you to take Harry and Sarah with you."

"No, Doctor!"

"Sarah, you've got to go with these people. You, too, Harry. I've got to get to the TARDIS and...take care of something. Marikan, you'll take care of them?"

"Like my own family, Doctor!"

"Good."

"Doctor..."

"Yes, Sarah?"

"N-nothing. Goodbye."

I grinned at her. "Don't worry, Sarah. I'll be back in no time!"

They vanished into the crevice, and I made my way to the lift, and up. The lower level of the city was deserted, the TARDIS standing right where I'd left it. That queer disturbance in the Temporal Vortex had me worried, which was why I didn't want Harry and Sarah with me when I went looking for it. Of course, if I failed, Harry and Sarah would be no safer in the hills, or even at the farthest rim of the universe, than they would be with me.

An entropic drain is not something to mess about with, and I was beginning to believe that an entropic drain was exactly what I faced here.

I set off to try to save the universe.

Go to **375**.

459

I ran down the ramp after the people I'd freed. "This way," Marikan yelled. The others were already slipping into a crevice behind a massive boulder on the far side of the lift tube. I pounded up the gentle slope after them.

Then the lift door opened, and a Dalek rolled out. Too late! It had seen me. Turning to look behind me, I saw more Daleks boiling out of the space ship and down the ramp. I was trapped, but I hoped that at least Marikan and his family had gotten away in time to prevent any more mischief by Elanin.

The Daleks led me back aboard the ship, and up to a cabin on the second level. Another pair of them waited for me there.

Go to **425**.

460

That was it!

How could I have been so blind? The answer had been staring me in the face right along! When you want to hide something, there are only four dimensions you can move it through, unless you want to leave the universe entirely. What I was looking for was not to be found in the three normal dimensions of space, so...

I touched the TARDIS controls, scanning. Yes! I adjusted the time control, drifted slowly forward, and then the

TARDIS materialized with its characteristic grinding thump. A city of gleaming crystal came into view, a city carefully and deliberately hidden by some unknown agency that had slipped it forward two and a half seconds in time.

Go to **470**.

461

They led Harry and Sarah away, but I knew not where. Me, they led up to a harsh-lit room on the ship's second level. The chamber was bare except for one table.

A pair of Daleks confronted me there.

You are sure Harry and Sarah are prisoners aboard this ship, and you have acquired Clue X. Go to **446**.

462

Marikan led us to a crevice among the rocks behind the lift tube. After climbing in, we were instantly plunged into a darkness thicker than the heart of a black hole, but we could hear Marikan pacing out the steps ahead. "Forty-SEVEN, forty-EIGHT, forty-NINE…Keep your hands on the wall to the left. We'll be turning that way soon. Fifty-THREE, fifty-FOUR…"

The passageway branched and rebranched, and then we could smell salt air and hear the pounding of surf on rocks. Light blinding in its unexpected brilliance splashed through a narrow opening in the cavern ceiling, where sand spilled down in a golden mound.

Inland, past the promontory where Tharesti was built, the ground grew warm under our feet and the perpetual fog cover closed in. Marikan continued to lead us, pressing on rapidly and muttering about the need to find Elanin before something terrible happened.

"Something terrible has happened, Marikan." I described the bodies we'd seen on the slope. "It looked like an ambush to me, as though all those troops had been climbing the ridge and run smack into a bunch of waiting Masters. Those Masters wouldn't have been waiting out there unless they'd known ahead of time that the rebels were coming."

Marikan's expression turned grim. "We shall see. But I must find my son, and I must talk with Latham." He paused, then added, "Thank you, Doctor."

After a time I stopped the march. "Marikan, I'd like a favor."

"Anything, Doctor. Name it!"

"I want you to take Harry and Sarah with you."

"No, Doctor!"

"Yes, Sarah. You too, Harry."

"Where are you going?" Sarah had a wild look in her eyes, one that I'd seen before. I hoped Marikan was on his toes.

"The TARDIS is right over there," I said, pointing. "I've got some...some business to attend to."

I was beginning to have a terrible suspicion about what had befallen Gathwyr, but I would need the TARDIS to find out for sure. If I were right, Harry and Sarah would be no safer on Earth or on the far side of the Galaxy than they'd be with the rebels. An entropic drain could mean the end of the entire universe.

I couldn't take my friends with me this time. If I was going to save the universe, I would have to do it alone.

If you don't already know it, Marikan points out the location of the rebel camp in the woods several kilometers southwest of Tharesti. This is Clue Y. Record it, then go on **375.**

463

Through the viewer, I could see movement along the rim of the valley. I increased the magnification.

Daleks!

If you have been working with the Daleks because the asked for your cooperation, go to 471. If you have NO been working with them, go to 478.

464

I knew that Harry and Sarah were being held inside th Dalek space ship. As I had both their biopatterns stored in th TARDIS memory banks, I should be able to use a narrowed field aperture scan to find out where. It would take som fancy piloting, but I ought to be able to pare things dow fine enough to allow me to materialize right alongside them.

You have some very tricky piloting to do. Make a Savin Roll against your TARDIS Piloting Skill. If it succeeds, g to 475. If it fails, go to 480.

465

I had to be missing something. I took the TARDIS int the Vortex again, leaned against the console, and went over all once more.

Before you go further, roll 2D6. If the result is 9 or mor go to 468. If the roll is 8 or less, you may try to puzzle o the mystery of this Gathwyran valley.

As before, add up the points for each clue you hav collected: A = 1, B = 3, C = 2, D = 3, E = 2, F = 3, G = . Add 1 point for each time you have collected a clue more tha once, and add 1 for each point of your MNT. Finally, roll 2D and add the result. If the total is 26 or more, go to 460. the result is less than 26, go to 456.

466

Microjumps can be tricky, requiring a keen head and a cool hand. As I set the ship in pseudomotion through the murk of the Vortex, the TARDIS began to shudder. It was not the normal tremor of dematerialization, but a wracking, straining shudder that wrenched at the hull and framework of the TARDIS.

I gripped the edge of the console, reading the instruments. It was as though we were poised at the lip of a black hole's gravitational well, or as though we were caught in the rush of a raging torrent that threatened to shatter the TARDIS hull like an eggshell.

An entropic drain! The TARDIS was battling energy, a torrent of temporal energy funneling through from the normal universe to the Vortex. It was as though a dam had been opened between the Vortex and space, creating a flood of wildly accelerating time.

"Hold on, old girl!" I patted the console, speaking soothingly. Somehow the old Type 40 would come through this. If she didn't...

Make a Saving Roll against your TARDIS Operation Skill. Add 4 to your roll because of the difficulty of the piloting problem. If the roll succeeds, go to **472**. *If it fails, go to* **483**.

467

TARDIS microjumps require precise maneuvering in the murk of the Vortex. The slightest miscalculation can transport you a very long way from where and when you want to be.

Odd, though. The TARDIS was drawing a lot of power as we began our pseudomotion. I could feel the beginnings of a shudder, a deep, frame-rending tremble rising from her depths, as though the TARDIS were caught in some vast, cosmic vise. I gripped the edge of the console, studying the instruments. It was like being caught at the lip of a black hole's gravity well, or like fighting against a torrential flood in some frail and fragile open boat.

An entropic drain! It was energy the TARDIS was battling, a torrent of temporal energy funneling from the normal universe into the Vortex, as though a gate had been flung wide between Vortex and space to create a damburst flood of accelerating time.

"Hold together, old girl," I said soothingly. If the old Type 40 couldn't stand those forces gathering around her hull, I didn't care to think of the consequences. "Hold together!"

Make a Saving Roll against your TARDIS Operation Skill. Add 4 to your roll because of the difficulty of the problem. If the roll succeeds, go to **482**. *If it fails, go to* **483**.

468

Odd. As I maneuvered into the Vortex, the TARDIS began drawing more power than she should, and the power loss was growing. First, there was a faint, distant rumble, then the rumble grew to become a shudder that howled through the TARDIS hull and gripped it as though in some vast, cosmic vise.

I clung to the edge of the console and studied the instruments. It was as though we were trapped in a black hole's gravity well, or in a small, open boat fighting against an unimaginable flood.

An entropic drain! Somehow, a gateway had been flung wide open between the normal universe and the Temporal Vortex, a damburst torrent of temporal energy was flooding through, a wave of rapidly accelerating time.

"Hang on, old girl!" I patted the console lovingly, spoke soothingly. "Hang on!"

If the old Type 40 hull couldn't take the strain...Well, I didn't care to think of the consequences.

Make a Saving Roll against your TARDIS Operation Skill. Add 4 to the roll because of the difficulty of the problem. If the roll fails, go to **483**. *If you succeed, you can choose your destination. Go to* **473** *to materialize back in the valley. Go to* **488** *if you want to try to rescue Harry and Sarah. Go to* **472** *if you want to go to the rebel camp, where Harry and Sarah are waiting for you if you have already rescued them.*

469

I sent the TARDIS hurtling back into the Vortex. I HAD to find Harry and Sarah before trying to solve this other, larger problem.

The shuddering began in the core of the TARDIS, then worked its way more and more violently through the hull, through every quark and quirk of her structure. The vibration was terrific, a howling, shrieking, battering torrent of noise and buffeting that had me clinging to the edge of the control console as I fought to bring the TARDIS back under control.

It was as though I were caught in a raging flood, trapped in a current against which I could work, but which I could never counter.

An entropic drain! Of course! It was as though a gateway had been thrown wide between the normal, four-dimensional universe and the Vortex. Through that gateway, there now hurtled a torrential damburst of temporal energy, a maelstrom of rapidly accelerating time.

"Hang on, old girl," I comforted the TARDIS, patting the console. "Hang together!"

If the old Type 40 failed, I didn't care to think about what would happen next.

Make a Saving Roll against your TARDIS Operation Skill. Add 6 to the roll because of the difficulty of the piloting problem. If the roll succeeds, go to **473**. *If it fails, go to* **483**.

470

The city shone with an inner light that made its spires and minarets glow like stars. By panning the view scanner, I could follow the course of those spires as they marched completely around the TARDIS, about as far from me as the rim of the valley had been in normal space.

In fact, they were *precisely* as far away from me as the rim of the valley, which explained the valley's curious regularity. Someone or something had generated a time field that pushed the entire city two-and-a-half seconds into the future from NOW. The place had not moved in space at all, but it was as far removed from that valley as the far side of the Andromedan Galaxy for anyone without a time machine.

Beyond the towers was darkness, an absence of light made jarring by comparison with those inner-lit towers. Closer at hand was a building that might be a temple. It was ornately graven with designs that intertwined to become a broadly spiraling tower that seemed to mark the precise center of the city. The entire structure was lit, ablaze with light radiating through its translucent crystal. Prismatic cuts in the stone created rainbow sprays of color. If there were any one place I might find some answers, that would be where to start looking.

The air was breathable, but warm and a bit stale. Though air must cross the temporal interface slowly, there would be no winds or storms here, nothing to disturb a timeless tranquillity. As I looked about at the crystalline perfection of this place, it occurred to me that here was the living image of the heaven of a number of religions, human and otherwise, a city of rainbow light beyond the bounds of normal time and space. There was an otherworldly stillness about the place, which was heightened by the sound of my footsteps as I crossed the paved distance between the TARDIS and the temple.

*If you are ever going to learn anything about this strange city, the temple-like building is probably the best place to start. You see a broad stairway leading to the building's entrance. You may walk straight in the front door at **505**, or you can look around for a less obvious, less direct way inside at **501**.*

471

The Daleks filed down toward the center of the valley from the distant rim, raising small clouds of dust as they moved. Allies or not, it gave me an uncomfortable feeling to see what amounted to a small Dalek strike force moving toward my TARDIS. As always, they were heavily armed, and were followed by a grav vehicle trailing a complex-looking assemblage of antennae and scanner gear.

This must be one of the Dalek search teams, out looking for the source of the temporal anomaly. I was trying to decide whether or not to go out to meet them when the light appeared.

A sun blossomed in the valley. The TARDIS was not at the precise center of the valley, but some distance off to one side. As the Dalek vehicle drifted across the center of the valley, I could see the expanding wavefront of light flare outward, racing to engulf both the hovering craft and the Daleks on the ground.

The TARDIS began to groan and tremble under the batterings of a ferocious assault. I hit the dematerialization controls, then clung to the instrument console as unimaginable forces swept over the craft.

Outside, in the instant before dematerialization, I could see the Dalek army. The aircar had crashed, and the Daleks themselves were scattered across the valley in confusion. And they were AGING. It was as though I were viewing a holographic time-lapse movie, but speeded up a thousand-fold. The Daleks were crumbling before my eyes, dissolving, the metal curling away and flaking into powdery rust in a space of seconds.

And around them, the scrub brush and bushes that had been the valley's only life forms seemed to writhe and twist with a hideous, crawling animation. They sprang from the dust, growing with blind, groping movements of leaf and branch, then dying and crumbling away to nothing, all in the space of a second or two.

By the time dematerialization had dropped me into the Vortex and wiped the image from the TARDIS viewscreen, thousands of years had passed in the valley outside.

Go to **483**.

472

The TARDIS materialized with a groan and a thump among the low canopy of trees surrounding the rebel camp. Among the ragged group of Latham's rebels who gathered outside my door were Harry and Sarah.

"Doctor, you're back!"

"Hello, Sarah...Harry. Yes, at least for the moment."

I was troubled about what to do next. Thus far, the valley had been a dead end, yet I KNEW it held the answers I was seeking.

You have another chance to puzzle out what is happening. Add up the points for each clue you have collected so far: A = 1, B = 3, C = 2, D = 3, E = 2, F = 3, G = 2. Add 1 point for each clue collected more than once, and add 1 for each point of your MNT. *Finally, roll 2D6 and add the result. If the total is 26 or more, you have solved the mystery. Go to* **477**. *If the result is less than 26, you still cannot solve the puzzle. Go to* **484**.

473

As I gradually eased the TARDIS out of the temporal maelstrom, the shuddering died away. With utmost care, I guided the old girl back into Four-D space, and rematerialized.

I was back on that lifeless, ancient plain, with nothing in sight but clouds scudding against the surrounding mountains and uninteresting tufts of scrub vegetation. This HAD to be the focus of the Vortex disturbance. If only I could figure it out! The answer was here, right here, right under my nose.

You have another opportunity to understand what is going on. Add up the points for each of the clues you have collected thus far. A = 1, B = 3, C = 2, D = 3, E = 2, F = 3, G = 2. Add 1 point for each clue collected more than once, and add 1 for each point of your MNT. *Now roll 2D6 and add it to the result. If the result is 26 or more, you know the secret. Go to* **474**. *If the result is less than 25, you haven't figured it out yet. Go to* **481**.

474

THAT WAS IT!

HOW in the Seven Rings of Santratheghast could I have been so blind? The answer must have been staring me in the face right along.

When you want to hide something, there are only four dimensions you can move it through unless you choose to leave the universe entirely, which is expensive and frequently self-defeating. Now, if that something is not hidden in one of the three normal space dimensions, there's only one dimension remaining in which to hide it.

Time, of course!

I touched the TARDIS controls, and dematerialized. The TARDIS scanners peered through the Vortex, tracing telltale eddies and currents of energy. The storm, time tempest, or whatever it had been was gone now, and the Vortex was almost eerily still. I scanned…then…Yes! Adjusting the controls once more, I drifted slowly forward. Then the TARDIS materialized again with its characteristic grind and thump.

A city of gleaming crystal came into view around me, a city that had been deliberately hidden by some agency that had moved it forward in time by two-and-a-half seconds.

Go to **470**.

475

It was very finicky piloting, indeed, but the TARDIS materialized in the passageway of the Dalek ship's upper level. I'd tried to enter the room where I was certain Sarah and Harry were being held prisoner, but the TARDIS protective circuits kept making her shy away. The room was cramped and it certainly would do none of us any good if I were to materialize in the same four-dimensional space occupied by a bulkhead, deck, or steel support.

The passageway was empty, at least for the moment. I strode across to the door and touched the central press plate. There was no response. It was locked.

Ah, but the TARDIS tool kit had supplied me with a sonic screwdriver to replace the one I'd lost earlier. I directed the concentrated beam of sound energy against the mechanical components of the door, and was rewarded by a click and a ping. The door slid open, and Harry and Sarah blinked at me from inside.

"Doctor! I knew you'd come for us!"

"Well, you know how it is, Sarah. I missed the conversation. Hello, Harry. How are you?"

"Fine, Doctor. Those metal monsters never laid a...er... hand on us. Just said you'd have to do what they said, or else. They talked a lot about extermination."

"Yes, well, they're like that. Come on, quickly!"

If you have already solved the problem of the Vortex Crystal, go to **509**. *If you have NOT solved the mystery of the Vortex, go to* **479**.

476

Marikan was there, his face grim. "What is it?" I asked, but already knew the answer.

"My son, Elanin."

"What about him?"

"Elanin was the traitor," Latham said. "It was he who led us into that ambush on the ridge, he who was giving away our movements to the Masters."

"What's going to happen to him?"

"I don't know," Marikan said. "He has vanished."

"Vanished? You mean he ran away?"

"He was seen leaving the camp before his family arrived," Latham said. "We think he is going to Tharesti. We plan to attack before more secrets are lost, and before he can betray us all."

I looked at Sarah and Harry, sitting by a fire and trying to stay out of the way. I didn't want them getting caught in the middle of a war. Especially not when the enemies were the

Daleks. I'd seen too many peoples exterminated, too many planets laid waste by those black metal legions.

Whatever was to be done had to be done quickly. There wasn't much time.

You may offer to help the rebels by transporting soldiers to Tharesti in your TARDIS at **489**. *Or you may leave Latham to fight his war, then take Sarah and Harry to a place of safety before going to solve the mystery of the Vortex at* **495**.

477

THAT WAS IT! By the seven thundering suns of Caligan, that HAD to be it!

How could I have been so blind? The answer had been staring me in the face right along. If you want to hide something, there are four normal dimensions within which to hide it, right? Other universes don't count, as they can be expensive to reach and are often a disappointment when you get there.

I'd been searching for something—I still didn't know what—within the bounds of the three spatial dimensions. But there was another dimension where I had not searched.

"Time!" I exploded.

"I beg your pardon?" Latham looked a bit confused.

"Time is the answer! Time! Whatever is causing the space-time disturbances is squirreled away in time somehow, and that's why I wasn't able to trace it! I've got to get back there right now, or rather, right then!"

Sarah managed to get out a "But Doctor..." before I stopped her.

"Still no, Sarah. Not this time." I hoped I didn't look and sound as grim as I felt. "Not until I know just what it is I'm facing here."

An entropic drain can be a nasty phenomenon up close. I might be able to handle a couple of quick centuries dropped on me by a time surge, but Sarah couldn't. I'd seen people trapped by time flow before, people who had aged into dust and dry bones after a shriek and a heartbeat or two.

Sarah and Harry agreed, reluctantly, to remain in that leafy glade, where I promised to return for them soon.

The TARDIS dropped into the Vortex, which was calm and tranquil once more. At the coordinates for the valley, I set the TARDIS scanners to tracing telltale eddies of vagrant energy, then adjusted the controls to allow a slow drift forward in time.

Got it! I touched the materialization controls, and felt the old girl settle into four normal dimensions with a grind and a bump.

Outside, a city drifted into view, a crystal city of cut glass and inner light, a city that had been carefully and deliberately hidden by some unknown agency who had slipped it ahead two-and-a-half seconds through time.

Go to **470**.

478

The Dalek column descended into the valley, moving toward the TARDIS. There were eight or ten of them gliding along on the ground, raising wispy clouds of dust as they travelled. Overhead, a grav flyer carrying at least two more Daleks and a couple of humans drifted at a leisurely pace. Antennae and scanner grids suspended underneath proved that the vehicle was engaged in electronic sensor work.

I increased magnification again. That was dimensional probe gear on that flyer. It was crude, but obviously designed to penetrate the Temporal Vortex.

Were they after me, or had they stumbled across me by

accident while searching for the temporal anomaly I was seeking? I suspected the latter. Still, they'd seen the TARDIS now. The grav vehicle accelerated, heading my way.

I had no desire to tangle with hostile or inquisitive neighbors at the moment. I touched the dematerialization controls, and the scene faded from view.

Go to **468**.

479

Within the safety of the TARDIS once more, I slipped through the currents of the Vortex, pondering my next move. Harry and Sarah were safe, but they would not remain so for long if my suspicions about the Vortex anomaly were correct.

I couldn't take them with me, not where I was going. Decision made, I touched the controls.

If you have met the rebels outside the city, you may take Harry and Sarah there, at **491**. *If you have not met the rebels (or if you prefer to do so alone), you can leave Sarah and Harry in a quiet, wooded area until you complete your task at* **495**.

480

The TARDIS was gripped by a shuddering tremor that seemed to rise out of the Vortex. I gripped the controls, easing her through the sudden temporal current. What was happening?

Skillfully, I adjusted my course through the Vortex. The current was accelerating, however, and I found it harder and harder to stay on course. Then there was a blow that rang through the TARDIS hull, hurling me to the deck. I picked myself up, then gripped the edge of the console, fighting... fighting...

The current was growing beyond all reason. It was a maelstrom of time gone wild, an entropic drain in which the natural flow of entropy was funneling from the normal universe of four dimensions into the otherness of the Space-Time Vortex.

"Hang on, old girl," I said. "Hang on!"

If the old Type 40 failed, well...

*Make another Saving Roll against your TARDIS Operation Skill. Add 6 because of the difficulty of the problem. If the roll succeeds, go to **488**. If it fails, go to **483**.*

481

It was no good. The valley remained as enigmatically silent as before. But, wait! There was something moving along the valley rim. I increased magnification on my viewer.

Daleks!

*If you are cooperating with the Daleks, they may be friendly (or as friendly as Daleks ever are). Go to **471**. If you are not working with them, they are certainly hostile. Go to **478**.*

482

The TARDIS materialized in the forest glade where Latham's rebels were encamped. I felt dried out, let down. Though I'd escaped from the Dalek masters of Gathwyr, Sarah Jane and Harry were still imprisoned, and I felt no closer than ever to solving the mystery of this world.

Latham met me as I stepped from the TARDIS. "Doctor! Welcome back."

"Hello, Latham. Why all the preparations?" The camp was in a state of turmoil. Men and women were running here and there, shouldering weapons, gathering equipment.

"We're moving against the Masters. Tonight! Do you want to come along?"

If you freed a prisoner named Marikan and his family earlier, go to **476**. *If you did not, continue this conversation at* **486**.

483

The TARDIS was hopelessly trapped by the temporal current, hurtling through a vast and whirling storm of unimaginable proportions. I was knocked to the deck and pinned there by the crushing force of that insane acceleration.

The TARDIS would not be able to take much more of this before she started to break up. When that happened, her atoms and mine would be scattered across all of Time and Space, and that would be the irrevocable end.

I had only two chances. The less risky course was to try to guide the TARDIS cross-time to where the power of the current weakened. Eventually, I should be able to re-enter normal space and time, though at a far-distant where and when. The laws of physics and temporal dynamics being what they are, I would not be able to return to Gathwyr in time to affect what was happening there.

In short, I could cut and run. Of course, that meant abandoning Harry and Sarah Jane—not to mention the rest of the planet—to the tender mercies of the Daleks, if the effects of the entropic drain didn't get them first.

More dangerous was taking the opposite tack. A Vortex storm like this one had an eye precisely like that of any hurricane that periodically afflicts worlds with more than a trace of atmosphere. That eye existed in ten or twelve dimensions instead of four, to be sure, but it would be a nonspace-nontime referent sheltered from the buffeting I was enduring now. And that center might lead me to the cause of the storm itself.

The only problem was that to reach the storm's eye, I would have to plunge deeper into the chaos that now held me in its grasp.

*You can also try to escape. Roll 2D6 and add 1 for each point of your TARDIS Operation Skill to the roll. If the result is 15 or more, go to **511**. If the result is 9 or less, go to **513**.*

*You can try to reach the eye of the storm. Roll 2D6 and add 1 for each point of your TARDIS Operation Skill to the roll. If the result is 19 or more, go to **487**. If the result is 13 or less, go to **513**.*

484

I still couldn't work it out. I was at a dead end, tormented by the unpleasant feeling that the answer to the riddle of Gathwyr was staring me squarely in the face.

"What is it, Doctor?" Harry asked.

"It's what to do next, Harry. I KNOW the answer is right in front of me..."

"Perhaps you can help us with *our* answer, Doctor," Latham said. He drew himself up proudly. "We go to attack the Masters!"

"What?"

"Gathwyr has endured the torments of the Masters and their puppet Kolav for too long. We strike tonight!"

*This promises to unleash a minor Armageddon upon this world. If you wish to escape, go with Harry and Sarah to **512**.*

On the other hand, things aren't quite resolved here, are they? You can try to figure out the puzzle again. As before, add up points for the clues you have collected so far: A = 1, B = 3, C = 2, D = 3, E = 2, F = 3, G = 2, plus 1 for each clue uncovered twice, and 1 for each point of your MNT. *Add to this the result of a 2D6 roll. If the final total is 26 or more, you have solved the puzzle of the valley. Go to* **477**. *If the result is less than 26, you may either quit by going to* **512**, *or decide to help the rebels in their campaign against the Daleks. If you helped a rebel named Marikan to escape, and you want to help the rebels in their fight, go to* **489**. *If you want to help, but haven't met Marikan, go to* **492**.

485

Following my guide, I approached the crystal.

There was something fascinating and hypnotic about it, as though its inner light probed spirit and soul, stirring memories, awakening fears.

There was intelligence there. I could feel its cold and calculating scrutiny, could sense its intellect, could sense too a deadly purpose, a hatred of things living, of order, of me.

It struck.

Go to **498**.

486

"I've got to get my friends out of there," I said. "If I can help you while doing that, I will!"

I thought furiously. Latham's determination to attack Tharesti worried me. I'd too often seen the disastrous results of resistance against a Dalek invasion, the slaughter of entire populations, the systematic razing of whole worlds. And Harry and Sarah could be caught in the crossfire.

"You're not planning on attacking the Masters with guns, are you?" The rifles and submachine guns Latham's rebels were brandishing wouldn't make a dent in Dalek armor.

"Guns for Kolav's Blackies," he said. "And these for the Masters." Latham hefted a large hand bomb like a grenade fitted with a magnetic grapple. "We've raided the Masters' field depots. They won't stand a chance!"

"How do you plan to get at them?"

"Through the cave system under the city. We'll come up through their basement!"

A good plan, but not good enough. Latham didn't know what he was facing.

"Tell you what," I said. "I can transport a strike force of your best troops into the Masters' ship. If you can take the ship, and cut power to the city defenses, maybe even blow up their entire base, that'll clear the way for the rest of your people to come in through the caves."

He looked doubtfully at my TARDIS. "How many men can you squeeze in?"

I smiled. "As many as you like. It's a lot roomier inside than you'd imagine. I'd suggest no more than twenty or thirty, though, or they'll be falling all over each other aboard the ship."

It was agreed. An hour later, thirty of Latham's bomb-carrying rebel commandos watched curiously as I set the TARDIS controls that would dematerialize us into the Vortex. With infinite care, I set the old girl for a microjump centered on the Dalek ship.

Harry and Sarah were aboard that ship. They HAD to be. A narrow aperture field scan confirmed it. I picked up their biopatterns, which were stored in the TARDIS computer, from somewhere on the Dalek ship's second level.

I held my breath, crossed my fingers, and we rematerialized.

Go to **494.**

487

Just as the vibrations wracking the hull of the TARDIS grew to an intolerable pitch, they stopped suddenly. I'd allowed the time currents to rocket the TARDIS into the very eye of the storm, which was relatively calm. I set the controls, and moments later, materialized on the empty plain in the mountains.

You may try to solve the riddle of this world. Add up the points for each clue you have collected so far: A = 1, B = 3, C = 2, D = 3, E = 2, F = 3, G = 2. Then, add to this 1 for each clue you have collected more than once, and 1 for each point of your MNT. *Roll 2D6 and add the result to the total. If the modified roll is 26 or more, you have solved the mystery of where the source of the time disturbance is located. Go to* **474**. *If the result is less than 26, go to* **493**.

488

The shuddering and bucking gradually subsided, I adjusted the controls and scanned for the telltale biopatterns of Sarah and Harry, which were stored in the TARDIS computer.

Ha! There! That confirmed it! They were somewhere aboard that ship, on the upper deck. Now to rematerialize without blowing myself and them into four alternate universes simultaneously.

Go to **475**.

489

It might be the beginning of Armageddon, but I could not stand by and watch the rebels attack the Masters and their puppets alone. I was concerned that Harry and Sarah be safe, but after that...

"I'll tell you what, Latham. I'm going to find a place where Harry and Sarah can wait this out, but then I'll be back. Maybe I can help." I looked across at his troops. "You're not planning to take on the Masters with guns, are you?" The submachine guns and rifles Latham's people were carrying wouldn't even dent Dalek armor.

"The guns are for Kolav's Blackies and the traitors who helped them. We've got these for the Masters. He hefted a kind of large grenade with a magnetic grapple attached to it. "The Masters' rule on this planet is finished!"

"Great. But you won't have a chance storming the city walls. I can carry some of your troops into the Masters' ship. If you can capture it, you can cut the defenses of the city, maybe even take out most of the Masters with one blow!"

Latham pulled at his lower lip. "We were going to enter through the caves...but yes, that would give us a real chance!" He eyed the TARDIS doubtfully. "But how many men can you squeeze into that thing of yours?"

I smiled. "More than you think. It's a lot bigger inside than out."

"Doctor, you can't leave us out of this!" Harry protested.

"I can and I will." Sarah started to speak, but I cut her off. "No, Sarah. Not this time."

I had my reasons. Under most circumstances, they would be safer within the TARDIS than elsewhere on this world, but there was a deeper mystery here, one extending within the Temporal Vortex itself. After we'd defeated the Daleks, I would have to face that mystery. And I didn't want Harry and Sarah aboard the TARDIS when that time came.

It took five minutes to transport my Companions to a safe spot in a wooded glade some kilometers from the rebel camp. If Latham and his men were captured, I didn't want them able to reveal where the offworlders were hidden.

Moments later, thirty of Latham's bomb-carrying commandos watched curiously as I adjusted the controls for a microjump to the Masters' buried space ship.

Go to **494**.

490

I wanted to do a bit of exploring. The bridge ought to be somewhere along this way.

I found the door to the bridge blackened by a bomb blast and forced open. The bridge was deserted, a tangle of burned-out wiring, smashed consoles, and overturned circuitry cabinets. On the deck lay the charred shell of a Dalek. At the center of the bridge, the lift shaft gaped open, and oily smoke rose from the pit.

Emergency power was coming in from somewhere, for some of the lights still worked, and some of the instrument screens still held images. I walked over to one of the screens and studied it.

There was a map there, its contours and features outlined in green light against black. Tharesti was easily recognizable on its cliff above the sea, with the ridge dwindling off to the west. Much further west were mountains. A perfectly circular valley among the peaks was highlighted in blue, and there were symbols that I knew represented Dalek parties.

One of the rebels stumbled into the bridge behind me, his gun high. "Oh, it's you, Doctor!"

"Hello, Larik. How goes the battle?"

"I think it's over."

"Eh? That was quick."

He kicked at the Dalek shell on the deck. "We've only found four of the monsters. The rest must be in the city above, or..."

"Or here." I touched the valley on the map. "Curious, but the Masters seem to have been taking a lot of casualties out there lately."

He nodded. "We've found something that looks like an assembly room for the monsters. And rooms with nothing but spare parts for those metal bodies of theirs. What does it mean?"

"It means that the Daleks have overstretched themselves here. They ran into something out west they couldn't handle." I arched an eyebrow at him. "Lucky for you they did. Daleks are hard to kill."

"I know." He wiped his forehead. "One of them killed four of my boys. Bullets had no effect on it. It took three hand bombs just to knock it down, and a satchel charge to destroy it."

Another soldier burst onto the bridge. "Sir! We've secured the cavern outside. The power leads are cut, as you ordered!"

Larik breathed a barely suppressed sigh of relief. "Then we've won! The city defenses are down, and Latham can lead his army in!"

It was clear that the messenger had more to say.

"Yes?" Larik prompted.

"We found the traitor...Elanin. He's dead."

"How?"

"Looks like he tried to attack a Dalek singlehandedly, almost like he had to prove something."

I turned toward the door. "Well, it looks like you won't be needing me here any longer."

"Where are you going, Doctor?"

I smiled in my best mysterious manner. "Oh, places to see, people to go. I'll be back for the medals and the victory speeches, never fear!"

I hurried back to the TARDIS.

*You have several choices, depending on the situation. First, you may still want to try to solve the mystery of the valley, if you haven't done so already. Add Clue G to your collection of clues. If you have rescued Harry and Sarah just now, you are concerned with their safety and will want to drop them off someplace before you go on to the valley. For this option, go to **495**. If, on the other hand, Harry and Sarah are already safe somewhere, go to **497**.*

*If you HAVE already solved the mystery of the valley, the adventure is nearly over. If you left Harry and Sarah somewhere, pick them up at **524**. If they are in the TARDIS already, go to **525**.*

491

The rebel camp was where I'd left it before, in a wooded glade some kilometers southwest of Tharesti. When we stepped from the TARDIS, Latham stood waiting for us.

"Doctor!"

"Hello, Latham. These are my friends."

His bushy eyebrows crawled up his face. "Snatched from the Masters? I am impressed!"

I was aware of a bustle of activity in the camp. Men and women were running back and forth, gathering weapons, tearing down tents. "What's going on?"

Latham grinned. "A small matter of a debt to settle, Doctor. We march to attack the Masters and their puppet Kolav!"

"What?"

"We've endured that burden long enough. Come with us!"

*This promises to unleash a minor Armageddon upon this world. You can take Harry and Sarah and escape to **512**, leaving this world to its fate. On the other hand, things are* *not quite resolved on Gathwyr, are they? You can try to figure out the puzzle again by adding up points for each clue you have collected: A = 1, B = 3, C = 2, D = 3, E = 2, F = 3, G = 2, plus 1 for each clue collected more than once, and 1 for each point of your* MNT. *Then, roll 2D6 and add the result. If the total is 26 or more, you have solved the mystery. Go to* **477.** *If the result is less than 26, you may either leave Gathwyr at* **512,** *or choose to help the rebels after first seeing to Harry and Sarah's safety at* **492.**

492

The rebels' fight against the Daleks was hopeless, of course. Too often, I'd seen human rebellions against Dalek conquest result in slaughtered populations, ravaged worlds. I remembered those still, ragged bodies on the slope of a fog-shrouded slope beyond the city walls.

And so, of course, I volunteered to help. I'd also seen many times the positive results of human battles against tyranny.

"I may be able to help, Latham. With my TARDIS, I could take a team of your best troops into the city, directly inside the Masters' space ship, in fact."

Latham looked across at the TARDIS, then back at me, and his bushy eyebrows seemed to crawl higher on his face. "Uh...how many people do you expect to squeeze into that blue box of yours?"

I laughed. "Oh, twenty or thirty ought to do it. Don't worry, the TARDIS is much bigger inside than it is out."

"Then perhaps we have a chance!"

"You're not going to try to take on the Masters with guns, are you?" The rebels' guns would not dent Dalek armor.

"The guns are for Kolav's Blackies. For the Masters, we've got these." Latham hefted a bomb similar to a large grenade, with an attached magnetic grapple. "We've been raiding their field depots. The Masters' rule on Gathwyr is finished!"

Although Harry and Sarah protested, there was a short delay while I ferried them to a secluded woodland glade some kilometers away.

"You can't mean it, Doctor!" Harry said. Sarah was furious. "You don't think you're just going to dump us in the wilderness," she said, hands on hips and fire in her eyes.

"I'm afraid so." I tried to keep the doom out of my voice. "In case one of Latham's people is captured and talks, I don't want you at the rebel camp where the Daleks could find you. You simply cannot come along." I had no illusions about the imminent battle with the Daleks.

Some minutes later, a band of Latham's bomb-laden commandos watched curiously as I dematerialized from the rebel camp, and set course for the Dalek spacecraft.

Armageddon had arrived.

Go to **494**.

493

It was no use. Whatever was causing the temporal disturbance was HERE, in this valley. It was not underground, not tucked away in some extra-dimensional twist or an unseen corner of the Vortex. No, it was HERE. But where?

Try to figure things out. Add up the points collected for clues: $A = 1, B = 3, C = 2, D = 3, E = 2, F = 3, G = 2$. Add to this 1 for each clue uncovered more than once, and one for each point of your MNT. *Then, add the result of a 2D6 roll. If the total is 21 or more, you have figured things out...at last. Go to* **474**. *If the result is less than 26, go to* **510**.

494

The TARDIS materialized in the upper deck passageway of the Dalek ship. As Latham's soldiers swarmed through the doorway, there seemed to be no one about, either Dalek or otherwise. The rebel leader was a fiery young man named Larik, with blond hair and a fanatic's eyes. Brandishing an explosive pack, he yelled "Death to the Masters!" Not very original, perhaps, but it had the desired effect. The rebel band shrieked out of the TARDIS and into the passageway, guns blazing, bombs at the ready.

I followed a moment later, hearing an explosion just around the bend of the passageway, and then a reedy cry of "EX-TER-MIN-ATE!" This was followed by more explosions and the yammer of gunfire. It sounded like the rebels were attacking the bridge, or one of the outboard cabins farther along the corridor.

The area around the TARDIS was now deserted.

If you are here to rescue Harry and Sarah, go to **496**. *If you have already rescued them, you will want to do some exploring. Go to* **490**.

495

A quiet, wooded glade ten kilometers from the city and beyond the chill, encircling fog, that was the ticket. The TARDIS materialized with a grind and a bump, and I stepped outside into sunshine with Sarah and Harry.

"This is a pleasant place," I said, dropping a rucksack in the grass. "I've left you some food here, just in case I can't get back as soon as I expect..."

"But WHY can't we go with you, Doctor?" Sarah asked. "You CAN'T just drop us off like...like unwanted parcels!"

Harry nodded. "Not quite the thing, old man."

"Don't call me old!" I said. "I'm only seven hundred thir..."

"And don't change the subject!" Sarah snapped. "You can't maroon us here!"

"Maroon? Who said anything about maroon? Look, I won't lie to you. I'm going somewhere that might be dangerous, and the TARDIS won't offer any safety. In fact, it's the TARDIS that could BE dangerous. I'm not taking you into that."

"We're not worried about being SAFE, Doctor."

"Look! I'm not taking you, and that's all there is to it! If something DOES happen, you'll be able to make contact with the rebels...live with them. They'll be rebuilding civilization here." I hope.

"Doctor..."

"Yes, Sarah?"

"I've...not seen you quite like this before. You're leaving us because you believe you might not come back."

"Sarah, you know that anything's possible! What is FACT is that I'm going to need to concentrate without being distracted. O.K.?"

"Yes, Doctor." Her lip was quivering. "Doctor...?"

"Yes?"

"You'll be careful?"

"I'll be careful." It was a solemn moment. I shook Harry's hand, kissed Sarah on her forehead, and stepped back into the TARDIS. Seconds later, I'd dematerialized into the Vortex.

I'd not told them the whole story, of course. If I failed, they'd not be safe in that glade. Indeed, they'd not be safe in the entire universe if that temporal anomaly was what I was beginning to think it was. That valley had the earmarks of a bridge—a hole, really—in the multidimensional fabric that held the four-dimensional universe away from the maw of the Temporal Vortex. That meant an entropic flow, an acceleration of time. It was on a limited and short-range scale, to be sure, but this temporal anomaly could threaten the stability of the universe itself. There was a definite chance I'd not be coming back for Sarah and Harry, but this was a pleasant enough world, soon to be rid of its Dalek population. My two Companions would do well here if they had to.

I concentrated on the task at hand.

Here was the valley again, dry, windblown, and utterly desolate. I was greeted by a brooding presence, as though the valley's mystery awaited me.

You may try again to solve the mystery. First, add Clue F to those clues you have collected so far. Then add up the points for the clues you have: A = 1, B = 3, C = 2, D = 3, E = 2, F = 3, G = 2, plus 1 for each clue gathered more than once, and 1 for each point of your MNT. *Then, roll 2D6 and add the result. If the total is 26 or more, you have solved the mystery. Go to* **474**. *If it is 25 or less, go to* **493**.

496

One of the outboard doors along the passageway was locked, but that presented no problem. One of the first things I'd done when I came aboard the TARDIS was to find another sonic screwdriver to replace the one I'd lost earlier. I directed its beam of high-frequency sound waves on the mechanical parts of the door's lock. There was a bang, a click, and the door slid aside.

Harry and Sarah came out.

"Doctor! I KNEW you'd come for us!"

"Hello, Sarah…Harry. Are you O.K.?

"They didn't DO anything to us, Doctor," Harry said. 'They just hustled us in here, saying that now you'd have to do what they said. Told us to behave or be Ex-ter-min-a-ted."

"Yes, well, that's their way. Come on, then. Let's get out of here!"

"Gladly!" I ushered them aboard the TARDIS.

I looked about. The sounds of battle, the yammering of automatic weapons, and the boom of explosions were growing more distant, and less frequent. The rebels must be winning. In any case, there was little I could do here for the revolution. Larik and his boys had that well in hand.

*If you wish, you may leave Harry and Sarah in the TARDIS while you check up on the progress of the rebels, and perhaps win some more information. This option is at **490**. You may also depart at once with Harry and Sarah. If you want to go find the mystery of the temporal disturbance, you can leave them at a place of safety, at **495**. If you have ALREADY solved this mystery, the adventure is almost over. Go to **525**.*

497

Latham's rebel forces had the battle in Tharesti well under control, but the biggest battle to be fought was right here in this valley. And I would have to fight it on my own.

The first step was to find the cause of the temporal disturbance. It was right here somewhere, not in some other dimension, and not tucked away in a fold of the Vortex. No, it was HERE.

*Try to figure it out. Add up the points for each clue you have collected: A = 1, B = 3, C = 2, D = 3, E = 2, F = 3, G = 2, plus 1 for each clue you have picked up more than once and 1 for each point of your MNT. Then, roll 2D6 and add the result. If the total is 26 or more, the mystery is solved. Go to **474**. If the total is 25 or less, go to **510**.*

306

498

You find yourself battling for your life and sanity as a cold, implacably hostile mind confronts yours in a silent struggle of will and being.

Haggling or *Negotiation/Diplomacy* skill count for little with a creature as alien as this Kronovore. You will have to rely on your CHA, which is another way of saying your ability to bluff and talk fast.

First, make a Saving Roll against your CHA. If it succeeds, you win a bonus modifier of −2. If you fail, the modifier is +3. Then roll 2D6 for the Kronovore's resistance to your pitch. Subtract this from your CHA score. This is the Kronovore's roll. Roll 2D6 for your own actions, and apply the modifier. If the result is less than or equal to the Kronovore's roll, you win. If it is greater, you fail.

If you succeed, go to 499. If you fail, go to 504.

499

The being's mind beat in upon mine with savage force, but I stood my ground and beat back with all my strength. As the struggle surged back and forth, victories were counted in the capture of bits of information. In that first, rushing attack, it learned that I was The Doctor, that I travelled in time, that I was here to prevent the destruction of the universe by the entropic drain from universe to Vortex.

And I learned things, too. As I'd half-suspected, the being I faced here was a Kronovore, one of those enigmatic denizens of the Vortex that feed in some inexplicable fashion upon Time itself. Once before, I'd met one—Kronos, the entity loosed by The Master on Atlantis, in Earth's Mediterranean sea a very long time ago. The Kronovore I faced here was stronger, more willful, and utterly dedicated to a chaotic destruction of the universe. It called itself Kali.

I could see the creature, a whirling whiteness against a crimson light flooding from the crystal. That crystal was its home—its prison. It was also the gateway through which the Kronovore was descending on Gathwyr, on the universe, from the Vortex.

Then the attack suddenly ceased, leaving me standing there, fists clenched at my sides. I lived!

You may make a mental counterattack immediately at **516**. *Or you may try to draw the Kronovore into conversation to learn more about him at* **500**.

500

"You're going to have to do better than that," I said. "Just what is it you're playing at, anyway?"

In answer, words rose in my own mind, as though from a cold, dark, chaotic pool. "You will be crushed, Time Lord. You and all your kind will be swept aside, dust motes before a whirlwind! I will be free!"

"Oh, come off it, Kali! If you could do it, you wouldn't be blustering about it." I had to learn more about this creature. "What's stopping you?"

"I have been imprisoned here since the beginning of the universe. These last fleeting seconds before creation comes thundering down upon itself are nothing next to my patience. Already, the entropic flow is increasing."

The crystal was a time gate, an opening between the normal universe of four dimensions and the Temporal Vortex. I looked over the edge of the platform into the abyss. It was dark and featureless, a nothingness so complete that it snatched at the mind, threatening to draw it into those endless depths. Somehow the crystal was the focus of forces that held open the gateway into the Vortex itself. I was SEEING into the Vortex, without the benefit of the TARDIS.

I could feel the crackle of immeasurable energies around me, energies that twisted time and space around the city itself in a closed time loop two-and-a-half seconds removed from Reality. Entropy lost from the universe flowed past, sensed as a gentle rustling into the depths. Somehow, Kali was reaching two-and-a-half seconds into the past through that crystal...reaching into the mountain valley on Gathwyr.

The Kronovore was reading my mind. "Each time those pathetic fools probe the Vortex with their primitive toys, I reach forth, gaining a foothold in that space. They sense me, as I sense them. They fear me, and I feed upon them, leaving them dust as the time rate accelerates, aging them by millennia."

So, the Daleks had been playing right into Kali's hand.

"But why, Kali? Why, when all you'll achieve is the end of a universe?"

Kali's voice within my mind was quiet, level, and utterly deadly. "At the dawn of creation, Time Lord, forces beyond your comprehension imprisoned me within the Vortex. This crystal they set as both doorway and lock. I am trapped within it until the flow of time sets me free."

"Ah!"

"I was helpless until these poor fools settled on this flyspeck world centuries ago. They found the crystal in its tomb of stone. I was aware of them, found I could communicate with them, at least in part. Their minds were tiny, incapable of understanding, but I am patient. The construct you think of as the Vortex Crystal gives me a special vantage point, one that bridges the Vortex and the space within which they lived. I showed them selected bits of their futures and past. I was worshipped..."

"You set yourself up as a god."

"I AM A GOD!" The voice was thunder in my head, a pain that drove me to my knees. "I planned to shape their civilization, to bring it to the point where they would learn how to free me."

I looked at the ranks of robed priests. They seemed frozen in time, which, perhaps, they were. Their facial expressions were rigid and unmoving. "It didn't work."

"No. There was war and revolution. Some of the fools rebelled against my authority. They left and set up a civilization of their own off to the east. Those who remained had little interest in science. Despite my urging, they were more interested in ceremony and ritual than in transdimensional physics."

"Yes, well, it's hard to cultivate scientific method among obedient slaves, isn't, it Kali? You'd have been better off with the ones who left."

"Perhaps, but it didn't matter in the long run. And I can wait till then. Eventually, those creatures called Daleks came drawn by tremors in the space-time continuum caused by my communications with the priests through the crystal. They brought with them probes that reached into the Vortex creating openings through which I could work. Each time they probed, I was able to widen the bridge between your universe and the Vortex. Each time I widened the gap, the entropic flow from universe to Vortex increased. Soon, the planet will crumble away, and with it, the crystal. And then I will be free again!"

You may try to further discuss the situation with the Kronovore at **515**. *Or you can attack him mentally at* **516**. *There seem to be few other options at the moment.*

501

No, that broad course of steps was a little too obvious, a little too direct, even for me. Until invited in, I would find a subtler approach to this house of mysteries.

There was a side door. It was closed and would have been almost invisible if not for the smaller flight of steps that wound up to it across the face of the temple. I climbed the steps, examined the smooth surface of the door, then applied my sonic screwdriver. In a moment, it slid noiselessly open.

It was dark inside, except for a vague blue glow coming from somewhere below. I seemed to be in a kind of railed gallery that circled a vast, open space. Dimensionally transcendent, I said to myself. Like the TARDIS, the building was larger inside than out. Curiouser and curiouser, said Alice.

I could not see the floor of the room. Instead, looking over the edge of the balcony, I seemed to be looking down into an infinite grey nothingness that was at once endless and palpable. The void was bridged by four slender walkways that arched across to meet at a central platform hung suspended at the point where they all met. The light was coming from there.

There were also people present, robed and hooded figures whose shadows were etched on the platform in a pinwheel radiating from that central blue light. They seemed to be engaged in some type of devotional, their hands outstretched, the air filled with a dirgelike chant. The object of their devotion was an upright pillar of glowing crystal, more than two meters tall, faceted and gleaming. The light inside the crystal seemed to pulse wth vibrant life like a coiled and powerful serpent waiting to devour the score of people that encircled it.

The words "Vortex Crystal" came unbidden to mind, and the hairs on the back of my neck rose.

You may remember having seen something like this before. Make a Saving Roll against your MNT. *If it succeeds, you remember. Go to* **502**. *If it fails, go to* **503**.

502

I remembered...the crystal...a super-human entity living within a crystal...the Vortex...

Yes! Of course! The Kronovores!

Once before, in an earlier regeneration, I'd met a creature known as a Kronovore, an entity called Kronos who was held prisoner in a crystal worshipped by the priesthood of Minoan Atlantis on Earth, thousands of years ago. The interference of The Master—the REAL Master and not these upstart, would-be Dalek Masters—had set Kronos against Atlantis and brought that Mediterranean civilization down in the flame and ruin that later ages attributed to the volcanic explosion of the island called Thera. I had managed to liberate Kronos. The true habitat of Kronovores is the Space-Time Vortex, where in some incomprehensible way they actually feed upon Time itself. I've often wondered if universal entropy—the fact that you can never break even in thermodynamics—couldn't be attributed at least in part to Kronovores nibbling around the edges of Time.

The crystal that once held Kronos prisoner had had only a partial existence in normal Space-Time. Its higher-dimensional extrusions had extended into the Vortex. Through the means of the crystal, the priests of Atlantis had been able to communicate with Kronos, albeit in a rather hazardous fashion. He had been a rather slippery god, sometimes answering supplications, sometimes ignoring them, and other times answering them entirely too well.

Very little is actually known about Kronovores, who traffic only rarely with lesser beings. Loosed in Space-Time, they are virtually all-powerful, or at least seem that way to mortals. They can control the weather, slow or speed the flow of time, destroy mortals with a glance. Kronos had been stopped by reason and by gratitude. If a Kronovore were feeling *un*reasonable, I knew of no way to stop or slow one.

I had to assume that the current Kronovore was of the unreasonable variety. The entropic drain could not be a natural phenomenon. In other words, someone or something was doing it—and risking the existence of the universe in the process. Kronovores have their own set of moral standards. Perhaps the rest of the universe wasn't important to this one. It might well be acting reasonably by its lights, if not by mine.

How DO you reason with a virtually eternal, omnipotent, omniscient being, especially when that being may be (by mortal standards) insane? Perhaps I was about to find out.

Your reasoning and memory have supplied you with Clue Z.

If you are sneaking into the building, go to **503**. *If you are walking in boldly by the front door, or if you have just been captured by a golden-robed priest, go to* **506**.

503

The ceremony around the crystal seemed to be reaching some kind of climax. The supplicants were on their knees, the light at the crystal's heart a writhing, living thing that pulsed with the beat of their incantation.

An image seemed to superimpose itself over the crystal, and I could see that it was the valley! And there were Daleks there, as well as black-garbed humans and a pair of grav flyers heavy with scanner equipment. Even from that distance, I could make out the Dalek temporal scanners, the equipment they used to probe the Vortex.

Then there began a breeze, a gentle movement of air from the closed, vault-supported dome overhead, moving toward the crystal below. Then the wind grew stronger and stronger.

I found myself gripping the balcony railing with whitened fingers, gritting my teeth against the blast. A hurricane wind thundered past me, filling the space with its roar, creating a cataract of power and sound.

Through slitted eyes, I saw the image of the crystal. I could see Daleks crumbling before my eyes, could see the flyers lying on the ground, flaking away into fragments in seconds. The humans were already skeletons, aged as if by the passing of centuries, the bones themselves softening, blurring, and dissolving into dust.

Time! I was witnessing the passing of millennia in seconds, as the entropic drain leeched the very fabric of Space-Time through a portal suddenly thrown wide.

The wind grew stronger, and I lost my grip on the balcony rail. With a shriek lost against the thunder, I reached out to grab hold again.

Make a Saving Roll against your DEX, *and add 4 because of the force of the wind. If the roll succeeds, go to* **514**. *If it fails, go to* **528**.

504

It was a battle of minds, a struggle no less desperate, no less fierce for the fact that it was conducted silently. I stood transfixed, fists rigid at my side, as the entity's mind beat down on mine. Victories and defeats in this motionless struggle were counted in bits of information won or lost. As

I resisted, I learned that the creature I faced called itself Kali, that it was a Kronovore imprisoned within the crystal I faced, that very, very soon it would be free, loosed upon our universe, that it would suck this universe dry, leaving chaos and death in its wake.

This last was supplied by the monster, not wrested from it. It knew who and what I was, and bore down upon me with a savagery I'd not imagined possible in a thinking being. It showed me what it was going to do to the universe in order to unnerve me, to beat me down. I was on my knees, lips drawn back from my teeth in a rictus that held me paralyzed, helpless. I was losing the fight, but had no choice but to continue.

At this point, reduce both your MNT and your END by 4. Then, make a Saving Roll against your END. If the roll succeeds, you get a bonus modifier of −2. If it fails, the modifier is +3. Now, roll 2D6 for the Kronovore's strength of mind. Subtract this from your MNT. This is the Kronovore's roll.

Next, roll 2D6 to represent your own performance, and apply the modifier. If the result is equal to or less than the Kronovore's roll, you have won. If it is more, you have lost. (If you have acquired Clue Z, this may help you in the struggle. You may apply an additional bonus modifier of −2 to your roll.)

If you lose, you immediately lose 2 points from your END and 4 from your MNT to simulate the toll this mental battle inflicts on your mind and will. Make this reduction before any subsequent mental combat.

If you succeed in your roll, go to **499**. *If you fail, go to* **519**.

505

Steps led to the open doorway. Within were vaulted arches that crossed an abyss of nothingness to a central altar suspended in space. Dimensionally transcendent, I said to myself. The place was larger on the inside than it was outside, an effect I was used to, of course, but it was spectacular nonetheless.

There were people at the altar, about twenty hooded figures whose robes caught the silvery light and transformed it into gold and fire-struck sparks. They possessed a curious sameness of face and feature. All, including the several women, had shaven heads, a dull blankness of expression, and each wore a hexagonal tattoo in blue ink on his forehead. With arms raised before them, they stood in a circle about the object transfixed above the altar, a two-meter tall column of faceted, polished crystal radiating a brilliance that bathed its worshippers and held the encircling darkness at bay. I could feel power emanating from the thing, a kind of throbbing, pulsing life that tugged at my coat and scarf, and stirred the still air around me.

"Who are you? Where did you come from?" The voice came from behind, startling me. I turned and faced another robed, tattooed, and shaven-headed man.

"Hello! I'm The Doctor! I heard there was a hole in time hereabouts and just popped in to see. Who are you?"

"We are the Servants of the Vortex Crystal, of course."

"Oh, of course."

"Long ago, we removed our city from the decay and strife of the world. Why have you intruded upon our meditations?"

"Well, I didn't mean to interrupt, actually...but, say! Did you know that you folks are tampering with the structure of the rest of the universe? If this goes on, the entire universe could collapse in one big rush of entropy."

"Your words are meaningless. We serve the Guardian of the Crystal. We do His will."

I grew serious. "Oh, I see. And who is this Guardian?"

The golden-robed man surprised me. He laughed. "Oh, you will meet Him very, very soon!"

Something is stirring in your memory, thoughts of an encounter you've had once before. Make a Saving Roll against your MNT. *If it succeeds, go to* **502**. *If it fails, go to* **485**.

506

I could sense the Kronovore within the crystal as the ring of robed supplicants parted and I was led through to face it. There was keen intelligence there, and restless power and purpose. I could sense, too, the opening between the Kronovore's universe and my own, a kind of sponginess in the texture of the barriers of space and time.

Sense them? Looking at the crystal was like looking into a hole, endlessly deep, filled with a pearly blue radiance that shifted with the thoughts of the entity hidden within. Those thoughts were malevolent and cold.

"So, what is it you want?" I said aloud. "Kronovores live in the Vortex and don't usually care to have dealings with mere mortals. What's all this about then, eh?"

Then the being struck.

Go to **498**.

507

Kali enjoyed thundering bluster. It was harder to get sense out of him than it was to get sense out of Daleks with their perpetual O-BEYs and EX-TER-MIN-ATEs.

In a muddy and roundabout fashion, the story eventually became clear enough. It was told through words, scenes, and rambling monologues spoken like thunder inside my skull.

An eon or two ago, Kali had been imprisoned, though he refused to say how or by whom. The Vortex Crystal was an artificial construct of very great age, an artifact that existed both in the normal Space-Time continuum and within the Vortex. The Space-Time aspect of the crystal had been set adrift in space. In time, it had come under the gravitational influence of the world Gathwyr, where it had fallen as a blazing meteorite. More ages passed, and humans came to Gathwyr. They found the crystal, which remained only a curiosity until someone gazed into it and saw visions of the future.

Well, that was easy enough for a creature of the Vortex to arrange. A subtle warping of the continuum. Not much, just enough to pass the photons bearing news of a future day, and the Vortex Crystal became an oracle. Later it became a god, complete with its own shaven-headed priesthood. Within the crystal, Kali bided his time. An eternal creature, he could wait, remaining patient for centuries if need be.

The humans were primitives barely able to harness simple fusion power, but they showed promise. Eventually, Kali might guide them to the point where their technology might free him. The Kronovore worked with infinite patience to—oh, so slowly—bring civilization to the humans.

Unfortunately for Kali, not all of Gathwyr agreed that their destiny should be directed by the visions of a priesthood and the pronouncements of an oracle. Not all agreed with the slow march of progress. There were even those who dared say that Gathwyr had fallen into stagnation, that invention, progress, and the striving for betterment had been sacrificed before the crystal. After all, why strive when the future is set and unchanging, when the oracle knows all that is to happen anyway?

The resultant civil war tore Gathwyr apart. Most of the people had followed the Reformists, those who'd wanted no part of the Crystal of Prophecy. They had left, determined to build their own civilization somewhere where tomorrow was still unknown.

But the war on Gathwyr continued. The numbers of the faithful were grieviously reduced. Losses in combat, added to the priesthood's willingness to give up procreation for the joys of meditation before the altar of tomorrow, had affected the community's already small numbers. They had pleaded before Kali, and Kali had removed them, twisting space and time to set their city in a place where their sundered brethren could never find them. Eventually, the war ended for lack of any common—or current—grievance.

The People of the Crystal emerged at times to trade gemstones and carvings for food, but they cared little for the untamed world of the outside. Better by far was the safe and celestial city ruled by the Crystal of Prophecy and its Guardian.

And the Guardian found himself a prisoner on his own altar. His worshippers could not be prodded from their meditations to create the technology he needed. Some of the Reformists knew about the People of the Crystal, but most thought of them as half-legendary, half-magical creatures of the mountains, a mere fairy tale for frightening children into obedience. Their traders and food caravans were glimpsed occasionally, but the location of their city was a mystery.

Then a spacefaring race (the Daleks) had appeared in Gathwyr's skies. They were attracted by the tremors in the Vortex that occurred each time the priesthood returned their city to the real world. The offworlders conquered the Reformist civilization in a bloody campaign that lasted days, then set out to locate the hidden city. Kali would not allow them to find it while he was still trapped within the crystal, almost helpless. But he could use the slender openings caused by the Dalek Vortex probes to reach through and stir the winds of entropy in that valley on Gathwyr. Dalek patrols vanished, aged millennia in seconds. More patrols came with more probes. Each time, Kali widened the portal he was forging from his Vortex prison to the universe of Time and Space.

Very soon now, the portal would be wide enough that Kali could escape his bonds. In escaping, however, the Kronovore would be dissolving the barriers in a cataclysmic transformation of mass and energy that would make the Big Bang look like corn popping. It would mean the end of the universe, of all creation, and the formation of an infinite sea of raw energy. In that sea, only beings such as the Kronovores would survive.

Kali planned to survive. The fate of lesser beings, of worlds, stars, and even his own worshippers mattered to him not at all. And the time of his release was fast approaching!

You still feel Kali in your mind. Go to **508** *if you want to try to talk Kali out of this course of action. Go to* **516** *if you wish to attack him mentally.*

508

"Kali, you can't destroy the universe to set yourself free!"

"And why not?" His words, which were forming in my own mind, carried little direct animosity. There was, however, his vast and icy disinterest in the affairs of this universe that chilled my blood. "I will soon be free, and will create a new universe that is all MINE!"

The mental thunder of that last word nearly drove me to my knees. How to fight against such supreme indifference? What argument is possible against a god bent on universal destruction?

Kali must be stopped. You might try to return to your TARDIS in hopes of creating a time loop or other technological foil against his plans at **520**. *Or you note that the Vortex Crystal rests on a support on the platform, and might be rocked free. If it fell into the abyss below the platform, it might be lost within the Vortex. This may be attempted at* **521**, *though it would obviously be an extremely risky course of action. You might also choose to attack Kali mind-to-mind at* **516**.

509

"Aren't you even going to drop in on those rebels," Sarah asked. "I mean, just to say goodbye, or help them with the rest of the Daleks, or whatever..."

"I don't think they'll be needing any more help, Sarah. The Daleks are pretty well wiped out already." The last surviving Daleks were being tracked down when we'd left, their ship a burned-out ruin, their underground base aflame. It was the human servants of the Daleks that concerned me. "I imagine there'll be a bit of a mopping-up operation against Kolav's people. As a Dalek puppet, he and the other 'wardens' must have made a good number of enemies."

I frowned, feeling curiously let down after all that had happened. "I don't really have the stomach to witness a massacre. You humans have a talent for them, but I don't much care for them myself."

"Here now, Doctor," Harry said. "You can't go blaming US for what's going to happen to Kolav."

Several retorts crossed my mind, but I shrugged them aside. "Of course not, Harry. Right now, I'm just happy to have you both back in one piece!"

"Were you worried about us?" Sarah's mischievous grin was much in evidence. "Did you miss us, perhaps?"

"Miss you? Why no, actually. I was too busy to miss

you. Saving the universe, you know, and all that!"

"Ah, but did you succeed?"

"What do you mean, Harry?"

"That Kronovore beastie you told us about. From the sound of it, that thing CAN'T be killed. What happened to it? Where did it go? Is it going to come back?"

Harry had touched the particular raw nerve that was troubling me.

"Hmmm. Good question."

"What do you mean?"

"Well, Kali is loose in the Vortex. That's where he belongs, after all. I doubt that he'll bother with mere mortals again."

Still, though, I was curious about the Kronovore's names—not that Kronovores have or use names as humans understand them. Powerful creatures like them only need a physical body or something like 'male' or 'female' in order to deal with mortal beings such as humans.

Had the Kronovore lifted the name "Kali" from my own mind, or was that a name it had used once before? Kali was also a name from the Hindu pantheon. Goddess of darkness, blood, and war, she wore a necklace of human skulls, and held a sword, a noose, a severed hand, and a flail in her multiple arms. Who had chained Kali in the crystal, and why? Had Kali been loose before within the normal Space-Time continuum, perhaps on a world called Earth?

Would Kali return there to clear up some unfinished business, perhaps?

No. Couldn't be.

"No," I said aloud. "Kali is happy in the Vortex, which is a very large place indeed. I don't think we'll hear from her again."

But I wondered.

Go to **544**.

The first tremors of the seismic quake began as an almost inaudible moan from deep within the TARDIS itself, a moan that grew louder and louder, accompanied by a trembling, wrenching motion that thrashed the TARDIS about the way a dog worries a bone. Outside, stones were dancing wildly across the ground, and dust was rising so thickly I could not see the far side of the valley.

And there was light, a pearly blue radiance coming from an ill-defined point some meters off, and several feet above the ground. Strangest of all, the ground was rising to meet it!

What was going on? I gripped the edge of the TARDIS console in an effort to stay on my feet. Outside, boulders were hurtling across the valley, leaping into that now-blinding radiance, then vanishing. The valley floor was softening, reforming, turning fluid under the incessant glare of blue light.

The TARDIS instruments showed what was happening. A gateway had opened through unseen dimensions and directly into the Temporal Vortex. All Gathwyr was now falling into the hole.

Cosmologists on Earth in the late 20th century were familiar with the concept of a black hole, a gravitational singularity where matter became so compressed under the force of its own gravity that it could wink down a crack in space-time to someplace else. Since matter and energy are interchangeable, it stands to reason that there might be black holes made of the infall of vast amounts of energy—ghostly physical abstractions called "kugleblitzes" by the cosmologists who predict them.

What I was seeing was a kind of black hole created by the collapse of Time. Time is, after all, a fourth dimension of matter. It can be measured, manipulated by the proper technology.

It was being manipulated now.

Around me, mountains were wearing down, crumbling to dust before my eyes. The sky had gone mad, a hurricane swirl of clouds funneling into the horror that was expanding now, reaching toward the TARDIS.

I dematerialized and dropped into the Vortex, only to find matters even worse. The hole in Space and Time had widened, was still widening, to receive the dissolving planet in a cascade of thundering raw energy. The Vortex currents were like a living thing, a vast and all-powerful creature reaching out casually to take the TARDIS in its grasp.

Through the viewer, I could see Gathwyr. How could that be? I was in the Vortex, which meant the planet should be invisible.

Unless...unless Vortex and the universe had become one.

Horrified, I watched the planet die in a single flash. The effect extended to Gathwyr's sun, which winked out in an explosion lost against the glare of a dissolving cosmos.

The TARDIS began to break up as the effect raced out to engulf the nearer stars.

Universe and Vortex merged in a final, apocalyptic thunder of light, heat, and energy. An Enigmatic Something was forming at the heart of the tempest, a growing sphere of pure energy far vaster than any star, a radiant orb that encompassed the cosmos. All creation— energy, fragmenting matter, the TARDIS itself—was spiralling toward an absolute and final doom.

A voice echoed in my mind with banshee shrieks as the TARDIS hull began to fail. "FREE! FREE! FREE!" A vast and shadowy figure stretched wings light years long across the light.

And then the TARDIS was dispersed across that infinite, raging sea of chaos.

My last conscious thought was that the energy in my body would make a very, very small contribution to the formation of a new universe.

The atoms of your substance have been converted to energy and flung across a dissolving cosmos. Despite your best efforts, the universe has been destroyed, and you along with it. Go to 542.

511

For what seemed like hours, I battled that surging current, until very gradually the TARDIS managed to pull away. Exhausted, I materialized at a point in space some millions of miles from Gathwyr. The planet was now only a point of light near the sharper glare of its sun, the stars a frosty scattering across the black velvet of space.

Then, suddenly, where WAS Gathwyr? I'd been looking at it a moment ago, but now it was gone!

Gathwyr's sun flared brightly, then a streamer of gas arced out into space, spiralling into the spot where the planet had been a moment before. Horrified, I watched as the sun ballooned, and became obscenely misshapen. The substance of that star was hurtling now into a blue-glowing whirlpool that occupied the point where Gathwyr had been.

Then the star was gone, and a wave of blue-pearly radiance was sweeping out to engulf the TARDIS. Automatically, I touched the controls that would drop me back into the safety of the Vortex.

But the stars were still there. From within the Vortex, I shouldn't be able to see them, but I could. What's more, that peculiar radiance was emanating still from a...from a SOMETHING that was expanding to engulf the cosmos.

The stars should be invisible and were not, which could only mean that the universe was somehow interpenetrating with the Vortex itself. I watched, numb and bewildered, as the universe was literally turned inside out, to plunge into that glowing horror that was devouring it. With magnification, I could see the shattered fragments of a universe, whole worlds. suns, and ragged streamers of gas spiralling into that sea of chaotic energy.

Then I no longer needed magnification. The TARDIS. too, was falling toward that Armageddon that was consuming creation. The vibration reached me through the TARDIS hull as a steady, thundering rattle. I tried to move, but any movement at all required an effort of will beyond my power.

The universe was dying, and there was nothing I could do to stop it.

In the heart of that glowing, central Something, mass was being transformed into energy, and a new universe—a universe of raw and seething energy—was a-borning. I couldn't help thinking that SOMETHING had gone very badly out of control, something I might have stopped, or reversed...if only...if only...

The hull of the TARDIS dissolved in fire and violence.

My final thought was that the atoms of my body would now contribute a tiny, tiny bit of substance to that newborn universe into which I was falling. I cannot say that the thought was comforting.

The universe has just come to an end, and so have you. *Go to* **542**.

512

Harry and Sarah were safe, and that was all that mattered at the moment. "Goodby, Latham," I said.

"But where are you going?"

"Oh, out there. That-a-way. See a dog about a man, you know." I ushered Harry and Sarah into the TARDIS, set the controls, and dematerialized.

The mystery of the valley was still bothering me, but I couldn't resolve it. Besides, there were more interesting things afoot in the universe. Why bother about one little temporal anomaly, eh?

"Doctor," Sarah said. "I've never seen THAT light flash before. What is it?"

"Oh nothing, nothing," I said with some abstraction. "Energy flux within the Vortex..." What I had just said seeped in. "What! An energy flux...where?"

"In the Vortex, you said..."

"Yes, yes, but WHERE...Oh, no!"

I had just caught sight of the viewer. Safely within the Vortex, beyond the bounds of normal Space-Time, we shouldn't have been able to view the universe. But it was there—stars scattered like glowing handfuls of sand, with Gathwyr a brilliant fleck next to its far brighter sun.

Gathwyr was growing brighter, which was odd. Odder still was the pearly blue light emanating from the planet, a brilliance suffusing space, entangling stars. Gathwyr's sun grew brighter as a single filament of glowing gas unwound from the star and spiraled gracefully around the planet, circling in, falling in...Then, suddenly the planet was gone.

"Oh, Doctor! It's beautiful."

I couldn't believe my eyes. How could this be happening? "I think a gateway has been thrown wide between the universe...and the Space-Time Vortex."

Harry looked puzzled. "Isn't the Vortex in the universe?"

"No, Harry. It's not. It would be more appropriate to say the universe is a small pocket in the Vortex, but now the two are interpenetrating."

"And that's bad?"

There was no way to answer him, except to nod grimly.

Where the planet had been, a glowing, growing, pulsing

spiral of light bathed space in opalescent radiance. The sun was gone. The near stars were winking out. The shards and fragments of a shattered universe drifted into the maelstrom. Worlds, stars, tattered streamers of incandescent gas, and then the TARDIS, caught in the Vortex current, was swept in toward the throbbing, living spiral.

"This is the end, isn't it, Doctor?"

"Yes, Sarah. I don't know if the effect is limited to just this corner of the universe, or if it's the end for... everything. But it's certainly the end for us."

She nodded, sad but still cool and very correct. "It's been fun."

Fun. I nodded, smiling. "Yes, it has."

Caught in pressures unknown since the Big Bang, the TARDIS dissolved, bursting outward in a spray of atoms and energy across an infinite sea of chaos. My last thought was that our mingled atoms would add a very small increment of energy to the new universe that was forming in the flux. But there wasn't much comfort in that.

You and the TARDIS have disintegrated, your component atoms sprayed across all of space and time. Go to **542**.

513

The vibration increased, a staccato drumming that threatened to splinter the TARDIS, to disintegrate it in a spray of its component atoms. I fought the controls, struggling to bring the timeship onto a course that would shield it from the worst of the buffeting. The shaking eased momentarily, and I believed I was going to make it. I was going to make it! Hold on, old girl...

At that moment, the TARDIS came apart with an eruption of light that filled the void.

The component atoms of you and your TARDIS have just been scattered across the breadth of space and time. Go to 542.

514

I was falling, plunging into the whirlwind that filled the chamber. Somehow I grabbed hold of the balcony railing again, grabbed hold, and clung to it for my life.

The wind passed. I scrambled back up on the platform, where a bald-shaven man in golden robes awaited me.

"Oh...hello," I said. "I'm The Doctor. You know, that's really quite dangerous. You ought to have..."

"What are you doing here?"

"Oh, just sightseeing," I answered cheerfully. "This is really a most impressive city. I especially admire the time engineering. Holding an entire city suspended in time must take..."

"We value our privacy, a holy solitude that you have entered unbidden."

"Oh, well, terribly sorry. Say, do you folks know that you are endangering the whole universe? I mean, opening up channels across to the Vortex—that could open a hole that'll suck your planet down like that!" I snapped my fingers for emphasis.

The man seemed unimpressed. He traced a sign in the air before his face. I noticed his brow bore a blue tattoo, a hexagonal symbol. "The Guardian would not permit that."

"Uh...I'm new here, remember. What Guardian?"

He pointed as we started to descend a stairway on the building's inner wall. At the central platform, the silent worshippers stood, watching us approach. "The Guardian of the Crystal."

"Oh, THAT Guardian." By the Novas of Pendragar, it was a Kronovore! We stepped out onto one of the slender, arched bridges and walked toward the crystal. "I'd like to meet him sometime."

The man startled me with a humorless smile. "Never fear, Doctor. You will, and very soon!"

He was right. I could sense the waiting intelligence within the heart of the crystal, a cold, malevolent intelligence. I could feel it probing my mind, claws of ice twisting in my brain.

I focused all my power to shut that presence out.

Go to **506**.

515

You are trying to talk to the Kronovore, hoping to convince it not to destroy the universe, and also attempting to find out what it wants.

Haggling or *Negotiation/Diplomacy* skills count for little with a creature as alien as this Kronovore. You will have to rely on your CHA, which is another way of saying your ability to bluff and talk fast. First, make a Saving Roll against your CHA. If it succeeds, you win a bonus modifier of –2. If you fail, the modifier is +3.

Then roll 2D6 for the Kronovore's resistance to your pitch, and subtract the results from your CHA score. Roll 2D6 for your own actions, and apply the modifier. If the result is less than or equal to the Kronovore's roll, you win. If it is greater, you fail.

If you have remembered an earlier encounter with Kronovores at Paragraph 502, you will have an advantage in your dealings with this one. Subtract 2 from your die roll in this encounter. If you are successful, go to 507. If you fail, go to 517.

516

I gathered my mental strength, my will, my purpose. I gathered it, marshalled it, then struck! Again a soundless, utterly motionless battle shrieked upon that platform. Kali HAD to be stopped! HAD TO BE!

Kali's mental thunderbolt smashed down upon me, and once again we were in mental combat.

If you have acquired clue Z and have remembered an earlier encounter with the Kronovore (in a previous incarnation), it gives you some additional leverage in the struggle.

Haggling or *Negotiation/Diplomacy* skills count for little with a creature as alien as this Kronovore. You will have to rely on your CHA, which is another way of saying your ability to bluff and talk fast.

First, make a Saving Roll against your CHA. If it succeeds, you win a bonus modifier of −2. If you fail, the modifier is +3.

Then roll 2D6 for the Kronovore's resistance to your pitch, and subtract the result from your CHA score. This is the Kronovore's roll. Roll 2D6 for your own actions, and apply the modifier. If you have remembered a previous encounter with the Kronovore, subtract 2 from the die roll. If the final result is less than or equal to the Kronovore's roll, you win. If it is greater, you fail.

If you succeed, go to **523**. *If you fail, go to* **519**.

517

"WHAT HAVE I TO DO WITH SUCH AS YOU?" The mental thunder drove me to my knees, blinding and deafening me.

"Kali! No! You mustn't destroy a universe just to…"

"I AM THE DESTROYER! AND I WILL BE THE CREATOR OF A NEW AND GLORIOUS CREATION. A

SEA OF ENERGY IN WHICH I AND MY KIND WILL BE FREE FOR ALL ETERNITY!"

I could feel the monster gathering its will, an avalanche of mental power poised somewhere in the light above my head.

Kali struck.

This struggle occurs entirely within your mind, and so it is your MNT and END that count this time. Make a Saving Roll against your END. If the roll succeeds, you win a bonus modifier of −2. If it fails, the modifer is +3.

Then roll 2D6 for the Kronovore's strength of mind, and subtract the result from your MNT. This is the Kronovore's roll. Roll 2D6 to represent your own performance, and apply the modifier. If the result is equal to or less than the Kronovore's roll, you have won. If it is more, you have lost. (If you have acquired Clue Z, this may help you in the struggle because you will recall an encounter with a Kronovore during a previous incarnation. As this gives you some leverage in the struggle, subtract 2 from your die roll.)

If you lose, you immediately lose 2 points from your END and 4 from your MNT to simulate the toll this mental battle is inflicting on your mind and will. This reduction must be made before any subsequent mental combat.

If you win this combat, go to **523**. *It you lose, go to* **519**.

518

I hit the crystal with driving force, then I was spinning away, falling into an endless abyss. Some part of my mind told me that this was part of an interface between the universe and the Space-Time Vortex. As I fell, the very atoms of my being were transformed into a spray of subatomic particles scattered across all space and time.

You have been completely disintegrated in your passage into the Vortex. The adventure is over. Go to **541**.

519

The Kronovore's mind smashed down, encircling and crushing me.

Doubt rose gibbering, helpless. What was I doing fighting an omnipotent, immortal being that could destroy mortals like me with a glance, with a thought? My own mortality confronted me, the realization as devastating a blow as any the Kronovore had dealt me.

I was on my knees, then on my back. I was falling into darkness, my mind fragmenting in shrieking wisps of unreason as I fell...fell...fell...

You have lost the battle, and are dead. The component atoms of your body have now scattered in a sea of subatomic particles across space and time, with no hope of regeneration. You have died. Go to **541.**

520

"Well, it really has been nice talking to you, Kali, but I've got to be going now. I didn't really mean to barge in here in the first place." I turned and walked through the ring of gold-robed attendants. If I could just make it to my TARDIS...

"STOP!" Mental thunder smashed me down on that narrow bridge arching across the abyss. "I SEE YOUR THOUGHTS CLEARLY, GALLIFREYAN! I WILL SLAY YOU...NOW!"

Only a stroke of luck can save you now. Roll 2D6. If the result is 8 or higher, go to **519.** *If the result is 7 or lower, go to* **527.**

521

"THEY COME!" The mental thunder caught me off guard. The light intensified, and the air around the crystal was suffused with dim and shifting images. I caught a glimpse of Daleks, a long line of them filing into the valley. There were humans with them, and a pair of grav flyers heavy with equipment for probing the Vortex.

I could sense Kali's distraction, the excitement of his human attendants. The Daleks were entering the valley again, with instrumentation that would open up a channel between Kali's prison and the universe.

"NOW IS THE TIME!" Kali's thunder had me holding my hands over my ears, though the voice echoed within my skull and not through my ears.

If I was to have any chance of defeating the Kronovore, now was the time for me as well.

The Vortex Crystal seems precariously perched on its stand on the platform. You can launch yourself against the crystal in the hope of knocking it off the platform and into the abyss below. Try this at **529**.

Alternatively, you can turn and run. If able to reach your TARDIS, there may be something you can do about Kali, using the TARDIS time controls. Go to **530**.

522

I hit the crystal with a blow that knocked the wind from my lungs. With arms and legs flailing, I grabbed hold and clung to it. The crystal swung far over at the impact with my body. My hands slipped from its polished surface, and I dropped insensible onto the platform below. Gold-robed priests surged forward and grabbed me, hauling me upright.

I found myself looking into the radiance streaming from that man-sized crystal. Behind the light, I could feel an intelligence that fixed me with cold and icy purpose. As the ringing in my ears died, I became aware that the hurricane had ceased. The air was still again, heavy and hushed with expectancy.

Fingers probed my mind. That I was in the presence of a Kronovore, I had no doubt. This being could swat me as casually as I might swat an insect. Panic began to rise in me, but I managed to control it. Pulling myself from the grip of the attendants, I reached down and picked up my hat, which lay on the platform. I saluted the crystal with it, and replaced it on my head.

"Hello! I'm The Doctor!"

For answer, I felt the being gathering powers of mind and will, a towering thunderhead of mental power poised within that blinding light. Then it struck.

And I resisted. The Kronovore's blow staggered me, but I recognized it for what it was—a probe.

The Kronovore was looking for weakness. "I AM KALI," a voice echoed through my brain. "KALI, THE DESTROYER!"

Your fall has reduced your END *by 2, and your* STR *and* DEX *by 4 each. (You hurt your arm in the fall.) Go to* **500**.

523

The terrible mental conflict faded, leaving me standing there among anxious-looking attendants. The light in the crystal was stilled, at least for the moment. It was obvious that the supremely powerful Kali was not used to taking no for an answer. My resistance must have shocked him into an omnipotent snit.

I no longer sensed his presence in my mind. If he were distracted, now would be the time for action. The question was, what action was there to take?

You know better than to assume that Kali has been stopped permanently. He is only momentarily distracted after his mental battle with you. The Vortex Crystal appears to be perched rather precariously on its mounting. A good, hard shove might send it off the platform and into the abyss, with unpredictable results. Try this at **529**. *Or you can try to slip away at* **530**. *If you can reach the TARDIS, you might be able to create a time loop to stop Kali permanently.*

524

I materialized in the wooded glade where Harry and Sarah were waiting. Sarah's reaction was predictable, perhaps, but no less welcome for that. "Oh, Doctor! You're safe!"

Harry took my hand. "You had us a bit worried for a time, old man. I'm not much in the rub-two-sticks together department, you know."

"I know, Harry. Next time, try matches." We stepped into the TARDIS and dematerialized.

Go to **525**.

525

The TARDIS travelled through the non-space and non-time of the Vortex.

"Then that Kronovore thing was really going to destroy the universe, Doctor?"

"I don't know, Harry. If it had been able to open the tunnel it was digging between its little niche of Vortex within the crystal and the rest of the universe, there would have been a cataclysmic interpenetration at the Vortex interface..." I stopped when I saw Harry's more-than-usual blank expression. "Let's just say the universe would have turned inside-out, all matter would have been turned into energy, and a new universe—a kind of energy sea—would have been the result. It's possible the interpenetration might only have been partial. Still, it would have taken a big bite out of the galaxy, eh?"

"Not to mention us," Sarah said.

"Not to mention us," I agreed. "And Earth's almost right next door, a few hundred light years off that way."

Sarah laughed. "So, the Doctor saves the Earth once again!"

"The galaxy!" Harry chimed in.

"The universe!" she cried.

"Pipe down, you two," I said from the TARDIS controls. "Speaking of Earth, I think we have a bit of vacation coming. Shall we see if the old girl's up to a bit of a jaunt back to Earth?"

Sarah gimaced. "Sure, if there are no dinosaurs with bloody big teeth running around!"

"Let's find out, shall we?"

If you have trapped Kali in a time loop, go to **545**. *If Kali was dropped into the Vortex abyss, go to* **532**.

526

The whirlwind caught me up, whipping me into the hurricane of wind. I grabbed for the rail, but missed and fell! I was plunging headlong into the crystal.

You have a chance to grab the crystal as you fall. If you miss, you will be hurled into the abyss. Make a Saving Roll against your DEX, *with a modifier of +4 because of the difficulty of the task. If you succeed, go to* **522**. *If you fail, go to* **518**.

527

Kali seemed locked in some violent effort of will and concentration. I scrambled across the narrow bridge, out the main door of the temple, and down the steps to the city pavement. A harsh, dry wind snapped at my scarf and coat, and the blackness beyond the city towers was mottled with patches of light resembling distant, roiling nebulae. From some direction impossible to define came a low rumble, like continuous thunder. Kali was marshalling his powers within the Vortex, with this city as their focus.

I raced into my TARDIS, reached the controls, and set them for dematerialization. I had an idea that I might be able to trap Kali in a time loop. If he were to spend eternity circling across the same few minutes of existence, he would pose little threat to the rest of the universe.

I hoped.

This is going to be tricky! Make a Saving Roll against your TARDIS Operation Skill with a modifier of +2. If it succeeds, go to **533**. *If it fails, go to* **528**.

528

If I could use the TARDIS dimensional transducer to warp the Space-Time field within the city, there was a chance, a slight chance. The difficulty came because the Space-Time field was already warped, bent out of shape completely by Kali's little trick in removing the Eternal City from normal time.

The TARDIS moaned and groaned, the task placing a terrible strain on her. I could feel the forces building. With a snap, the TARDIS lost its delicate balance between those cataclysmic, warring forces in the Vortex around it. I was hurled to the deck as the timeship went careening across

Space and Time. A vibration was building within the hull, building to a thundering roar that tortured my brain and threatened to disintegrate the TARDIS hull.

I fell through a universe gone mad.

Make another Saving Roll against your TARDIS Piloting Skill with a modifier of +2. If it fails, go to 513. If it succeeds, go to 531.

529

I lunged forward, throwing my full weight against the crystal. The crystal was far more massive than it looked, something I would never be able to budge normally. Besides, its mounting was well-braced against the seismic disturbances that afflicted Gathwyr.

I had already measured the crystal by eye, however, and so I hit it high above its center of gravity, and in a direction that profited by the fact that it was tilted backward slightly in its support.

I hit it and plunged into a sea of flame.

Make a Saving Roll against your STR. *If it fails, go to 534. If it succeeds, go to 535.*

530

I took advantage of Kali's distraction to back away, push past the ring of attendants, and race out onto the bridge. I needed only a few precious seconds. With luck, Kali wouldn't even notice I'd gone...

With Kali distracted, it is a matter of chance whether or not you escape undetected. Roll 2D6. If the result is 8 or more, go to 519. If the result is 7 or less, go to 527.

531

Step by step, I fought the TARDIS back under control. Despite the ship's bucking and trembling, I goaded the old Type 40 back up the Vortex currents. Could I do it? The trembling increased, an avalanche of sound and fury. I set out to construct the time loop again.

Make a Saving Roll against your TARDIS Operation Skill with a modifier of +2. If it succeeds, go to 533. If it fails, go to 513.

532

I wanted to get back to Earth quickly. Despite the gaiety, I was beset by a lingering worry.

There is no way to kill an immortal creature like Kali, and my encounter with the Kronovore worried me. Where was it now? Loose in the Vortex, or still a prisoner within some hyperdimensional remnant of the Vortex Crystal?

And the name "Kali"—was it a name drawn from my own mind by a super-being who had no need for names, gender, or any other convention, save when it had to deal with dim-witted mortals? Or might it have used that name before?

It was familiar enough. Kali was a deity of the Hindu pantheon, goddess of war, blood, and darkness. She wore a necklace of human skulls, and her multiple arms wielded a sword, a noose, a severed hand, and a flail. Who had chained Kali within the crystal, and why? Had Kali been loose once before within the universe of space and time? Loose, perhaps only a few hundred light years away on a world called Earth? And if Kali were free, might he return to that world to attend to some unknown, unfinished business?

I had a strange feeling that I might meet the Kronovore again sooner than I wished.

Go to 544.

33

The vibration subsided, replaced by a low, melodic hum. A blessed, rapturously welcome peace returned to the Vortex.

I looked down at the controls, scarcely daring to breathe, scarcely daring to hope. The time loop was complete. The Vortex Crystal, itself a prison, was entrapped in a never-ending loop of time that effectively segregated it from the rest of creation. Within it, Kali would recognize nothing wrong, would not realize he was living the same five seconds over and over and over for all eternity.

Go to **536**.

34

When I opened my eyes, I was lying flat on my back, looking up at the crystal towering over me. The artifact was far more secure in its cradle than it had looked, and its radiance burned like fire.

Somehow, I managed to get back to my feet. The voice in my head was silent. Was Kali preoccupied with something else? If so and if I were lucky, perhaps…

Your STR *and* END *have each been reduced by 2. How lucky are you? Roll 2D6. If the result is 8 or more, go to* **537**. *If it 7 or less, go to* **530**.

35

I was engulfed in an explosion of darkness, invisible fire, and the sense of a universe cascading upon me in a nightmare of pain and horror. My vision did finally clear, enough to find myself rolling off the edge of a precipice into terrifying nothingness. The Vortex Crystal landed with a crash close beside my arm as I scrambled to cling to the edge of the platform. For one horrible second, I thought the artifact was going to roll down on top of me.

Then, with a deafening noise, it hurtled past me, off the platform and into the abyss.

Make a Saving Roll against your DEX *with a modifier of +2. If it fails, go to* **538**. *If it succeeds, go to* **539**.

536

The TARDIS materialized in the normal universe near the center of that bowl-shaped and barren valley.

It was barren still, but no longer empty. The crumbling ruins of a once-great city surrounded me. At the exact center of the valley, the temple of the Vortex Crystal lay, a heap of crumbling stone and dust. I estimated the age of those ruins at a thousand years, at the very least.

Kali's power was broken. When the pocket of time holding the Eternal City had been opened, the city returned to the normal universe. But it had aged in that return, aged millennia, and had instantly crumbled into ruin. A human skull grinned at me from among the splintered shards of the temple steps. There was no other trace of life.

If Harry and Sarah were rescued earlier and taken to a place of safety, go to **524**. *If Harry and Sarah are still prisoners of the Daleks, go to* **540**.

537

"YOU WILL DIE, GALLIFREYAN. NOW!"

This, apparently, was just not my day.

Go to **519**.

538

A whirling darkness of vertigo, pain, and fatigue surrounded me. I wasn't even aware of it when I slipped from the edge of the platform and hurtled into the abyss below. The passage into the Vortex reduced the component atoms of my body into a spray of subatomic particles across all of Space and Time.

You are dead, but you may have just saved the universe. Go to **543**.

539

Through blinding waves of pain and fatigue, I managed somehow to cling to the rim of the platform, managed to drag myself back over the edge.

The temple seemed to be collapsing. Jagged pieces of rock were raining from the dome overhead, and the narrow spans of the bridges across the abyss were rocking and swaying as though caught in a high wind. The attendants were gone. There was nothing left of them but a sandal and one crumpled, golden robe. Outside, Armageddon had arrived.

I made the last part of the trip across the bridge on my hands and knees. I was too weak and the structure was swaying too wildly for me to run. As I reached the safety of the far side, the bridge crumbled away behind me, the individual shards of rock flashing into the nothingness of the Vortex. From the look of things, the interface between the universe and the Vortex was closing off. Good news for the universe, perhaps, but very bad news for this city perched at the apex of precariously balanced forces that could disrupt all of Space and Time.

That balance was being realigned now that the entity who had performed this cosmic balancing act was hurtling down into the Vortex itself.

I reached the door as the temple collapsed behind me in a pile of rubble. The sky looked strange. Once a uniform black, it now was blotched by cancerous-looking patches of light. The ground shook incessantly.

I raced for my TARDIS. Once inside it and with the door shut behind me, I slipped into the relative calm of the Vortex. There were currents flowing there, too, but not the raging tempest I'd experienced before. As I watched my instruments, the storm abated.

Go to **536**.

540

The TARDIS materialized in the forest glade where Latham's rebels were encamped. I felt dried out, utterly exhausted. The universe might be safe, but my companions were still prisoners of the Daleks. There was no knowing how many of the black horrors had survived Kali's time-twisting game. Nor were those survivors likely to feel pleasantly disposed toward upstart humanoids who came knocking on their spaceship door demanding the release of hostages! I felt no closer to rescuing those two than I had when they'd been separated from me.

Latham met me as I stepped from the TARDIS. "Doctor! Welcome back!"

"Hello, Latham. What's all this?" The camp was feverish with preparations. Men and women dashed back and forth, striking tents, shouting orders, passing out weapons.

Latham grinned. "Something's happened in the city. Whether a revolt, a breakdown of Blackie authority, or we don't know what. But it looks like this is going to be our chance to shake free of the Masters once and for all!"

"You're attacking?"

"Tonight! You want to come along?"

You may restore END *and* STR *lost due to wounds or fatigue (but not from regeneration). Go to* **486**.

541

You are dead.

What's worse, Harry and Sarah will also probably be dead soon, if they're not already. Still worse, forces that you have glimpsed only dimly during the course of this adventure will soon bring the entire universe to an end.

Well, even Time Lords aren't perfect. Perhaps in an alternate universe you'll manage better, when once again you confront the Vortex Crystal.

542

Well, you escaped the Daleks, and you've learned a great deal about the nature of the threat to the universe. The Kronovores are extremely powerful, almost godlike entities that inhabit the Temporal Vortex, feeding on Time itself in some way incomprehensible to normal, four-dimensional beings. One of these Kronovores was long ago imprisoned by unknown forces and for unknown reasons within an artificial hyperdimensional construct called the Vortex Crystal. That entity has been using the Vortex probes of the Daleks to open a channel between its prison and the rest of the universe.

Unfortunately, you were not able to prevent the Kronovore from completing that channel. The interface between the Temporal Vortex and the universe (which may be visualized as one fold within the many dimensions of the Vortex) has collapsed, allowing the universe and the Vortex to interpenetrate.

The result is that the known universe has come to an end, its matter transformed into a vast sea of energy. What has been created is a universe of different physical laws and properties where Kronovores, but not life as we know it, can exist. Despite your efforts, you, your Companions, and all the rest of the universe have been destroyed.

Well, even Time Lords have bad days. Perhaps you'll fare better in an alternate timeline, when again you must confront the Vortex Crystal.

543

You have just saved the universe, but your victory has resulted in the loss of the Vortex Crystal somewhere within the Temporal Vortex. If Kali had been able to open a channel from his prison to the rest of the universe, the interface between the Temporal Vortex and the universe (which may be visualized as one fold or pocket of the Vortex) would have been destroyed. The universe and the Vortex would have interpenetrated, and that would have been the end of known reality. All matter would have been transformed instantly into energy, creating a new universe of radically different physical laws and realities, a universe within which Kronovores could live, but not life as we know it.

Unfortunately, your victory demanded of you the ultimate sacrifice. In the battle, you fell into the abyss, an extra-dimensional route to the Space-Time Vortex that was created by Kali when he removed the Eternal City to its hiding place two-and-a-half seconds in the future. When you hit the interface, the atoms of your body were flashed into their component particles and sprayed across all of Time and Space. Perhaps this is a fitting end for a Time Lord who labored so long for freedom and justice throughout the cosmos.

4

The Eternal City, balanced at the cusp of unimaginable temporal forces, depended on Kali for survival. With Kali's departure, the city will return to the barren valley in the western mountains, aged millennia as thwarted temporal forces are loosed on that single, remote spot. As for the Eternal City and the robed attendents of Kali, only scant traces remain.

Harry and Sarah are stranded on Gathwyr, of course, with no way to get back to Earth. They are alive, however, and will survive well enough as the Gathwyrans set out to rebuild their shattered civilization. So many Daleks have been destroyed by Kali's tinkering with the time flow of the valley that rebel forces will have little trouble overthrowing the Dalek's puppet government. Marooned in this new society, the two time travellers from Earth will eventually make a life for themselves in this new society, though they will always remember you with sad fondness.

Your heroic sacrifice has saved the universe, and the lives of Harry and Sarah. This attempt to solve the mystery of the Vortex Crystal was a definite victory, but purchased at a high cost.

How well will you fare next time?

544

Congratulations! You have defeated Kali, freed Harry and Sarah, and won liberty for a planet that had been conquered by the Daleks.

Had you failed, the universe and the Vortex would have interpenetrated across the escape tunnel Kali was opening for himself. In moments, all matter would have been transformed into energy, creating a new universe whose physical laws and properties would enable Kronovores to live, but not life as we know it.

Your victory is marred only by the knowledge that Kali is not dead, and, in fact, might even be free. Might he return to Earth in the future, or take enough of an interest in the mortal affairs of the universe to pose a threat at some future time?

Even Time Lords don't know everything. All you can do is wait and see.

545

You have managed to trap Kali within an endless time loop from which the immortal demigod will never escape. You have also rescued Harry and Sarah. Meanwhile, the humans of Gathwyr have overthrown their Dalek masters, and their world is at peace again.

Nothing could be more satisfactory. Congratulations on a splendid victory!

But the universe, as one Terran cosmologist stated, is not only queerer than we imagine, it is queerer than we CAN imagine. Even Time Lords should heed that warning, for Space and Time are very deep. It may be that within the complexities of the Vortex, Kali will find his escape at last, or perhaps the entire episode will be played out again in some other, different universe.

You have won this round. Only Time will tell how well you will fare next time you must face the challenge of the Vortex Crystal.

EXPLORING THE SHIP

Level 1

The only way to board the ship is through the **Entrance Ramp** at **S1**. This leads into the first, or lower, level of the vessel.

S1 (Entrance Ramp)

This five-meter long ramp leads from the ground to an open doorway in the lower half of the ship's hull. It is designed to fold back into the ship behind a sliding door when the ship is ready for take-off.

Stepping onto the ramp, you detect a distant throbbing, more felt than heard, which seems to be coming from the ship. Somewhere aboard are power plants feeding energy to those cables snaking across the cavern floor.

Go to **S2**.

S2 (Airlock)

Just behind the outer door is a second sliding door, and beyond that, a third. The second and third doors divide a passageway leading into an airlock. The room is bare of equipment, suits, or other devices, though there are hooks for hanging equipment along one bulkhead. All three doors are open. A small control panel on the airlock wall with self-explanatory buttons allows the crew to open or close various combinations of airlock doors as needed.

Go to **S3**.

S3 (Passageway)

This is a passageway that curves away to left and right, and seems to circle the core of the ship. In the outer wall is the door to the airlock, with another set of airlock controls beside it. Opposite is a closed door with a single button set into the wall alongside.

If you want to push the button, go to 383. If you want to follow the passageway, go either right or left to S4.

S4 (Passageway)

The pasageway continues to curve around a central hub. There are three outboard doors, all closed, each with a large button or touch plate set into its center.

If you went right to S4, you may try to enter any one of the doors to S6, S7, or S8. If you went left to S4, you may try the doors to S10, S11, or S12.

You may also turn around and go back to S3, or continue on to S5.

S5 (Passageway)

The passageway continues. There are two doors, one set into the inner wall, one opposite in the outer wall. The outboard door has a pressure plate in its center. The inboard door has a single button on a panel alongside.

If you want to try the button next to the inboard door, go to 383. If you want to try the outboard door by pushing the touchplate, go to S9.

If you prefer, you may go back down the passageway, either right or left, at S4.

S6 (Store Room)

Pushing the touchplate to this room causes the door to slide open. You find a room filled with stacks of hard black plastic crates with hinged lids.

The room is dimly lit and seems to be a place for keeping stores or cargo. There is a single door leading back to the passageway, and another with the same type of central pressure plate in a bulkhead leading to the next compartment at S7.

If you wish to open one of the crates to find out what is inside, go to 384. If you have already been to paragraph 384, go instead to 397. Otherwise, you may continue through the passageway at S4, or go to the door in the bulkhead to the next compartment at S7.

S7 (Store Room)

Pushing the presssure plate on this door causes it to slide open, revealing a room stacked with hard black plastic crates, each with a hinged lid.

The room is dimly lit and may be a storage room or cargo hold. There are three doors, one on the inboard bulkhead leading back out to the passageway, and one on each of the adjoining bulkheads, apparently leading to the compartments on either side of this one.

If you wish to open one of the crates to see what is inside, go to 384. If you have already been to paragraph 384, go instead to 397.

Or you may return to the passageway at S4, or try one of the other two doors leading to S6 or S8.

S8 (Storage Room)

Pressing the button on the door to this room causes the door to slide open, revealing stacks of crates. The crates are made of hard black plastic, and have hinged lids.

The room is dimly lit and seems to be a cargo hold or storage area of some kind. There are three doors. One, in the inboard bulkhead, leads back to the pasageway outside. The other two, on the adjoining bulkheads, probably lead to the compartments on either side of this one.

If you wish to open one of the crates to see what is inside, go to 384. If you have already been to paragraph 384, go instead to 397.

Otherwise, you may go to the passageway at S4, or try the adjoining compartments at either S7 or S9.

S9 (Storage Room)

Pressing the button on the door to this room causes the door to slide open. The room is empty, though apparently once served as storage for something. Marks in the dust on the floor suggest that boxes or crates were once stacked in here.

Along one wall is a long table covered with bits and shards of metal and plastic. As you examine them, you realize that these fragments are the remains of Daleks—of several Daleks—and that the pieces are hundreds, perhaps many thousands, of years old.

Curious. What were Daleks doing on Gathwyr thousands of years ago?

The room has three doors, one on the inboard bulkhead leading back to the passageway, and one each on the two adjoining bulkheads leading to the compartments on either side.

You have picked up Clue E. Record this with other clues you may have come across.

You may either return to the passageway at S5, or you may go to an adjoining compartment at either S8 or S10.

S10 (Storage Room)

Pressing the button on this door causes it to slide open. At first, you jump back in shock, your hearts racing, until you realize that the sinister, black Dalek shapes within are merely empty shells. The room is filled with Dalek paraphernalia, deactivated travel machines, dozens of black plastic crates, racks of Dalek manipulator arms and optical tubes, machine parts, spare particle beam weapons (which, unfortunately, require a power source not available here).

This room seems to be the Dalek spare parts room, either for repairing the metallic bodies of Daleks when they wear out, or to provide shells for the organic bodies of new-born or new-grown Daleks. You wonder if the Daleks might be planning to open an assembly-line nursery for their own kind on Gathwyr.

There are three doors in the room, one on the inboard bulkhead leading to the passageway, the others on adjoining bulkheads leading to compartments on either side of this one.

If you want to search more thoroughly among the crates and boxes, go to **385**.

Or you may go back to the passageway at **S4**, *or through either of the other two doors to* **S9** *or* **S11**.

S11 (Storage Room)

When you press the button on this door, it slides open. Inside is a room filled with massive steel racks, and each rack holds ominous-looking cylinders tapered at each end. There are also numerous hard black plastic boxes stacked around the walls of the room.

There are three doors in the room, one leading to the passageway, the others on adjoining bulkheads leading to compartments on either side of this room.

If you want to investigate the contents of this room more carefully, and have not investigated it before, go to **386**. *If you have already been in this room, go instead to* **398**.

Otherwise, you may return to the passageway at **S4**, *or choose one of the other two doors leading to* **S10** *or* **S12**.

S12 (Storage Room)

When you press the button, the door slides open, revealing an empty room. There are signs that heavy objects of some sort were stored here once, and faint stains and tire tracks on the deck suggesting that machinery was used to wheel it out.

There are two doors, one on the inboard bulkhead leading back to the passageway at **S4**, the other in an adjoining bulkhead leading to the compartment next door.

You may go back to the passageway at **S4**, *or you may go through the other door to* **S11**.

S13 (Bridge)

This room appears to be the bridge or central nerve center for the ship. The walls are lined with viewscreens, control panels, and endless racks of sophisticated electronic equipment. The ring of instrument panels is broken by four evenly-spaced doors, one of which you have just come through.

The overhead is a large, blue-tinted dome through which can be seen the rock ceiling of the cavern, and the silvery elevator tube leading up through the volcanic chimney into the darkness above.

At the center of the room is a kind of dais surrounded by a low, gently sloped, circular ramp, with a dish-shaped section and what might be a pressure-sensitive plate in the middle. To one side is a raised area, like an open balcony with a railing half way around it, which are the throne and citadel of the Dalek commander.

And there are Daleks here.

Go to **387**.

S14 (Passageway)

This is a narrow passageway between banks of bridge instruments. If the pressure plate at the center of the door is pressed, the door slides open, revealing a curved passageway outside.

Go to **S15**.

S15 (Passageway)

This is a curving passageway much like the one on the lower deck. Inboard is the door leading to the bridge. Outboard is a single closed door with a pressure plate in the middle.

You can go along the passageway to either **S16** *or* **S17**, *or you can try the door at* **S23**. *If you want to go back to the bridge, (which is through the door at* **S14**) *go to* **419**.

16 (Passageway)

The passageway continues to curve around the central ridge. Outboard are two evenly-spaced doors with pressure plates in them.

You may try one of the two doors, either **S18** *or* **S19**, *or you may continue along the passageway to* **S15**.

17 (Passageway)

The passageway continues to curve about the central ridge area. Outboard are three doors with pressure plates in their centers.

You may try to enter any one of the three doors, at **S20**, **S21**, *or* **S22**. *Or you may continue along the passageway to* **S15**.

18 (Communications)

The door slides open at your touch. Inside is a small room crowded with electronic equipment that your trained eye instantly recognizes as communications gear. Leading to the next room is a door with the usual pressure plate lock as well as a door leading back into the passageway.

There is a Dalek here, his optic tube swivelling about like a tank's turret gun.

Go to **388**.

19 (Communications)

The door slides open at your touch, revealing a small room filled with electronics gear. The purpose of the room is obscure, but the equipment appears to include temporal scanning equipment and diphasic dimensional penetration apparatus—the sort of equipment needed to jury-rig a crude vortex probe.

There are two doors, one to the passageway and one the the next room.

*If one or more Daleks are pursuing you, you may g[o]
through the door to the next room to S18 or through th[e]
door to the passageway to S16. If you choose S18, read th[e]
description above, then go to 388. If you choose th[e]
passageway, read the description at S16 above, then go t[o]
389.*

*If no Daleks are pursuing, you can either go straight t[o]
the passageway at S16 and on to explore the ship further, o[r]
go directly to S18.*

S20 (Locked Door)

Press and pound as you might, the doorway to S20 wi[ll]
not open.

*The fact that this door is locked suggests that the Dalek[s]
may have something or someone locked up inside. You ma[y]
record Clue X with the other clues you have collected.*

*You may continue to try gaining entrance to S20. If yo[u]
do, go to 391. Or you may keep running to S15. You ma[y]
also go to the next door in line at S21.*

S21 (Locked Door)

The doorway to S21 will not open, no matter how yo[u]
hammer on it.

*That the door is locked suggests that something o[r]
someone is locked up inside. Record Clue X with the othe[r]
clues you have collected.*

*You may continue trying to get in by going to 391. O[r]
you can go to either S20 or S22 to try to enter there. O[r]
you can continue along the passageway to S15.*

S22 (Compartment)

The door slides open at your touch, and you barge into [a]
bright-lit room barren of furniture except for a single, ova[l]
topped table.

There are Daleks here.

Go to 392.

356

S23 (Compartment)

The door slides open at your touch.

Daleks! The room seems filled with them, all rolling toward the door, their gun arms leveled at you. This, you realize, is what passes for quarters aboard a Dalek ship, the place where they come to rest—or whatever it is that Daleks do when they're not driving slaves.

Go to **393**.

S24 (Engineering)

This is the engineering core of the ship. The elevator brings you down into the center of a room filled with vast angles of piping, machinery, conduits, wires and cables, and the looming, massed array of vast, throbbing power plants. You recognize the usual Dalek-type power plant. Even as you look at those monstrous generators, three or four distinct ways of sabotaging them occur to you.

You don't have much time to ponder sabotage, however. There is a Dalek here, drifting toward you through the high-tech jungle of wiring and circuitry.

Go to **394**.

SECTION III: Exploring the Ship

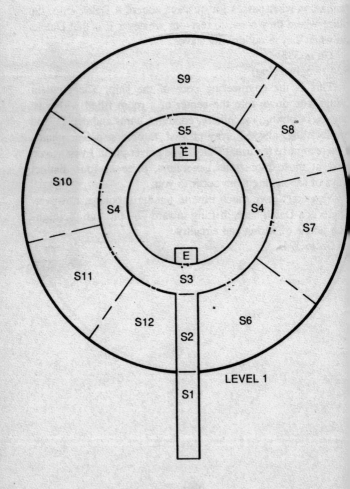

S9

S5

E

S8

S10

S4

S4

S7

E

S3

S11

S6

S12

S2

LEVEL 1

S1

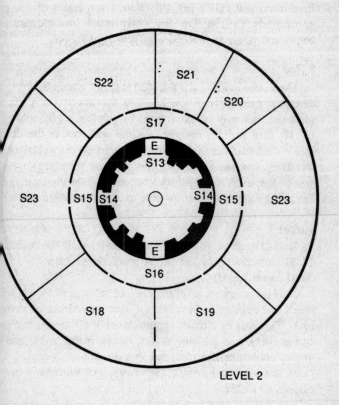

LEVEL 2

EXPLORING THE TOWER

Attempts at exploring the tower generally begin in a lift. Each time you call a lift, roll 2D6. On a result of 12, go immediately to **250**. On any other result, the elevator is empty and you may proceed with your explorations.

Lifts

There are six lift shafts grouped together within the central core that runs through the heart of the tower. Each lift is identical, and may be summoned by passing a card through the ID card scanner mounted on the wall beside the door. Inside each lift, there is a panel of buttons on the wall next to the door, numbered 1 to 50. Simply push a button to take you to the level indicated by your initial 2D6 die roll. (The Doctor, it should be noted, is able to read Gathwyran script.)

Level 1

Roll 2D6 as soon as you enter this level. If the result is 12, go immediately to **251** before proceeding further.

T1 (Lowest Level)

This is the lowest level that the central core elevators will reach and appears to be a storage area carved out of native rock. The area is circular, approximately 80 meters across, and is filled with packing crates, boxes, metal tanks, and a motley collection of rusting and long-disused machinery.

*If you wish to examine the crates and machinery more closely, go to **252**.*

T2 (Underground Tunnel)

This is the opening to an underground tunnel two meters tall and four meters wide, which appears to slant downward into the darkness. A cool, damp breeze that smells of the sea blows faintly through this opening.

*If you want to enter the tunnel, go the **300**.*

LEVELS 2 AND 3

*Roll 2D6 as soon as you enter either of these levels. If the result is 11 or 12, go immediately to **253** before continuing with your explorations.*

T3 (Cell Block)

This area is a prison cell block. Six corridors branch out from the central core to a passageway that circles the area. Each corridor is lined with cells approximately two meters wide and four meters long, each with an electric light, a pile of straw, and comforts such as waste buckets and water jugs. About half the cells are occupied and locked, but an observer can look into the cell through a small sliding peep slot in the upper part of the door. A key (which you do not have) is needed to unlock the cells.

If you try to speak to any of the prisoners, you will get little response beyond curses, hurled buckets, or stony silence. They tend to think that anyone addressing them through the peephole is a guard taunting or attempting to trick them.

If the Doctor is taken prisoner in this adventure, he occupies a cell on Level 2, which is marked on the floor plan.

*If you want to examine cells looking for Harry and Sarah, roll 2D6 for each cell examined. If the result is 10 or less, the cell is either empty or occupied by an imprisoned rebel. If the result is 11 or 12, go to **255**.*

Level 4

Roll 2D6 as soon as you enter this level. If the result is 7 or higher, go immediately to **260** *before continuing with your explorations. If the result is 6 or less, the area seems to be deserted.*

T5 (Interrogation Room)

Level 4 appears to be an interrogation room. There are numerous banks and consoles of electrical apparatus, cables snaking across the stone floor, and several metal racks with manacles positioned to hold a prisoner spread-eagled during questioning. There are also chairs with manacles on the armrests and legs, and racks of miscellaneous surgical and torture instruments.

Nearby is a table with pieces of metal on it that crumble and flake in your hand when you pick them up. Examining the metal pieces more closely, you realize with a start that they are from the metal shell of a Dalek, and appear to be many hundreds—perhaps thousands—of years old!

But what were Daleks doing on Gathwyr thousands of years ago?

You have stumbled across important information. Add Clue E to the clues you are collecting.

If you decide to examine this level more carefully, roll 2D6. If the result is 8 or less, go to **257**. *If the result is 9 or more, go to* **277**.

T6 (Office)

This is a small room that opens into the larger interrogation room. Cluttered with papers, a writing machine like a typewriter, and books, it appears to be an office. Most of the books appear to be medical texts.

If you wish to examine this room carefully, roll 2D6. If the result is 9 or higher, go to **277**. *On any other result, go to* **262**.

Level 5

Roll 2D6 as soon as you enter this level. If the result is 5 or less, go to 264. If the result is 6 or more, go to 267.

Level 5 is a large, open public rotunda. Along one wall is a set of glass doors leading to the outside. Along the opposite wall are other glass doors leading to what may be offices. Looking up, you see two railed catwalk balconies circling the rotunda, which is connected by fenced-in pedestrian bridge-walks to platforms around the elevator column.

T7 (Public Offices)

These appear to be public offices for government workers in the building. Through the glass doors, you see a counter separating a reception area from an office area where people are working at desks. Signs indicate that Gathwyrans come here to obtain various official licenses and permits and to pay their taxes.

Levels 6 and 7

Roll 2D6 as soon as you enter one of these levels. If the result is 9 or more, go to 259. On any other result, nothing happens immediately.

A railed platform surrounds the elevator column, and a narrow, railed pedestrian catwalk leads across open space to a gallery running completely around the circular room, which is about fifty meters across. Looking down, you see you are either one or two stories (depending on whether you are on Level 6 or 7) above the entrance rotunda, where dozens of people, both soldiers and civilians, are coming and going.

If you cross the catwalk from the lift to examine the balcony more closely, go to 265.

Levels 8, 9, and 10

*Roll 2D6 as soon as you enter one of these levels. On a roll of 11 or 12, go to **266**. On any other result, go to the description below.*

These levels seem to contain storerooms for documents and records. Near the elevator are several desks where men and women are working among stacks of papers, but no one seems to take any notice of your presence.

Each room is filled with floor-to-ceiling filing cabinets. If you make a surreptitious attempt to try to open one or more, you will find them locked.

*You may return to the lifts by going to **Lift** at the beginning of this section, or you may approach one of the desks to question the young lady working there by going to **297**. She may know something about Harry and Sarah's whereabouts and might be able to tell you about the layout of the Tower. You will have to be careful, however, not to let her know that you don't belong here. [NOTE: If you have already questioned a young lady on another level, this desk will be unattended. Proceed to the elevator.]*

Level 11

*Roll 2D6 as soon as you enter Level 11. On a roll of 10 or more, go to **266**.*

Level 11 is a reference library furnished with stack upon stack of books and a desk to handle check-out of library materials.

T8 (Reference Library)

Among the bookshelves here, the title of one book, *Myths of the Crystal City*, catches your eye. It seems to be a compilation of legends about the beginnings of Gathwyran civilization. Skimming quickly, you learn that the coastal cities, including Gathwyr, were founded by settlers escaping from religious persecution in their native place, known as The Crystal City. There are repeated mentions of something called the "Vortex Crystal", the "Oracle", "Guardian", or "Voice of the Crystal", and the text refers to those who refused to obey the tyranny of the Voice. This led to war and a rupture between the coastal cities and the Crystal City. Sometime after this, the "Guardian of the Crystal" hid the Crystal City from men's sight, though its emissaries appear from time to time to trade gems and carvings for food.

The text concludes that there may be some kernel of truth in these legends, but attaches little importance to them. The Crystal City, if it ever existed, has long since crumbled to dust.

If you have examined the book, you have won an important clue. Add Clue A to the list of clues you have collected so far.

You may, if you wish, approach a young woman at the front desk and question her at 297. [NOTE: If you have questioned the woman at the front desk on another level, this desk will be unattended. Proceed to the elevator.]

Levels 12 – 18

Roll 2D6 as soon as you enter one of these levels. On a roll of 9 or higher, go to 266. On a roll of 6 or less, go to 272.

Levels 12 through 18 are offices for the Gathwyran government bureaucracy. All seven floors are similar, bustling with men and women working behind desks.

You may approach a desk near the elevator and question a young lady working there at 297. [NOTE: If you have already questioned a young lady at a desk on another level, this desk will be unattended. Proceed to the elevator.]

Level 19

Roll 2D6 as soon as you enter this level. On a roll of 12, go to **272**.

Level 19 is a kind of 'garage' for grav vehicles. There is a crude square opening that seems to have been blasted through the ceiling. Grav vehicles entering Level 20 can drift down through this opening to parking areas on Level 19.

The grav vehicles here now are of several varieties, from two- to eight-seaters, some with twin-mount weapons in open turrets. With power off, the vehicles rest on the floor.

If you wish to try to steal a grav vehicle, go to **310**.

T9 (Service Area)

This is a mechanical/electronic service area for grav vehicles. A grav two-seater with its wiring and internal mechanism exposed is up on a rack.

If you wish to make a careful study of the service area, go to **271**.

Level 20

Make a 2D6 roll as soon as you enter this level. On a roll of 11 or higher, go to **272**. *Otherwise, go on to the description below.*

Level 20 is the building entrance for grav vehicles. A slot about three meters wide and high has been opened into one wall, apparently with blast torches of some kind. Through it, you can see the Fog Sea west of the city, and beyond that, the purple shadow of distant mountains.

There are a number of deactivated grav vehicles parked around the perimeter of this level. In the floor is a large, square opening leading through to Level 19.

If you want to try to steal a grav vehicle, go to **274**.

Levels 21 – 30

As soon as you enter any of these levels, go to **282**.

Levels 31 – 33

As soon as you enter any of these levels, go to **283**.

Levels 34 – 35

As soon as you enter any of these levels, roll 2D6. On a roll of 8 or more, go to **288**. *Otherwise, go to* **290**.

Levels 36 – 50

As soon as you enter a request for one of these levels in the elevator control board, go to **286**.

SECTION II: Exploring the Tower
(Levels 21-50 need no maps)

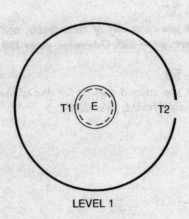

LEVEL 1

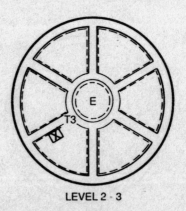

LEVEL 2 - 3

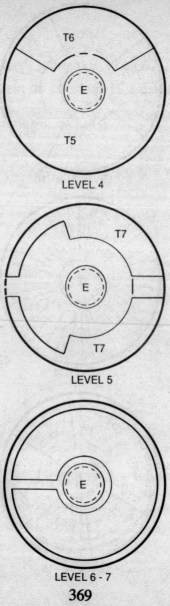

T6

E

T5

LEVEL 4

T7

E

T7

LEVEL 5

E

LEVEL 6 - 7

369

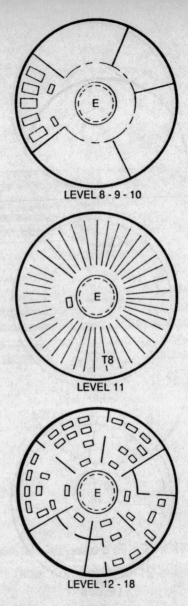

LEVEL 8 - 9 - 10

LEVEL 11

T8

LEVEL 12 - 18

4

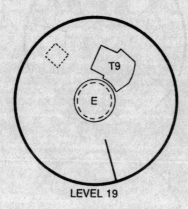

LEVEL 19

LEVEL 20

SECTION II: Exploring the Tower
(Levels 21-50 need no maps)

371

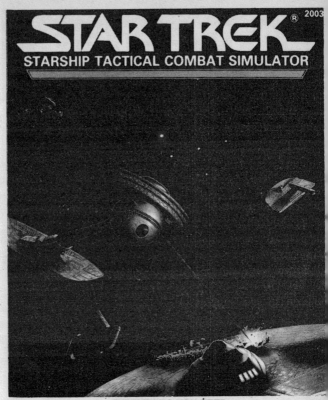

THE SWORD AND THE DAGGER

BY ARDATH MAYHAR

MechWarriors believe that the only way to kill a
BattleMech is with another 'Mech...
But Generals know that the best way to kill an army of
'Mechs is with a well-placed dagger.

Hanse Davion is Prince of the Federated Suns, the largest of the
five warring Houses... an idealistic man who has had to learn that politics
is neither honorable nor straightforward.

Ardan Sortek is the commander of Hanse Davion's personal guard.
Although a long-time friend of Hanse's, he has not yet learned the lessons
of power. Through a chance series of events, he stumbles upon a plot of
such magnitude that it threatens the balance of power of the Inner Sphere.
Unfortunately, no one will believe him... Indeed, they think he is quite mad.

. Is Ardan crazy or is someone trying to kill Hanse Davion?

THE SWORD AND THE DAGGER $3.95
Stock #: 8602   ISBN#: 0-931787-77-7

BATTLETECH NOVELS
"Die MechWarior! Die"

Grayson Death Carlye had been training to be a MechWarior since he was 10, but his graduation came sooner than he expected. With his friends and family dead, his regiment vanished, young Grayson finds himself stranded on a world turned hostile. And now he will have to learn the heardest lesson of all: it takes more than armored weaponry to make a MechWarrior.

To claim his title, he will have to build a BattleMech regiment from the ground up. All he has to do is capture one of those giant killing machines by himself.

If it doesn't kill him first.

DECISION AT THUNDER RIFT $3.95
Stock #: 8601   ISBN#: 0-931787-69-6

Become a part of the action with the **Doctor Who Role-Playing Game**. This novel game lets you, the fan, become a Time Lord and travel the galaxy fighting evil and encountering new worlds and races. It is a game designed to allow you to create your own episodes.

Each game includes:

The Players Manual

This easy-to-read 48-page book explains how to create your own Time Lord character and Companions.

A Sourcebook for Field Agents

This 64-page book contains the Doctor Who time lines and history as set forth in the TV series.

Game Operations Manual

This 80-page book has all the information required to run the game and create the monsters and aliens to be encountered.

THE DOCTOR WHO ROLE-PLAYING GAME $17.00
Stock #: 9001   ISBN#: 0-931787-90-4

Something was seriously wrong with history...

And the disappearance of a psychiatrist and his patient from the 20th century was only the beginning. In this plot-your-own Doctor Who adventure, The Doctor and his Companions travel back to America at the time of the Civil War. There, they learn that a time-loose rebel soldier has discovered how the war turned out and is hard at work making certain that this time around, the South wins.

DOCTOR WHO AND THE REBEL'S GAMBLE   **$3.95**

Stock #: 8901   ISBN#: 0-931787-68-8